D0555157

Other works by Greg Triggs

The Next Happiest Place on Earth, A Novel

Blog posts at www.GregTriggs.com

Columns at www.RiverReporter.com

THAT WHICH MAKES US
STRONGER

GREG TRIGGS

REDHAWK
PUBLICATIONS

ISBN: 978-1-952485-53-4

Redhawk Publications
The Catawba Valley Community College Press
2550 US Hwy 70 SE
Hickory, NC 28602

Library of Congress Number: 2022934942

For my brother Art Radke,

our sister Emily Sobiek & our grandmother Emma Fiore.

Make the world a better place.

Convince a kid their future is full of wonderful possibilities.

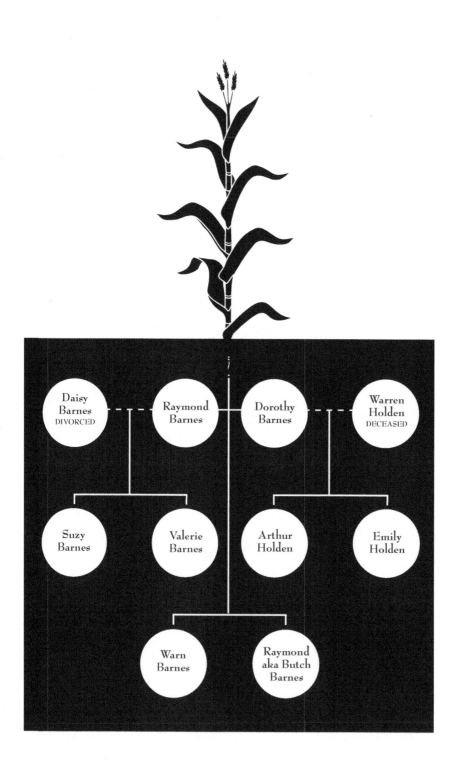

PROLOGUE

FUNERALS & FARMING

Memories are unpredictable. Lurking. Always ready to pop up. You never know how, where or when. The rusty edge of an autumn leaf might remind you of a former lover's hair. The pitch of a beautiful melody might remind you of his voice. The knife with which you're cutting your dinner might remind you of the one she plunged into your heart.

You get the idea. We've all been there.

My memories are of the Instagram variety. There's an image, but it's filtered. Prettier perhaps. Certainly, more intense. Clearer. Black and white-not in coloration, but in judgment.

Insta might not be the best allusion. This story takes place in the 20th century. Long before the world went digital; but, as the world changes, so does the context of memories.

This story exists in two times. Present and future, or past and present. Your choice. While reliving it I'm a child and an adult. I'm both, as we all are in the moments when memories come back to life. You remember the feelings with a mature voice because you know the consequence. You are briefly omnipotent.

Like most lives, mine was swirling in motion before I was even born. It starts at the funeral of someone always present but gone long before I arrived. In fact, his death made way for my birth.

For these moments I rely on family stories, piecing them together like my grandmother's quilts. I cannot be where I did not exist as more than two separate cells waiting to be introduced.

This story begins at the end of another.

"Art," says Great-Uncle Nick, straightening my future half-brother's clip-on bow tie as they walk toward the casket, "your dad is gone."

My future half-sister Emily, so blonde that her nickname is Chick, points to the casket, the memory of which will always make my Grandma chuckle. "No, he's not," she says. "He's right there."

Three-years old, and already she doesn't suffer fools.

In the 1950s gender usually wins. Nick Caruso, a perfectly wonderful man whose intentions were always good, keeps his attention on Art. "You're the man of the house now."

And so, a seven-year-old boy is forever burdened.

Emily, toddler-chubby and adorable, stations herself at the casket. She is playing with a doll on the edge of the metal box, riding the narrow margin between life and death. The stuff of drama. Thrilling. Were the casket pink, it could be sold as Barbie's Dream Box. Art grabs her hand and walks away. "C'mon," he says in his big brotherly, forever patient, now evidently a man, voice.

They sit in the front row as assigned by Mr. Gunderstoon, the funeral director. He's sincere in a very Midwestern way, working hard to make sure you know how bad he feels for you. Sympathy is his Olympic sport. His non-existent chin tucks into his neck like a turtle as he nods empathetically toward the woman who will become my mother. "Shall we begin?" whispers the man who knows the importance of being earnest.

The kids keep time with the organ hymns by bouncing their legs up and down. A blurry parade of mourners file by until Mable Franklin, the divorced blonde with brown roots from around the corner and across the street, stumbles up to pay her respects.

As she bends down to kiss the body's forehead, an ample breast pops out of her low-cut dress. Art's jaw goes slack as though he's just witnessed a miracle. After quickly composing herself, she puts her right index finger, painted with pink polish, up to her matching pink lips and says, "Shhhh. Our secret."

There's an upside to everything, I suppose. Instead of being the day Art buries his dad, it becomes the day he sees his first exposed breast.

Like most funerals in America's Dairyland, this one ends in a sturdy Protestant cinderblock basement. The service has been at the nearly new Moravian Church on Tulane Avenue, nestled between an irrigation ditch and the elementary school. In the narthex, a plaque with the names of dead parishioners can be seen to this day. Warren Holden, the deceased, is #2. If he died just six days earlier, he could've been #1.

Bad timing. It'll follow you forever.

Most of our family is Catholic. We're Moravian, which according to Sunday School, is the first Protestant faith, having started in the fifteenth century in Moravia, near Bohemia. Just a little more creativity and the church could've been called Bohemian; a term rarely associated with Christianity. I would have liked that.

We're Moravian because it's the church closest to our house. Spiritual, and practical. Were the Pope Midwestern, he'd probably be Lutheran if the church were half a block closer than the Catholic parish.

The church motto is, "In essentials, unity; in nonessentials, liberty; and in all things, love." I will always be thankful to proximity for leading my family to this church. There, I met friends I have to this day. I was given support I can still feel. It's in my DNA. My Christmas tree will always carry the Moravian Star.

Warm, generous women with shellacked Final Net hair and needlepoint aprons protecting stain-impervious dresses, ladle gravy over open-faced roast beef sandwiches. They serve watery Kool-Aid. There are desserts which these kind women woke up before dawn to bake from scratch to honor their own—the man whose name floats above their heads on a plaque, one-story up.

Eventually, all the prayer cards are distributed. Flowers have been given to the nursing homes where elderly relatives are waiting to join the young father who art now in heaven. Kids are given carnations to press into Sunday School Bibles.

I don't understand keepsakes from sad times. Open a book. Out falls a dead flower and an obituary. Boom. You're wistful and sad. Foolish perhaps to everyone but my mom. You can't pick up a book in her house without a family tragedy floral keepsake falling out. Her home library can trigger a hay fever attack.

Leftovers are sealed in wax paper. The parcels are loaded into a dark pink station wagon, which the family calls Dusty Rose. Warren's mother blocks the doorway, sobbing loudly enough that Emily starts crying too, which is mistaken for grief rather than the pain of young ears. Emily scores several butterscotch candies from the old ladies before making her escape.

The for now smaller family drives down Dennett Drive and over Olbrich Creek before turning left onto Johns Street. Three blocks later, Mom turns into her driveway, passing maple trees planted by her late husband. The trees are tall, strong, and intact to this day. They have deep roots.

The kids run up to the small, white, well-tended, crisp Cape Cod house. After several attempts, Emily's little hand twists the knob to open an always unlocked door. Grandma Caruso, my mom's mother Emma, is already there.

The first time I see the Panama Canal, I will be reminded of her waist—a narrow band bordered by two much larger things, the Atlantic and Pacific Oceans. In Grandma's case, her upper and lower torso.

For my fourth Christmas, I will get a set of Weebles from Santa, whose handwriting looks just like my mom's. I'll rip through the paper and rush to open the Fisher-Price box. Upon pulling the first one out, a bottom-heavy old lady, I will say, "Look, it's Grandma!" In a room of frozen smiles, my dad will laugh loudly. I will quickly be handed another box, lest Emma gets a chance to say something.

Today her concerns are more practical. "Wipe your feet. I'm sad enough without dirty floors making it worse."

Her commitment to cleanliness doesn't take a day off for anything as common as a funeral. Emma Caruso has been gone for a million years, but I can still hear her voice saying something like, "Change out of those clothes and head outside. Play while there's still light. Land sakes, do I have to tell everyone what to do around here?"

Yes. You do. It's your nature, Grandma. We loved you for it.

Good clothes form a little mound on the floor of his bedroom as Art grabs a Batman sweatshirt and some patched jeans, which surely belonged to a lot of other neighbor kids before they were his. Soon he and Emily are playing clothesline badminton, which I'm still sure my family invented. Art holds back his game because he's been trained not to beat his three-year old sister.

At the clothesline next door, Florence Nabors puts up her bedsheets. Her name led to brief childhood confusion on my part. I sort of expected everything to be named by their function in my life. Neighbor Nabor. Teacher Teacher. The dynamic was further compounded by Marshall the Marshall, Channel 27's kiddie-show cartoon host.

The cartoon host everyone in Madison remembers is Howie Olson. He and Cowboy Eddie were on Channel 3. Mr. Olson was a ventriloquist, and Eddie was his dummy. They were my friends, but I digress.

Back to the Nabors.

Florence is the rare 1950s career woman of our neighborhood. She works as one of the secretaries to the Governor. Each morning, Monday through Friday, her Mandarin Red Buick pulls out of the driveway and ferries her downtown to the state capitol. She worked in Washington D.C., during the war. Terribly glamorous. Very stylish. An impressive woman. With a nod of her blonde helmet, Florence calls the kids over to the fence, which had been put up by their dad not all that long ago.

"How are you doing?" she asks, brushing away some invisible lint from the tailored black dress she wore to the service.

"Fine. We're fine," responds Art.

"Good funeral." she offers. Emily nods, as though children have opinions about such things. Today the funeral would have a 5-star Yelp rating. Back then, the reviews came from the neighbors. More reliable. Just as political.

"Let's play," Emily whines, tugging at Art's sweatshirt, causing Batman's face to temporarily have a post-stroke droop.

Florence intervenes. "You probably shouldn't. People will get the wrong idea." The woman who advises Governors then says, "Act sad." Art quickly scans the glasshouses of our neighbors, surrounded by people with no room to judge - bad parents, a womanizer, the new family rumored to be from Nebraska. The kids aren't sure why they are supposed to care what these people think, but they follow Florence's always wise counsel. Toys are left to wait for a more appropriate time.

Having been warned by Grandma not to come back for at least an hour, Art and Emily sit invisibly in the shadow of the house lest they be seen smiling by Mr. Hillingham's hunting beagle, Trixie.

Art has a couple of well-worn comic books in his back pocket. He reads an old Captain America. Emily, a few years shy of reading, looks at the pictures in Archie. For the moment, they have everything they need.

The kitchen window is open. They overhear a conversation not meant for children.

"Dorothy, you haven't cried," observes Grandma, always concerned with appearances. "Do you want people to think you're cold?"

The response is punctuated by a weary voice and the clatter of Pyrex casserole pans, "I've got two kids to think about. Am I supposed to crumble?"

Grandma, ever practical, clarifies her point. "Your father, may he rest in heaven, left next to nothing when he passed. I can't help you with money. What are you going to do? Kids got to eat, Dorothy." Terms like car payment and mortgage start getting thrown around. Heavy stuff for young eavesdroppers to process.

I can picture Art. My big brother. One of my heroes. My biggest hero. He stops breathing for a second, his habit when confronting a new thought. His head tilts to the side like a puppy. Determination floods his jaw. He has a plan.

Months later, that summer, as the family comes home from their daily trip to the C & P Grocery Store, Mom spies something odd in the front yard. She lifts her white pre-Jackie O. Jackie O. sunglasses to see more clearly. Her dangling cigarette keeps time with her words like a metronome. "What the heck is that?"

She and Grandma cautiously walk through the yard like it's a minefield. They hunch down to look more closely at a rogue plant. Grandma, having grown up on a farm, is the first to speak. "Corn. Dorothy, that's corn."

Art appears from the side door carrying a battered, well-used water can. "Did it come up? Let me see!" He plows past the ladies with a big smile on his face. Gently watering his crop as he'd seen his father do, he explains. "I saved up my allowance to buy seeds. I didn't say anything in case they didn't take, but they did! They did!"

"You don't have to worry, Mom. We have corn."

Warren may not have indulged in Art's surprise. By all accounts, he was a yard fanatic. Wonderful Mom is different. Out comes the Cub Scout manual and a well-worn Almanac. Together they go to the library to learn about farming. Placed at odd intervals, essentially separate, the stalks are unable to hold each other up. They're tied to poles, resembling scarecrows randomly placed throughout the yard, watching over my still-in-the-future family.

The crop is overseen by a boy who understands that despite weeds and chaos, there is always the chance for something delightful to grow. In the autumn, they have corn.

Like all sweet things, it is gone far too soon.

THE BEGINNING, 1969

CHAPTER ONE

DRIVEWAYS

A lot has changed since the funeral. My mom started dating. My dad got divorced. Then the two of them started dating and got married. They blended their families, like *The Brady Bunch*. Then I came along. Sixteen months later, my little brother Butch was born. He's asleep on the lawn chair next to my rollaway in the room we share with our oldest brother Art.

The adults don't seem to realize I don't sleep as much as a five-year-old should. My mind refuses to shut down for the recommended ten hours. I'll listen to the radio or look at a comic book. Sometimes I'll practice my alphabet. Color. Anything to stay awake until my dad gets home.

When I finally hear a car pull up, it's time to get to work. I push aside my thin orange bedspread and faded Superman top sheet, lifting myself off the field of roses on my mismatching, well-worn fitted sheet. Quietly I make my way toward the window which overlooks the driveway.

I crouch like Kilroy, who was way before my time. I know who he is because my parents are of what will come to be called the Greatest Generation. Someday I'll be proud of that, but not yet. Right now, I only know concern. I rest my arms on the windowsill and watch my breath cloud the glass. If the car is straight, I can finally go to sleep.

Far more likely, the car is crooked. That means my dad is drunk. The more severe the angle, the worse he will be. The worse he is, the more I'm needed downstairs. I'll pretend I was having a bad dream or need a hug which I can't believe they don't see through. I'm not a hugging kind of kid.

If he picks a fight with Mom, I turn it on thicker, getting worked up to the point of tears. I grow up to be an actor, so that's money in the bank. Instinctually, I already know the only way to make a bad situation better is by learning something from it.

"Use it," as my acting teachers will someday say.

Tonight, it's not the bronze Buick we call Champagne Betty. It's my big brother's car, the light blue Chevy convertible we call Sky King. Art is home. Things will be better. I hear him mumble a hello to Mom, followed by the squeak of the door which hides the carpeted stairs leading to the second floor where the boys sleep. Twelve steps later, he's in our room.

Through fluttering eyelids, I watch him put away his things. At that moment, he stands straighter than he will later when we're both adults. He is tall and lean with wavy chestnut hair. He has huge, earthy brown eyes, different than my green, which are more like trees or moss in the spring. His nature is to be kind, patient, and self-sacrificing. My brother. Arthur Bradley Holden. A. B. Holden. A beholden man.

My name is Warn. I'm named after my mom's first husband, which strikes me as odd. It was my dad's idea. Story has it my birth certificate was filled out by a Norwegian social worker who was writing in her third language. Her mistake, missing the second R and an E, would've cost $25 to fix, so no dice. A verb I remained.

warn /wôrn/ ver to provide insight of problems or danger before there is consequence.

Try living up to *that*.

Our last name is Barnes. British. My dad was born in London but in the pre-makeover Eliza Doolittle way. So, I'm named Barnes in Wisconsin. The jokes write themselves. My middle name is Gregor, after an uncle who passed away. Being named in honor of two dead guys can be a burden, but I do the best I can.

We live in Madison, Wisconsin, near Lake Monona, in a little Cape Cod house. Whiteish. Fading to gray, but consistently so you probably wouldn't notice it. Cobwebs and moss, easily washed away, gather, and stay between the slats of the house's aluminum siding. The edges of the foundation are crumbling a bit. The house needs attention. My dad owns a small construction company. We should have the best-tended house on the block, but we don't.

Emily, my middle sister, is in high school. She doesn't seem to go very often. The fights about that carry throughout the house, which only creates more tension. I don't see what Emily gets out of it. That's one of the blessings of being younger. You watch things play out, thinking,

"That'll never work." So, you're spared from making the same mistakes. It's very efficient, being one of the youngest.

Emily is beautiful. Teenage chic. She's smart but less disciplined about that than her looks. Each morning I watch her go through the ritual of getting ready. She has long, beautiful eyelashes. They come from Rennebohm's Drug Store. The plastic case rests on unopened textbooks. While she glues them on, we listen to songs like "Lazy Day" by Spanky and Our Gang or "Sitting on the Dock of the Bay" by Otis Redding. That song is so good that sometimes you forget his plane crashed into the lake near our house and he died. *Boom*. A plane. In the lake where I take swimming lessons. I probably drank some of his blood when I learned how to hold my breath underwater.

I figure that's why I'm a pretty good singer.

I pet our cat Ming while Emily uses something called a hot brush on a wiglet, which matches her brown hair perfectly and gives it a little bump. We have the same coloring. Our eyes are green. Everyone else's are brown, except Valerie. One of her eyes is brown. The other one is a milky blue.

Valerie, my youngest sister, is blind. Totally. She can't see anything. To be fair, she's a lot of things, but blind is probably the first thing you'd notice. Because of that, she goes away to school but is with us almost every weekend. Necessity demands her looks be simpler. Pixie cut. Plain clothes, all of which are basically the same color, so they always match.

When we walk down the street, I guide her like a seeing eye dog. People forget that we're not both blind. They make no attempt to hide their staring. I want to tell them to knock it off. She's my sister, not a charity. Worry about yourselves, please. We're just fine.

Maybe it's easier for Val because she doesn't have to see it. I sure hope so. To know how we're looked at by people would make her sad.

I think about what it's like for her a lot. I walk around with my eyes shut or a sweater pulled over my head. Once I fell down the stairs. Another time a neighbor almost hit me with their car, but I made it to the mulberry bush on the corner. It's not as hard as you'd think. You get used to it.

Still, it doesn't seem like I can really know how being blind feels. Even while I'm pretending, I know when I open my eyes or pull down the sweater, I'll be able to see. Imagine if you knew you couldn't.

My oldest sister Suzy moved away in the middle of the night. We don't see her often. She's beautiful too. I often overhear women say, "too beautiful for her own good."

What a stupid thing to say. There's no such thing as too much beauty.

Art stops breathing for a second. His head tilts to the side, looking over to make sure I'm really asleep. I don't want to be told I stayed up too late, so I keep my eyes shut and breathe evenly to match Butch.

Butch. He's youngest, so there's not much of a story there yet. He's smaller than me, of course. He's always in motion, even his brown eyes. They dart around the room, like he's excited or trying to make sense of something he doesn't understand. His real name is Raymond, after my dad. Why they call him Butch, I couldn't tell you. It's a funny name, right? Years from now, my friend Bruce will meet Butch and laugh, saying, "Oh my God. What if they'd named you that?"

Butch is butch. I'm not.

My family is complicated. Lots of people think theirs is, but mine truly is. Suzy and Valerie have a different mom named Daisy. She lives in Michigan. That must be farther away than it looks on a map because she never comes to visit. She calls occasionally, so I've heard her voice, which is low and quiet like she's telling a secret. We've never met. Never will. She dies the summer I'm sixteen.

Val will say, "Poor soul. What's for dinner?"

Art and Emily's father was the first Warren. He's dead. My dad, Raymond, is still very much alive. Grandma says Canadian Club and Camel cigarettes are the secret formula to immortality. She rolls her eyes and says, "Land sakes. Just Dorothy's luck: this one will live forever."

My parents went to high school together but married other people. Dad married Daisy after the war. She was a nurse in an army hospital. Which war I couldn't say. From the sounds of it, there've been so many.

My mom married the first Warren. He was the printing foreman for the *Wisconsin State Journal*, our hometown newspaper, where Mom also worked. Imagine knowing you helped make sure the entire city got the news. What an accomplishment. Outstanding.

Warren was also a saint. That happens to most people who die young. Since they have less time, they don't age or disappoint. He was tall with sandy blonde hair, and kind; although ultimately, I guess he was just plain unlucky since he was thirty-seven years old when he died.

Something called Melanoma made my mom a widow at the age of thirty. Two kids left fatherless. Newspapers left unprinted. Dickens in Wisconsin. A Tale of Two Farms. A rotten break for all involved.

Years from now my spouse will be critically ill. The only person with whom I'll want to talk about it is my mom. What did she do right? What does she regret? What would she do differently? How did she get through it? I'll be unable to see that path for myself. My mom is always good at seeing the path.

Sometimes I pretend Warren is my real dad but seeing as he'd been dead more than eight years when I was born, that seems unlikely.

My dad, Raymond, will occasionally say: "I'm going out for cigarettes," at which point he's gone for hours. Either he's lying, or he buys his cigarettes in Chicago. It's kind of embarrassing to watch. I mean, the five-year-old and your blind daughter both see through your story. Exactly who do you think you're fooling, Dad?

Not my grandma. She just clicks her tongue and stares at the door. "Warn, did I ever tell you the story of your mom's first husband and his funeral? Cars lined up around the block. A line of mourners out the door. If your dad died, there'd be three people there, and he'd owe two of them money. I don't know how your mother ended up with such a man."

I do.

My parents were reintroduced by a mutual high school friend living clear over on the other side of town. It's about a 10-minute drive away, on the highway. My mom, who didn't learn to drive until her first husband got sick, avoids the highway like the plague, when the plague was the plague and not just an allusion to things people fear.

I don't know the matchmaker's name. She stopped coming around after my parents got married. It's like she thinks she made a mistake or something. If she hadn't done that, I wouldn't be here, so thanks, lady I'll never meet.

"Dorothy," I can imagine her saying, one hand on the receiver, the other holding a cigarette and a clip-on earring. "You wanted to get some work done on the house, right? You should call Raymond Barnes, remember him? Good looking!"

About this, she isn't wrong. My dad is a good-looking man when he's sober. When he's drunk, he gets sullen, and his face contorts. It turns beet-red. Sadly this is more his norm. So, referring to my father as handsome wouldn't be correct. He has the potential to be handsome, but his potential is unrealized.

Tall, with an athletic build, looks are important to my dad. He keeps his thick, dark hair neatly trimmed. He tries to dress stylishly. His stomach is flat. His bloated liver, however, gives the illusion of a belly.

Wikipedia before Wikipedia continues. "Ray Barnes! He graduated two years ahead of us. He's back in town. Started a contracting business." Heteronormative nameless classmate knows how to bring it home.

"He's divorced!"

So, Raymond came over and literally raised the roof, adding a second story to the turning more-gray-everyday house on Johns Street in Madison, Wisconsin.

My dad is an excellent card player. Almost a shark. His ability to play poker and gamble will get us through lean winters when there's no construction work. Like most excellent card players and addicts, my dad knows to play his cards slowly. Deliberately. Lulling the other player into a false sense of security to get the desired outcome.

The first few dates, he's a gentleman, no drinking. On the third date, he starts asking about her kids. A month in, it's time to get them all together, which goes well. After that, maybe it's okay to have a beer over lunch, a drink or three with dinner. Less than a year later, they're engaged.

Eight months after the wedding, I show up prematurely, which makes sense. I'm the kind of kid that hates to miss anything.

CHAPTER TWO

RAINBOWS & A FLASH FLOOD

"Warn. Warn!" whispers my sister Emily. "Wake up. I've got something to tell you."

She has no way of knowing I only fell asleep about 15-minutes ago. "What? What is it?" I say in a groggy whine.

"Judy Garland died."

"Who?"

"The lady who played Dorothy in *The Wizard of Oz*."

We watched that movie for the first time this spring on our color TV. At first, I was bored, because it was old fashioned black & white. Then she sang, "Somewhere Over the Rainbow," and on some level, I understood what she meant. There's a bigger world beyond the one in which you're growing up. If you're a certain kind of person, you want that larger life even though you love your home and the people with whom you share it.

Then it morphed to color after the tornado. As an adult, I understand the artistic choice. As a child, I figured color film was invented during the making of the movie.

"She died? She's so young."

"Uh Warn," says Emily, "that movie is super old. She was the same age as your dad," she adds with an eye roll, implying that, of course, a five-year old should know how old this dead lady is.

"Anyway, I just thought you should know. Since you loved that movie so much and all." She starts to rise. As she kisses me on the cheek, a strong gust of wind comes through my open window, rustling the curtains.

"Em, I think she's here," I say with wide eyes.

"That's a nice thought," Emily responds. "Lots of people think that spirits are carried on the wind."

"What's a spirit?" I ask.

"Gosh, that's a big question. It's, well, I guess it's the best part of us. The force that keeps us in touch with God. The force that keeps us alive forever. Even after our bodies die," she says.

23

For the rest of my life, I'll be glad that Emily woke me up to tell me that Dorothy Gale went back to Oz. I love that I know exactly where I was that night. I love knowing who I was the week the Stonewall Riots began.

I love feeling spirits swirl around me when I'm caught in the wind.

It's time for kindergarten. Preparations begin. One morning after Sunday School, Art takes me to buy new clothes at Arlan's Discount Department Store. After that, we hit Copp's Family Department Store & Grocery. Very high-end. It's next door to the petroleum storage tanks near our house.

The polyester making up my new shirts will endure past the millennium. Polyester, which comes from petroleum, the storage tanks for which are next to Copp's Family Department Store. Don't tell me there's no order in the universe.

Art says I need a notebook. I instinctively reach for a blue one. Art shakes his head. "Why not?" I ask.

"Every boy in the school is going to grab that notebook. Get something different, so you know it's yours."

So, with my new Fantastic Four notebook and matching pencil case, we head toward the lunchboxes. Oh. My. God. The lunchbox aisle is amazing. There's Snoopy, Mystery Date, The Monkees, Sesame Street—which seems way too baby to me. Then I see it. The one I want. Wonder Woman.

"You mean Batman, don't you? Or Superman?"

No. I meant Wonder Woman, but something in the tone of Art's voice makes me nod. "Yeah. Batman."

Emily teaches me the alphabet and how to write letters, of which there are twenty-six. When I put four of them together, I can write my name. W-A-R-N. Revelatory! My parents are proud, assuring me I'll be ahead of something called "The curve." A funny look passes over both their faces as they turn their attention to Butch. The silence is heavy while they stare at him, in a manner I'll later learn to call wistful.

Some people hate silence, thinking it's because they've failed to inspire conversation. Not me. Silence is confidence. Silence is being left to draw your own conclusions rather than being *told* how to feel.

Each night during what my mom thinks is my bedtime, she'll tuck me in and offer a variation on, "Remember, all anyone expects is for you to do your best." Adding, "as long as you do that, there's nothing to worry about."

Art lingers in those moments, waiting for her to leave. After the door shuts, he looks up from his book and says, "You always do your best. Don't worry, Warn. You're going to do great in school." Then he kisses me on the forehead or tosses me a comic book and asks me to read it to him.

I don't get all the words, but enough. Superman's girlfriend Lois Lane is trying to figure out his secret identity again. I like this one because she's starting to look more modern. More like a girlfriend. Less like a mom.

The big morning finally arrives. My mother and Art take me to Herbert Schenck Elementary just across the street from our church. It, and the attached middle school, are named after a local shopkeeper and politician from something called the Progressive Party. I like parties, so that's okay with me.

I've never been in a school before. The hallway is dark because there are no windows past the entrance. When we walk into my classroom, it's full of moms and dads. One lady assumes my mom is my grandma and that Art is my father. They don't correct her, so I do.

I try to sound polite. I really do, but as always, something betrays me. "He's my brother. She's my mom," I say with a tone that might've included a sigh.

But the lady ain't wrong. I never noticed it before. Mom is a little older than the other mothers.

"Warn! Don't be rude." My mom says in her scolding voice. "Never mind. It's an easy mistake to make." Why is she apologizing? The other lady is wrong. I don't get accepting blame for something that's not your fault.

Then, years before the term drama queen is invented, I meet my first drama queen. We're standing next to a girl who is hyperventilating through her tears. The little nametag we were each given says her name is Paula. I can read this because my family taught me the alphabet. I can already tell Paula is a cry-baby. We will never be friends.

"Do you want us to stay?" Mom asks me, with a small quiver in her voice.

"No." While Mom looks for a tissue, I notice that Art has a huge smile on his face. He gives me a little nod and messes my hair up a bit before they leave.

That Paula girl is still crying. She's exhausting.

Mrs. Milbauer, the teacher, assigns us places to sit in three rows of seven kids each. It must be alphabetical by first name because I'm sitting in the last row next to a nice-looking boy named Wayne. He's a little taller than me. His hair is just a little bit longer, so it falls in his eyes.

Warn Wayne. Like there's something wrong, and Wayne needs to know.

We're also sharing something out in the hallway called a locker, in which we're supposed to put our coats, boots, and mittens when it gets colder. It looks like Wayne and I will be spending a lot of time together. Good thing he seems like a nice kid.

Mrs. Milbauer, wearing a smart tartan plaid wrap-around skirt and a crisp white blouse, is very careful to make eye contact with each child while she's explaining things to us. She's wearing one of those wiglet things, but the color doesn't match as well as Emily's does. And her eyelashes are real. You can tell because they're kind of stubby and thin. I should tell her where Emily gets her false ones.

She explains something called recess, which seems to be another word for playtime. I can get behind that. We take a nap each day. Whatever. I'm not a napper. I'll run the alphabet in my head. There's also a milk and graham cracker break each morning.

The chubbiest of the three boys in my class named Mark raises his hand. "Mrs. Milbauer, will the crackers be regular or cinnamon?" She very patiently explains to us that there will be a choice of either. Mark seems relieved.

Encouraged by my classmate's success, I raise my hand.

"Mrs. Milbauer?"

"Yes?"

I point to my nametag with the gender imprinting truck on it. "My name is misspelled."

And for the first time, I hear something I will be told during pretty much every roll call of my life. "No. W-A-R-R-E-N is the proper spelling of Warren."

"No, Mrs. Milbauer, my name is spelled W... "

My ability to spell, which is clearly impressing the less prepared students, is unexpectedly interrupted by a bunch of kids scooching backward. As I look beyond them, I see a river of urine rushing toward us,

accompanied by now familiar gasping tears.
  That Paula kid is the worst.

CHAPTER THREE

NOBODY'S DUMMY

I rush home from school, pants dry, which is more than I can say for some people. If I run home, I can make it for the end of *Dark Shadows*, the scariest and best thing that has ever been on television or anywhere else.

It's about a vampire named Barnabas Collins. He lives in this creepy old mansion. Barnabas spends a lot of time with a psychologist, Dr. Julia Hoffman, who thinks drinking blood is psychosomatic or something. She screams a lot too. Always scared or terrorized. She's not very good at her job. If someone is sucking the blood out of my neck, I'm guessing it's a real vampire, not some guy working through childhood issues.

When *Dark Shadows* is over, *Cowboy Eddie's TV Circus* comes on. It's the greatest cartoon show in the history of television. Howie Olson, the ventriloquist, is the host and his best friend Cowboy Eddie is the dummy; but he's not a dummy. He's smart. They're on Channel 3, where Art works as a cameraman.

Howie and Eddie always have bleachers full of kids celebrating birthdays and stuff. I've never been on. They require kids to be of school age. I pointed out I've been school age since I turned five in January, but Art says they mean you have to be *in* school, which only just happened today.

They could be clearer.

Anyway, between Binger Bunny, Daffy Duck, and Porky Pig, they ask some of the kids in the audience the question of the week. Those kids get to talk on camera! For appearing on the TV show, all the kids get an orange drink from McDonald's and a loaf of Wonder Bread, which to me sounds awesome.

We get our bread from Barnes' Bakery, which is owned by my grandpa on my dad's side. You can only get Wonder Bread in the grocery store. I'm a kid, so I want the bread from the store. It's enriched and helps grow healthy bodies in twelve ways. I don't know how my grandpa's bread helps me grow a healthy body. Maybe it doesn't. Maybe his bread is *hurting* me.

Little do I know that years later, I will wonder if Wonder Bread is even bread. I have no idea how much I will yearn to taste my grandpa's bread again. Donuts. Cakes. Any of the delicious things he baked.

After the question of the day, Howie always shows the latest episode of "Clutch Cargo," which is just about the worst cartoon ever. It's not even really a cartoon. It's a series of still pictures that people talk over. To make it look like the character in the picture is moving, they put human lips on the drawings. The whole thing is super creepy, so I usually go get a glass of water during that part of the show.

After my television fix, I head outside and tell the rest of the kids about my first day at school. They've all been through kindergarten, so they get it. We play until their suppertimes, at which point the neighborhood becomes a symphony of moms yelling, "Time for dinner!" followed by a friend's name.

We eat later than most people because Art is a cameraman for the WISC-TV, *Channel 3, Evening News at 6pm*. It's an important job. It's totally worth the wait and our own small contribution to making sure that Madison, Wisconsin, stays in the know. We watch the *CBS Evening News with Walter Cronkite* while Art drives home.

When Mr. Cronkite says, "And that's the way it is," we start eating.

Art usually gets home just as we're hearing how many soldiers were killed someplace called Vietnam. My dad always says, "Lord love a duck," when the number is announced. I have no idea what that means or why saying it makes him feel better. All I know is after he says it, my mom puts her hand on his shoulder and gives it a little squeeze.

Art walks in and stands in front of the TV. Rude. Butch, sitting next to me on the couch, cranes around to keep watching. I'm not sure why he wants to see Mr. Cronkite so badly. Butch is four-years old. I doubt he can understand the news as well as me.

"Warn, how was your first day of school?"

I tell him about the locker I share with Wayne, the awesome toy trucks in the play corner, and end with Mrs. Milbauer's wiglet, which is really the best part of the story. His smile gets huge, and then he says, "How would you like today to get even better?"

Uh, yes, please. "Why? What? What's going on?" I ask with a child's enthusiasm, which makes sense since I'm a child.

"A school group was supposed to be on Howie's show tomorrow…"

"You mean Cowboy Eddie's show."

Art's brow furrows for a second, and then he says, "Okay, Eddie's show. Anyway, the school group is quarantined because their teacher broke out in chickenpox today. We don't have enough kids for the show."

"That's too bad," I say with total sympathy. I've already had chickenpox and it's no picnic. Mom says it's good to get it over with though. That must be why she had me and Butch hug Valerie when she came home from school with it.

"We need some extra kids, so ..." and then he says something I've been waiting my whole life to hear, "How would you like to be on the show tomorrow?"

I don't know it yet, but this watershed moment and a bit of nepotism will lead to being one of the regular kids on the show. I'm only five, but I learn an important, lifelong lesson quickly. It pays to know people.

It's going to be a restless night. I'm too excited to get any sleep at all.

In the vague light of our room, I can see the outfit my mother has chosen for my television debut. "Look, Warn," she had said. "All the kids are wearing solid shirts and blouses. You're going to wear stripes!"

The dinner table becomes a rehearsal hall. "You're going to be asked a question," said Art. That's HUGE! Most kids don't get to talk. They just sit there looking glassy-eyed. I'm going to be a star. A star!

Art continues, "Ringling Brothers bought commercials, so we're promoting it. When they ask you what you like best about the circus, you have to say the clowns, okay?" I nod solemnly, knowing that never before has a more important question been asked.

Here's the thing, though. I hate clowns. To me, clowns celebrate the moronic. Any idiot knows there is confetti in the bucket, that all those guys aren't going to fit in the little car and that the wooden beam needs to go through the doorway lengthwise, not across.

I really hate clowns. When I was about three, I dreamt that my parents were having my birthday party at an old, imposing church downtown. I was getting ready to blow out the candles on my cake. A clown was there, carrying a huge knife. I thought he was going to cut the cake. Instead, he chased me through the church, eventually catching me on the altar and holding me down. Just as he raised the knife to stab me, he pulled off his mask. It was my father. I woke up screaming.

I'm sure many of these clown people are hardworking artists with a vision of how they can make the world a more joyful place. That's fine, I suppose. I'm just saying, they're also iconic symbols of the horror film genre.

But that's showbiz, baby. If they want me to say clown, so be it. Clown I shall say.

School drags by. My attention span is even shorter than usual. We must've started math that day because I was never good at that. Even then, my career was forcing me to make compromises. "I have no time to learn about addition. Someday there will be calculators, Mrs. Milbauer. Now, if you'll excuse me, Cowboy Eddie is expecting me!"

Art picks me up in Sky King right after school. My freshly ironed shirt is hanging on the little hook in the backseat. There's a chocolate donut back there too.

In an early "food is love" lesson, my stage brother says, "You can have that donut if the show goes well."

Make no mistake, Mr. Donut, you will be mine.

We get to the TV station. Art pulls into the employee parking lot. Unlike the other kids I see lined up outside a different door like cattle, we walk in through the newsroom. I've been here before. People remember me. Judy Saunders, the sultry red-head host of the *Farm Hour* comes up to me, gives me a little hug, and kisses me on the cheek. Seeing she left a lipstick stain, she takes out a handkerchief, licks it, and vigorously rubs it away.

Another star, Michael Lerners-Weife, comes over. You're expecting that to be a man, right? Wrong! It's a *lady*. The world of TV is crazy. Whenever you hear her name announced on TV, you're expecting some big German guy to come onto the screen, and you're wrong. She's a petite brunette with the same wiglet my kindergarten teacher wears.

Like an entourage, the adults walk me toward the TV studio. We pass the picture-perfect news anchor, Rick Fetherston, who looks up from his papers to smile at me. "Stripes," he says, returning to his reading. "Smart choice Warn. Most of the kids wear solids."

I'm quickly seated, separate from the rabble, with the other featured kids. We're down front and therefore easily reached by the microphone. We're given Dixie Cups of McDonald's orange drink. It's even more delicious than I imagined.

Howie Olson walks into the room. He's shorter than I expected and he's wearing glasses. He doesn't do that during the show. All the kids applaud, so I join in. It seems the polite thing to do; but, come on. We all know the real star is Cowboy Eddie.

Mr. Olson waves to us, smiling. "Welcome to the circus, kids!" His smile disappears as he bends over with a grunt, moves aside the skirting surrounding his desk, and pulls out a trunk. Since I'm seated on a level higher than where he stands, I can see inside.

There in a twisted, pretzel-like contortion is Cowboy Eddie.

I suppose I always knew that he was a doll, a dummy if you want to be cynical, but it's hard to see just the same. Even now, all these years later, I don't understand why no one took precautions to protect the illusion. Why didn't anyone care?

Cowboy Eddie was like Mr. Rogers, Mickey Mouse, and Binger Bunny. He was one of the stars of my childhood. Eddie was carved by the same man who made Charlie McCarthy for Edgar Bergen. My Cowboy deserved better. So did his fans.

The light on the camera has turned red, which they told us means we are on the air. The show is going well. Classic Howie. Then one by one, they start asking kids the question of the day. I go last. Art is the cameraman. Ever so slightly, he comes in closer on me than the other kids. After saying I love those stupid-ass clowns, Mr. Olson shocks me by asking a follow-up question.

"Why?"

Not being prepared, I answer quickly, without filter. "Because they have red noses, like my dad."

Cowboy Eddie's head pops up, his jaw drops, and his head spins around. Mr. Olson is stifling a giggle well into his introduction of a Clutch Cargo.

On the ride home, I enjoy every bite of the chocolate donut.

Mom greets us at the door, "You did so well!" She offers my second lipstick stain of the day. I proudly hand her my loaf of slightly squished Wonder Bread. She looks over my shoulder at Art while she shakes her head. "Raymond didn't see the show."

Butch is behind her, jumping up and down. "You were in the TV!" he says, clapping. As always, my mom asks me to interpret. I'm the only one who seems to understand what he's saying. Probably because we're brothers. That makes sense.

The next morning, I go into the kitchen for breakfast which includes toasted slices of my paycheck. I am literally a breadwinner for my family.

As usually happens when you're on TV, people you know tune in to watch. For my birthday and many years after, I will be gifted with clown figurines. People always assume kids like me tell the truth.

CHAPTER FOUR

DOROTHY'S ALL-GIRL POSSE

I'm not the only entrepreneurial member of my family. Mom makes tiny doll dresses she sells at the True Value Hardware Store on Cottage Grove Road. Farmers and blue-collar guys shop there, stopping in the basement toy department to pick up a surprise for their kids. A 4x6 pegboard displays Mrs. Dorothy's doll fashions. Couture creations made from material scraps Mom's girlfriends give her. Next to them are handmade Raggedy Ann dolls brought to life on her Singer Featherweight sewing machine, which I'm told was a gift from the first Warren.

Mom sees opportunity where others don't. Even now, at five-years-old, I'm so proud to be her son.

Next door to the shopping center is the Lakeview Tavern, a simple neighborhood bar, which does not offer a view of the lake. Perhaps the name is aspirational. Very dark, it is dominated by two pool tables, Skee-Ball and an Addam's Family pinball machine. There are always pickled eggs and venison jerky for sale on the counter. Normally, my mom wouldn't go to such a place, much less take her kids there, but the day bartender is one of her best girlfriends, Shirley.

Shirley is an Amazon. Genetically superior, imposing, and strong. Naturally tall, she makes no attempt to hide it. She accentuates her height with two-inch heels and a blonde beehive hairdo. Her ex-husband Jerry, with whom she lives but refuses to remarry, has no choice but to look up to her. He is six inches shorter.

Shirley is a magician, often seen pulling coins from her cleavage. "Your burgers will be ready in a few minutes. Play some games, kids." Implied message, I want to gossip with your mom. They whisper conspiratorially to avoid the prying ears of children and the drunks of the Lakeview Tavern.

I think of Shirley each time I hear the Addam's Family theme song.

My mom is a girlfriend magnet. Men may come and go, but not Mom's all-girl posse. They're here to stay.

Aunt Lil is a family friend, so she's an aunt by choice, as opposed to lineage or marriage. Like my mom, she became a widow in her early 30s. Our families share a backyard fence anchored by a telephone pole that has been greased so none of the kids could climb it.

Both women, to use their words, settled into new marriages, counseling each other through the dicey waters of second love.

Aunt Lil is on the short side, so she wears her hair high to compensate. Each year the salt in her salt and pepper hair gets a little more dominant. She wisely doesn't attempt to cover it up. The white sets off her beautiful smile and olive tone skin. She is a little on the bottom-heavy side, so she waddles like a duck. She's got five kids, so maybe it's better to say mother hen.

Lil has been an industrial clothing presser at Nedrebo's Tuxedo Shop, ensuring wrinkle-free proms and weddings in Madison, WI. She was an elevator operator at Manchester's Department Store, Madison's version of uppity. Now she has a job cleaning rooms at the Mayflower Hotel, which will cause back problems for the rest of her life.

Lil loves indulging the people she loves. Her children dress beautifully. I know because when Tim the youngest, is through with them, his clothes end up in my dresser. Aunt Lil has an electric organ bigger than the one in our church. She will play whenever anyone has the time to listen or sing along.

She accompanied me when I sang "Those Were the Days" at her daughter's wedding. Super 8 movies from the day prove we were spectacular. My first standing ovation.

Aunt Lil's conversations with Mom plant little seeds, which will stay with me forever.

"Why do people treat an elevator operator like she's invisible?"

"Why does my boss have to be so horrible? Isn't standing over an iron for 8 hours a day hard enough already?"

"Why don't people use a paper towel to wipe up the soapy, milky water on the edge of the restroom sink? They're thoughtless."

Each Christmas and Easter, a florist drops off a centerpiece for our small table with a card signed in Lil's distinctive handwriting. As an adult, I will wonder how many rooms she cleaned to make that gesture. How many elevator buttons did she push? How much milky water did the pine boughs cost?

I think of her each time I clean up a small splash of water after washing my hands.

Rounding out the group is Lillian McKay. Everyone calls her Mick. She works nights downtown as a waitress at Crandall's, home of Madison's finest fish fry. She can make smoke rings, which adds to her overall mystique. Mick is never far from her pink cigarette case with the gold clasp and a compartment for her lighter. It's usually in the same hand as the beer stein she carries wherever she goes, but her drinking doesn't seem to cause problems. Liquor is my dad's addiction. Mick's is tobacco.

Mick is an optimist in the best and kindest sense of the word. She loves to laugh and has an infectious cackle. Her brown eyes light up, anticipating the punchline of a joke or the ending of a funny story. Her reaction will start as a low giggle, building to an all-out guffaw, until she starts to cough and begins gasping for air.

I think of her each time I see someone on oxygen.

I sit at the kitchen table, connecting the dots in my coloring book while they talk in code, underestimating how much I understand. Their coffee inhaled as fast as Mick's lipstick-stained Virginia Slims. Florence Nabors would be there too, but she's busy helping the Governor.

When there was neither time nor money for the more professional version, these friends became each other's counselor. They all live within ½ a block of each other and could be at each other's home within 60 seconds if they were needed.

The first time I hear, "It takes a village," these are the women I will picture.

CHAPTER FIVE

CROSSES TO BEAR

Life falls into a pattern. School feels ordinary instead of new or fresh. Wayne and I walk home together, crunching orange, red, and golden leaves along the way, usually laughing about something that happened in class. Most of the time, his mom is waiting for us on Dennett Drive, the first street we'd have to cross without a safety patrol. When I mention this to my mom, she smiles slyly and says, "Wayne is the oldest, isn't he?"

I learn to tie my shoes. Mrs. Milbauer begins spelling my name correctly. Paula's then Indian-Style, now more thoughtful, "crisscross apple sauce" accidents are less common. Growth and progress abound for nearly everyone.

Nearly everyone. My dad is drinking more. I wish that surprised me, but it doesn't. The angles of his car are getting more severe. Last night the Buick was almost perpendicular to the driveway.

Art was taking classes to become a history teacher at the UW Whitewater, but he stopped. He's working at the TV station full-time. He's been dating a girl named Nancy. She looks like Ali McGraw, with long, straight auburn hair parted down the middle. She wears jeans with penny loafers and thick woolen sweaters. I heard her say one of her sweaters came from Ireland. Imagine that. Nancy's got a sweater which will probably see more of the world than me. She's studying at UW Madison to become a teacher.

Nancy always asks about my lessons at school and writes down what I say, which makes me feel kind of important. Yesterday, she taught me what comes after 99. It was confusing, but then she mentioned *101 Dalmatians*. So, from now on, when I'm confused by a math problem, I'll visualize dogs. That'll help. I love dogs.

All the grown-ups are glued to our TV watching something called lottery numbers get pulled. They say that since Art dropped out of school, he's got to worry about the draft. I don't get it. My dad orders draft beer. His contractors talk about a kind of drawing called drafting. Houses that are breezy have a draft. Which one do they mean?

Emily is going to school part-time now. She scored an afternoon job at a really cool office building downtown. All glass. She's something called a receptionist. It sounds less stressful than when she was working at Kentucky Fried Chicken. I used to beg her to tell me the secret recipe, but she said, "No. The Colonel would find out. I'd get in a lot of trouble." So, maybe it's good that she's moved onto something new. Who could handle that kind of pressure?

Mom and I meet her bus each evening and drive her home. I get to carry the plaid bag with a zipper that holds her work shoes. Very sophisticated. Very *That Girl*.

There's tension between Mom and Em. That's probably why they want me to tag along. It's during *The Flintstones*, but I try to be a good sport about it. Hopefully, things will be better by the time they get to the Great Gazoo episodes. I'd hate to miss those.

"Emily," says Mom between puffs of her cigarette, "a couple of college catalogues for you came in the mail today."

"So?"

I hear them arguing late at night while I'm on my Kilroy vigil. Mom says things like, "Your father's Social Security will help pay for it. Please go to college.' She follows that up with one of the saddest things I've ever heard anyone say.

"Do you want things for you to turn out the way they did for me?"

Emily gives the classic teenage response. "I don't want to be anything like you," which she punctuates with a slamming door. From my window, I can see Emily get into a waiting car and ride away. It's the same car each time. A red Oldsmobile Cutlass with a white vinyl roof.

How could anyone not want to be like my mom? I mean, I know I'm only five, but she's the best person I know. She's so smart. There's always an open book near her. Jacqueline Susann to James Michener, so she's well-rounded. She reads the Bible, but she also studies reincarnation. Sometimes we read *The National Enquirer* together. Last week we read Mia Farrow might be going back to Frank Sinatra. I haven't heard anything since, but I'm hopeful.

Mom likes to play little word games on a scratch pad while she's talking on the phone. She has beautiful handwriting. I can't read cursive yet, but I like looking at her little grids and wondering what they mean.

Once I heard her say she had wanted to be a doctor. Her dad, my Grandpa Sam, an Italian immigrant who passed away before I was born, told her, "Those jobs are for men. It's a waste of money to send a girl. You'll quit working when the first baby comes."

Instead, she went to secretarial school. She graduated with honors. I know that because she keeps her framed diploma on the wall of the office facing the desk.

She pretty much runs my dad's company, Barnes Home Improvement. Mom does payroll, handles the bills, deposits the money, tells the workers where to report, manages inventory, and handles customers when they complain, which happens a lot.

My dad goes on the sales calls. That's about it. The rest of the time, his car is in front of one of the bars between our house and the grocery store. Sometimes we pass the Electra driving home from Sentry Fine Foods. I say, "Look. Dad is at the office."

Everyone laughs, which is good.

My mother is rail thin. She says it's because she's "Too nervous to eat." She has beautiful skin, which you can see because she doesn't wear much make-up. Just deep red lipstick and a little powder. She wears her nearly black hair modern and simple, not like the other mothers who constantly perm, curl, re-curl, and spray, spray, spray. Maybe they have more time for those kinds of things.

Mom usually wears crisp white blouses which smell like starch and capri pants with flat ballet slippers like Laura Petrie on *The Dick Van Dyke Show*.

Her purse is huge and seems to carry anything you could ever want. Pens, Kleenex, band-aids, rubbing alcohol, pliers, lifesaver candies, aspirins, waxed dental floss, tape, it's all in there. It's *Let's Make a Deal*, come to life!

The most beautiful thing about my mom is her kindness.

The men my dad hires are sort of broken. Once I heard a customer call them losers, which made me sad. No one should be called that. Yes, most of them smell of cigarettes and stale liquor. Their tempers are quick. They can be unreliable. Sometimes, one of guys will sleep on the old couch in our basement for a couple of nights because his wife threw him out. That doesn't make them losers. We wouldn't be friends with losers.

I'm too young to know it yet, but I will always love that my parents are not judgmental people, especially my mom. She listens. She encourages.

She makes sure those guys have a hot meal. She's patient and kind, sometimes to her own detriment, but that's Mom's nature.

When Emily says she doesn't want to be like her, I think she's making a mistake.

One day, trees bare, autumn in full swing, a moving van pulls up two houses down. Grandma Caruso is at the window looking for, or more likely snooping on, the new family.

Suddenly she gasps. "Well, there goes the neighborhood," she says before dissolving into a percussive round of tsk-tsk-tsk.

Mom hurries in from the kitchen. "What? What's wrong? Looking out the window herself, she looks back at Grandma with confusion.

"Dorothy, the new family is colored." Then she whispers, "They're negroes."

"So?"

Grandma's eyes get bigger than her cat-eye eyeglasses. The dishtowel in her hands gets twisted and knotted while she continues to stare out the window, as though she has heat vision like Superman and can stop the family from moving in with a flash of her eyes.

My grandma is many things—loyal, opinionated, judgmental, a good cook, a master gardener, and an incredible needleworker. She can size someone up and call a situation within the first five seconds.

She can also be prejudiced.

Grandma has a fear of things outside of her own experience. She grew up on a Christmas tree farm in rural Wisconsin. She didn't see anyone from a different race until she was nearly twenty years old. I'm grateful not to be growing up that way.

We discussed racism and prejudice at school last week. A beautiful woman named Mrs. Marlene Cummings came to talk with us. She brought two puppets with her. They were bunnies. One was brown. The other was white.

"Which one is better?" she asked. No one said anything, although Paula's hand was in the air. Mrs. Cummings called on her, which I knew was a mistake. Paula is one of those kids who raises her hands before the question is even done. So annoying.

Paula paused, of course. Then she started blushing. I thought for sure she was going to wet her pants. Instead, she nervously grinned and shrugged her shoulders.

Mrs. Cummings smiled. Her eyes crinkled like my mom's when she's trying not to cry. "No answer is the *right* answer. We don't know which bunny is better just by looking at it! Their only real difference is color."

There was a moment of silence before she added, "Color doesn't decide who or what is better."

Her tone shifted. It had a little more weight. "It's the same with people."

Then she explained that there are differences in skin color because of something called … okay, I can't remember what it's called, but it's the only difference. Just something inside us that decides which color skin we'll have.

Melanin. It's called melanin. Some people have more. Some people have less.

I wish Grandma could meet Mrs. Cummings. Maybe then she and my mom wouldn't be arguing right now. When things get like this between them, I'm invisible, so I walk out of the living room, into the little foyer, twist open the always unlocked door, walk through it and head two doors down.

A nice-looking lady with an easy smile and big brown eyes is watching the movers carry things in. "Thank you, thank you, thank you," she says as each workman passes by with a box or lamp. I wait for her to stop before tugging on her jacket.

"Hello. I'm Warn Barnes. I live in the white house two doors down."

Her head cranes. She looks a bit confused. "White house?"

"Gray. I meant gray," pointing toward our house.

"Oh, I see it. Hello, Warn. I'm Geneva Smith."

She puts out her hand. As we shake, I notice how neat our hands look together. Kind of like the cover of that Three Dog Night album I'll have someday. The ink is black. The page is white. Together they learn to read and write.

"Mrs. Smith, do you have any children?"

Her smile gets even bigger. "Do I have any children?" she repeats. Just then, three kids who I will later learn are named Jerry, Genie, and Clint come out of the back door. I invite them to our yard, where we begin to play a wicked game of front path Badminton.

Through the big picture window, I can see into our house. My grandma's jaw is slack as Mom brings us each a cookie from the bakery.

But it's hard to hate someone you know. At a cookout, months from now, I will hear Grandma praising Geneva Smith's potato salad. That's her highest form of praise.

Emma Caruso, a very practical woman, will die believing you can't change the color of your skin, but you sure as hell better know how much mayonnaise to use in a salad.

One night while waiting for Champagne Betty to pull up, I spy the by now familiar Cutlass instead. Whoever is waiting for Emily has pulled ahead a little farther and therefore more into my line of sight. As she gets into the car, the little overhead light engages. I can see the driver.
He's black.
No big deal. Emily is the white bunny. The driver, whose name I later find out is Charlie, is the brown bunny. My dad gets home soon after. His car glides into view at an appropriate angle. Downstairs I can hear my parents greet each other warmly, followed by the shutting of their bedroom door. I go to bed unworried and get a full night's rest.

Other nights are more restless.
For some reason, Mom has taken to locking the doors lately. She is hyper-vigilant about it, almost obsessive.
Julia, an awesome show starring Diahann Carroll as a single mother, ends. Mom gets up and walks toward the kitchen to get some water.
"Butch, clean up your marbles. Warn, make sure the front door is locked." I hesitate for just one second. "Please, Warn. Now!"
"Okay. Jeez."
I head to the front door thinking about Julia's son Corey on the TV show. Is it better to have a dad who's dead or a dad who doesn't want to be around? Maybe Corey is the lucky one. Raymond went out for cigarettes hours ago. He's probably in California by now.
PS, there's a full carton on the dresser in his bedroom.
I walk across the foyer and twist the doorknob, three concentric circles with a brass finish, to make sure it's locked. It is. It always will be after tonight. I begin to turn away when something in the narrow rectangular window catches my eye.
"Mom, something is wrong."
Butch, always curious, wanders toward me. He's about to look out the window when I instinctively put myself in front of him. Mom, on her

way towards us, stumbles over a few of the marbles she had asked to be put away.

It's a small detail that will seem unimportant in five seconds.
I can feel her fear and confusion as she looks out the window.
A cross is burning in our front yard.

Red lights and sirens alert the neighbors who have yet to notice the fire. Mom is too preoccupied to move us away from the window. So, we watch until the cross falls to the ground. As it lands, little sparks fly away from the debris, like new angels trying to reach heaven before falling back to earth, too weak to escape the gravity of the situation.

Art arrives with a crew from the station, sent to cover what is being called a crime.

The firemen and investigators automatically assume the real targets were the Smiths, two doors down. Something in their tone implies that it's understandable, to be expected when a black family arrives in a white neighborhood.

I can see in my mother's eyes that she doesn't agree.

The scorched earth will be a reminder of the ugliness for weeks to come. Anyone walking past our house, postman or Jehovah's Witness, will be able to see what has happened, especially now, in the autumn when things aren't growing as quickly.

For years, Dorothy Barnes will wonder which of her neighbors wanted to hurt her family. In the back of her mind, she has no doubt that burning the cross was meant to be retribution for a red Cutlass which can be seen into when the overhead light is on.

"Dorothy, what did you expect?" asks my grandmother.

Doubling down, Mom suggests, "Warn, why don't you go outside and play with the Smith kids?" Staring at her own mother, she adds, "do you have anything else to say?"

Eventually, the memory of this will blur and begin to feel almost imaginary. An appropriated memory from a book or a movie. Perhaps it didn't even really happen. Half a century later, my sister will be reminded that it did.

At Emily's high school class reunion, a nondescript man will walk up to her and offer an apology. "I'm the one who burned the cross in front of your house." She won't know what to say. Her silence will be taken as permission to keep talking, so he does. In doing so, he asserts a thousand assumed privileges without any sense of irony or regret.

"I wanted to date you. Then I found out you were seeing that black guy." To his credit, he will stammer a little. Perhaps feeling ashamed, although that seems unlikely.

"I wanted to scare you ... you know, so you'd stop seeing him. So, I could step in. You were so pretty. Still are. Always will be."

What a fool. Assuming a beautiful woman can't be strong. It's a mistake to underestimate Emily's will and strength. Ask any of her ex-husbands.

The confessor seems to think of it as a prank. Nothing serious. The consequence of unrequited love instead of realized hatred. Typical, stupid guy.

In a home within a block of our own, a teenage boy was able to gather wood and build a cross taller than himself, wrap that cross in rags, drag it down our street, douse it with gasoline, light a match and set it on fire.

Scary for us. Scarier for the Smiths who had worked hard and saved for years to buy a home where their kids could feel safe and secure. Relaxing just a little when a friendly neighbor kid introduces himself. Relaxing more when their children are given cookies by a kind woman.

To watch it go up in flames in the middle of the night. To not be sure if it was meant for them or the neighbors who welcomed them. Losing with either interpretation. In America. In 1969. 104 years after the Civil War ended.

All because a kid didn't have the guts to ask a girl out on a date.

Each time there's a school shooting or another type of uniquely American tragedy, our country seems blindsided. People react as if they didn't know whatever it was, was possible, although clearly, it is possible because it has happened before and will happen again.

On some level, that means we haven't lost our empathy. Perhaps that's a good thing, people clinging to the illusion that children are safe. It's terrifically naïve, but I like to think it means most people aren't cynical.

I can't say the same for myself.

In those moments, a small part of me comes back to the surface. I'm five years old, making sure the front door is locked, thinking, "Here we go again."

CHAPTER SIX

TRICK OR TREAT

"Warn, we've been here for half an hour," Mom says impatiently. "DECIDE!"

I honestly don't know what she expects from me. "This is an important decision," I say as I look up and down aisle four of the Ben Franklin Store. After all, it's an entire row of Halloween costumes.

I could be a cowboy or a pirate.

I could be Charlie Brown, who I've always thought is kind of a downer. So, no.

Casper the Friendly Ghost. Not scary. Kind of baby.

All the costumes are cheap imports with a plastic facemask secured by a thin piece of stapled elastic with a one size fits all something or other that slips over your street clothes. It's basically a themed medical robe, tying in the back, made of shiny nylon, and guaranteed to be fireproof because it will melt before it burns.

"You've got until the count of three," Mom says. As she's rounding two and three-quarters, I shrug. Mom takes the hint, "Okay. That's it. Let's go."

She grabs my arm and starts moving toward the door like a linebacker, which, if I'm not mistaken, was one of the costume options in aisle four. I hesitate, acting like dead weight. "What? Did you finally decide?"

"No. You forgot Butch. He's in the pet section by the goldfish and birds."

My mother blushes. We go grab the kid she forgot. As we move to leave, Butch has a small tantrum. "Slow down, baby. Use your words. Good Lord—you're the only one who can understand him. What is he saying, Warn?" My mom asks, smiling nervously at an older, judgy woman near the cat toys.

"He wants a fish," I say, wishing I had thought to say puppy instead.

Dammit, Warn, next time say puppy.

We stop to pay for the goldfish swimming in artificial, toxic, stolen from Love Canal, blue water. Soon we're in Dusty Rose heading toward the small home Shirley shares with Jerry, her former and now common-law husband. There is a pile of old Halloween costumes in the center of the paneled living room.

Oh. I get it. We're here because Mom is trying to save money.

"Warn," says Shirley with her eyes square on my mom, "why don't you look through my kid's old costumes? There's a lot of good stuff in there."

This pile of costumes is like my record collection, all of which belonged to Art, Emily, and Suzy before me. Everything is at least ten years old because Shirley's kids are older than me. Instead of cool things like H. R. Pufnstuf, there's a bunch of junk from the Eisenhower Administration. I'm surprised there isn't a Senator Joseph McCarthy costume in there. Not so fun fact: he represented Wisconsin.

Howdy Doody? No thanks. Roy Rogers. Who's that? Next!

Shirley holds up a matted fake fur coat with little tufts of bald spots. "My daughter Tammy wore this the year Alaska became our 49th state." Then in a textbook display of what will someday be called cultural appropriation, she adds, "She went as an Eskimo."

Then, it happens. Over her shoulder, I see the perfect costumes.

This is going to be the best Halloween ever.

Halloween has different meanings for different people. I like the candy and getting dressed up. It's fun to see what people choose for a costume. Other people like the scary part, sometimes too much if you ask me.

Even though it's almost the end of an episode of *The Lucy Show* and Mr. Mooney is in the middle of yelling at Mrs. Carmichael, Mom says, "Warn, turn off that TV. Art and Richard…"

Richard is Art's best friend. Great guy. Super smart. He's a gymnast and computer engineering major at the University of Wisconsin. Sandy blonde hair. Athletic build. Good looking. Kind of shy, but not in a boring way. He's shy in a "what isn't he saying?" way. He's Florence's son. Earl's too, but I don't know him as well.

Mom repeats herself the way she does when she thinks I'm not paying attention; but I was. Really. Anyway, she repeats herself. "Art and Richard said to meet them next door in the basement. No one else is home, so just walk in." A crack of thunder reminds her of something else. "It might rain. Hard to tell because it's dark. Wear your rain slicker just in case."

Halfway next door, it starts to rain. It becomes even harder to see. Luckily, I have the sidewalks memorized from all the times I've pretended to be blind. I know where the tree roots have pushed up the sidewalk. I know where it's crumbling and worse for wear. I turn left and walk up the Nabors' empty driveway, stumbling once on some wet leaves. I open their pristine storm door, which I keep open by wedging my body against it. I twist their spotless brass doorknob, clockwise and the door opens. Once inside, there's a little landing separating the stairs to the basement from the rest of the house. I take my coat off, shake away the rain and close the doors. The coat rack is too high for me, so I use my hood to hang the coat off the end of the banister.

I start walking down the stairs as I was told. Their rec room looks like the Montgomery Ward catalogue. They have a pool table, a stereo, and a bar with a sunburst mirror hanging behind it. The matching chairs and couch look like they were made from old barrels. The only light in the room comes from a Hamm's Beer clock with the infinity waterfall. Years from now, I'll think it is kind of tacky. Right now, it's awesome.

Art and Richard don't seem to be here.

Suddenly there is a clap of thunder. I jump a little. My heart begins to race. It's beating so loudly I can barely hear the ghostly moan filling the room. The lights briefly flash on.

Was that a ghost? I think it was. It was too quick to tell. I gasp and start backing away. The lights flash on again. There is something behind me, blocking the stairway. The lights flicker again. Instinct kicks in. Saturday mornings spent with Scooby-Doo pay off. If that's a ghost, I should be able to walk right through it.

Leading with my head I charge toward the stairs and hit something solid. A body. I didn't expect that. Only one thing to do, start slapping and hitting wildly.

The ghost begins laughing, which confuses me for a second. Someone from behind me forces my arms to my side. With no other option, I do what kids have done since the beginning of time. I raise my knee until it makes contact.

The lights come back on, revealing that it wasn't a ghost. It was a costume, and part of it has fallen away. The ghost is Art, doubled over in pain but still laughing.

"Warn! Warn," says Richard. "It's us!" Before giving into their explanation, I hit him once for good measure. Despite myself, I start to tear up - more from relief than fear.

Once Art can stand upright, they explain everything.

"See? I got a reel-to-reel tape machine for the sound effects. We unscrewed most of the lightbulbs, so they'd flicker better. We didn't mean to scare you that much. It's just a prank."

As scary as that was, part of me is thrilled. Someone loves me enough to frighten me. I'm a lucky boy.

It takes a lot of pouting, but Art, who is taking us trick or treating, is now on board. He and Mom help me get ready while Emily and her mad make-up skills work on Butch.

In the back of my mind, I'm vaguely aware that I haven't seen my father in two or three days and for some reason, decide that now is the time to ask. "Where's Dad? He should see our costumes."

I notice a quick look between Art and Emily. Mom keeps working on my costume, and complicity says, "He's out getting cigarettes."

Again, with the cigarettes. They come with second-hand smoke, and second-hand lies.

Us three brothers are placed in front of the china buffet, which we keep in the living room because the kitchen is too small. Val is home from Badger School for the Blind because it's the weekend. She's the first to speak. "You guys look great!"

The rest of us kind of look confused, but she can't see it.

"Just kidding," she says with a big smile. Val cracks me up.

Emily, too cool to dress up, breaks out her Polaroid Swinger camera to take a picture. Mom is so excited she applauds. As she hands us our candy bags, she says, "I don't think there have ever been better Halloween costumes."

And with that Batman, Robin, and the Joker head out the door.

Here's the backstory. Shirley already had the two superhero costumes, but we couldn't leave Butch out of the theme. I mean, it's not like you can have Batman, Robin and then randomly grab the Lone Ranger or Mamie Eisenhower from Shirley's 1950s stash. Mom spied a purple and green clown costume, which grossed me out until she said the keyword: Joker.

The rest is Barnes' family history.

It's hard to tell which one is bigger, Butch's real smile or the one Emily painted on.

I'm Batman, which means Art is Robin. He said the costume was too tight, so he's wearing his gym shorts instead of Robin's acrobat trunks.

So far, we've been given mini Nestle's Crunch, party-sized Lemon Drops, Good and Plenty in little cellophane baggies that don't open unless you use your teeth, an apple which will have to be inspected for razor blades, Dum Dums, Jolly Rogers, candy corn and a penny from Mrs. Christensen three doors down.

She's a widow without much money. I don't think many kids knock on her door. Mom said to make sure and stop there because she'd want to see our costumes. "Just say hello. Don't ask for anything." Mrs. Christensen insisted, so I'm going to put my penny in the UNICEF carton at school.

Mick, who lives next door to Mrs. C., smiled when she opened the door. She looked around to make sure no other kids were around, grabbed candy from a secret stash, and gave us *full-sized candy bars*. Mine is a Nestle's *$100,000 Bar*, which is the best. No coincidence. Mick knows it's my favorite.

Florence Nabors gave us jellybeans and three pencils. "See?" she said, "the Governor's name is engraved on them ... in *gold*."

Within half a block we have our routine down. Art hangs back, because he's like 20 years old. Everyone still gives him candy, which is nice of them. I'm in charge of saying, "Trick or treat," while Butch sits in his stroller looking cute. It's a plan that works. We're doing very well. My bag is almost too heavy to carry.

When we get to Aunt Lil's house one block over, we all get into position. I step forward to knock on the door and take a deep breath, getting ready to ask for candy. As the door starts to open, Butch leaps out of his stroller, jumping up and down excitedly. When Aunt Lil pops her head out of the door, somehow his giggles morph into words. Real, recognizable words.

"Trick or treat."

It's perfectly understandable. Clear as can be. All three of us just stare at him dumbfounded, happy, and proud. It's a Halloween miracle.

Aunt Lil starts crying and gives him three pieces of candy before kissing him on the cheek. Her red lipstick leaves an impression on the Joker's clown white face.

We're wrapping things up and are about a block away from home when Nancy's awesome emberglo (that means dark orange in car talk) Mustang pulls up. "Hi boys!" she says from the driver's seat. "I've been driving around looking for you. Great costumes!"

Nancy pulls over to the side of the road and jumps out to give me and Butch quick hugs before kissing Art. "Nice legs, Robin." Their kiss lasts longer than the hugs; that's for sure. Come up for air already. Now I'm the only one without lipstick stains. He holds her close, looking toward the inside of the car like there's a magnet inside it or something.

"Warn, it's close enough for you two to walk home. I'm going to hang out here with Nancy. You guys head back to the house, okay?"

"Sure." My mind starts plotting. We can stop by Mrs. Quamme's house again. She's giving out freshly baked brownies. In fact, we can do our whole street again. If anyone says anything, I can play the scared kid card and pretend we lost Art.

I practice whimpering under my breath just to be sure I'm prepared.

Butch and I start turning the corner back to our block. In the corner of my eye, I see a flash of metal. A car jumps the curb. I pull Butch's stroller away just before we're hit with a spray of gravel and dirt. The car missed us by inches. I quickly check on Butch, who's giggling as though he just got off a carnival ride. When I look up, I see the back of the car. Even if the tires didn't screech before turning into our driveway and parking at a severe angle, I'd know the driver of that bronze Buick Electra anywhere.

It's my dad.

Upsetting? I suppose. A surprise? Not really. Why dwell on it when there's candy to be gathered. Butch and I get home about fifteen minutes later, our bags overflowing. Crumbs of Mrs. Q.'s brownies quickly brushed away just before we enter the side door.

"Where were you, boys?" my Mom asks.

She follows up with another lie. "Your dad came home right after you left. He just went to bed. He waited up to see your costumes, but he was too tired."

We are quickly given a bath, Mom using food coloring to dye our water the same color that Butch's already dead goldfish used to swim. Mom tells us about some of the other kids and the costumes she saw.

"Wayne was here. He was a scarecrow. His little brother was Bucky Badger. Paula from your class was here too. She was dressed as Raggedy Ann."

Barf.

We're each allowed to have a little candy. We share with Val. She loves Sweet Tarts, so I give them all to her. Our cat Ming meows at the door to be let in and follows me to bed. He makes a little nest between my calves and settles in for a snooze.

I hear Art come in a few hours later, in a very good mood. He's humming a little tune to himself while he reads. He smells of Nancy's perfume.

The next morning there's Sunday School. I sneak some jellybeans into my pocket to help get me through. Our teacher, one of the more conservative parish members, warns us about the dangers of Pagan holidays. Krissy Thomas raises her hand. "I think you're a little late, Mrs. Dyer. Halloween was yesterday. Do you mean Thanksgiving? Many people don't realize it, but that's a pagan holiday too."

She's a preacher's daughter and Paula's best friend.

Mom is putting the finishing touches on Sunday dinner when Art and I get home. My nose immediately tells me she made fried chicken. She's mad. My dad *hates* fried chicken. Whenever we have it, he says, "We aren't god-damned poor Dorothy. Once a week, we can have a roast."

When she's done setting the table, she tells us to get settled. Then Mom heads toward their bedroom, pounding on the door real hard. It's *loud*. Like the Nabors next door can hear it loud.

"Raymond! Get out of bed. You slept the morning away. It's time to eat. The kids are waiting."

He grumbles a reply.

"You missed Halloween. You're not missing this," she says with a voice she normally reserves for misbehaving children. No room for negotiation. Case closed. Do as I say.

There's a pause, followed by a groan, followed by a slouching man who looks a lot like my father. His hair is pointing in a million different directions. His eyes are puffy, narrow, little slits. He's wearing a white t-shirt and worn boxer shorts. The rest of us are wearing our Sunday best. Val may not realize it, but she's wearing a freaking bonnet.

Soon, the clatter of knives and forks is filling the air. Emily praises the fried chicken. She should know. She worked at KFC. Art is watching the clock. He's expected at the station in time for the 2 pm airing of *Dairyland Jubilee*, a super boring TV show featuring Freddy Terpening and the Accordocats. It's basically a bunch of old people doing the polka. Gag.

As always, the Barnes' Home Improvement message book and a pile of little notes are on the dining table, wending their way through the various plates and bowls. My father absentmindedly starts looking through them when he comes upon the picture Emily took yesterday.

"What's this?" Raymond asks.

"A picture of the boys from last night," responds Mom in an annoyed voice.

His eyes get wide. "Batman and the clown," he begins to say.

"Joker. Butch was the Joker." Why doesn't anyone get that? I continue explaining, "You see, Shirley had a clown costume, so…"

He cuts me off. "That's what you went dressed as last night? That was you? You and Butch?" He looks at Mom. "Oh my God Dorothy, I almost…"

Stopping himself from finishing the thought, he quickly gets up. Putting one arm around me and the other around Butch, he kisses our faces over and over. His lips are dry. His beard is scraping my cheeks. I can smell the whiskey on his breath. I want to pull away, but I don't. Somehow, I feel sorry for him. He's trying not to cry. The rest of the table is quiet, unsure what to make of all this.

Butch breaks the silence.

"Trick or treat," he says. "Trick or treat!"

CHAPTER SEVEN

A BRIEF THANKSGIVING

My dad hasn't had a drink since Halloween. It's been almost two weeks. Each day is weirder than the last. We've eaten together as a family every night. Emily and Mom looked through a college catalogue together. My dad plays with us. He even took me to Arlan's to buy me a baseball glove. I think it's the only time we've ever been alone together. Thank God for car radios.

I can see some of the neighbors spying from their windows, mouthing, "What the hell?" to each other when they see my dad giving me baseball lessons. Can't blame them. I feel the same way.

We start a couple of feet apart from each other, just tossing the ball back and forth. It lasts about five minutes. The only time we talk is when he corrects my form. He keeps using words like acceleration. Hello? I'm five years old. I don't know what that is.

Finally, there is an attempt to break the silence. "So, how are you doing?" he asks.

I immediately have the impulse to start looking around to see who it is he's talking to when I realize it's me. My father is asking me a question. I pause before answering, because I'm sure I'm not supposed to acknowledge being kind of creeped out. "I'm fine," is the best I can do.

Awkward pause. "I'd like us to do more of this."

"We don't have to," I say.

His jaw stiffens. "Don't say that." He takes a deep breath and visibly relaxes before inhaling again. "Why? Why do you say that?"

"Well, you never wanted to before," I mumble, staring at my new best friend, the ground.

Just then, Sky King pulls into the driveway. Art is carrying a bag from Ben Franklin. Somewhere in that bag, there are comic books. I break the heavy silence by throwing my glove to the ground and running after my brother.

After a few minutes Dad comes into the kitchen, quietly puts the baseball glove on the table next to me, opens the cupboard under the sink, moves aside the Comet, Pine-Sol, and Lysol, all the Sols really. He finally finds his treasure, a hidden bottle of Canadian Club.

I anticipate the next move. Grab a glass from the cupboard. Instead, he opens the bottle and pours it down the drain. As he does so, my mother comes over, puts her arms around him, and kisses his cheek. They stare at each other for a moment or two before Dad grabs his car keys.

"Where are you going?" she asks in a concerned voice.

"There's a meeting I should go to," he says while putting on his coat.

The next day my dad asks me to play ball again. We manage to catch and throw from a farther distance. Despite being farther apart, I feel closer to him. My game begins to improve. He notices and encourages.

"You're a good spotter, Warn. You make the ball go where you want it to."

We play a little longer each evening until the weekend when Valerie comes home from school. He asks her to join us. She looks confused before beginning to laugh.

"Very funny, Dad. I can't play catch."

"Why not?"

"You know why … I'm *blind*."

"Yes, you are. You're blind. That'll make catching harder, but nothing is stopping you from *throwing* the ball." With that, Valerie stands up and leads us to the front yard. The game begins. Each time she hears the ball she has thrown land in a glove, she giggles. Butch is our cheering section. He sits on the steps waiting to be old enough to get in the game.

Evenings get chillier. Days get shorter. Thanksgiving arrives, which is always a special holiday at our house. This is the happiest one I will ever have. Waking up to pancakes, the kitchen is already humid from boiling potatoes. The turkey is roasting in Mom's enameled Nessco oven. The pies my grandpa sent over are waiting on the Formica counter. We have so much tradition going that there should be a fiddler on our roof.

After the Macy's Thanksgiving Day Parade, on which I will someday work, Mom bundles me up in my new coat with the shearling collar. Just before Art and I walk out the side door, she says, "Wait! I almost forgot. Grandma Caruso made something for you boys!" She quickly returns with a small box. Immediately an old lady cologne of spicy lavender joins the cornucopia of Thanksgiving scents already filling the kitchen, getting stronger as each layer of tissue paper is peeled away.

From the box, she pulls two knit caps. The grown-up-sized one for

Art is shaped like a roasted turkey, with drumsticks popping out from his temples. Mine, the kid-sized cap, has a colorful cascade of knit turkey feathers fanning out across the back. The gift is completed with matching mittens for me and gloves for Art. Fun and more playful than I think of my grandma ever being.

When I'm an adult, I will pull these from the same box and wear them with Art's kids. As I push the hats onto their tiny, perfect heads, I'll tell them all about the best aspects of their Great-grandma Emma, who would've loved them very much.

For some reason, our little house is the one everyone comes to for the holidays. As such, Art and I climb into his car to pick up all the widows and spinsters - a word which we have yet to learn is diminishing to women choosing not to marry. I try not to use that word, even though I am using it now, in the historical context.

Our first stop is to the home of Great-Aunt Louise. She's a firecracker. Aunt Louise has buried three husbands so far, one of whom was named Bunny. How and why was a grown man named Bunny? How I wish I'd asked. Maybe Marlene Cummings named him.

We listen to "Alice's Restaurant" on WHA, which will become another tradition. We will listen to it each Thanksgiving we're together while making the widow run.

I have the chorus memorized and begin to sing along with it.

"You can get anything you want at Alice's restaurant ... "

It's a long song. We collect Aunt Louise well before it's over. She sings along in her sharp, church lady soprano. After the song ends, she puts her hand on Art's shoulder, sneaks up behind us from the backseat, and says, "What a foolish war."

"By the way, boys," she adds. "I love your hats. I'd recognize Emma's needlework anywhere." Holding up her own gnarled, arthritic hands, she looks a little wistful. "Oh well. Still so much to be thankful for—happy Thanksgiving!"

When we get home with Aunts Louise, Judy, Judy, Addie, and Gladys, the nice lady who works at Grandpa's bakery, our house is bursting at the seams. Nancy is passing out trayed appetizers she made herself. Canapes, I think they're called. Boy is her family fancier than ours. My sister Suzy is here with, "A long-haired hippie type," according to my Uncle Philip who is here from Minneapolis. Both grandmas are helping Mom cook in a friendly alpha matriarch competition.

My Grandma Barnes. Tiny. Birdlike. Always well dressed in a dotty, older British lady way. She desperately loves my grandpa, which explains the blonde rinse she puts in her hair once a month. Thick glasses exaggerate her expressive eyes.

She is perhaps the most family-oriented person I will ever know. I love her so much. How I'll miss her when she passes away in ten years.

She and my grandpa met when she was a dance hall singer in London during World War I. As I understand it from others, she never would have told me herself; she was also a model. I have a beautiful photo of her wrapped in furs which was sold as a postcard all over England. Doughboy soldiers carried Phyllis Tinkum Barnes into fox holes throughout Europe.

As an adult I will keep my copy next to the souvenirs she brought home from the coronation of Queen Elizabeth.

Grandma and Grandpa married in England. They moved to America after their second son, my dad, was born. In total, they had six boys. Phyllis Barnes was the only woman in the household. Perhaps that's why she always seems just a little bit nervous. Keeping them all in line had to be draining.

Her fourth son, Gregory, is drafted into service during the Korean War when he's nineteen-years old. He's the first soldier from Wisconsin to be killed. His young body will never be recovered. She will spend the rest of her life combing newspaper obituaries so she can attend the funerals of soldiers who died in battle. She needs to see for herself that the other bodies come home, I suppose. Who knows? Grief isn't rational. Keeping a list of the fallen, she prays for them while clutching her well-worn rosary.

When my grandfather passes away, six years and four months from now, she will be sad in a way that will never end. She'll stop visiting the bakery. She will wear his robe to bed. She will cry each time his name is mentioned, so much so that, for a while we will stop talking about him. When she realizes what we're doing, she will say, "Please don't do that. I don't want the world to forget my Billy."

Afterward, her heart will be a little lighter—not for herself, for her family, and to hear his name said by someone other than herself.

A converted Catholic, she will suffer a major stroke while attending church the Monday after her final Mother's Day. Her last words will be to a priest administering last rites.

"Don't worry about me, Father. I'm going to be just fine."

In her will, she leaves me the money I will use to go to college.

Her funeral will be led by my Great-uncle Father Francis. My two Great-aunts, Sisters Alma Rita and Mary Rita, will play their guitars. Butch will accidentally say, "Pray their guitars." They'll be thrilled and say it that way for the rest of their lives.

Service families will be standing at the back of a packed church.

I will be a pallbearer. For weeks afterward, I'll wonder if I did a good enough job for her body to have been laid to rest perfectly, as she deserved.

That is years from now. Today she's sneaking a little more salt into Mom's corn casserole. She's mad at Grandpa because he's at the bakery making sure people can pick up their last-minute orders.

"I said, 'Billy, how many family holidays are you going to miss'?"

Aunt Louise, three times a widow, solemnly nods.

Aunt Judy #1 hands Mom a bottle of red wine. A quick look of tension passes over her face as she takes it. A beat later, she remembers to say, "Thank you," before placing it in the hallway linen closet behind her Kotex. No liquor will be served today.

Dad is off to the side making gravy. He holds up a spoon for me to try it. Tastes like gravy, so I make an m-m-m-m-m sound and give him a thumbs-up before heading to the TV. As I pass Aunt Louise and Grandma Barnes, I overhear her saying, "It's been almost a month. I hope he can keep it up this time." She follows it up by pulling a crucifix on a thin gold chain toward her mouth and kissing it.

One day I will go on to play the Stage Manager in Thornton Wilder's *Our Town*. Mr. Wilder was originally from Madison. Hometown boy done good. Pulitzer Prize winner, for *The Bridge of San Luis Rey* and *Our Town*, in which, spoiler alert—the lead female dies. Sorry, not sorry. You've had a long time to see it. Your fault if you haven't. Anyway, in the third act, the dead woman newly settled in the town cemetery is offered a chance to relive one day of her life.

This Thanksgiving is the day I'd choose. Except for my own wedding,

I will never again be with so many people I love, when I loved them, at the same time in the same room.

I'd choose this moment because, by Christmas, all of it is gone.

CHAPTER EIGHT

SON OF A SANTA

Christmas is a restless time. So much anticipation! Shopping. Carols. Decorations. Presents. And get this. Mrs. Milbauer just told us we get two whole weeks off from school.

"It's called winter break," she says.

A kid, Tim Maustin, who sits next to the only Jewish boy in our class, immediately raises his hand. "You mean Christmas break."

Mrs. Milbauer pauses before pressing forward, "Some people call it that, Timmy, but not everyone in our class celebrates Christmas, so I prefer for us to say winter break."

"Well, I'm going to say Christmas break!" retorts the five-year-old who will become a father his sophomore year of high school.

In my notoriously subjective memory, Danny Stein mouths the word "schmuck" and rolls his eyes toward heaven.

I don't know it yet, but this Christmas will be my most memorable. It starts in December, the day before the first snowfall of the year. My dad, doing his best to keep busy, idle hands, and all that, brings me into what feels like a very adult plan.

"Warn," he says, holding my coat, hat, and mittens, "Turn off the TV. I need your help." I happily comply, despite the fact I'm watching *Bewitched* and it's a Serena episode.

I follow him to the front yard, where a ladder, extension cords, a long string of lights, and a garden clipper with a telescoping handle await us. Dad starts trimming the tree in the literal sense, doing his best to make sure it is shaped well. He's trimming it before trimming it. Chopping here and there as offending branches reveal themselves.

My job is to snake the multi-colored lights across the yard to ensure there are no tangles. Luckily, they were put away carefully last year, so it's fairly easy. Soon the lights are stretched out past the point in the yard where the cross was burnt. The cords are so long they nearly reach into neighbor Nabors' yard.

"Now, Warn, you stand next to the ladder, right here," he says, gently placing me into position. I'm going to start winding the lights around the tree. It's your job to hold them up and keep the line moving." He then patiently demonstrates what he means. It's like a mime pulling a rope, but instead of a rope, it's a cord, and instead of miming it, there's something to hold.

As dusk settles in, the lights are evenly spaced out and in place.

Mom comes outside without her coat on, which she'd yell at me for doing. She does that little jump up and down that people do when they're trying to stay warm. She also rubs her hands together. For circulation, I suppose. Honestly, it's just easier to grab your coat from the pegboard by the backdoor. As she stands next to me, Dad connects the extension cord and moves toward the outside outlet he installed last week. "Okay, family," he says with a smile, "count backward from 3!"

"3-2-1!" we say together. Dad plugs in the cord, and ... nothing.

That doesn't stop Ray Barnes. Like the mechanical genius my father is, he slaps the side of the circuit box, and there is light. We all clap, including Butch, who is watching from inside, with our cat Ming, who also looks impressed. For real. He stopped licking himself the minute the lights popped on.

For a second, I forget to breathe. Our tree is perhaps the most beautiful thing I've ever seen. I'm unable to imagine anything better for all of ten seconds. Then something even better happens.

"Warn, I have one more job for you," says Dad. He opens a box I hadn't noticed before. After pulling away several layers of yellowed, fragile-looking tissue paper (my family loves wrapping things in tissue paper), he pulls out an angel tree topper.

"This is from England, where I was born. When I was your age, I used to put this on top of the tree, but now it's your job. Do you promise to be careful?"

Nodding my head very solemnly, I say, "I do."

"Good. This was given to me by my grandma. Someday it will be yours."

My dad leads me up the ladder, holding my waist as we both climb. When I get to the highest wrung, he lifts me into the air. Mom hands me the angel. I fly higher than I've ever been and gently place the fragile figurine on the top of the tree. As my dad pulls me away, I notice she's just a little crooked. I'm back on the ground before I can say anything.

I can't be sure but, in my memories, we were the first family in our neighborhood to have outdoor lights. As other homes begin to decorate, I'm silently sure everyone else is copying my dad. Each time I stare at our tree, awash in Christmas colors, I'm proud to be the son of the man who invented outdoor Christmas lights.

Time keeps moving forward, as time does. The Christmas season inches closer, molasses slow. Holiday cards start arriving. One by one, they are hung up on the thin fishing wire stretched across our living room walls, near the ceiling. As Mom puts them in place, she makes little marks in her correspondence book so she knows to whom she should send cards next year. This need to keep an inventory, as though each stamp is priceless, is one I will not carry forward. Keeping score that way. I don't understand it. If I want to wish you happy holidays that's what I'm going to do.

About a week later, on a Saturday evening, without any warning, Butch and I are given a thorough scrubbing and put into our finest clothes. Both of us are in dress pants, starchy white shirts, and little clip-on bow ties. Matching cardigans complete the JC Penney's on clearance look. Val, home from school for the weekend, is in a beige plaid dress—a Burberry knock-off long before I knew what Burberry or knock-offs were.

A bag and a suitcase are placed in the back of Dusty Rose. The car carries us to the shores of Lake Waubesa and the grandest house I've ever seen. Old. Stately. It's what I will judge other grand homes against for the rest of my life.

Whoever lives here has clearly stolen my dad's outdoor Christmas lights idea and taken it to a whole new level. Huge, old-fashioned golden lights faithfully follow the lines of the soaring roof. The house glows as if it has a halo.

In the front yard, a huge horse, thick with a winter coat, is strapped into a harness attached to a sleigh. A man in top hat and riding boots waits to give rides. Currier & Ives has come to life.

My father pulls the car to the side of the house, which is flanked by catering trucks and a few workers stealing a smoke. My mom's wonderful cousin Frances is there looking at her watch before we enter her peripheral vision. A look of relief comes over her warm and classically Italian face. She is a Hummel figurine come to life.

"There you are!" she says. "Dorothy, help Ray get ready. Kids, you follow me." She grabs Butch and me by the hands, forgetting for a moment that

Valerie is blind and in a strange place. She drops my hand, grabs Val's, and moves forward looking over her shoulder before adding, "Warn, keep up!"

One winding path and a heavy oak door later, we are in the most alive, beautiful room I've ever seen. High ceilings, gleaming wooden floors, classic American furniture, a tinseled, flocked Christmas tree, and a roaring fire that crackles whenever people stop paying attention to it. Along the mantel, bubble lights percolate in random rhythms. An elegant, older woman, wearing a mink stole and a feathered hat, sits at an upright piano playing Christmas Carols. Between songs, she takes liberal gulps of what I'm guessing is a punch made purely of booze. Her playing gets worse throughout the evening.

Val is singing along with "Frosty, der Schneeeman." How does she know the lyrics? They're in German. I've got to remember to ask Val about that someday. Cousin Frances finds us a small clearing to position ourselves. She taps an older gentleman on the shoulder.

"Yes?" says the silver-haired, distinguished man in a real tweed suit.

"Kids, this is Mr. Healy," says Frances. "He and his lovely wife are our hosts for the evening. Say thank you."

"Good evening, Mr. Healy. We're Ray and Dorothy Barnes' children. Thank you for having us over tonight," I say as was drilled into me in the car on the way here. I think I got every word perfect. I must have. He's smiling.

"No need to thank me," he graciously says. "This is for all the heroes. Men like your dad," he says with a gleam in his eyes.

"Huh?"

"Your dad and other men who got wounded in the war. This party is in their honor. Every family in Madison with a Purple Heart recipient was invited."

"Mr. Healy, my dad's heart is red just like anyone else's," says Valerie.

Our host chuckles. "That's true, I'm sure. A Purple Heart, the way I'm using the term, means a medal that is given soldiers for exceptional service that resulted in an injury ... or death. Your dad, for example. He was shot..."

Wait. What? My dad was shot. My dad was *shot*?

"... during World War II, in Italy. 1945. From what I've heard, he still has shrapnel in his legs. Poor guy. I imagine he's always in some sort of pain." Mr. Healy gets a faraway look in his eyes. He breaks his own trance by offering one final thought. "Guys like me owe men like your dad a lot."

"Heroes sell aluminum siding?" I ask.

"Yes, some of them do. This room is full of heroes."

Mr. Healey gives us a second to look around and appreciate the weight of what he's just said. He smiles warmly and offers, "Wow. That was some grown-up talk, eh? Those aren't my stories to tell kids. If you want to hear more, ask your dad," says our host. A woman, instinct and her diamond earrings tell me it's Mrs. Healy, comes up beside him. He kisses her lightly on the cheek before speaking. "Dearest, these are the Barnes' kids. Let me see if I can get this right. Butch, Valerie and, and…"

"Warn! I'd recognize you anywhere," says Mrs. Healey. "Your dad called the day you were first on TV, so we watched. You did a very nice job! I didn't know we'd have such an attractive television star at the party tonight!"

She playfully adjusts her hair and then straightens my bow tie before handing me a little porcelain clown. "I bought this for you at Goodman's!"

That's a nice jewelry store on State Street. The nicest one in town, I think. I don't know why a jewelry store sells clown figurines, but okay.

"Thank you, Mrs. Healey."

One of the catering staff shows up with a tray. Mrs. Healy grabs three bags. "Kids, these are a little treat from us to you. One for each of you. We have a big supper planned. Don't let these treats ruin your appetite!"

I look inside my plastic bag. There are five nuts still in their shells, a few red and white starlight mints, and an orange. I smile and say thank you, but I'm pretty sure my appetite is safe. Grown-ups have some funny ideas about so-called treats.

Then we are all ushered into a large foyer, with a Beverly Hillbillies like staircase winding its way up to the house's second level. Me and a bunch of the other kids are corralled toward the front, so we don't have to look over the adults. Val, standing next to me, faces in the opposite direction, confusing the grown-ups in the next row.

A woman in a black leotard with her hair pulled into a ballerina-like bun starts applauding. It's my cousin the dance teacher, Mary Esther, Frances' daughter. The rest of the crowd joins in as she puts the needle down on a high-fi. Hawaiian music fills the room, and the lady says, "Aloha! We take you from Wisconsin to the sunny shores of our 50th state, Hawaii!"

A group of young girls float down the stairway. Some are in time. The others, not so much. They're dressed in tropical bikini tops and grass skirts. The girls without long hair wear wigs of Halloween quality. As the intro music plays, they distribute little fake flower leis, saying, "*Mele Kalikimaka*," in thick midwestern accents. Adorable, hilarious, or both, depending on your mood.

Oh boy. Paula is one of the younger dancing girls. I resist the urge to throw one of my Brazilian nuts at her. She sees me and waves, but I ignore her. I am, after all, a TV star. Mrs. Healy said so.

The girls do a nice job. Sincere applause is followed by a cascade of flashbulbs as the troupe takes a curtain call. On their final bow, the music changes. When the girls are once again standing upright, we can see they have put on Santa hats, which look kind of silly with a bikini top and a grass skirt.

"*He's making a list and checking it twice. He's going to find out who's naughty or nice. Santa Claus is coming to town.*"

The girls wave to the top of the stairway. All eyes follow up in time to hear, "Ho-ho-ho!" Mr. and Mrs. Claus have arrived. Valerie and Butch start cheering. Something doesn't feel right to me. I squint and immediately see my dad's face underneath Santa's white beard.

As he and Mrs. Claus, AKA, Mom's cousin Frances, make their way through the crowd passing out gifts, the kids around me get very excited. One kid looks like he's about twelve, but okay. To each his own.

I resist the temptation to shout, "He's not real. That's my dad, you idiots!"

What good would it do? I don't want the believers to be sad or feel stupid. Then it strikes me; I've never believed in Santa Claus. Not the way other kids do. I just went along with it because it's what the adults expected.

I look around at all the kids cheering for my dad, and feel a bit sorry for them, getting so worked up over something that isn't real. I'm the lucky one. I already know something they won't figure out for years. As my parents once said, I'm ahead of the curve.

Then I look at my dad, handing out presents, looking so happy and playful. As he hands me my present he says, "I saved a special one for you, my boy." Immediately feeling better, I rip through the wrapping paper, knowing there's something special awaiting. Inside the package is every child's dream, a shoehorn on a long stick.

Nuts, mints, an orange, a clown, and a shoehorn—a masterclass in what not to give kids. How the children in my life have benefitted from that lesson.

I watch the man in red jiggle through the crowd. My dad is Santa

Claus. He can string Christmas lights and sell aluminum siding while maintaining sobriety for over a month. He won World War II for the United States and has a Purple Heart to show for it. There's nothing my dad can't do.

For a nanosecond, I believe he can make reindeer fly.

Later that night, Art and Emily come upstairs to hear about the party and see my shoehorn, about which they pretend to be very excited. I give them my snack baggie. Their enthusiasm seems to equal my own. Thanks for the orange, rich people on the lake.

Feeling as though I'll burst if I don't tell someone, I share the news.

"Santa Claus was there, but it was Dad."

Art and Emily look at each other before Art starts speaking. "He was just helping Santa out. We talked about this. Kris Kringle can't be everywhere. He has helpers."

Maybe they're not ready to hear the truth. I decide not to push it. I put a little bow on things by saying, "All I know is we're lucky to be his kids."

Art's posture changes. It's slight, but he pulls away an inch or two. Emily's lips frown. "Warn," she says with a pause as though she's been reminded of my name's weight. "He's not my father or Art's. You know that."

"Yeah, but we're still his kids."

Art joins in. "You are. Butch is. And the four of us have the same mom, but he's not our father. That's why we call him Ray instead of Dad."

"Then why is your last name Barnes?"

"It's not. Our last name is Holden," says Emily. "I thought you knew that."

Suddenly something has irrevocably changed. For the first time ever, I feel separate from them. How can we have different last names? They're my family.

Art must sense that I'm uncomfortable and confused. His tone quickly changes. "Hey, it's just a name. You're our brother," he says before kissing me on the cheek. While Emily tucks in my sheets, he walks over to Butch and gives him a little tickle. "You, too!"

Butch is still giggling as they leave the room.

I fall asleep hugging my shoehorn.

CHAPTER NINE

FLYING CHRISTMAS COOKIES

The house smells so good. Mom spent the entire day baking traditional Italian cookies, and the sweeter frosted American kind. I got to help this year, so some of the treats probably look better than others. A few Santa cookies look like they have Bell's Palsy. The snowmen might look as though they were done by Picasso, but every cookie on the table is a homemade labor of love.

They're stacked all over the kitchen table. Mom says they've got to set, which I suspect means dry, so they can be put in last year's tins without sticking to each other. We will do that tomorrow. Then they'll get delivered to friends and family. I hate to see them go, but even at five-years-old, I know that we are likely to get just as many in return.

"Warn, come here; I have something to show you," says Mom as she rushes through the door. She seems excited and hopeful, so I am too. I follow her to the bedroom.

"We have to hurry. I'm running late," she says, staring at her watch. "The beauty salon took longer than I thought it would, and … well, just hurry!"

She unzips a plastic garment bag and reverently pulls out a new dress. The garment is built on a foundation of heavy, ivory color brocaded silk. The high collar has sequins that manage to catch the little bit of late afternoon sun streaming in through the windows. Below that and down to the hem, there are what I will someday know are called bugle beads. One end of each bead is sewn onto the dress. The other end falls free, so there is a rustling sound with each movement of the garment.

"Do you like it?" she asks.

I'm silent for a second, trying to capture the right words. "Mom," I say solemnly, "that's the prettiest dress in the world."

"Oh, good! It was on sale, so … oh, you don't care about things like that. Go on now. Your dad will be here any minute. I have to get ready for the party tonight!"

The party tonight. An adult only affair. A date night, before the term has been coined. It's nice to see Mom so excited. Girlish. Wanting to be pretty for her husband. Everyone should see their mother like that, at least once, excited to look her best for the person she loves. Fathers too.

My dad lights up when he sees her. Having arranged for Emily to babysit, they leave arm in arm. He even opens the car door for her. Something I will only ever see him do this once. They are a beautiful couple.

I have relaxed my Kilroy vigil since Dad stopped drinking nearly two months ago. I'm not at the window as they arrive home. Hearing loud grown-up voices awakens me. I must have been in a deep sleep. I'm momentarily disoriented. Immediately wanting to feel safe, I look to my right. Art's bed is empty. He's not home.

As I've done many times before, I throw off my bedding and rush to the window. Dad's car is back. It's in our driveway, parked on a diagonal, wandering into the neighbor's yard as though it's trying to escape.

A tight knot forms in my stomach. I rush down the stairs. Through the crack in the door, I see my mother run toward their bedroom. The door begins to shut. My father kicks it open despite the constant pain caused by the shrapnel I've heard his leg supposedly carries.

"Stay away from me, Raymond," I hear her say quietly. Even when she's frightened, she thinks of her children first. Threatened but unwilling to wake anyone up while defending herself. As her fear builds, she repeats herself more strongly. "Stay away!"

He advances despite her protests. I reach the door just in time to see him rip the world's most beautiful dress off her body. My mother is left standing in an ivory-colored slip as a thousand bugle beads fly over my head and hit the wall. I gasp, which in hindsight is a mistake.

My father's fist is in the air, poised to hit her when he hears me. His anger changes target. He pushes my mother to the floor. I turn away, my weight already on my front foot. I begin to sprint, barely eluding his grasp. I run into the hallway toward the kitchen. He's right behind me, just like in that dream about the clown.

I slide onto the linoleum floor but not toward home plate. I'm headed underneath the table covered with Christmas cookies.

He pushes aside his chair at what we all assume is the head of the table despite it being round. He bends down to yell at me. "Get out from there." When I don't, his anger grows. "Come here, goddamn you!"

His arm lunges toward me, but I'm balled up, just out of reach.

For once, having an older father pays off. I'm certain he won't crawl under the table to get to me. It's too much effort. Instead, he walks over to the other side of the table and pushes that chair aside. By then, I've moved back to my original position, still just out of his reach.

I believe Wonder Woman has a golden lasso that compels people to tell the truth. I believe that Thor has a magical hammer that can summon lightning. I believe that Superman can fly. What I can't believe until this very moment is that my father could willfully want to hurt me.

Ignore me, yes.

Choose other things over me, absolutely.

Act violently toward me, no. Never. Not in a million years.

That's not possible.

Is it?

Raymond, tired of our cat and mouse game, stands his ground for a moment. Growling like a bear. Pacing while he decides what to do. Suddenly both his hands appear underneath the table. I hear a grunt. The two legs against the wall begin to rise. My dark little cavern underneath the table is flooded with light as the table begins to take flight. Christmas cookies fly into the air until they hit the floor, ruined.

Everything is ruined.

He has underestimated the trajectory. Instead of allowing him to reach me, the table has created a new barrier. I start to run back toward my mother. Raymond attempts to follow me but instead slips on the cookies. As he falls, his jaw hits the edge of the table, and I'm glad. He begins bleeding, but that doesn't stop him. He's up on his feet, angrier than ever. He's just about to enter the doorway when Emily blocks his path.

"What the hell do you think you're doing?" she asks in a resolute voice.

To her right is a tiny table with a beige trim line phone on it. He sees it and realizes that help is just a phone call away. He picks it up, wraps some of the cording around his fist, and yanks. The phone wires and a big chunk of plaster fly out of the wall, ricocheting back toward the fallen table and Christmas cookies.

Emily looks at him with dispassionate hate.

"I already called the police."

Sirens can be heard in the distance.

Butch wakes up and joins us just in time to see Raymond put in handcuffs. As the cops lead him out of the house, I see my little brother sorting through the cookies, trying to find one that hasn't hit the floor. He's biting the head off a reindeer as the door shuts.

I stare out the window, confused, as my former, temporary hero is pushed into the squad car. Sirens. Flashing lights. Neighbors. My attention diverted from the car as I look up and notice that although it's past 1 am, every house on our street has lights on and curtains cracked.

They all know.

Everyone knows.

It's not going to be a secret.

Mom and Emily set the table back into position, I notice the place where I usually sit is now chipped and cracked. It will remain that way until I buy my mother a new table the day after Raymond dies.

I won't truly forgive him for tonight until about 30-seconds after he's dead.

My father, having been arrested and booked, uses his one phone call to contact his brother. In a stunning example of loyalty over common sense, Uncle Foolish heads down to the police station to bail him out. For $50, Raymond Barnes is released into his own recognizance. Uncle Comeonnow proceeds to drive him back to our home, to the literal scene of the crime. My dad is dropped in front of the house. Uncle Whatthehellareyouthinking pulls away before Dad makes it to the front door.

My Uncle's work is done. The Barnes family has been reunited.

Inside, on the other side of the wall, Mom, Emily, Butch, and I are huddled together. Butch is stopped from going to the door and letting Raymond in. I'm hyperventilating, afraid that my breathing will betray our location. Mom, still in her ivory slip, starts to panic.

Emily looks completely calm.

"Don't worry. I have his keys. He can't get in, and he can't drive."

Art arrived as the police were pulling away. He's blaming himself. When he saw the kitchen and the aftermath, he kept saying, "I should've been here. I should've been here." Now, he is outside, acting as bodyguard blocking my father's path.

"Goddammit Dorothy, it's cold out here. Let me in!" says my father in an angry voice. The silence is met with a long, steady, strong round of pounding against every surface not protected by landscaping.

"Come on. It was just one night. One night," he whimpers. "I fucked up again, didn't I? I ruined everything."

No one is arguing with you, Dad.

The tree we lit together provides just enough light for me to watch him through the sheer curtains in the bedroom. I can see him pacing along the front of the house. Anger and contrition having failed, he tries empty promises.

"Come on, sweetie pie. Let me in. I'll be fine. I promise." He gets tired, sits on the front steps, and pulls a tiny flask out of his breast pocket. He drains it quickly, smacking the bottom to release any small drops that might be clinging to the sides or pooled at the bottom. Once confident he's had all there is to have, he throws the flask toward the window from which I'm looking.

He's too drunk for his throw to break the window. Instead, there is a dull thud. Flaccid failure. The flask slides down the side of the house and hits the ground.

I make out a figure walking across the street. One of our neighbors kindly lifts him up, before heading across the street, where I assume Raymond will spend the night.

And so, our little house loses another father.

As Art, Emily and Mom straighten up the kitchen, I unlock the front door, open it and walk outside. There's no need to sneak. Their attention is elsewhere. Despite the darkness, I easily find the flask my father threw. I pick it up, take aim and throw it into the air.

The quiet of the night is broken by the sound of the angel on top of our beautiful tree breaking before it falls to the ground, beyond repair.

CHAPTER TEN

LOVE AMERICAN STYLE

It's April. We just came back to class from spring break which Timmy Maustin insists on calling, "Easter break."

I heard Danny Stein's parents found out. Mrs. Gasser, the school secretary, says everyone was worried they might sue, whatever that means. In the end, nothing came of it. Mr. and Mrs. Stein were like, "Eh. We've got bigger gefilte fish to fry." All that drama for nothing.

Art and Nancy are going to get married in June. I'm going to be something called a ring bearer. That means I get to walk down the aisle of the church with Nancy's cousin Sherri, the flower girl, like a mini bride and groom. She has the easier job for sure. Sherri just throws flower petals at people, which I'd do for the fun of it. I've got to carry two slippery rings on a slippery pillow from the back of the church to the front and walk in time with the music.

Mom doesn't wear her engagement or wedding rings anymore, so I practice with those. My parents are getting a divorce. I'm not supposed to know. No one has told me. I just overheard Mom talking with Grandma.

"Land sakes, Dorothy don't worry yourself about it. The only thing people will be asking is why you waited so long." Putting the dishtowel back on the drying rack, she adds, "This is the first divorce I've ever been in favor of."

I haven't seen my dad since the night he threw the table at me, or away from me, whatever you want to call it. Although if you ask me, "My dad threw a table away from me," doesn't describe it very well. I've asked Wayne and some other friends at school. None of them have had a table thrown away from them. I'm pretty sure I'm in a unique situation here—but not in the good sense of the word. The bad kind of unique. Wrong.

Raymond hasn't tried to see us. He hasn't apologized. He's just gone.

Last week I threw a ball at Butch, and it was a whole big deal. "Apologize to him, young man!" said basically everyone who saw me do it. Throw a ball in this family, and it's a big deal. Throw furniture and everyone acts as though nothing has happened.

Grandma Caruso came to live with us, so our rooms got shuffled around. Emily is sharing the upstairs bedroom with Grandma and Butch. Art is sleeping in the small bedroom on the first floor.

Val isn't living with us. One morning before Christmas, her stuff was just gone. I accidentally overheard Mom say, "Raymond arranged for Valerie to stay with Gladys," the nice lady from the bakery who was here for Thanksgiving.

It's weird, right? No one has said anything. I think life would be a lot easier if my last name were Holden. There's nothing easy about being a Barnes.

My sister Suzy moved back to live with Dad. I know this not because I was invited to visit or because they've come to see me and Butch. I know this because we were in McDonald's since I was on *Cowboy Eddie* again and had gift certificates for orange drinks. I was walking ahead of Mom when I stopped, dead in my tracks. Mom plowed into me.

"Warn!" everyone sounds so angry all the time, "why did you stop like that?" I pointed as Suzy climbed into her olive-green Ford Thunderbird. Mom stared for a second before absentmindedly saying, "Oh. Yes. That's where she and your Dad are living."

Maybe we should've stopped by and said hello. I could've given them my loaf of Wonder Bread as a housewarming gift.

It's probably a good thing Dad isn't living with us. I can't see the driveway from my new room. Me and Mom are sharing the big bedroom, which I usually have to myself because she's working the late shift cleaning the Madison Gas and Electric office building near the State Capitol.

I hardly ever get to see her. When I do, she says, "Now Warn, when you go to bed, slide over as far as you can. That way, I won't wake you up when I'm getting into bed, okay?"

I've been ignoring that because, and I think this is very clever of me, if I sleep on the outside edge, she's got to wake me up to get into bed. Then I get to see her. I leave toys on the bed too. That way when she gets home, I get to hear her voice when she complains. "I clean an empty office building all night long. Now I've got to put toys away too!"

Sometimes I hear her saying to Grandma, "Why does he do that?"

Duh. I do that because I wouldn't see her otherwise. I'm not seeing my dad. Seems to me a kid has the right to see at least one parent regularly, even if you've got to trick them into it.

It annoys Grandma, but I run around the house, turning off lights whenever I can. That way we use less electricity. That means people at the power company have less work to do. That means their offices don't get as dirty. That means less work for Mom. That means she might get home earlier. Maybe before I go to bed even. It hasn't happened yet, but maybe it will someday. Maybe.

Years from now, I will ask her why she chose to work overnight. She'll say, "I needed the quiet to think. Also, it paid more. I got an extra $.25 an hour to work that shift. We needed the money."

Forty quarters. $10 a week. $40 a month. That's why I'm not seeing my mom.

When a single mother is scrambling for an extra $.25 an hour, you can be sure the man in her life is a deadbeat. He's an invisible, pathetic, awful man. A loser. He's probably not giving her alimony or child support because he thinks that by doing so, she will feel powerless and weak. Most likely, he's trying to force her to let him come back.

Maybe not always, but I think that's what my dad is doing.

Take it from me; being a selfish ass won't make your family more receptive to you.

There's more bad news. I had to get glasses. I have something called astigmatism. I wanted cool, little round gold ones like the Beatles wear, but Mom says they're impractical. My glasses are like the ones old men wear. Horn-rimmed. Plastic. Gross. No one seems to remember, I'm six-years-old. Being practical isn't my top priority.

And why are they called horn-rimmed? They don't have horns.

Not that any of it matters. I know what it means. I'm going to go blind, just like Valerie. So why wear the stupid glasses? I managed to lose one pair, but this time Grandma had them put my name and telephone number in the glasses, so they're harder to ditch. Some stupid guy found my stupid glasses in his stupid shrubs and just had to call my mom, so he could return them.

Telephone numbers are stupid too. We had to get a new one. I'm not allowed to tell my friends what it is, so my dad doesn't find out how to call us. Again, stupid. It's not like we moved. If he wants to see us, he knows where we are.

Good thing he's not coming around. He might see the inside of my glasses and know how to call us.

I wake up alone in bed. My mind floods with an infinite number of things that might be wrong, so I sprint into the kitchen.

Grandma is making scrambled eggs and ham. Mom is dipping toasted Wonder Bread into her milky coffee. We always have Wonder Bread now. There haven't been deliveries from the bakery since Dad moved out. Since I'm on the show two or three times a week now, there's always a loaf around the house.

"Aren't you going to say, 'good morning'?" says Grandma.

I pause to make sure I sound suspicious before saying, "Good morning."

Mom looks up, "What? Why do you sound funny?"

"Why do you *look* funny?" I ask.

Grandma glares at me. If looks could kill I'd be lying dead on the floor.

Mom pulls out the little pocket mirror that's usually on our table. She says, "Why do you say that?" as she checks her teeth for food and her lipstick for smudges and smears.

"You're all dressed up. How come?"

Mom says, "No special reason,"

Grandma says, "To go to the courthouse."

Not wanting to talk about it, my mom takes her final bite of toast, gulps her last bit of coffee, and heads out the door. Just as I'm about to ask Grandma what she meant she plops down a plate of scrambled eggs in front of me.

"Don't talk with your mouth full."

I walk out of school with Wayne at the end of the day. Art is waiting out front.

"Hi, guys." He quickly grabs the stuff I'm carrying. My Batman lunchbox, a few corrected assignments no one will look at, and a field trip permission form are tossed into Sky King, whose top is down because the weather is nice.

"I'm going to take Warn to feed the ducks at the pond. Want to come with Wayne?"

"No, thank you. I have a cold." He holds out a handkerchief as evidence that he's telling the truth.

"Okay, Wayne. Just for future reference, I would've taken your word for it."

WISM-AM is playing "Cherish" by the Association as we drive to the duck pond. Art loves this song. He's singing along. I'm counting the number of Bucky Badgers I see. Wisconsin loves Bucky Badger. I'm almost to fifty when we pull into the parking lot.

"What about bread?" I ask. "Why didn't we stop at the bakery like we usually do?"

Art grabs the Wonder Bread he stashed in the trunk. "No need."

I love the duck pond. It's right off a busy road, but you wouldn't know it. It's quiet here. Mossy trees filter the sunshine. Light dances on the water as ducks ripple through it. There's a beautiful rock wall that I'm now tall enough to jump up on by myself instead of needing Art to lift me. I bet my Grandpa Sam, or my Uncle Greg or Art's dad Warren came here before they died. That means I'm looking at things they saw too. That makes me feel like I didn't totally miss out on getting to meet them.

We just sit for a while, tearing off little pieces of bread and throwing them to quacking ducks, battling for position. I like throwing to the littler ones that won't fight to get into the fray. Someone's got to look out for those guys. Pretty soon they relax. The quacking stops as they enjoy their unexpected meal.

The silence is nice, but temporary.

"Warn," says Art. "there's something I think I should tell you.

When has any good come of that opening? I can feel myself get smaller to protect myself. I contract as though that's going to accomplish anything. Not by choice. It's just instinct, learned from too many moments like this. "What?"

"Ray, your dad," yeah. I know his name. "He and Mom went to court today. They had some very grown-up things to take care of. Your dad was late. When he showed up, he'd been drinking."

What a surprise.

"He got angry in the court. Then the judge got angry. Your dad tried to hit him."

When I look back on this, and I will, I'll wonder why Art thought this information is something a six-year-old needed or could process. I'm sure his intentions were good. They always were, without fail. He probably wanted me to stop expecting my dad to show up. To understand why he wasn't around. I'll never know.

"Warn, your dad is in jail."

CHAPTER ELEVEN

BATBOY & BROKEN TAIL

Unexpressed anger changes a person. It can cause cruelty. It can motivate retribution or violence. It can be twisted into other emotions. It can also inspire humor. So, with all that in mind, I'll just say this. Having Daddy in the big house hasn't affected things around here all that much.

Mom is still working at the power company. Because my dad is gone, she also runs Barnes Home Improvement. Art goes on the sales calls when he's not at the TV station. He measures the houses or specs the scope depending on what the customers want. Then he brings the information to Mom, who comes up with the pricing, which Emily types up. If the customer says yes, Art goes to deliver the sales contract, which my mom signs as, "D. Barnes."

I was working on homework at the chipped kitchen table when I heard Emily say, "It's ridiculous to bring Art into this. You should be getting credit for all the hard work you're doing. Besides, he's only twenty-one, what do you think…"

Mom doesn't let her finish. "The lights are on. That's credit enough. I wouldn't be a very good mother if I let you fool yourself, Emily. It's a man's world. No one would commit to a remodeling project sold to them by a woman."

I would. I will. I want to be the kind of man who would.

From what I've been able to eavesdrop on, Raymond was going to go to jail even before he tried to hit the judge. There were also charges of being physically violent toward a spouse and dependent child. I think that means because he pushed down my mother and threw furniture at me. He's lucky they didn't know he almost hit me and Butch with a car.

I can't be sure, though. *No one is talking about it.*

However, I'd like to pull a President Nixon. Let me be perfectly clear about something. In no way do I feel responsible for what has happened. For the rest of my life, I will see films during which a crying child will say, "Is your divorce my fault?"

I just roll my eyes at the bad writing.

"Warn, will your father be attending the end of the school year father and son picnic?" asks Mrs. Milbauer.

"No ma'am, he won't," I say, trying to look very wholesome and perfect. "My dad is in jail, so he can't. May I please be excused to go to the bathroom?"

It's fun to watch an adult have reactions they can't express. I can see how startled she is. It's all she can do to say, "Of course."

I knew she wouldn't say no. She wouldn't say no because I'm pathetic. Not in the far-flung sense of the word. I mean, my clothes aren't tattered. I have all my limbs. I simply mean I am one who inspires pity; thus, I am pathetic. Divorced parents? Poor kid. Blind sister? How sad. Father in jail? Oh, my goodness.

Put them all together, and you can get away with murder.

Again, not in the most far-flung sense of the word.

I don't have to go to the bathroom. I walk past the boy's room at the end of the hallway and go through the double doors that lead to the schoolyard. Whoever designed this building sure did me a favor. The walls are made of brick. There are no windows looking out onto this part of the playground. Once through the door, all you have to do is walk three feet toward the gym, and you become invisible.

I've been coming out here a few times a week. The feral cats in the neighborhood hang out here, waiting for kids to come out for recess. We're friends now. I sneak some of Ming's treats into my pocket and feed them. I pet them. Talk to them. Tell them what's going on at home. They purr and rub up against me. For a little while, we all feel less alone.

Luckily, I'm slightly allergic to cats, so when I come back to the classroom, with red eyes Mrs. Milbauer will assume I've been crying. She won't challenge why I was gone for so long. That might embarrass me. Or, God forbid, make me cry again.

Sure, I'm being manipulative, but here's the thing—so what? There's an upside to manipulation. It can score you 10-minutes with your new best friend, a one-eyed orange cat with a broken tail.

As I walk back into the room, I spy Mrs. Milbauer looking at the clock. Perhaps I was gone longer than she expected. Looking heavenward, she takes a deep breath, smiles, and walks to the front of the classroom, with the chalkboard behind her.

See? No consequence.

As she speaks, I'm doing my best to listen. At the same time, I'm also imagining that I'm Batboy, son of Bruce Wayne. Waiting behind the chalkboard are my Batboy costume and a 10-speed bike which spits out flames at anyone chasing me. I fight crime during recess with the help of Broken Tail, the Batcat. Paula, one row in front of me is my arch-nemesis. Her code name is the Wetter.

"And that's that, kids. Most of you will be passed onto First Grade. Others will be sent to another year of part-time school called Junior Primary. If that's the case, please know it was a decision made after talking with your parents. It doesn't mean you're not smart. Sometimes it's about your age or just needing another year before full-time school. It's in your best interest."

What. The. Hell. You can *fail* Kindergarten? They waited to tell us about that until now, at the end of the school year. Nothing can be done about that now.

Wait. She said that it had been discussed with our parents. I know my mom hasn't been here. Mrs. Milbauer can't talk to Dad because he's doing time. Besides, she said parents. Two. Plural. The only people who have talked to both my parents are lawyers. I think I'm fine. I'm going to pass.

"Now go to recess. Have fun!"

All the kids nearly trample me on their way out the door. It takes me a little longer because I was lost in my thoughts. I get up as Mrs. Milbauer passes. She smiles down at me. "Now, Warn," she says, "don't you worry about any of that. You're doing great in class which is impressive considering how much is going on at home. Speaking of which, how about we get together this weekend to break your dad out?"

Okay, she didn't say the last part, but wouldn't it be awesome if she had?

I start to head to recess. Paula walks out with me. Even wrapped up in my own thoughts, I can see how sad she looks.

"You okay, Paula?"

One thick, fat tear falls from her eye. I don't know if it's left or right. They don't teach us that until First Grade.

"My parents told me last night," she says in a hoarse whisper. "I'm one of the kids going to Junior Primary."

I'm surprised. My first urge is to hug her, so I do. I'm going to miss her.

CHAPTER TWELVE

I DON'T

So now it's summer. The first one I've earned, I suppose, having survived Kindergarten. I can only imagine what First Grade will be like, but that's months from now. There's much to do before then. I've got cook-outs and picnics to attend, zoos to visit, TV to watch, swimming to do, and of course Art and Nancy's wedding.

The three of us are at a restaurant called the Jolly Roger. It is the best restaurant ever. You walk in, and it's like being on a real live pirate ship. The world hasn't begun to evolve past sexism or misogyny yet, so the waitresses are called "wenches." The man who seats us has a wooden leg, but that might be from necessity rather than the theme. I'm not sure.

"Hello me mateys," says our waitress, wearing a peasant blouse. Weird that I could call her a wench here, but away from the Jolly Roger, it just wouldn't be right. So, why's it right here? Weird. Anyway, my thoughts interrupted her. She continues.

"What may I bring ye land lubbers today?"

Nancy orders a salad and iced tea. Art orders a double cheeseburger and fries. "With a coke."

"And ye, my young scallywag?"

"I'd like the shrimp cocktail, please." Everyone looks surprised. I ordered it because it has the word cocktail in it. I know that means drink, so I thought if I ordered it, I'd have a better idea of why my dad likes cocktails so much.

"Why don't you try something else, buddy?" offers Art.

"Okay. Parrot nuggets and onion straws, please."

Don't worry. They're not really parrot nuggets. They're chicken nuggets. They just take the theme past the point of logic.

"Are you excited about the wedding?" asks the groom.

I nod.

"Me too," says the bride. "Not only do I get to be Art's wife. After the wedding, I'll be a member of your family. I'll be your sister!"

This throws me. I didn't know that weddings changed the boundaries

Greg Triggs

of a family. Not that our family has ever been big on boundaries. We haven't. I'm just surprised, is all.

"Oh, so families can get bigger?"

"Yes!" says my soon-to-be sister-in-law.

"They can get smaller too, right?"

Art looks confused. "What do you mean?"

"Like, when my dad left. He's not part of the family anymore."

Nancy frowns and kisses the top of my head. Art rubs my back the way he does when he thinks I'm going to cry. I'm not, but it still feels good. I think we'd all still be in those positions if the wench hadn't come back.

"Here's a complimentary flagon of root beer for me first mate who looks so sad."

It's funny looking back in hindsight on two people you love and who love each other, and a day full of hope knowing it didn't last. The sadness in knowing that doesn't replace the joy you felt when it was happening. The feelings co-exist, even if the couple can't. It's like combining Count Chocula and Rice Krispies. They're both in the same bowl, floating in the same milk, but in the end, they're two separate things.

It's the actual day of the wedding. So exciting! I'm in the wedding party, which is called a party even though there aren't balloons or games. I think they could come up with a better name for it.

The wedding is in the afternoon, so we guys are just hanging out right now. Art's best man Richard Nabors has a brand-new Kodak M9 motion picture camera, so we're making a movie. It's something called stop action.

"Okay, Warn," says Richard, who is being kind of bossy considering it's Art's wedding day. "You're going to pretend you're driving a car all over the yard. Art is chasing you, and you're trying to get away. Just before Art catches you, we'll pretend you're climbing up my ring tower." That's the tall metal apparatus upon which Richard practices his gymnastics. It's impressive.

In the future, I'll learn it stands 19 feet high, per collegiate regulations. Today it looms as tall as the building Emily works in downtown. I am thrilled and scared at the same time.

"The last shot will be you, in the air, holding the iron cross position."

"What's that?" I ask.

Richard, a gymnastic expert, explains. "That's when you're in the air, holding yourself in position with your arms fully extended."

88

"I don't know if I can do that."

"You can't," says Art. "We'll be on a ladder. I'll be holding you in place."

My first movie, even if it's not listed on IMDB. All these years later, I know where my copy is, but I can't bring myself to watch it. A great memory that's too hard to revisit.

Happier thoughts of happier times.

Em is one of Nancy's bridesmaids. She's wearing a buttery yellow dress with see-thru sleeves and a matching netted hat. Shoes dyed to match, which was a big deal. We had to go to Manchester's Department Store to get them.

Everyone seems to expect I can dress myself. Usually, I can, but this is something called a tuxedo. The pants are fine, but they have straps in them I don't understand. The shirt doesn't button. There are a bunch of little metal button-like things that I ignore. There's an elastic something or other. Art's wearing one just like it around his waist, but how did he make it work?

No one is paying attention to me. In just my underpants, I climb on top of a chair, take a deep breath, and scream, "CAN SOMEBODY HELP ME PLEASE?" Unfortunately, the photographer is in the room with his camera. This moment is captured on film and will follow me for the rest of my life. Regardless, the strategy works. One of the groomsmen agrees to help me get dressed.

Before I know it, we're standing in the back of the church.

"Warn, please hold my hand when we walk down the aisle," says Sherri.

Somewhere in the back of my mind, I'm pretty sure that means I'm pledging to marry her when we're grown-ups, but she seems nice enough. She's sweet with downy blonde hair and icy blue eyes. That's okay by me. I'm not going to worry about it. "Sure."

Mom, in a beautiful pink dress, stops to kiss Art on the cheek before an usher walks her down the aisle by herself. Alone. Someday I will realize this leaves her feeling vulnerable and not completely in the moment during her eldest son's wedding. As she makes her way toward the empty seat down front, how can she not think about the first Warren and all he has missed? How can she not wonder what people are thinking about my father's absence?

Uncle Nick is in the parking lot. He's on lookout for Dad, who has been released from jail, back living in his McDonald's adjacent apartment. Everyone except me, and maybe my fiancée Sherri, are worried that he'll show up here drunk and ruin another family occasion.

Just tell him Butch and I are here. He won't show up.

We all start to promenade down the aisle. Sherri hits Aunt Josie square in the mouth with some rose petals. Hilarious. We keep walking. It's harder to concentrate on the music because I want to laugh but was told I shouldn't, because grown-ups live to inhibit joy. Once all of us are at the altar and facing the congregation, the pipe organ crescendos. Nancy appears at the back of the church, looking glorious in the second most beautiful dress I'll ever see. Little daisies float on chiffon sleeves. A tulle veil explodes off the crown of her head and cascades to the floor. She is breathtaking. Everyone in the church stands up, not because they were told to, but because she is respected and loved.

There are hundreds of people inside the Nakoma Golf Club Party Pavilion. I don't get to talk to Art and Nancy much during the reception, but I can see them. They're floating around the room, alone and together. Nancy's side seems to dominate. Perhaps that's because her parents, a doctor and his wife, are throwing the party, not the cleaning lady running a small construction company from her chipped kitchen table.

I can see Mick dancing with her husband, Bob. Grandma is nearby, teaching Butch a step or two. I caught Florence sharing a laugh with Earl. Aunt Lil is discussing the centerpieces with her husband Robert, who is trying his hardest to look interested. Shirley, who it turns out works here part-time, opted to bartend rather than attend as a guest. Sherri and I are getting pops at her bar when she says, "Hey, kids. I was just outside having a smoke. There are a bunch of deer grazing on the golf course. I saw a fox too. You should check it out."

Forgetting entirely about the cokes Shirley just poured, we run hand in hand through the dance floor obstacle course, past Howie Olson standing by himself on the edge of the crowd, to the outside. There's a full moon and a breeze. The music can still be heard over the crickets and frogs.

A group of deer are happily using the rough of the golf course as a buffet. Another pack of deer can be seen playing together near the 18th green. In this uncommon to me, beautiful setting, Sherri takes a deep breath and puts her lips on mine.

A boy dressed in a tux and a girl dressed as a miniature bride share their first kiss while the grown-ups dance behind them. Her lips are soft and warm. She smells like the roses she has been carrying. It's hard to think of a way in which it could be more perfect. When it ends, she is out of breath. I am not.

The next morning, we all head to Art and Nancy's tiny one-bedroom apartment by campus. Tiny is a generous description, but it's affordable. Everyone walks up three flights of crooked, creaky stairs and angles their way in. The small space is overwhelmed by wedding presents and the catering staff Nancy's parents hired for the brunch.

It's time to open wedding presents, which sounds more exciting than it is. All the presents are very grown-up, so me and Butch wedge our way into the bedroom to eat our eggs benedict. We are between the queen-sized bed and the wall, in a little niche just past the radiator. There are lots of oohs each time a package is opened. Occasionally someone with an uncanny sense of children's interests will come in to show us a sugar bowl or a fondue pot.

Nancy's mom, wearing what I will someday know is a Chanel suit, comes in and sits down. Despite her obvious elegance I can tell she loves children. I like her a lot.

"Are you boys having fun?" she asks.

That seems like one of those questions to which no one wants an honest answer. "Yes. Very much, thank you."

"The menu was very adult. You've been good sports, so I snuck you extra big slices of cake," she says, handing them to us.

"Hanku," says Butch.

Nancy's mom looks a little confused.

"He says, 'thank you.'"

"Oh. Thank you. You're very good with him, Warn."

"Hanku," I say.

Nancy's mom gets it and laughs.

"Look what I've got. It was a present for Nancy and Art from my mother," she says. Out of her pocket, she pulls a tiny bear made of glass. "It's crystal," she adds. "Look what he can do."

Nancy's mom puts the little bear in a sunbeam coming in from the window. When the light hits it, colors begin to swirl and move as she twists the bear.

"It's called a prism," she instructs. "Sometimes things just need to be put in the right light to show the world what they're capable of." She looks at Butch. "Never forget, boys, everyone has a secret strength or special talent. Sometimes it's only a matter of the light hitting it in just the right manner."

Most of the guests go downstairs to bring in the next round of presents. Nancy stays behind to keep an eye on Butch. I offered to do it, but Nancy said she'd stay to help.

"Did you like the presents from me and Butch?" I ask.

"Oh, yes. Clue, Trouble and Candyland. That'll be a lot of fun when you come over to visit."

"I chose them myself," I say.

"Really? Well, we loved it."

"What's that?" I ask, pointing to a picture leaning against the wall.

"A present. A painting done by my parent's neighbor, Mrs. Miller."

I tilt my head from side to side. It's unlike anything I've ever seen before. It's not realistic. I think I see trees without leaves. Like new growth after a forest fire. It's rainy, so there's fog, but the sun is breaking through.

Or it's just a bunch of lines. Who knows? I'm six.

Art walks in and says, "It's the first real painting I've ever owned! What do you think?"

"I don't understand it," I admit.

"Maybe you're not supposed to."

"Then Mrs. Miller did a really good job."

The painting now hangs in my dining room. I love it. It's Art.

CHAPTER THIRTEEN

DEPENDENCE DAYS

Art and Nancy pick me up in her little Mustang. The top is down, so Nancy hands me a pair of oversized sunglasses and a cap. "So, you don't get sunburnt."

"Where are we going?" I ask.

"It's a surprise," says Art, who I can see winking through his sunglasses. We follow the labyrinth of roads behind the airport. For a second, I indulge the fantasy that we're going to Chicago on an airplane, knowing it can't be that. Grandma would've sent me with fresh underpants.

We pull up to a concrete block building, painted white with blue doors. A sign outside says, "Dane County Humane Society."

"What's a Human Society?"

"Humane," says Nancy. "See the 'e'?" That changes human into a whole new word." Anticipating my next question, she adds, "Humane means to be kind or generous. It's an important word."

"Then I'll be humane."

They each grab one of my hands, and we walk inside. There is a strong smell and lots of noises the minute we cross in. An orange cat walks up, rubs against my leg, and keeps walking. "Is this a pet shop? Why are we here?"

"You're going to help us pick out a dog!" says Art.

Nancy stops to look at a few small dogs, but they're super yappy. She asks to hold a little toy poodle who snaps at me, so she hands it back.

"We have small children in our family; it probably wouldn't work out."

As we head toward the bigger cages, the barking gets louder and deeper. Art is here. We'll be fine. I just cover my ears. They stop to look at a German shepherd named Sarge, who seems sweet but kind of stupid. I know Art isn't going to choose him. It says "untrainable" under the notes on his little ID card.

While they're busy with him, I see a little flash of gray velvet peeking out from a shadow. He's scared. Probably from all the other dogs and noise. I crouch down and put my hand on the chain-link fence. He slowly inches over to me, finally arriving to sniff my hand just as Art and Nancy arrive. When they crouch down to our level, his tail starts wagging, and his eyes get brighter.

Name-Bo.

Breed-Weimaraner.

Art looks at Nancy. "What do you think, hon?"

"He's awfully big for our small apartment."

As they're pondering, a grandpa looking volunteer comes by. "Sweet dog. A little skittish, but I'm sure the right home can correct that. "You should decide soon. He won't be here tomorrow."

"Is someone else interested?" asks Art.

"No," says the volunteer in a solemn voice.

"Welcome to the family," says Nancy.

Before I know it, it's July.

"Dorothy, would it be alright if we take Warn with us to the fireworks?" asks Mick.

Mr. Mick, or Bob, put me to work. "If you're coming with us, you got to help us get ready." That's how I ended up in their backyard garden helping get the fruits and vegetables for our picnic dinner. Bob is a big believer in education, so as we harvest, he gives us a little quiz.

I hand him a potato. He says, "What's the greatest country in the world?"

"The United States!"

His daughter Laurie and I fill up a tub of raspberries and turn them in. Bob asks, "Who is the best President ever?"

We say, "Nixon!" because that's who we hear the most about.

Bob laughs before adding, "What a couple of knuckleheads! You're Americans, so you get to have your own opinion, but that's not the name I was looking for. Now Abraham Lincoln…"

Before I know it, we're spreading out blankets on the lawn of Vilas Park and Zoo. Yeah. It's *both*. Mick is putting down the last of three coolers we brought. I helped Mr. Mick and their son Mike carry the heaviest one because that's what we guys do.

Coleen, their oldest daughter, sneaks off with her boyfriend Jeff to make out. Me and Laurie have caught them at it before. We'll catch them again. No doubt. They're in love.

"Aren't we here kind of early?" Mike asks.

"Oh no," says Mick, briefly pausing to light a cigarette, "if you want the good spot, you got to get here early, or all those goddamn west-siders will take 'em."

You don't have to tell me twice. Eastside. Best side. Although it does bring up the question, if the east side, where we live, is best, why are we coming to the west side to see the fireworks? And what are fireworks? I've never seen any.

Daylight wanders into dusk. Mick gifts me with an Uncle Sam hat. Laurie is given a pair of patriotic glitzy sunglasses. I suspect we look adorable. We wander into the coolers, enjoying the delicious meal we all worked on together. After dinner, Mick puts her arms around me and Laurie. "You kids take a quick nap, so you're awake for the big show."

I don't know how I could sleep. All the people. The Italian Workmen's Community Band playing in the gazebo. It's going to be impossible.

When we wake up about an hour later, Mick's arms are still around us. Years from now, when I visit her in the hospital, I will realize that this moment on the 4th of July is the longest I've seen her go without a cigarette.

"Kids? Kids," she says, gently shaking us a bit, "time to get up." As we slowly transition from groggy to giddy, she kisses us both on the cheek.

Ten minutes pass, during which Laurie and I get to share one can of Coke. It's sweet and cold, wet and satisfying. The caffeine is just kicking in as the sky begins to explode. Literally. Explosions. The sky is on fire!

I hope everyone is lucky enough to remember the first time they saw fireworks. Sitting here in the dark, around people I love and trust, people who represent the best of our country, couldn't be more perfect. Red, white, and blue, in addition to green, purple and gold, fill the sky, and it all feels like it's being done just for us.

I can feel each burst. It's like I am part of each color. I've never seen something so beautiful. Did everyone know about this? Why didn't they tell me? Why did it take until I was six-years old to experience it?

It ends way too soon.

As we pick up from our day, "Always leave the park cleaner than you found it," says Mr. Mick, the crowd begins to thin. "It'll be a long wait to get out of the parking lot."

"Who cares?" says Mick. "It was worth it."

On the way back to their car, a two-tone Plymouth Valiant station wagon, we run into a rather buttoned up looking fellow who turns out to be Mick's manager from the restaurant. "Lillian, I didn't know you had a little boy too."

Mick smiles and gives me a quick wink before turning back to her boss. "Oh, he's one of ours for sure. He's one of ours."

My smile might be brighter than the fireworks.

As if today couldn't get any better, Mom waited to do sparklers until we got home. She, Grandma, and Butch are waiting for me on the front steps. Mick and her family join us, so it's a regular party. Mom even has ice cream, which is the only thing today has lacked.

Butch burns himself on one of the hot sparklers, but he doesn't cry. Mom kisses it and says, "Did it hurt, baby?" Butch gives her an answer, but Mom can't understand him. "What's he saying, Warn?"

"He says, 'he's fine.'"

I can tell everyone is worried. I feel my own younger version of it. Butch hasn't added many new words to his trick-or-treat burst of vocabulary. That was nine-months ago. Even I know things should be getting better.

It's Monday morning. Grandma is pouring coffee into a Styrofoam cup for Jack, the roofer, when I walk into the kitchen. He leaves with his orders. Grandma makes me some toast and eggs. It's an efficient morning in Emma's Diner.

"Where is everyone?" I ask with my mouth full.

Grandma looks at me disapprovingly before answering. "Your mom and Butch are at school getting him registered for the fall. They left first thing, so they'd be first in line."

They return just as Grandma is finishing lunch. Butch runs inside to eat, but Mom stays in the car. When I start out the side door to check on her, Grandma's arm gently blocks my way. "Give her a little time by herself, Warn. Your soup will get cold."

When she finally comes inside, Mom seems burdened and overwhelmed. As she gets ready to go to work at the power company, the door to our room is shut, but I can hear her crying. Sobbing is hard to hide in a small house.

Using an eavesdropping technique perfected by children everywhere, the picture comes into focus. The grown-ups are using words that will be with us for the rest of our lives. Words from the 1970s which will grow into kinder means of assessment someday.

Due to oxygen issues at birth, my little brother has irreversible, permanent brain damage, commonly known as mental retardation.

So that's what it is. That explains why no one can understand him. That explains why I knew the alphabet when I was younger than he is now. It's not that I'm special. He's special, but we aren't evolved enough to use that word yet. Instead, we have words that define people's limitations instead of their potential.

Okay, so the issue has been defined. Now people can start to help him. Help us all help him. He's still my little brother. I love him. We all love him. Nothing has changed. We just found out something we may have already known.

I don't get worried until my dad comes over.

Butch and I come running in from outside. Raymond is sitting at the kitchen table. The purple ashtray my parents got as a wedding gift is in front of him. It was clean when we went outside. Now it's brimming with fired matches and cigarette butts. The air is thick with smoke, but no one thinks anything of it. That's still normal.

Grandma is at the sink vigorously scrubbing a mug which I'm assuming my father just used. Mom is standing near the tea cart full of Grandma's African Violets. Art and Nancy sit between them. Art is on a chair. Nancy resting on his thigh. We are lucky to have a teacher in our family. Nancy will help us figure this out.

Butch lights up like a Christmas tree and pushes past everyone when he sees our father. He squeals, "DeeDee!" his word for dad and jumps into Raymond's arms. My dad hugs him hard. In my memory, Raymond's eyes are red, but that seems out of character.

The adults are distracted. I take advantage of that and slip between the chair my dad is using and the refrigerator. I go into the living room and sit in what used to be called "Dad's chair." I pull a Wonder Woman comic from my back pocket and start to read, wishing I had an invisible plane that could take me anywhere away from this house.

"Butch, you run and find out where Warn is. You two play, but stay inside," says Grandma. I can tell she doesn't want Raymond here either because she pronounces my name as "Warren." For a woman who only went through 4th grade, she's awfully smart. Butch is excited to see I've already pulled out his beloved marbles. He starts building one of his Rube Goldberg-like ramps, happy as can be.

For 30-minutes or so, there are hushed voices. I hear a chair scrape across the floor, followed by the familiar groan of a man in his 40s who doesn't take care of himself. Please just let him leave. Just let him leave. I sense the energy in the room change. No such luck. He came into the living room.

He dismisses Butch quickly. "Buddy, can I have a few minutes alone with your big brother? I think your grandma has a piece of cake for you." Butch takes the bribe and leaves me alone with my dad.

"I suppose all this is a little confusing. You're probably wondering what's going on." I say nothing, but slowly shake my head from side to side. "Oh, you understand?" I nod my head up and down.

"Anyway, there's a lot to figure out right now. That probably means there's going to be less time and attention for you," says the man I haven't seen since before Christmas.

Less he said. Less. Is there less than nothing?

"I hope you understand." I shrug my shoulders.

"Anyway, how are you? How have you been?"

I hope my face is as deadpan as it feels. "I'm fine." He doesn't talk, probably hoping I'll say something. There is an awkward silence. He's waiting me out, as though he's selling me aluminum siding. He wants me to talk. I've heard him say it a million times. The guy who talks first loses. I'm not sure that's necessarily the case.

"How was jail?"

I stare at him unflinchingly, which is a word I don't know yet. Then I see it for a moment. That familiar flash of anger. He hasn't changed. He's learned nothing while he's been gone. We both know he can't make a scene or yell at me. His tension twists into a smile. He exhales before saying, "I'm glad I saw you, son. I'm sorry it has been so long."

A lifetime of learning through negative example has just begun. I am resolute and totally sure of one thing. I will be nothing like my father.

The rest of the day is ordinary. There is no discussion of Raymond's visit. Mom leaves for work. We order pizza from KC the Rolling Pizza Man, who cooks the pizza on its way to being delivered to you. We watch a little bit of a too grown-up for me movie about Russian spies. I get bored, so Art and Nancy teach me what all the little symbols on playing cards mean. We organize them according to suit in order of rank until I can do it without their help. They head to their tiny apartment near campus. Butch is sent to bed. I take a bath per Grandma's rigid schedule. I'm heading to bed in my pjs when she says, "Let's sit on the stoop for a while, yes?"

I can tell she figured I'd agree. When we get out the front door, there are two sweaty glasses of ice water and a little bowl of popcorn.

As we enjoy our snack, Grandma points to different stars and planets.

"Do you know which star is most important, Warn?"

"The sun?"

She laughs. "That's a good point! Do you know the *second* most important star?"

"No."

She carefully unfolds the celestial map tucked inside the pocket of her hand-embroidered apron. "Your grandpa bought this for me at the World's Fair in 1939."

"Should we get a new one?"

More laughter. "No. The stars are permanent. This one is fine." Then she takes her finger and runs it across two dotted lines until they intersect. "See here? This is the North Star. If you can find it, you'll always know your way home." Then she looks up into the sky. "Land sakes Warn, just think, man has been up there."

"I know. They've been talking about it since before I even started school."

"I suppose they have. You're growing up in a world very different from the one I did." She kisses me on the forehead, saying into my hair, "I wish it was easier for you. I wish it was all easier."

Then she gathers herself, kind of morphing back into the usual version of herself. She points to the evening sky. "Now, let's see if you can tell me which one of those is the North Star."

It takes a couple of guesses, but I get it right.

I kiss Grandma goodnight, and creep upstairs as quietly as I can so as not to wake up Butch. He's asleep. Smiling. Content. His own, unique version of perfect.

My mind flashes to the movie about Russian spies.

Butch isn't mentally retarded; he's a spy.

A foreign government has sent him here to check on our typical

American family and report back. He's not retarded. Butch is a spy. That's the only explanation.

Surely God wouldn't do this to my perfect little brother.

CHAPTER FOURTEEN

MITZVAHS

"Hello, Dorothy."

"Hello, John," Smith of the family two doors down.

"Me and the kids were wondering if Warn would like to join us tonight. I'm umping the amateur baseball games at Olbrich Par..."

"Yes. Yes! How soon does he need to be ready?"

That's how I became one of the boys of summer. Mr. Smith was kind enough to invite me to his games. He's an umpire. I didn't know what that was. Turns out the ump is the decider. He watches the game and decides who gets points, who isn't behaving, and pretty much controls who wins. The umpire is in charge. Mr. Smith is in charge.

4-nights a week if I want to, the Smith kids and I get in the backseat of John's (he said I could call him that) car and drive all over town to ball fields. One time I even saw Grandma Barnes there, which was nice. I haven't seen her since her son, my dad, moved out. She offered to buy me whatever I wanted at the snack bar, but something in me said, "No, thank you," even though I was hungry.

The games don't always hold my attention. Especially if I don't know the players. Most of them are nice guys, dads trying to relive glory days. Some of them are really good, especially John when he plays. You can hear some of the guys saying things like, "Back up everybody. Here comes Smith!" He's the best player, but he's not cocky. He's never showing off. He's just enjoying the game. I wish he were my dad.

Most nights, Mom or Grandma will send a snack or treat along with me. It makes me happy to have something to share. It gives me a reason for being there. Somewhere in the back of my mind, I know I'm just a tagalong. I'm only invited because the Smiths feel sorry for me. I don't know it yet, but it's going to take years for me to get past a nagging feeling that I'm nothing more than a pity date.

I lay my bike down behind my mom's car. I hope she doesn't run over it, but I'm so thirsty. I've got to get some water. The minute I walk inside, the air is cooler and feels great.

Well, this is a surprise.

"Grandma Barnes?"

I walk over to hug her, only remembering I'm hot and sticky once I'm in her arms.

"So, Dorothy," she says, sounding more British than ever before. I guess I've been away from her accent for too long. "Do we agree? May I tell Warn the news?"

She didn't leave Mom with much of a choice after that, did she? I guess Mom agrees because she nods.

"Your Grandpa and I missed your birthday this year."

"Yeah. It was right after Dad moved out."

"Yes. Well, we missed it."

"Probably because Dad moved out. That's what I thought when we didn't hear from anybody."

"Well," she seems a little flustered. I can tell. I was just being honest. I didn't mean for her to feel bad. Just sharing how I looked at it. "For whatever reason, we weren't here. That was wrong. So, I'm here with a present now."

"Grandma, my birthday was a long time ago, in January. It's August. You don't have to do anything for me. Just remember next year."

"Well, this present has to be now. Your Grandpa and I signed you up for Saturday morning acting classes at Edgewood." That's the Catholic Church my grandparents go to. It also has a school and a college. Seriously Catholic. No meat on Fridays Catholic.

Looking back on it, it's funny. The grown-ups found a place for me to deal with the feelings they weren't up to the challenge of discussing with me. Don't get me wrong. This was one of the biggest gifts I received in my life. I'm forever grateful. However, on some level, this takes midwestern avoidance to a whole new level—the British level.

"Hello, Warn. I'm Miss Charlotte," says my new drama teacher, dressed in a leotard and flowery, flowing robe something or other. Her bangs are blonde, but the rest of her hair is jet-black. It, like the class, is dramatic.

"Hello, Miss Charlotte," I say in return.

"Char-LOT."

"That's what I said."

"No, Warn. You used the American pronunciation. A common mistake."

"But we're in Ameri…"

"Yes, but I grew up in Milwaukee, so I use the more urban version. Char-LOT, not Char-LIT. We must work against getting trapped in our regional quicksand."

And so, despite an air of pretension, my world begins to get a little bigger.

As she leads me toward the rest of the class, she adds, "I've seen you on the Cowboy Eddie program. How did you get that?"

With that indoctrination, classes begin in earnest. For two-hours each week, I'm not stuck being me. I can play Oliver Twist or pretend to be a cow grazing in a field. Like most young actors, I can only escape being me so much. My Oliver is almost too carefree. Sure, he's a hungry street urchin living in an orphanage, but I'd trade places with him.

It's easier to transcend myself when we pretend to be animals.

My cow, I've chosen the name Borden after a local dairy, wants to enjoy the grass but is painfully aware that the rest of the world sees her as a bull.

The inevitability of the slaughterhouse is welcomed compared to living a life mired in the judgment of others. To her emotional baggage, I can only offer the most existential of moos and chew on my cud.

"Warn. Come here," demands Mom. Demand might be too strong a word, but there was no negotiating. I've got to stop what I'm doing, so I'll just trust that Bamm-Bamm gets adopted by Betty and Barnie.

"Yes, Mother?" I ask, doing my best to sound exasperated.

"I need you to promise me you'll be as well behaved as you've ever been."

When am I badly behaved? "Okay. Why?"

"Your grandma has a doctor's appointment, and no one can take her. Art and Emily both have got to work. Nancy has a class. I've got to take Grandma. I'll take Butch with me, but someone has to stay home to answer the business phone."

"What about Dad? It's his business. Shouldn't he answer the phone?"

"Let's not dwell on 'shoulds' today, okay? You've got to stay home and be very careful. I can't worry about you and get everything else done. If anything happens, run over to Mick's house for help—but nothing bad is going to happen."

I nod.

"Don't let anyone who calls know you're a kid, okay? Try to sound grown-up."

I force my voice a little lower but kind of end up sounding like a drag queen. "Okay."

"And what do we say when we answer the business line?"

"Barnes' Home Improvement. Vinyl is final. May I help you?"

"Yes! Good job! And then ask for a phone number and name. If it's a hard one, you can ask them to spell it. Write it all down here," she shows me the message pad that has every tavern in town written on the inside cover.

"Got it."

"Okay," she says, kissing me on the forehead. "I'm sorry to leave you like this. I wouldn't do it if I weren't desperate. They're all waiting in the car." She kisses me on the forehead again and starts to leave. Pausing at the door, she turns around as if she has something to say. Her lips purse for a second. She stares at me with sad eyes before smiling. "Bye. I love you."

I stare at the phone, anticipating it will ring at any second. It doesn't. There is, however, a shift in the room. No longer is it a kitchen. It's my office, and I'm a receptionist, like Emily.

I think about acting class. I guess that means I'm a lady, which is good because my voice doesn't sound like a grown-up man. I'm wearing a skirt and blazer with a ruffled blouse. My hair is brown, but I frost it like the ladies on TV. I am beautiful.

I have long fingernails, like Emily. What color polish? Red seems kind of cheap, so not that. Maybe a soft pink. That sounds perfect.

The phone begins to ring. Oh, my goodness! I reach to pick it up, but my inner office professional immediately knows that seems needy. I wait until the third ring. Picking up the beige receiver, I flash on a lesson from my acting class.

"You've only got one chance to make a first impression!"

I clear my throat and clearly say, "Barnes' Home Improvement. How may I help you?" Shoot! I forgot the vinyl part. Okay, I'll remember next time.

"What did you say?" says the woman on the other end.

I repeat it, remembering the vinyl part the second time.

"Oh. I'm sorry. Wrong number." Hang up. Dial tone. Over. Easy enough.

Two other calls come in and go perfectly. My inner receptionist is starting to realize this job is just a stepping-stone to bigger and better things. Through my interactions with the public, I'm sure to meet an eligible young bachelor. He won't want me to work, but I'll insist. After all, he knew I was a career girl when we met.

The phone rings again. This time I pick up a Barnes branded ballpoint pen for the taking of messages. I am, after all, the communication hub for the entire operation. I will not allow myself to keep our important customers waiting.

"Hello. Barnes' Home Improvement…" blah, blah, blah.

"Is Ray Barnes there?" asks a gruff voice with a thick Wisconsin accent.

"No, but I'd be happy to take a message. He, or someone else from the company," AKA my mom, "will get back to you as soon as possible."

"Really? Because this is the fourth message I have left, and I've yet to hear back from him. His wife and stepson have called, but I want to talk to the owner," says the sexist man who doesn't know he's better off talking to my mom anyway.

"I'll do my best to make sure…"

He cuts me off. "Lady, your best isn't good enough. You may have to put up with this shit, but I don't. Tell that asshole you work for that no one showed up on the start date as listed, so I'm canceling the sales contract," says the man who doesn't know he's talking to a child.

Hang up. Dial tone. Over.

Left in the silence after that call, I just want to quit.

Emily broke up with the lifeguard she met at the beach in Lake Mills. "Last summer fling," says the new high school graduate. Now she's dating a cab driver named Dave. He gives her free rides to work. She's working full time. Sometimes she sleeps at his house, which probably saves them both a lot of time.

I got to see Valerie. She came over for a birthday supper last week. She said I sounded taller, and she's right. I grew almost 3 inches this year, which is more than the United States average for a boy my age. I think I'm going to be one of the taller kids in my class this year.

"Hello, class. I'm Mrs. Langenkamp." Whew. What a name. Remembering how to write down her name is going to be like a spelling test. She goes around the room introducing herself to each of us one by one, as teachers do. No wiglet this year. My new teacher has a short pixie haircut and wears mini dresses. The 70s have begun!

Wayne and I are still in the same class, so we're sitting next to each other. "I bet it happens again," I say to him, just before she gets to our row.

"Hello, Warren."

This year we are at desks. So, there are no wetting of pants incidents. Although I did hear at lunch that Paula broke down in tears during introductions over at Junior Primary. I'll look for her during recess. Sounds as though she could use a friend.

"Class," says Mrs. Langenkamp. "We're going to jump right in with a test today. There is no reason to feel scared. It's just a test to tell me which reading group you'll do best in. Everyone has a sharp pencil, correct?"

The room floods with brand new, freshly sharpened pencils thrust into the air.

Mrs. L. holds up an answer sheet with lots of little rectangles. It's our job to look at the booklet, read the multiple-choice questions to the best of our abilities, and then fill in the corresponding letter for each answer we think is correct. Simple enough; except, then I start thinking about Butch. Tests aren't easy for him.

When the results come in, I'm placed in the middle of three reading groups. Wayne and most of my friends in the class are in the highest level, which stings. Looking around my group, I see a lot of nice kids. I wait for them to raise their hands when questions are asked, but none of them respond. I'm the only one participating.

If I'm being honest, the lessons bore me. I concentrate on helping the kids that are struggling.

Butch has started school, but not with me. He's on the other side of town, in something called a temple. So now Mom collects me at school, we pick up Butch, she takes us home, Grandma meets us in the driveway, we jump out, and mom heads to her overnight shift at the power company. On days I have Cowboy Eddie, Art picks me up from school.

Sometimes Mom says, "I wish they'd let first graders drive."

I say, "Me too!" knowing that will probably never happen, but I start paying attention just in case. All the lines on the road. They mean something. I'm going to figure it out, but that will have to wait. Today, Butch's teacher wants to talk to Mom.

She quickly looks around. "Warn, you wait here," placing me in a pew toward the back. "Hopefully, this won't take too long. I can't be late for work."

I brought my spelling list with me, so I begin studying. With. *With* is a spelling word. Who doesn't know how to spell "with"? I let go with a dramatic sigh, trying to multi-task and work on acting and spelling at the same time. I must've been effective. The nice-looking, cardigan-wearing man passing by stops and looks at me, raising his glasses. A little black beanie covers the back of his head.

"Hello. May I help you?"

"Hi. My name is Warn Barnes. I'm waiting for my mom and brother. They're downstairs." I pause to give the situation the weight it deserves, "talking with his teacher."

"Ah, your brother is in special education then?"

"He doesn't go to a regular school like me. He goes to school here," I say, trying to make sense of whatever this church-like place with a different name is. "So, if this is special education, yes."

"You look confused."

"This place feels like a church, but I don't think it is."

"You're observant. That's good. No, this is not a church. It's a synagogue. Temple Beth El."

"What does that mean?"

"This is where Jewish people come to worship."

I want to repeat this new word correctly. "Jew-ish. What's Jewish?"

Someday I'll know he is a Rabbi, but not today. I just see a kindly man who is willing to listen and talk with children. I like him. Whatever he has to say seems worthy of my full attention.

"Eh. What's Jewish? Ask ten people. You'll get twelve answers. How to answer for the smart little boy willing to ask? Let's see ... do you go to church?"

"Yes, sir, I do. Most of my family is Catholic. I have an uncle and a cousin who are priests. Two of my aunts are nuns. Sister Alma Rita and Sister Mary Rita. I wish they didn't share the name Rita. I can't tell which one is which." Am I rambling? I think I'm rambling. Wrap it up, Warn. "My mom, my sister, my brothers, and me, we're Moravian."

"Such a story! So, you're Moravian - a fine church. Reverend Boettcher or Reverend Graf?"

Visualizing our minister, a bearded young man, I answer, "I don't know. We call him Paul. My Grandma calls him, 'The hippie.'"

The Rabbi laughs, which echoes in the nearly empty sanctuary. "That is Reverend Graf. He's a fine man. Very open-minded. He'd be glad we're talking." He looks at me with a smile, "Which brings us back to your question. What is Jewish?"

"Yes, sir."

"Jewish or Judaism is another type of faith. Older than Christianity. Basically, we don't believe that Jesus was the son of God. A fine man, yes. A prophet, surely. The son of God? No." He starts to ramble. "Of course, many say we're all the children of God, but…"

I must look confused because he changes tactics. "In Sunday school, what do they tell you will happen when the messiah comes to Earth?"

"Things will be better. Perfect."

"Are things perfect?"

Something about this man makes me think my answers matter. I dig deep inside myself before saying, "Not at my house. No."

Again, laughter fills the temple.

Years later, I will find out this man is named Rabbi Manfred Swarsensky. He emigrated from Berlin to the United States after the war. His synagogue was burned by the Nazis in 1938. Afterward, he was imprisoned in the Sachsenhausen Prison Camp. Somehow, perhaps through God's good graces, he made it to Madison, Wisconsin, and stopped to talk to me.

To a little boy given a grateful reprieve from an unchallenging spelling list, he is a mitzvah beyond measure. I will always be thankful he took 5-minutes to talk with me and plant a few seeds.

"Well, just you remember Warn Barnes, there's more than one path into the garden. Choose yours wisely."

CHAPTER FIFTEEN

READING THE ICE

Good intentions can lead to bad results. Bad results can lead to good outcomes. Of course, I don't know that when Mrs. Langenkamp calls me up to her desk. I'm no sooner there; then my mom walks in.

"Thank you for coming in, Mrs. Barnes. We seem to have troubling results with one of Warn's test results."

Immediately not wanting to burden Mom, my stomach twists in knots. "What do you mean? I don't copy. I never have! You've got to belie…"

"Warn," she says patiently, "relax. I'm not saying you cheated. You did the opposite. It appears you got questions wrong on purpose."

Mrs. Langenkamp then goes on to tell us I read at a third-grade level and have a fifth-grade vocabulary, but every fourth question on my test was wrong. Therefore, the mainframe computer used by the school system rejected my test.

"If he knew even two of those questions, he'd be in the higher reading group. So, we'd like to move him to the more advanced program."

Mom looks at me with confusion.

"He's missed six weeks of work. He'll have to make that up at home to catch up. If you do two lessons a day, it shouldn't take that much time. You and Mr. Barnes shouldn't have any problems helping him."

Yeah, lady. My dad'll jump right on that.

The ride to Temple is a little tense. "It's not going to be easy. It means me going to sleep later and you getting up a half-hour earlier so we can do the lessons before breakfast. There's only one thing I can't figure out."

"What?"

"Why would you do such a thing?"

Mom's question hangs in the air. I turn to look out the window.

"Warn, answer me."

Despite my advanced vocabulary, I have yet to learn the word coincidence. "It was just a weird thing. No reason."

My mother knows disapproval is my kryptonite. She waits me out, even turning off the radio, so the lack of noise bears down harder. Can waterboarding be far behind?

The tension becomes unbearable. I finally break.

"I did it for Butch."

Mom briefly stares at me incredulously before realizing her attention should be on the road. "Please explain what you mean."

"I figured if Butch was going to have problems in school, like you said, then I should slow down and not show off. I didn't want him to think I thought I was any better than he was." Again, my mother's temptation to look at me gets the best of her. She turns into a parking lot. I notice we are at a Barnes' Bakery as she turns off the car and hugs me. Hard. Like my face is squished up against her coat, and I can't breathe hard.

"That was very kind of you, but don't ever hold yourself back again. You'll do no one any good pretending to be less than you are. Not Butch. Not me. Especially not yourself. Do you hear me?"

I nod.

"Okay then. Good." She searches through her purse, digging to the bottom. She smiles as she pulls out one sticky quarter and three hairy dimes, all of which she hands to me. "Run inside and get yourself a treat. If they recognize you, don't let them give you anything for free."

I get each of us a little frosted cookie for $.15 apiece. I return one of the dimes to my mom.

The next morning my lessons begin. Grandma is already up and made us a special breakfast. Two eggs. *Three* slices of bacon. Toasted Cowboy Eddie Wonder Bread. "Land sakes," says Grandma. "This looks fun. I think I'll pay attention too if you don't mind."

So begins the most time the two of them ever spent with just me. On weekends Art and Nancy help. I will come to think of this as one of the most generous things the four of them ever did for me. I hate needing the extra attention; I love getting it.

The rest of the semester flies by. Each day new lessons. Each day something that I feel the teacher is doing just for me. Wayne and I add Jeff Quamme, Kurt Weinberg and Jim Petersen from our reading group to our afterschool gang. If we were on TV, we'd be called the Dictionaries or the Brainiacs. I don't think I'm being stuck up or anything, but we're all pretty smart. I'm lucky to have made bright, challenging, good friends.

There's no Purple Heart Christmas party this year. I'm guessing we didn't make the cut because we no longer live with my dad. Mom does her baking at Aunt Lil's house. We did go to the East Side Shopping Center to get our picture taken with Santa. Mom had a coupon. She let me wear my blue buffalo plaid flannel shirt that laces up the front, so I had kind of a lumberjack pirate thing going on. Pretty cool.

There are fewer presents under the tree, but who cares. Ming has plenty of ribbon to devil. Butch gets marbles, even some huge cat eyes and tri-lites, which he loves. I get a Batmobile pedal car and some skates. What could be better?

I'll tell you what could be better. After Christmas comes my birthday.

"What do you want to do this year, Warn?" asks Mom. I know she means business because she's got a Barnes' Home Improvement pen and a notepad in her hands. She's taking notes. "Keep in mind, the cheaper, the better."

"Well, how about a skating party?" I say.

"The skating rink costs about a buck a head."

"The one by the park is free."

Mom smiles. "Now you're thinking, kid!"

"We could also do the toboggan run."

The toboggan run is amazing. It's sponsored by Oscar Mayer, one of the biggest and best-paying employers in Madison. Each year, not far from our house, they set up a wooden toboggan run that is lined with ice. Two kids and an adult can ride at one time. It's best that way because if you have an adult's weight, you can slide onto the frozen lake.

Anyway, it's great fun once you get past your fear. God bless the Oscar Mayer Company for sponsoring this wonderful lawsuit waiting to happen. My bologna will always have a first name.

"Great idea! You were born in the winter. Let's lean into it!" says Mom. "Everything but the cake and a thermos of hot chocolate will be free."

The big day finally comes. I miss my father. Not because I miss Dad. I miss having the things that other kids have, so I wish he were here. I might as well wish for my own space capsule. The odds of getting either are equal.

The Smith kids, Laurie Mick, Wayne, Jim, Jeff, Kurt and my cousin Lee Ann are all coming. We're all doing the slide and then meeting at the warming house at Olbrich Park for cake and hot chocolate before going skating. I don't know it yet, but inviting Lee Ann was a mistake. Her dad is my dad's brother. By inviting her, my dad finds out about the party.

Miraculously, no one hurts themselves on the toboggan. Despite being the thin, cheaper kind of watery hot chocolate, everyone enjoys it. I mean, I don't want to sound ungrateful, but it's not even Swiss Miss. It's an off-brand knockoff. Mademoiselle du Norway or something like that.

Grandma can't send anyone home with a chocolate-stained face, so she chases after each kid with a napkin wetted with her spit. It's fun watching them try to run away from her. I should tell them not to bother. Grandma always wins.

My cake isn't one from Grandpa's bakery like it has always been before. Mom made it from a yellow cake mix. It has simple chocolate frosting and my name spelled out in sugary letters from the grocery store. When I first saw it, I was disappointed, but as an adult, this is the only birthday cake I'll remember. Mom for the win.

Everything is served on white paper plates. No color. No special writing or design. I'm disappointed in a childish way, but I get it. No discussion needed.

I'm not a good skater. No one has ever taught me how, so I rely on instinct. I pick up tips by watching the other kids. Art comes over and offers a few adjustments, which help. I improve throughout the night, but I'll never be great.

Our big, chubby kiddie cheeks are red and frozen from laughing. The air is cold, but our bodies are warm. Butch wears training skates. His natural athleticism allows him to keep up with the older kids. He's thrilled. All my friends are happy.

I've never been to a party like this, and it's wonderful.

From the ice, across the street and past the toboggan run, you can look across the lake and see the state capitol lit up. It's the best view in town, one that true Madisonians never stop loving. We even have laws limiting the height of new buildings to guarantee the capitol dominates the skyline. It's beautiful. As I stare out, a familiar figure is backlit against my hometown pride.

My father is stumbling toward us.

I instinctively break away from the group and head to the front edge of the skating rink. He stops, but I can tell he's here to see someone else. Not me. He offers a "Happy birthday" as he passes me a brown paper bag. I can smell whiskey on his breath. He's drunk.

I look inside the bag, which is from the True Value Hardware Store where my mom sells doll clothes. I pull out a plastic gunslinger belt and two cap pistols. It's an afterthought. A gift for any little boy, not *his* little boy. Not this boy.

He gives me a lazy smile before ripping the packaging open. He fumbles to put it on me, but he starts to lose his balance on the ice. "You're the smart one. Figure it out," he says before handing me the twisted belt.

I stare at him as he walks away across the ice. About halfway toward my mom, he turns into a cartoon. His legs and arms start flailing through the air in a frantic attempt to not fall. He fails, landing on his tailbone as gravity claims its latest victim of the night.

"Son of a bitch!" exclaims the man who doesn't appear to realize he's surrounded by children.

As he stumbles up with John Smith's help, I notice little clumps of packed snow and shards of ice interrupting the pattern of my dad's plaid pants. I hope falling hurt. Badly.

After giving my mother two sloppy kisses, she pushes him away. Art and Emily conspire to get him home. As they walk by me, Art stops, kneels, and says, "I'm sorry this happened, but I don't think anyone noticed." We look out into the crowd of slack-jawed, dumbfounded faces and laugh at his lie. Art kisses me on the cheek and runs to catch up.

Embarrassed guests quickly make up excuses and leave. It should probably feel like a big deal, but I'm used to it. Butch and Grandma catch a ride home in John Smith's forest green VW Bug, which must be part accordion or simply bend to John's will. If he says he can make you fit, you'll fit.

Now it's just me and my mom. "I'm sorry, but we have to wait, honey. Art and Emily will be back soon with my car. Do you want to talk about this?"

"No," I say, followed by a headshake that makes the pompom at the end of my long stocking cap hit me in the face.

"Okay. We don't have to, but there is just one thing I'd like to say. Is that alright?"

I shrug my shoulders.

"I just want you to remember that bad things happen sometimes. There's nothing we can do about that. It's just the way life is. It makes us stronger."

"Like Superman?"

"Yes," she says kissing me on the cheek. "You're my little Superman.

None of this is your fault. What really matters is how we get over it. You've got to pick yourself up and show some grace."

"Like when you pray at a meal?"

She smiles. "No. It's a different kind of grace. You'll understand someday."

"Okay."

"Would you like more hot chocolate?"

"No thanks Mom. Let's just skate."

Together, just the two of us on the ice, I manage my first spin and a figure 8.

CHAPTER SIXTEEN

FREE FALLING

It's summer again.

Me and the guys are taking swimming lessons at Olbrich Beach. We already got certified to swim by ourselves. Clint Smith is the best swimmer, but I'm not far behind. Jim Petersen is pretty good. Wayne wears a nose clip, which keeps falling out, so I don't see what good it does. One way or another, you're going to ingest Otis Redding's blood. It's mixed in with the water, plain and simple.

Paula was in our swim class because it's divided by age instead of grade, but then she decided she'd rather be with her friends from class, so she went back a year. Seems like that's her habit.

Mr. Mick pays me a quarter and slips me a bag of vegetables each time I help him in his garden. I told him the story about Art and the corn and asked if we were going to plant any of that. He says no, because "It takes up too much space. Besides, the yield is usually only one ear per stalk. Piss poor results for a home garden if you ask me."

I'm glad Art didn't let that stop him. Sometimes passion has got to win over logic: otherwise, what fun would the world be?

Today is Valerie's birthday. There's a big party. It was my dad's idea. He's just trying to use it to wear down my mom. Both my grandmas have been cooking since before I woke up this morning. We've got baked beans, seven bean salad, potato salad, coleslaw, tomato salad, carrot salad, ambrosia which is gross, hot dogs, hamburgers, steaks for the grown-ups and a big sheet cake my grandpa sent over. It's supposed to say, "Happy Birthday Valerie," I think. The writing is in braille which I've been teaching myself. I think Grandpa got the V and B confused, so it really says "Happy Virthday Balerie."

⠠⠊⠞⠄⠎ ⠎⠥⠍⠍⠻⠂ ⠃⠕⠽⠄ ⠠⠍⠑ ⠯ ⠮ ⠛⠥⠽⠎ ⠁⠗⠑ ⠞⠁⠅⠬ ⠋⠕⠗ ⠎⠺⠊⠍⠄

Val's birthday party is much bigger than mine was, but that's okay. I can see, so everything kind of evens out. Besides, a skating party in August wouldn't be much fun.

Our yard is packed with everyone from the neighborhood, my Aunts, Uncles, and cousins. Emily brought her cab driver boyfriend, Dave. I can't stop looking at him. He's got curly brown hair and a compact, athletic build. He's cute. Nancy's parents are here. Just about everyone I've ever met. There's a sense of fun in the air. I even caught my parents laughing together, which I don't think I've ever seen before.

Butch runs by like the Flash yelling, "It's Valerie's birthday!" I catch my grandmothers as they share a look and grasp hands.

"That school they found is doing him a world of good."

"He's getting better, isn't he, Emma?" says Grandma Barnes. "I wish Billy could see it. We light a candle for that boy each time we go to Mass."

"Well, Phyllis," says Grandma Caruso, "keep at it. It's working."

Ming jumps up on the table and starts to sniff the potato salad before Aunt Louise shoos him away. The cat runs to the side door with impeccable timing. It opens just as he arrives. In walks my sister Suzy with whomever she's dating right now. I think his name is Stoney, which is a weird name. He looks like he belongs on an album cover.

This whole thing with my parents has been hard on Valerie. She's living with Gladys, a very nice woman who worked at the bakery. The work was physical and getting too hard for her; she's frail. Now she's sort of Val's caretaker. They're kind of isolated. The TV is on at their little apartment all the time. It's like a third roommate.

Valerie is loving all this attention today. She's holding birthday court in the living room. The cousins sit around her, hanging on every word.

"You guys, it's so sad. My friend Kim is in love with Dan, but he was already married. He finally told his wife he was leaving her, during a big storm. He was on his way to Kim, but a tornado came through. When he finally got to her, Kim had been injured. When she woke up, she had amnesia."

"Wow!" says Cousin Lee Ann.

"Wow," says Emily, "you guys are gullible. Valerie, tell them the truth."

Val starts laughing. "It's a soap opera."

Art and Nancy are the last to arrive. When they do, I hear my dad say, "Everyone is here, and I've got my Polaroid. Let's get a family picture!"

I leave the room, pretending I didn't hear him. For the rest of my life, I will regret that there isn't a single picture of all of us together. Lesson learned. Try to hurt someone else, and you end up hurting yourself, but I can't help it.

As I sneak out of the house, I see Bo, Art, and Nancy's dog.

Don't get me wrong; I love our cat, Ming. But he's a cat. He likes to prowl alone. Dogs can go anywhere. One time, Bo even let me ride on his back. It was like having a horse or something. Can't ride a cat. I know. I've tried.

Skittish in crowds, Bo still makes his way to me with his tail wagging. He loves catching frisbees. We go to play in the side yard where people are less likely to see us.

I throw high. I throw low. He never misses! Pretty soon, I forget all about my dad.

I keep throwing to Bo until I think my arm will fall off.

"Bo, I've got to take a break," I say as though the dog can understand. He whimpers but follows me to the front yard, where I find the Smith kids. We share a summer lament echoed by every child ever.

"I'm bored."

"Me too."

"Let's walk to the store and look around."

There's a garden center at the end of our block, just before the gas station, a body shop, and a bunch of small industrial spaces housing God only knows what. As Bo follows, we walk toward the entrance. There are three bins of gravel to climb over. One was recently gouged by a front-loader. The gravel, various shades of white and grey, has been baking in the sun. The remaining rocks have formed a little cliff, so Clint and I climb up there, wondering if our combined 80 lbs. might cause an avalanche.

After 10-seconds or so, our patience pays off. We start to feel the earth beneath our feet shift and rumble before breaking away. The gravel starts to fall, taking us with it. We fall on our backs, riding the gravel tidal wave to the bottom of the bin. We are giggling and coughing from the gravel dust we've kicked up. The more we laugh, the deeper we breathe. The deeper we breathe, the more we cough. The more we cough, the more we laugh.

We brush ourselves off and head toward the front entrance. We are well known to the staff. No mention of the dog following us. Inside the much cooler store, it smells fertile-plant food, fertilizer, and end-of-season plants fill the air. We pass the candy and cigarette machines, kept side by side, and head toward their small toy section. There we find our end-the-boredom tonic. On clearance for $.10 a piece are four kites perfect for the four of us.

Hot Wheels for Clint.

The Milwaukee Bucks for Jerry.

Barbie for Genie.

I'd like that one but know better than to grab it. There's one just as good, if not better. Batman. Dark blue background with his yellow and black chest symbol in the middle. It's like having my own personal Bat-Signal.

I have a quarter, as does Genie. Clint and Jerry have $.75 between them. We've got plenty of money so we can get string too. We grab the kites and four bundles of string, gushing about the fun we assume awaits.

There are things you understand as an adult that a child just can't see. The kites were on sale because there's no wind. It's August, which is not a month known for kite flying in Wisconsin, but no matter. Our moods are breezy. That's enough.

We set up a little kite-making workshop in the front yard. There is a mishap or two solved with a little paper and glue. Soon we appear to be in business, nearly.

"You guys," I say urgently, with my own version of string theory. "We need sticks to tie our string around. Remember? In the spring, I lost a box kite because the string came off the spool. We've got to find sticks to tie the string to."

So, we fan out in search of twigs and fallen branches. For once, my yard is in perfect order because my dad sent workers over to get everything ready for the party. This is going to take some figuring out.

Butch's old tricycle was left next to the taller maple tree in the front yard. Sticks come from trees. There must be something up there which I can use.

Bo spots me, waiting at the bottom of the tree. I shimmy up quickly, with confidence. I swing from branch to branch, searching for an elusive twig until I'm about 12-feet in the air.

I see a stick. Gnarled in the middle, smooth on the ends. A kid, likely me or Butch, broke off whatever part is missing during an earlier climb. I try to break it off, but it's determined to stay put.

Quickly using my computer-like problem-solving skills, I devise a plan. My 40 lbs. of weight hanging off the stick as though it were a Jungle Jim bar will cause the stick to crack off from the tree. As soon as I hear the cracking, I will grab an adjacent branch and safely climb down with my treasure.

Branch chosen, I hang from the branch and wait.

And wait.

Just as I twist to see if there are any other easily accessible branches, I hear the crack of breaking wood. I begin to fall. I start bouncing off branches twisting into new positions, my head quickly taking the lead and now speeding toward the ground.

I see Butch's tricycle and wonder if it might break my fall. At the last minute, I instinctually understand that hitting it would be worse than flat ground. I shift my weight to land farther away. The tricycle, from decades prior, has other plans. The uncovered end of the handlebars catches my right cheek, ripping the length of it.

The shallow scar it will leave one day motivates conversation with casting directors. "How did you get that scar? I love it. Gives your face character!"

I place out my dominant arm, the right, to break the impact. Break it does. There is no other answer for the searing pain running up the length of my arm to the shoulder. This must be what Wile E. Coyote feels when he falls.

I'm not scared, but I am in pain. Probably in shock. I do nothing but ponder what just happened. Sweet Bo has other ideas. He begins running back and forth between me and the driveway, barking frantically, gathers a group of grown-ups led by my parents.

"Oh my goodness," says my mom.

"Fuck," says my dad.

I look down and see my arm twisting in directions it probably shouldn't. I look like the Elongated Man.

My parents are frozen. Thank God for grandmas. Caruso props me up. Barnes starts cleaning up my gashed cheek. She has Iodine. Where did that come from? They must give it out at grandma training camp.

"I'll take him to the hospital," comes at me in stereo. My parents said it at the same time. The mix continues. "No. I will!"

Before I know it, the argument about who will take the victim is getting more attention than the victim. A fight worthy of a pay-per-view. Emily and her handsome boyfriend finally break through the crowd.

"I can grab my cab!" says Dave.

"No. We're not his parents," says Emily. "These two need to get it together. Warn is hurt. What are you going to do?"

They look at her in stymied silence.

Grandma Barnes seeing an opening, says, "Take him together."

They flank me on both sides as the Buick pulls out of the driveway. WISM-am kills the silence. We are serenaded by the top hits of the summer including, "Candy Man," "The First Time Ever I Saw Your Face," and "Daddy Don't You Walk So Fast."

Each time the chorus comes around I find myself thinking, "Let him walk, kid. Let him walk away as fast as possible."

We pull up to the Emergency Room entrance. An attendant is waiting for us.

"You must be the Barnes family." We all look confused, so he explains. "Mrs. Barnes called ahead. She was kind enough to tell us the bakery would send a pastry and donut buffet for us next week if you could follow up on that. Allow me to lead you to pediatrics. It shouldn't be too long a wait."

We stoically sit until my father, who needs either a dozen cigarettes or a gallon of whiskey, can no longer take the silence.

"Thank God I was there."

"What did you say, Raymond? Thank God you were there?" repeats my mother. "I'm sure I could've figured out how to get him to the hospital. I've been figuring everything else for…"

"All I'm saying is that a boy needs two parents at a time like this."

"When has he ever had two parents?"

The conversation is flying over my head like a badminton birdie flies over a clothesline. The lobs come right and left. Served and returned. In fact, it takes on such rigor that I'm not sure they remember I'm here until a kind looking nurse comes into the room.

"Barnes? Warren Barnes?" she asks.

I start to correct her, but my dad is quicker. "Warn. His name is Warn Barnes."

"Oh. I'm sorry. I thought that was a typo."

"It was, but then it stuck," says my mom incredulously.

I begin to sob. Sob. Gut-wrenching, I can't breathe, sobbing. All my fear, my pain, and the tension of the day come vomiting out. My parents both rush to me. My father gets there first, dammit. I collapse into his arms. Putting my arms around him causes more pain, which makes me cry harder. Perhaps for the first time ever, he hugs me and buries his head into my small shoulder. My back is to my mother, but I know they're looking at each other. I can feel their chemistry. Their connection.

They let me sob for a few more seconds. Him hugging me. Her

rubbing my back. When the embrace breaks, I can see tears have welled up in his eyes. I'm already too cynical to believe those tears are in any part or measure for me.

For a quick second, he's exactly who I need him to be. Strong. Available. Completely present. Gently patting my arm to make sure the pain has subsided, he says, "I've got an idea."

"Wh-Wh-What?" I say while trying to recover my breathing.

"After this is over, we'll stop at the store, and you can get any toy you want."

My breathing recovers. The tears stop.

"Any toy? From Arlan's? They've got the biggest toy department."

"Yeah. You just get through this best you can, okay? They're going to help your arm get better, but you've got to be a big boy."

"Okay."

What were they thinking in the 1970s? They didn't let my mom come back to keep me company. I am put on a gurney and wheeled away. By myself. Alone.

The nurse looks at me oddly. "What?" I ask.

"Haven't I seen you on Cowboy Eddie?"

The surgery goes well. Yes, the *surgery*. It turns out there were multiple fractures with displacement issues if I heard correctly. The arm had to be set. Full plaster cast from hand to shoulder. I awaken groggy but with no sense of trauma or pain. My parents are in the room with me. The first thing I see is my dad giving his card to one of the nurses.

"Yes, ma'am. Vinyl is final. Have your husband give me a call if you want to hear about the special offer we're running." Noticing I'm awake, Mom kisses me on the cheek.

"I heard you were so brave!" says my dad.

"I was asleep."

"Well, the nurses said you were a very good patient. I'm proud of you," says Mom.

"Let's go see about that toy," says my dad.

I am out of the car like a shot.

"Whoa. Whoa, son. You just broke your arm. No need to break a speed record."

More slowly than I'd like, we make our way into Arlan's and toward the toy department. My dad pauses near sporting equipment and Hot Wheels racing tracks, but I keep walking. He follows until I turn right at aisle 10.

Dolls.

"You said any toy," I remind him, just as Mom is catching up.

"That's true. You did say that Raymond," she echoes.

I begin to scan the Barbies. There is a carrying case with a dozen dolls in it, but I don't want to be greedy. I certainly don't want to hand him a reason to say no. Then I see her. Amongst all the blondes, an ash blonde. More subtle. Elegant. Amongst the twist and turn versions, a classic girl with straight hard plastic legs that wouldn't stain or break. Amongst the ordinary, a star.

Francie.

"I need an outfit for her."

"What?" says my dad.

"Warn, I can make her one," offers Mom.

"Okay, thank you. I need one today, though. I'm not taking her home with just a swimsuit. My dad slips away while Mom and I look through the outfits. There's a lot of showy stuff. Trashy. Puffy sleeves, shiny material, headbands, bad choices abound. Then I find it. Classic black skirt with a high collared white blouse. Riding boots. A crop. A simple cameo broach at her swan-like throat.

"Francie and I like this one, Mother. May we have it, please?"

Mom nods just before my dad reappears, carrying many boxes.

"What are those?" I ask.

"Francie's boyfriends, G.I. Joe, and the whole goddamned adventure team."

They waited to cut the cake until we got home. It's awkward trying to eat it with my left hand, but it's cake, so it's worth the effort. Emily draws an ivy vine across my cast on a diagonal, leaving room for everyone in the family to sign it. Em writes her name in beautiful, distinctive handwriting. She guides Butch's hand while he holds the pen. He must like it. He claps when they're through. Val makes a big X, which doesn't stay within her area, but who cares. Art and Nancy sign their names, and Bo's pawprint, inside a little heart-shaped cluster of ivy. Suzy is still here to sign her name. Both my grandmas write "Grandma," but their handwriting is very similar. It's hard to tell which is whose.

Mom writes, "I was so proud of you today! Love, Mom"

My dad writes, "Raymond." When Emily points that out, he gets flustered.

"Let me redo it."

"It's plaster," says Emily. "There are no do-overs in plaster." She manages to sound disgusted and patronizing at the same time. She's amazing.

Mom slips her arm through his. "Ray, it doesn't matter. Don't worry about it." Then she kisses him on the cheek, and the room goes silent. Even Val notices it.

"What just happened?" she asks.

Mom blushes and defers to him. My dad steps forward. "We all know it's been a tough couple of years, but Dorothy and I talked while Warn was in surgery. We're going to give it another go. I'm going away for a little while, but when I get back, I'll be moving back in. We're going to be a family again."

I don't quite know what to say, or how to feel. On one hand, I'm glad. I won't be the kid without a father anymore. On the other hand, I can't help wondering what the last year and a half has meant. Did we go through all this for it just to end up like it was before?

In my heart, I know we're moving backward, and that's the wrong direction. Nothing is going to be different. There's no point in acknowledging it. No one has given me a vote. I smile, but my eyes are dead.

Breaking my arm isn't the worst thing to happen today.

CHAPTER SEVENTEEN

IS THERE A DRAFT IN HERE?

By "going away," my dad meant treatment. He's in an in-patient, ninety-day addiction clinic in Minnesota. Once again, no one told me. Get this. They said he's "At a clinic for heart problems." Yeah, right. They're looking to see if he has one.

I will eventually learn you can't get over a problem you're not willing to openly talk about. The anger and shame won't resolve. They're still there, unacknowledged, waiting to spill over into other areas, but I don't know that yet.

My new favorite thing to do is come into a room where everyone seems to be in a perfectly good mood and say one little thing to change the tone. Something like, "Art, are you still going to buy that new camera lens?"

"Yeah. I think so," says Art.

"That's kind of expensive, isn't it?" says Mom.

"We're using some of the wedding money," explains Nancy.

"Oh, really?" says the woman working overnight to make an extra quarter an hour until her husband in the expensive in-patient addiction treatment center returns home.

And so, it begins. Perfect fun for a rainy Saturday afternoon.

As fun often does, this ends quickly. Sensing the tension in the air, Art decides to rip the band-aid off and changes the subject. "I have some news." Looking to Nancy and sadly smiling, he corrects himself. "We have some news. It affects all of us." Nancy steps next to him and puts her hand on his back.

"Art's draft number came up. He's reporting for basic duty in two-weeks."

Two sentences. One thought. Everything is different, just that quickly.

Having heard everything, Grandma Caruso hurries into the living room. "Warn, you go play with Butch upstairs."

"I want to stay."

"Listen to Grandma," says Art.

"Okay."

Climbing the stairs, I consider staying there to listen, but it doesn't feel right. Art asked me to let the grown-ups talk. This seems like a time to respect his wishes above all other things, so I keep climbing.

Over the next two weeks, I spend a lot of time watching Walter Cronkite. Grandma is cooking. Mom is working. No one thinks to stop me.

Over 6,000 American soldiers were killed in Vietnam last year. Uncle Greg died in Korea. In WWII, Dad was wounded, which sounds better, but he's in constant pain. Both those things happened in our family. It can happen again.

Six-thousand people, and that's just the *Americans*. What does that really mean? I remember Emily said her high school had 2,000 students. So, 6,000 means more people than both our schools combined, including teachers.

I try not to think about that too much. What's a kid going to do about a war that no one can explain? Besides, if I think about it too much, I'll miss the time we have before Art leaves.

"Happy just us day!" says my brother.
"I've never been to this big a city before!"
'Warn," says Art. "We're not even in Milwaukee yet."
"You're kidding, right?"
"No. These are just the suburbs."
Wow.

"Okay, if we're going to try and see as much as we can in one day, so we've got to stay focused."
"What's focused?"
"Concentrate. Stick with the plan. We aren't going to be able to do things like this for a while, so we've got to make today count."
I'm not going to get sad. I'm not going to be scared. Smile. Enjoy being here.

We pull into a parking lot, at the far end of which there are three glass domes built with a framework of metal girders. I've never seen anything like it. "We're here!" Art says as he puts the car in park. "Grab the bag lunches Mom made."

He pulls a pamphlet from his pocket, unfolding it and carefully smoothing it out before he reads.

"Feel the heat of a desert oasis, the humidity of a tropical jungle, and the bright colors of a floral garden. Three of the world's dominant ecosystems come together in one destination at The Mitchell Park Horticultural Conservatory, better known as The Domes. Visit a living museum filled with plants from across the globe without leaving beautiful Milwaukee, Wisconsin."

"You mean this place is like getting to go on a trip around the world?"

Art is so much older than I am and married. It's easy to forget he's barely in his twenties himself. "I think so. There are plants from all over the world. And they control the atmosphere in each one. It's exactly like being in a desert or a jungle." Art's eyes grow larger. "Let's start with the desert."

"Let's not drink the whole time we're in there, so we know what it's like when people in the movies have to cross the desert with no water."

"Great idea."

We start trekking across the world in our own small way. We pass the desert airlock and immediately feel the driest heat either of us has ever experienced. Despite the warning signs, we touch giant cacti, because when are we ever going to see giant cactus again? We don't touch the huge lizards, even when they ask for volunteers. Some people have a very odd sense of fun.

We snake our way through the deserts of North America, South America, and Africa. I promise myself, someday I'll see the real thing. I will travel the world.

I stop at a particularly huge prehistoric looking plant. Looking around, I realize Art is not beside me, but I'm not scared. We will find our way back to each other, no doubt. I just keep following the path toward the exit signs, where he's waiting for me.

We stop at the first bubbler we see. It's one of those side-by-side kinds, where one is at a lower level for kids. We can drink at the same time. My throat constricts at the first cold burst of water. It's delicious. I stop drinking first and watch Art continue to gulp several times more before coming up for air.

"Are you hungry?" says Art. "I know it's a little early, but…"

"Sure. Let's eat. Mom gave me $1.50 for a souvenir. We could get snacks instead if we get hungry again."

Art finds us an out-of-the-way spot on the floor right underneath an air conditioning duct. We don't have AC at home. It feels so good. Mom made me a peanut butter and jelly sandwich. Art got Oscar Meyer ham and cheese loaf, which was on sale at the C&P Grocery Store. Cowboy Eddie Wonder Bread completes both sandwiches. I got a bag of Frito's. Poor Art got regular old Lay's chips. We split a can of 7 UP from a vending machine, passing it back and forth without wiping it because we're brothers.

One dome has a "come back and see us again after we're done planting" sign up, so we head to the Jungle Dome. As we walk in, we're hit with dank air. It is humid in the best sense of the word. A student choir is standing on risers singing "Edelweiss" which Art says is from a movie called *The Sound of Music*. I've never seen it, but the music doesn't sound very jungle-like to me. Inside there are huge palm trees and flowering vines. Giant moss-covered boulders form a waterfall. The air is floral and sweet. You can feel the potential for life.

"This is a jungle, right?"

"Yes," says Art.

"Vietnam is a jungle too. Is this what it will be like?" I ask.

We both take a second to look around at the lush landscape and listen to the rushing water of the waterfall. It is peaceful and idyllic.

Art looks me in the eye and says, "Yes. When you think of me in Vietnam, picture this. This is exactly what it will be like. Don't let anyone tell you any different."

This time Art hands me the pamphlet. Having been carried through the desert in his pocket, it is a little damp, but I manage to smooth it out without ripping it. "Read it to me," he says.

"Okay. I'll try," I say, hoping the writing isn't too grown-up. *"As one of the country's finest animal … sanctuaries, The Milwaukee County Zoo will educate, entertain and inspire you! Visit over 2,100 mammals, birds, fish, and reptiles in habitats spanning 190 acres. The zoo is a place where everyone can laugh and learn!"*

We pull into the parking lot. There's a tram thingy that gives rides to older people, but Grandma isn't with us, so me and Art decide to walk to the entrance.

"So, what kind of animals do they have?"

"What kind of animals do you want to see?"

"Giraffes."

"They've got 'em."

"Do they have chickens?"

"In the petting zoo, for little kids. Babies."

"I was just asking. I don't need to see chickens. Do they have gorillas?"

"Do they have gorillas?"

Art leads us through paths like an expert. "How do you know where we're going? I'm holding the map!"

"I've been here before."

"Really?"

"My dad brought me."

I stop. "Your dad? The first Warren?"

"Yeah. The first Warren."

I can't stop myself from asking. "What was he like?"

"Well," says Warren's son, "I don't remember that much. He was tall."

"Like you?"

Art smiles. "Like me. He spent a lot of time with Emily and me. He was usually in a good mood. He loved to laugh. I'm pretty sure I remember his laugh. He was a good guy."

"Did he drink?"

"Not that I remember. So, if he did, it couldn't have been much."

"I think he'd be proud of you."

I can't be sure I said that part. I hope I did. It's the truth.

The Primate Path ends at a wide hallway open on both sides. The entrance is dark. The exit is well-lit and obvious. Between those two points is an angled glass wall framed by thick stainless-steel beams. Behind that are walls covered in subway tile. The wall is long and smooth.

Inside the enclosure, pacing back and forth, owning his space, is the most beautiful animal I've ever seen. A silverback gorilla, a powerful, natural contrast to the locker room-like quality of his environment. His strength has anger underneath it. I can tell he's not happy. He's trapped. The life he's living has been handed to him by something outside of himself. Two boys from Wisconsin stare at the gorilla in silence until Art says, "This is Samson."

Samson. That's perfect. "Who named him?" I ask.

"Someone at the zoo, I guess," replies Art.

I see someone who looks like they work at the zoo. "Hey, Mister! Mister, can Samson sign my cast?"

The man, heavyset with thinning hair, smiles. "I'm sure he'd love to, buddy, but gorillas can't write."

"Really? I thought maybe they could. He seems really smart."

"Son of a gun. Look at that! Samson followed you over here. He likes you," says the kindly zookeeper, who like Samson, has exceptionally long and furry arms. "Tell you what ... I've got a marker with me. Can I sign for Samson?"

"Yes! Thank you."

And so, he does. He signs right next to Art's signature.

"We've got to get going if we want to see any of the other animals," says Art.

Samson and I catch each other's eye. I feel like I'm saying goodbye to a new friend. On the way out of the building, I put my $1.50 into a collection bin for gorillas in the wild.

It's the day before, the day before Art leaves.

"Warn! Come on! Dave is here to take us uptown," says Emily. "He was nice enough to pick us up. Let's not waste his time."

Total lie. Emily doesn't mind keeping people waiting if it means getting her eyelashes perfect. Especially if it's a man. She was giving people delayed gratification before the term delayed gratification had been invented.

Soon enough, we're in the cab. Emily is sitting with Dave in the front seat. I'm in the back. We're on our way to get Art a present. Emily read that clothing was a good thing to give soldiers on their way to basic training, so we're getting him socks and underwear. Emily didn't know what kind of underpants to buy, but since I used to share a room with Art, I know he likes boxers. Butch and I wear briefs. I don't get boxer shorts. They bunch up in weird places. You look like an old man. It's what Art likes, though, so that's what we should get.

Dave drops us off at Kresge's on the square, across from the State Capitol. We find red, white, and blue striped boxers and a big box of black and white cotton socks. I give Emily $2.00 from my birthday money toward my share of the present. She pays for the rest. I think I got a good deal.

Kresge's has a luncheon counter, so we each get a cherry Coke. Emily runs into Kathy Olson, her best friend. She's got the biggest brown eyes ever, like one of those kids on a Hallmark card. She wears her hair bobbed, like Doris Day and Mary Tyler Moore. Everyone calls her KO. She's super cool. So, we hang out with KO while she eats a tuna melt. Pretty soon, it's time to go.

Everything outside has changed. There are a bunch of people carrying signs. Policemen are trying to move them away from the capitol. People start pushing and shoving us. We nearly get separated. Luckily Emily and KO are each holding one of my hands, and they're strong.

Amongst the "make love, not war" and "protest is patriotic" signs, someone is carrying one that says, "soldiers should burn draft cards, not babies." I break away from KO and Emily to talk to that guy. Or his back. He's facing in the other direction, toward the center of the protest.

"Your sign is wrong. My brother is a soldier. He's leaving next week. He'd never, ever burn a baby."

The protestor starts to fight with me before he turns around. "Oh yeah? Fuck you and your brother. Hold onto your old ideas and morality all you want. He's going to come home changed if he comes home at all!"

He finishes turning toward me as his tirade ends. By the time he realizes he's talking to a child, it's too late. It's too late because it's literally too late. He's finished talking.

It's also too late for him because Emily heard it all.

"What is your problem?" asks my strong, beautiful sister. "You're talking to a child."

This guy, Art's age, maybe younger, doubles down. "He shouldn't be here."

"That's what you've got to say for yourself? We were inside the store minding our own business when all this started. What about peace and love, asshole?"

"Now, who should be watching how they talk in front of children?"

"Kiss my ass, you shithead. He's my fucking brother."

"Yeah! I'm her fucking brother!" is the last thing we say to him before walking east toward home with KO.

We make our way to the bus stop about two blocks away. "Can I ask a question?"

"Yeah. Of course."

"What's fucking?"

"Don't worry about it," says KO.

Emily adds, "Just never say it in front of Mom." They're still laughing when the bus arrives. Because they're laughing, I don't have their attention, which gives me time to think.

I saw signs with a naked girl running down the street with smoke from a fire behind her. There was a picture of Vietnamese people lining up like they were going to get shot. There was another picture of a pit filled with

dead soldiers.
>   Where's the beautiful jungle?
>   Where is Art really headed?

CHAPTER EIGHTEEN

THE PARTY IS OVER

Today is Art's going away party.

Mom's all-girl posse kicked into high gear. Yesterday they were over here cleaning under Grandma's leadership until the place shined. Their husbands were outside mowing, pruning, painting, and whacking weeds. Shirley even cleaned the gutters. Our house has never looked better.

When I walk into the kitchen, Mom is frosting a cake. Aunt Lil is attacking stubborn soap scum on our kitchen faucet. Geneva is making potato salad. Mick is pounding hamburger into perfect patties. Shirley is making sausage and peppers in the Nesco, just like at the East Side Businessmen's Fair. Florence is checking off items on her to-do list.

"Ladies, we're 10 minutes ahead of schedule! Well done," adds the Governor's secretary.

Aunt Lil says, "Good morning, Warn."

"Hey, sweetie," says Shirley. "Can you help me carry this out to the picnic table?"

As we carry the sloshing, enameled portable roaster outside, we do a little sidestep dance as people inevitably do when there's a height disparity. I stretch. She squats. As she does, the blouse she is wearing over a tank top slips over her shoulder.

"Hey Shirl, how did you get those bruises?"

I can't tell if the look of frustration that crosses her face is because of my question or our task. "Bruises? Oh, that," she quickly recovers. "I had to throw a drunk out of the tavern. He pushed me up against a wall before I was able to give him the old heave-ho."

Guests start arriving around 11 am. Art, Nancy, and Bo pull up at noon. Everyone cheers as they walk up the driveway. Art smiles. "We'd have been here sooner, but we had to park three blocks away."

Under her breath, I can hear Grandma say, "People love him. Just like his father."

"Warn, can we talk to you for a minute?" asks Nancy.

We sit down on the front steps, Art next to me at the top, Nancy sitting one step down. Bo lies on the ground, where he can keep an eye on all three of us. Good boy.

"We need to ask you a favor."

"Okay."

Nancy places Bo's leash in my hand. "Take care of Bo."

"Okay. I'll be right back. You can tell me the favor then."

Art smiles. "That is the favor. We'd like Bo to stay with you while I'm gone."

"I'm going to be busy in classes. Our apartment is too small for the dog to be cooped up all day long," adds Nancy.

"So, what do you say?" asks Art.

"It's okay with Mom?"

"It's even okay with *Grandma*."

"Wait. What? Bo would live with us?"

Both nod their heads. "If you say yes."

"Yes. Yes! Oh my God, yes!"

Bo, who must sense my enthusiasm, breaks his vigil and runs to me with wagging tail before giving me a sloppy, wet, wonderful kiss on the cheek.

Amongst the crowd are familiar faces from the TV Station. Rick Fetherston, Michael Lerners-Weife, and Judy Saunders are all here. Everyone else is trying to play it cool, but I know they're impressed.

Just when I think it can't get any better, it does.

Howie Olson, dressed in a spiffy one-piece jumpsuit, walks up the driveway with a box full of Wonder Bread hotdog and burger buns. He's carrying something else in a red case, but I don't want to think about what might be inside. If he wanted me to know, he'd tell me.

Uncle Nick and Aunt Josie make a beeline to him. "Mr. Olson, it's a pleasure to meet you! I'm Josie Caruso. Arthur's Aunt. This is my husband, Nick. We watched you with our kids all the time. And I swear each time you were on, I'd say ... oh jeez. What would I say, Nicky?"

"She'd say his lips ain't moving. He's good!"

Mr. Olson smiles, and says, "Thank you," without moving his lips.

A few minutes later, Rick Fetherston shuts one of several beer coolers and stands on it. I can see my Grandma's displeasure, his dirty shoes on her clean beer cooler. She's about to say something when Mrs. Smith asks her to try the potato salad. Grandma says, "You just saved a man's life, Geneva," as she is led away.

Mr. Fetherston, whose hair seems summer-blonder, waits for the yard to settle before raising a PBR bottle into the air. "All of us at Channel 3 are proud of Art for doing his patriotic duty. We're going to miss you, Private, so hurry back. It won't be the news without you."

The crowd cheers. Mr. Fetherston continues. "Now we adults need to get down to some serious drinking." No one laughs. Wrong crowd. Post-Traumatic Raymond Barnes Syndrome is too fresh. Reading his audience, he plows through. "So, let's do something special for the kiddies. Boys and girls, how about a hand for Mr. Howie Olson and Cowboy Eddie!"

Oh. My. God. The cheering from the kids on the east side of Madison, Wisconsin, surely shattered some windows and more than a few eardrums. The other kids aren't veterans like me. They've never been with Howie and Eddie before. I used to be a fan before I was on the show, so I get it.

Mr. Olson does a whole routine for us, which is hilarious. Cowboy Eddie, dressed in a matching one-piece jumpsuit, is getting the best of him all over the place. He says Mrs. Olson is something called a hen pecker. She wears the pants in the family. Howie tries to get the upper hand back and says, "Oh yeah? What about your wife? Is she a hen pecker?"

Cowboy Eddie says, "No she's not. She's no spring chicken, and I ain't got a pecker!" I don't get the joke, but most of the grown-ups crack up. I can tell it's racy because Grandma's lips disappear.

They can't show cartoons, so I don't know what they're going to do after their comedy routine. Mr. Olson surprises me by calling me up.

"Folks, we want to call up one of the regular kids from our TV Circus. How about a hand for Warn Barnes?"

I get shy and fold into Grandma's apron, but she pushes me forward. I arrive next to Mr. Olson and Eddie just as the applause is ending.

"Warn, how are you doing today?" asks Eddie.

I can't lie to Eddie. "I'm sad, I guess."

Mr. Olson joins in. "Why?"

"Because Art is leaving tomorrow."

Mr. Olson, who may have been a soldier during the Spanish-American War, for all I know, chokes up a little. "We all are Warn. We all are. Kids I want you to remember that it's guys like Art Holden who make it possible for the rest of us to enjoy beautiful summer days like this. His sacrifice and honor make everything else possible."

Then, in a way that is both surreal and touching at the same moment, Cowboy Eddie leads the entire backyard in "God Bless America."

While everyone is focused, my Grandma shocks me and stands up to talk.

"Hello, everyone. On behalf of me, Dorothy, and our whole family, thank you for coming over to wish Arthur well. Now Lord knows, I'm not one for talking, but it wouldn't be right to not say what an honor it is to be his grandmother."

She pulls out a handkerchief she embroidered herself and dabs her eyes.

"Art, from the first day I knew you were coming, you've brought so much love to us all. You're a wonderful grandson, son, big brother and husband. Now you'll be a wonderful soldier. God bless you. Come home to us safe."

Mom adds her own thoughts.

"Art, I already miss you, and you haven't even left. I can't imagine what it's going to be like while you're gone. You had to grow up so quickly. I hope the maturity and selflessness you've always shown serves you well while you're away. Your father, a proud veteran himself, can't be here with us, but I know his spirit is here. I can feel him standing here next to me. We're both so proud of you."

She raises a glass of ice water. "To our son."

Grandma hands her a handkerchief, and they fall into each other's arms.

The anxiety I've been feeling since yesterday starts to build, becomes harder and harder to ignore. I spy our plastic pool, flipped over in the corner of the yard. While the others are preoccupied, Bo and I quietly walk over, lift a corner of the pool up and scoot underneath.

Inside, the air is still and humid. The sun shines through the plastic, giving everything a blue glow. The grass is sweaty. There's enough light to read. I have two issues of *The Fantastic Four* with me. I get through the first one okay, but then I get drowsy. I use Bo's ribcage as a pillow. He nestles in, resting his head on my shoulder before we both fall asleep.

I awaken to hear people yelling my name. I don't know how long we've been napping. A chorus of, "Warn! Has anybody seen Warn?" gets louder and louder. I want to pop out of the pool and stop their worrying, but I don't want to get in trouble, so I stay put.

Someone, maybe Shirley's husband Jerry, says, "has anyone looked underneath the pool?" I can tell from the shadows that people are walking toward my hiding place. I squat with one knee in front of me; and my back leg extended, ready to run. When the pool starts to rise, I run. Bo follows. Everyone is momentarily startled, so it's easy to get past them before they chase after us. We rush into the garage, which is empty.

I jump up and pull the garage door down with my good arm. I then twist the lock and hear a click. I try to open the door. It doesn't budge. Good. They can't get me. I have time to think.

Art is the first one to reach the door, followed by everyone else. There must be at least thirty people watching this unfold.

"Warn! Warn! Open this up!"

"No."

"No one has a key. Open this door."

"NO!"

I see Art's jaw set. He takes off the sports coat he's been wearing and tightly wraps it around his hand. "Okay then. Have it your way. Stand against the back wall of the garage."

Even though I'm confused, I do as he asks. I grab Bo and walk backward, crashing into some dusty tools.

Art takes a deep breath, pulls his arm back, and then crashes his fist through the garage door window. Nancy gingerly taps away stubborn shards of glass still trapped within the frame while Art unwraps his hand. His skin is unbroken. His jacket is, however, shredded. It's ruined.

Art decisively disengages the lock and lifts open the door. As he walks in, I rush into his arms and wrap my body around his. We bury our heads into each other's shoulders.

"Why would you do that, Warn? Why?"

I can't stop myself from answering his question. I've got to tell the truth even though I know it's the wrong thing to say to a new soldier the day before he leaves for war. I can't keep the words or the feelings inside.

"Why did you do that?"

"Because I don't want you to leave. I don't want you to die!"

And then I cry. Deep, heaving tears of which only children and Italian widows are capable. Nearly all the tears are for Art. I'm scared he won't come back or that he'll be a different person when it's all over.

Somewhere, I also know I'm crying because when Art leaves tomorrow,

I'm going to be alone in a new way. Alone as I've never been before.

Still bundled in Art's arms, everyone circles us and begins rubbing my back or offering the tired clichés kids have been handed since the beginning of the first war, whenever that was.

"Don't worry. Everything is going to be fine."

Beyond the mob, I spy a familiar car coming up the driveway. After only three-weeks of what was supposed to be a 90-day in-patient treatment plan, my dad is home.

My dad is home, and the car is parked at an angle.

THE MIDDLE, 1979

CHAPTER NINETEEN

TEENAGE WAISTLAND

Stupid alarm clock. I've hit snooze three times. You think it would get the hint. I don't care if I'm on time for my stupid algebra class. The clock is the constant. I am the variable. Thanks, algebra. I get it.

Half an hour later, I stumble down the stairs. Barnes Home Improvement Command Central is in full mode. As I pour myself some store-brand Frosted Flakes, I see Mom giving assignments to the crews, most of whom are more interested in their cigarettes, coffee, and surviving today's hangover.

Speaking of hangovers, I can hear my dad stirring in the bedroom. He's groaning as though he's surprised to be waking up dehydrated with a headache. The implied subtext of "who did this to me?" is clear to everyone but himself.

You. You did this to you.

Some dads are accountants. Others are firemen. You're an addict.

You're a *daddict*.

Pouring sugar onto my cereal before inhaling it, I steal some orange juice fresh from concentrate and head upstairs. Before choosing my clothes, I splash water onto my cut to be feathered hair. Pushing aside my closet door, I choose from a rainbow of flannel shirts and grab a pair of painter's pants, which I buy at Fish Lumber Supply, using my dad's company charge account.

Forcing the pants over my chaffed thighs, I notice they don't button easily. Grabbing a Twinkie from the stash I keep in my room, I ponder other options. These might be tight, but they're what all the other kids are wearing.

I'll just keep my shirt untucked. No one will notice.

Passing the mirror, I see that my hair has fallen into place well enough. I slip on my leather Nike Cortez sneakers, grab my backpack full of homework I didn't get around to doing, and head back downstairs. I wave to my mom, who is handing out checks. Workers are blocking the doorway, so I cut through the kitchen.

141

"Good morning, Dad!" I say with loud enthusiasm, enjoying his wincing. "You have a great day!" Not waiting to see if he mumbles something back, I open the door before closing it loudly.

I get to the bus stop. The metro is pulling away, heading toward LaFollette High School. Oh well, another one will be here soon enough. Might as well get something done. I plop myself inside the alcove of the Lake Edge Tavern to break the winter wind. I pull a notebook out of my backpack and begin working on the English paper that's due third period.

Just as I get into a groove Doug Brace, the rare senior who is also a nice guy pulls up in his light blue Mercury Bobcat. "It's cold! You want a ride?" he asks.

Inside I can see a couple of jocks. "No thanks. I've got to finish some work." Doug smiles and nods. He begins to pull away from the curb.

As they leave, I hear the tall guy whose name I no longer remember say, "See you later, fat ass." He's the assistant manager of a tire department now, so he's doing great.

Another one, high fiving, says, "Good one." He's in prison last I heard.

I finish writing just as the bus pulls up. I deposit my $.15 fare, and we are on our way to the hallowed halls of obligation.

I stop by the locker I share with Wayne before heading to class. 14-4-10, the master combination lock slides open as I get a whiff of the stale air inside my locker. Better take the gym clothes home and get them washed. As the door fully opens, a note in very expressive handwriting flutters to the ground.

I'll meet you for lunch in the QRA, ♥ *Skipper.*

Something to look forward to. My mood brightens a bit. I walk up the stairs with a little bounce in my step until I'm body checked. My fall is broken by the stair railing.

"Faggot."

There you have it. First faggot of the day. 9:15. Everyone is running late today.

I hear teenagers can be self-loathing. Someone is looking for negative attention.

"*No lo sé mi amigo … Tu hermana no se quejó anoche.*"

"What? What are you saying, queer?"

"Can't speak Spanish, and your English isn't much better." I pass by them, trying not to show that my ribs hurt. "*Si me disculpan, tengo que ir a la clase de español.*"

It really seems to bother my father that I'm taking Spanish, which makes me enjoy it more. "What the hell do you need that for? People should just speak English." No point in telling him I take language courses because I want to make sure I don't stay in Wisconsin. Surely speaking Spanish means someday going somewhere Spanish is spoken.

My teacher Mrs. Jung is young. She dresses as though she's immediately leaving to go out to a club after school. I like her.

"You can learn Spanish by rote. Memorize a list. Learn how to apply the vocabulary, but that's shortsighted. *Miope.* Better to think about what you want to say and then learn how to do it in Spanish. Language isn't about conjugating verbs. It's about *communicating.*"

There are a lot of things I'd like to say, but what's the point? Nothing around here is going to change. Really. Significantly. Permanently. Better to keep my eye to the horizon. Get through it and have a little fun when I can.

The bell rings. A purgatory of classes continues until lunch. Time to meet Skipper.

I walk out of Advanced English with Mrs. Erickson, where several of the student's are struggling with apostrophes'. Wondering exactly what the criterion for Advanced English is, I start heading over to the QRA, or Quiet Reading Area, where all of us super cool kids hang out. The QRA is a big, open room with high ceilings and lots of windows. It's also kind of a hallway connecting the lunchroom with the humanities wing.

Humanities and food. The summation of my high school experience.

Everyone passes through so you can say hi to people. Butch is a freshman this year. Lots of the special ed classes are in this area, so hanging out here gives me the chance to check on him without him realizing that's what I'm doing.

Skipper and I meet here for potluck every day. He still feels the need to leave me notes in my locker reminding me, but that's Skipper at his skippiest.

Throwing a package of Hostess Ding Dongs and a few smooshed HoHos from my backpack onto the table, I say, "I brought dessert. And here are the appetizers," adding a bag of Frito's to the pile.

"Well, you certainly outdid yourself today Warn," says Skipper with an over-the-top earnestness. "I'm almost embarrassed to show you what I brought." With that, he quickly scans the hallway to make sure the lunch rush is on the wane and begins gathering the books and papers he used to ensure we'd have our own table.

He then smooths his already perfect hair before smiling to pause for effect.

"Today in chef class … "

"You mean home ec."

I am confronted by resting bitch face before the term resting bitch face was coined. Perhaps Skipper invented it. He exhales and starts again, "Today in chef class, we made Mediterranean Chicken Casserole." He puts a picnic basket on the table, carefully extracting two small cast iron skillets, covered with gingham, red and white checked, matching my mom's kitchen curtains, cloth napkins.

Which matches his red Izod polo shirt.

Next, he pulls out a thermos of very strong coffee, before handing me my own Tupperware-protected side salad, marinated in a light lemon Green Goddess dressing he and his mom made last night.

Lunch has begun.

"Do you want to come over to my house tonight?" Skipper asks. "*Monty Python* is on!"

"I have a rehearsal tonight."

"Oh wow! Thanks for reminding me." Pulling out his day planner and the pencil always tucked behind his ear, Skipper begins writing. "Me and the rest of the costume crew are supposed to be there tonight for fittings."

Getting things right is *very* important to Skipper. He exhausts himself, corralling chaos. Probably because his dad is a big drinker. Good friends with my dad. Sometimes, late at night, we'll compare atrocities.

"My dad ran over my bike."

"Big deal. At least you weren't on it. My dad could pull nickels out of the pores in his nose."

Oh, how we laugh.

There's an upside. I suppose there always is. We're both kids that give off the aura of being good. No one thinks we'd do anything wrong. So, we've been granted a kind of emancipation. Our parents will let us go to the midnight showing of *Rocky Horror*, no problem. As long as we wake up in our own beds Sunday morning, they don't even ask how we got home.

The important curating of our active social calendars is interrupted when Bijon arrives, per normal 5 minutes late. Skipper sees him before I do and begins preparing the other servings still warming inside the thermal compartment of his picnic basket.

Skipper's lips purse in judgment. "You really should try to be more punctual. I'm reading *101 Teen Tips for Young Lutherans*, and it says ... "

"Wait. Aren't you Methodist?"

"Yes, but I believe in the power of diversity."

Bijon, the third member of our QRA clique, is Muslim. It's November of 1979. Together Skipper and I aren't vulnerable enough, so we've become best friends with our only Iranian classmate during the hostage crisis.

Skipper is very put-together. Being the head of the pep committee, he feels it best to lead by example. His red shirt is coordinated with gray slacks, as he usually dresses in our school colors. His deep brown hair almost perfectly matches his big, expressive eyes.

Bijon is attractive, too, but in a more thrown together way. A Beatles fan, he wears his hair long. His compact, wiry frame is hugged by a John Lennon t-shirt and old jeans that have almost morphed into a second skin. Girls are crazy about him.

We're a subset of the group I think of as, "The Dichotomies." Together we're a group of devoted nonconformists, which seems to undermine nonconformity. Skipper, for example, likes to sew. I am an actor. Bijon does calligraphy. Separately those things are not thought of as being particularly cool; however, take us to a renaissance festival, and we're Diana Ross and the Supremes.

Other Dichotomies include the editor-in-chief of the yearbook, the captain of the forensics team, most of the drama department stagehands, and the foreign exchange students. Our friend Tommy Cambridge is on the volleyball team, but we hang out with him anyway. It's just the right thing to do.

Butch and his friends walk by. He pretends not to know me. Mostly I think it's because he doesn't want to only be a little brother. He wants to be independent. Part of me suspects it's also because he's kind of a jock.

"Hey, Butch," he stops while motioning to his friends that he'll catch up with them.

"Yeah?"

"You've got Special Olympics tonight, right?"

He nods.

"I'm in rehearsal. I'll meet you at the bus stop at 4:30. We can ride home together."

"I can get home on my own."

"I know. I was just thinki…"

"Don't worry about me. I'll get home."

Butch runs to catch up with his friends. I return to our table as Skipper passes me the last Hostess HoHo. I start to take my first bite as Paula walks over, wearing the pink sweater I gave her for her birthday. She bites the other end, and our lips meet in the middle, a la Lady & the Tramp.

"Look at the lovebirds," says Skipper.

"Get a room," says Bijon.

"Stand still!" says an exasperated Skipper, with his hand and a tape measure upon my thigh.

"I can't help it!" I reply. Twisting to get a better angle, his hand brushes the fly of the pants he has given me to try on. Skipper gasps and giggles nervously.

"Sorry!"

Michael Drake from the stage crew passes by carrying a flat, taking note of Skipper's hand. It's impossible not to notice his reaction.

Onstage Paula and two other girls are working with Mr. Burdick, the director of our production of *Sweet Charity*. She's playing Nickie, Charity's best friend. It's kind of a big deal because Sophomores (Paula) and Juniors (me) don't normally get featured roles in the musical.

I'm playing Herman, the owner of the Fandango Ballroom. It's not the lead, but it's the best male part. I told my parents I was going to be in a musical about taxi dancers. Mom said, "Is that appropriate for high school?"

When I asked why she said that, my dad chimed in.

"Warn, they're basically hookers. When I was in the service, you'd go to those dance halls, and the girls would give you a hand job. Some would actually bl … "

He went on to describe the action in more detail than I cared to hear. Mom slowly backed out of the room. I memorized the pattern of the kitchen floor. Can't beat family time. It was a scene Norman Rockwell forgot to paint.

Paula and the other girls are doing the full run-through of "There's Gotta Be Something Better Than This", with lights and costumes.

"Isn't her dress amazing?" asks Skipper, whose hand, for some reason is still on my thigh. "That was my sister's ice dancing dress when she and I went to sibling figure skating camp in Sheboygan."

Paula is the best dancer of the three girls. Everyone knows that, including the other two girls on stage and several of the pervy dads working on the set. One of them is rubbing his hammer in a way that's almost as gross as my dad's story about the dance hall girls.

Her dirty blonde hair, perfect, parted in the middle and curled away from her face, spins like the blades of a helicopter as she twirls during the number. Her smile, framed by the picket fence of her braces, is sweet. Her eyes are twinkling but searching. She looks to the small audience of parents waiting for their kids for a little approval.

At the end of the number, Paula runs offstage, directly to me. "How was it?" she asks in a completely unguarded, trusting way. Everything about her is adorable, sweet, and incredibly guilt inspiring.

"You were awesome," I say, totally meaning it. Then remembering I'm her boyfriend, I take it a little farther. Acting classes pay off when I add, "and so hot." I want to talk about the design of the dress, the fabric, and color; instead, I say, "Your tits look amazing," hoping I don't sound like Paul Lynde.

I'm kind of embarrassed to say that, but she must like it. Paula grinds into me and uses years of dance classes to stand on point, making her tall enough to initiate a long, lingering kiss.

Despite liking it, I know there's got to be something better than this.

CHAPTER TWENTY

WE ARE FAMILY

Rehearsal ends. Paula's mom picks us up in her car. When Paula moves to sit next to me in the backseat, we hear, "I'm not a chauffeur." Paula begrudgingly moves to the front seat. So, that's one less kiss tonight. Thanks, Mrs. Pellham.

We pull up to my house. The driveway is full. Something's wrong.

I give Paula's shoulder a quick squeeze and blow an air-kiss, quickly slide out of the car. My pace is molasses-slow approaching the house. Why rush? Whatever stupid bullshit awaits certainly won't resolve before I make it inside. It's like the Streisand version of *Gypsy*; unlikely to happen.

I open the door. A wall of cigarette smoke stings my eyes. The smell of burnt coffee stings my nostrils. Now, years later, were someone to invent a candle combining these scents, it would be a quick trip home.

"Where have you been?" asks Art.

"Rehearsal," I answer, pausing to grab a brownie off the plate next to the blue and white Corningware percolator.

Art, holding his swaddled daughter, responds in a cooing voice, which always makes baby Kristina giggle. "Well, he could've let someone know, couldn't he?"

I point to the rehearsal schedule being held up by a Wisconsin is for lovers magnet on the refrigerator and walk to the living room. Everyone follows me like a conga line. They silently stare at me long enough that I start to wonder what I've done.

Mom breaks the silence.

"Your father was in a car accident."

"Did he hurt anyone?" I ask.

"No one was seriously hurt," she replies, leaving me to wonder at what point injuries become serious.

"Okay. That's good, I guess."

"Aren't you going to ask how he is?" says Ruth, Art's not-so-new, second wife. When will her optimism die? Tall. Lanky. Kind. Her Dorothy Hamill haircut is 70s perfect. I would like her even if she wasn't married to my brother.

Acting class pays off. I do my best to keep my tone light. "I can hear him snoring, so I'm guessing he's fine. He's sleeping like a baby." A drunk baby that smokes three packs a day. "You're the ones who are stressed out. I'm more worried about you."

Mom, suddenly exhausted, slumps down onto the couch. We all sit in silence.

The TV is always on. Loudly. Tonight is no different. Somehow, as a unit, we've learned to ignore loud things. Emily's baby-faced husband Martin, a blonde jeweler cuts through the wall of noise.

"Look, everyone. A special report."

We all turn toward the huge television in the carved wooden cabinet, taking up a space larger than Kristina's crib. An older, still blonde, Rick Fetherston's face fills the screen. "Breaking news from the WISC-TV, Channel 3, weather department. A major ice storm will descend upon the Channel 3 viewing area within the hour, expect bad driving conditions, possible power outa ..." and just like that, the screen fills with light that quickly contracts into a little dot before blinking out altogether. One beat later, the power goes out. The hum from the compressor of the refrigerator winds down to punctuate the moment.

Ruth, my sweet sister-in-law, is closest to the curtains. A practical farmer's daughter, she opens them to hold vigil through the living room picture window. "Every house is dark. Looks like it has already started. Art..."

"I know. We've got the baby with us. We probably shouldn't drive in this weather."

Emily calls it. "I guess we're all staying here."

The phone rings, so that's still working. Good. Mom picks it up.

"Hello? Hi Mick! Yep. Sure thing. No problem. We'll take care of it. Bye." Mom takes a drag off her cigarette before updating us. "Mick and Bob are home alone. His blood sugar is low. She doesn't want to leave him. Wondering if we were going to do a grocery run, which is a great idea. Boys, get your coats and boots on. I'll make a list."

Art and I climb into the heaviest vehicle, my dad's 1975 Ford F-150 pickup truck. Years from now, the incongruence of me in a pickup truck will make me smile, but tonight it's just ordinary. Typical. A dented cage. The body is so bruised and battered that it's hard to tell which wound is freshest.

As always, the passenger side is a mess. I brush crumpled sales contracts, fast food bags, and cigarette ashes onto the floor of the cab. I kick my father's tape measure underneath the seat, where he'll have a hard time finding it. Its momentum stops when it hits an empty pint of Canadian Club.

Ruth runs out, jumping up and down in a way I've come to think of as wifely. Art rolls down the window. Ruth hands him a list of things they'll need for the baby, my goddaughter, the adorable Kristina. She thanks him with a kiss. I get a wave. Art starts the truck. The clutch engaged, he forces the uncooperative transmission into reverse, and we're on our way to Woodman's, the 24-hour, no-frills grocery store near the highway.

We listen to the radio while I review the list. A Barnes Home Improvement ballpoint pen falls out of its tucked away perch wedged between the sun visor and roof of the cab. I can mimic my mom's handwriting and add a few items of my own.

The truck slides a few times, but we recover. The roads aren't too bad yet. As we pull into Woodman's spartan parking lot, WISM-AM starts playing, "This Guy's in Love with You" by Herb Alpert. It's Art's favorite song. My friend Andrew will sing it at my wedding. We park. I move to open my door.

"Let's wait for the song to finish."

I'll always be glad we took that moment. When it's over, our eyes connect, Art takes a deep breath, and we head toward the grocery store's fluorescent lights.

We're nice guys from the Midwest. So, as we walk-skate over the slippery pavement, we stop to pick up a few stray shopping carts. Growing up without money creates a very specific kind of imagination. We make a game out of it. Art wins, capturing two more carts than I do.

Out of breath, we enter the chaos of provision shopping, making our way up and down the familiar aisles. Several kids from school are here. I plot our course to avoid them. Art grabs supplies as we pass them, slowing at the Coke and cheese displays to load up on his favorites. Only now, in my memory, do I realize he looks ten-years older than he is. Why didn't I notice it then?

Obviously, we can't buy many things that will spoil, so I lead us to the Hostess baked goods. Dammit. They're out of Twinkies.

"Grab some Little Debbie's" offers Art, trying to be helpful.

I begrudgingly do so. "It's not the same. Hostess is better."

"Really? I can't tell the difference."

So, there on aisle twelve, while harried shoppers make their way around us, I patiently explain to my brother the hierarchy of industrial bakers. "Hostess is the best. After that, you've got your Little Debbie's and Dolly Madison's, neither of which are as good. They don't taste as fresh. They clearly use the ingredients Hostess rejects. Then there are the knock-off versions."

"Knock-off versions?" asks Art with an incredulous look.

"Yes. With bad names like Twink-ohs! Snowbells. Bing Bongs instead of Ding Dongs, which is just stupid. Ha-Has instead of Ho-Hos."

What did we miss talking about while I pontificated? The time wasted talking of inconsequential, stupid things which don't matter in the long run. That's another lesson I've yet to learn this evening at Woodman's Warehouse Discount Grocery Store.

After patiently explaining the difference between Doritos and the new, infinitely better Tostitos, we get in the longest line ever. Eventually. We. Get. To. The. Front. I see a worried look on Art's face but ignore it. No need to talk about anything unpleasant with Lisa Iverson only two aisles away. She is the queen of the cool kids. A Farrah-haired, designer jean wearing icon in a Bruce Springsteen t-shirt.

Mrs. McKenna is our check-out lady. Her husband and brother-in-law sometimes work for my parents. She's much nicer to us than her last customer, but I think it's because she likes us, not because she's got to be. She's one of the prettiest moms in our neighborhood, and her kids are very nice. Her fingernails are a pink blur as she scans the barcodes on our groceries.

"That'll be $62.28, boys."

Art's jaw gets tense the way it always does when he's nervous.

"Art, why don't you put the money you owe me toward the groceries? I can kick in. Here's another ten bucks."

"Really?"

"Yeah, no problem. That's why I've got a job, right?"

His jaw relaxes. "That's a help. Thanks, Warn."

"Good luck with the storm, guys."

"Thanks, Mrs. McKenna. Get home safely."

She crosses the fingers of her left hand and waves goodbye with the right before scanning the next customer.

The parking lot has gotten icier. We slip, slide, and laugh our way to the truck, hoist the groceries into the camper shell and return the cart. Key inserted, the truck starts up first try, which is rare. We bop up and down in the cold cab as the truck warms up. Art doesn't put it in gear.

"We should probably get going before the roads get worse," I say.

"We should," responds Art, doing nothing.

"Or we could stay here and listen to music for a while," I offer.

"Yeah. Let her warm-up. It's what's best for Ray's truck."

Joe Walsh sings, "Life's Been Good to Me," as little pieces of ice bounce off the truck in rhythms impossible to predict.

CHAPTER TWENTY-ONE

FRIGID

I wake up, but the light in my room is different. Sleepier. It's like being underwater. I slowly turn my head toward the blank alarm clock. Weird. It's not on. Butch is still asleep on the other side of the room. Taking care not to wake Bo, asleep, on my bed snuggled between my legs and the heating register, I rip open the envelope of warmth created by my sheets and bedspread, stand up, stretch, and walk to the window, which I cannot see through.

The ice from the storm has formed a layer that totally covers the glass. I can hear little pings as the house continues to be pelted. The storm isn't over. School must have been canceled. I head downstairs in no particular rush, just like I would were school in session.

None of the construction guys are here. Emily is sitting alone at the table reading yesterday's newspaper, sipping one of the Cokes we put in the cooler. The radio, powered by batteries, drones in the background.

"Good morning," she says without looking up.

"Yeah. Okay. What's going on?"

"Worst ice storm in the history of the state. The temperature was just right. The rain freezes as it lands. Everything is coated. It doesn't appear to be stopping anytime soon. So far, about an inch of ice covers everything. Everything." She looks up from the paper smiling facetiously "And it's going to get worse!"

"Power?"

"Out."

"Phone?"

"Still working. Go figure."

"How did you get ready? Your make-up is perfect."

"Priorities," she says, smiling. "Like Lincoln studying by candlelight."

"Where is everyone else?"

"Asleep. What's the point of being awake?"

"Where's Martin?"

"Who cares?" she says in a deadpan style. "Mr. Excitement is asleep in the basement. Art, Ruth, and the baby are in the small bedroom. Val called. She's fine."

I look behind Emily at the kitchen counter, which is loaded with stuff normally kept in the fridge. Emily notices me noticing. "The radio said we could be without power for weeks, so I got the things I thought we'd need out of the fridge, so it would stay cold longer. Less opening and closing. This is going to be a long haul."

The house, covered in ice, starts to feel like the Fortress of Solitude from the Superman movies, only without the solitude. Instead of regal Marlon Brando as the father, I'm stuck with drunken Ernest Borgnine. Luckily, the small awning over the backdoor has kept the door from being iced over, for now. I've got to get out of here.

"I'm going for a walk," I say to Emily as I grab Bo's leash.

"Wear your skates," she suggests in a very helpful voice, not looking up from the paper as we walk outside.

We turn left at the end of our toboggan run of a driveway. Gliding about two blocks, we walk past Shirley's house on Clover Lane, Bo's ancient tail wags slowly. His curiosity is engaged; he stops to marvel at the sight of a world covered in ice.

It takes much longer than usual, but we finally arrive at the Drake house. We slowly climb their inclined driveway before knocking on the door of their home.

"Good morning, Warn!" says Mrs. Drake in her best June Cleaver voice. "You and Bo get out of the bad weather! Come in! Come in!" she says, opening the door wider before smoothing her ruffled apron.

There's something about her Stepford Wife perkiness I just don't trust. She's a less sincere Sandy Duncan if that's possible. It's like all hell would break loose were she to find a broken Wheat Thin.

"I was just going to see if Michael wanted to hang out."

Passing a mirror, she pauses to fluff her already perfectly in place hair. "He's in his bedroom!"

Perfect.

Sandy Duncan continues. "I was just on my way to give him his coffee. Here's some for you too! Thank the Lord for generators!" she says, pouring Folger's into a spotless cup and saucer. "I'll just put them on this tray, so it's easier to carry." Handing it to me, she adds, "Bo, you go play with the puppy! Warn, head downstairs! Michael will be so happy you're here!"

I make my way down the not rickety stairs to Michael's bedroom, with which I am very familiar. The hum of the dehumidifier drowns out the many long talks Michael and I have had down here, ensuring we aren't overheard by parents or siblings. It is private.

I knock on the door. "It's me. Warn."

"Come in."

I start to juggle the tray, attempting to open the door. Hearing the clatter, Michael says, "Don't worry! I'll get it." I hear the rustle of bedsheets and bare feet slapping against a linoleum floor. The door which opens into the room causes Michael's shaggy blonde hair to billow like the mane of a super-model during a photoshoot.

It could be argued I'm biased.

"Good morning," he says with a smile and blue eyes so dazzling that it takes a few seconds to notice he's naked. In a begrudging effort to avert my eyes, I look down toward the floor, where I can see a pair of blue briefs in the path between the bed and the door. I'm left wondering if he slept nude or took them off on his way to let me in.

Michael stands there for a moment, owning that he's everything I'm not. Lean. Exercised. Athletic. I'm taller, which helps restore a little bit of my self-esteem. Handsomer, although doughy. Smarter too, but since when is smart sexy? Smart helps, but everyone would choose Jaclyn Smith before Kate Jackson.

I'm sixteen. Michael is seventeen. A senior.

Teens, when pondering your sexual choices, always be the younger one in the relationship. With just a little preplanning, you can ensure the word statutory is kept at bay.

"Come in," he says, throwing the door open and making a grand gesture. He turns around, giving me an uninterrupted view of the other side. I quickly put the tray on the nearest flat surface and sit down on a big, overstuffed chair lest the front of my pants betray my reaction. He bends down and picks up his briefs before turning around to put them on.

"What's up?" he says, sitting down next to me as he finishes pulling on a thin tank top in the middle of winter. In a cold room. His chest looks amazing. Nipples peeking through. I've never wanted to be a Wisconsin Dells tank top more.

He repeats himself. "Hello?" waving his hands near my face, "what's up?"

"Nothing. I couldn't handle being stuck with my family all day long. I had to get out for a while."

"The restaurant called." We work together at Taco Palace, the least authentically Mexican restaurant in all of Wisconsin, which is saying something. "They're closed until further notice." He slides toward me, whispering in my ear, "What are we going to do with all the extra time?"

My mouth, already warm from his mom's perfect yet creepy cup of coffee, gets even warmer when he starts to kiss me.

"Quit fooling around, Michael," I say in an out-of-breath voice. Reaching for my bookbag, I add, "Run *Sweet Charity* lines with me."

He opens the libretto. Looking up over the edge of the paperback, he says, "I thought kissing you would be the gayest thing I did today."

Michael kisses me again. I use that time to steady myself against the roughness of his face, which needs a shave. The bristle is a punishment and a reward at the same time. Having been gently moved to the corner of the old sofa in his bedroom gives me a foundation to shift my weight. I lean into his lips and his body, moving on top of him. His head hits the table, causing his mother's coffee cups to clatter against each other.

Hearing a threat to her dinnerware is like sounding an alarm to someone like Mrs. Drake. Her brisk steps can be heard coming down the steps. She stops midway.

"Is everything okay, boys?"

Michael leaps up and cracks open the door. I watch from behind him, taking the opportunity to steal Paula's trick and grind into him. "Yeah, Mom. Everything is great." He pauses to catch his breath and exhale. "We're studying. One of my books … hit the tray. It hit the tray, is all."

"Oh, thank goodness! My imagination! I was worried something might've broken!" Her voice moves upstairs. Michael keeps guard until she's out of sight. I use the time to return his briefs to the floor, remembering the first time this happened.

Before I get to that part, let me be frank. Taco Palace is a bad restaurant. It used to be the Castle of Fish, which had a king's banquet hall kind of look. When it went out of business, the owner of Taco Palace just put up paper flowers and acrylic burro blankets. The décor is tacky and cliché. The lighting is dingy. The food is bland. When Mom asks me to bring home tacos, I drive to Taco Bell to get them.

Michael is the assistant manager of Taco Palace. Being 17 with a fake ID, he can hand the rare customer a beer when it is ordered. He even has a key to the front door. Heady stuff, the raw power of a key. It can provide somewhere to meet late at night.

Being a people person, I was hired to work the counter. Michael can fill in for any responsibility since he's got to cover call-ins, etc. We work with a crew of three - counter person, cook, and dishwasher. One night, October 10th of last year, Michael sent home Jorge, who I think is here illegally. Right after he left, we got a surge that lasted until closing time. We had to stay late to clean.

Michael pulled a cassette out of his bookbag. Elton John and Kiki Dee started telling us not to go breaking their heart through the surprisingly good speakers, left over from the space's tenure as a Long John Silver's wanna-be.

We'd worked harder than we normally do. We were sweaty. Clammy. Frankly, we were kind of gross. Michael's Taco Palace rumba shirt was soaked through. He took it off so it could soak in the sink. I handed him my poncho.

"We should celebrate. Why don't you grab a couple of beers from the cooler?"

Passing by sour cream past its expiration date, generic shredded cheese, and beige cilantro, I made my way to the corner of the cooler where the beer is kept. I was reaching for two Pabst Blue Ribbons when I heard the door open. Michael walked in, sans poncho, moving me farther into the corner. Reaching over me, he got on tip-toe and said, "I think we deserve something a little better." He grabbed two Coronas and a couple of limes. After getting the beers, feet back on earth, he lingered. He held eye contact as he smiled.

Back in the kitchen, I noticed he had turned off the lights in the restaurant to discourage anyone from thinking we might still be open. Beer signs and the backlighting from the sad menu gave the room a nice glow. "Cut those in quarters," he said.

I did as he asked. Michael grabbed the lime wedges and squeezed them into the beer bottles. Then he forced the limes into each bottle. He handed me my Corona, grabbed his own, clicked them together, and took a long swig, before using his wrist to wipe his perfect mouth.

I was too nervous to drink mine.

I could taste the lime on his lips the first time we kissed.

Despite Mrs. Drake's Sue Ann Niven's like protests, Bo and I leave just before lunchtime. The dog, with his four legs and lower center of gravity, keeps his attention on my slipping and sliding, wondering if it's a new game. It takes us about ten minutes to walk the two blocks.

No one else is stupid enough to be out. Just me and my sweet dog. It's cold, but I'm warm. Someday I will learn this is called afterglow, a lingering post-coital sweetness. I can still smell him. I can still feel the weight of his body on top of my own. I try to use the lips he just kissed to form the words, "I'm gay," but I can't. I know I'd only be acknowledging the truth, alone, for only me to hear, but I can't say it.

The words won't come. Saying it would mean saying goodbye to too many things. The kids I imagine having someday. My friends. My already burdened family.

If I don't say it, it's not true. This is just a phase. A phase that takes my breath away. A phase that makes me feel alive. A phase that makes me feel more myself than I've ever felt. A phase.

I read in a magazine that there's something called conversion therapy. Gay people can be cured if there's early intervention. The article said you've got to get help by the time you're eighteen. So, I've got two more years to enjoy this. 2 more years before I lose the chance for a normal life.

Bo and I slide our way up the drive.

I open the door to an empty house.

There's a note from my mom waiting for me. She put it on top of the last box of Twinkies where I'd be sure to find it.

Dear Warn—there was a break in the weather, so we're running the baby home as neighbors say Art & Ruth still have power. Emily, Martin & Butch came with me. Hot showers! Be back soon. Love, Mom

The pelting pinging of the rain starts anew, and then the phone rings. "Hello?"

"Hello Warn. It's me. Your mother."

Despite good intentions, my inner-teenager kicks in. "Yeah, Mom. I recognize your voi …"

"The weather has gotten a lot worse over this way. We're going to wait it out here at Art's house."

"Okay," I say, trying to sound cheerful.

As I place the phone in its cradle, I can hear a door scraping the pile of my parent's wall-to-wall carpeting. The air and energy of the room change as my father stumbles in. My father. And me. Dad and I alone together while the storm rages on.

CHAPTER TWENTY-TWO

DAD VISITS CANADA

Disheveled. Unshaven. Hungover. Somehow, my father is still attractive the way a shirt that has been wadded up on the floor of your closet can still be stylish. A month in detox, a good shave and haircut, a facial to shrink his pores, a thorough Silkwood shower, and he'd be very presentable in his next mug shot.

"Whereiseveryone?" he asks in a raspy voice. He must be frantic with worry. He cared enough to crane his head from side to side. That hurt - if the empty bottle of Canadian Club in the trash is any indication.

"There's an ice storm. The city is shut down."

"Oh. That's why you're home. School canceled, huh?" He smiles. "Got to like that."

"I'm thrilled. Would you like some breakfast?" I ask.

"That sounds nice."

"Too bad. That was hours ago." I head to the cooler and grab, gag, a liverwurst sandwich my mom left for him. I also codependently grab a snack bag of Lay's potato chips, his favorite. "Here's your lunch."

Being as close as we aren't, he doesn't thank me. In his midwestern dad way, he doesn't say please either. When he adds "Coffee," there's no effort to raise his voice at the end of the sentence. That might imply it's a question rather than an order.

Classic Dad. What fun.

"The power is out, so there's no coffee." I steal a Coke from Art's dwindling supply and toss it to him, secretly hoping it got shaken up. He opens it without explosion. Oh well. I'm used to disappointment.

I grab a ham and cheese. Better than wurst. Hm. No Fritos. Thanks, universe. We eat in silence. When he's done, liverwurst remnants cling to his unwiped lips. "Well, I should go buy some cigarettes."

"Don't bother. The bars are closed."

Dad doubles down, which is hilarious. "Bars? Who said anything about a bar? I just need to get some smokes."

The kitchen is small. I can reach the junk drawer from my place near the crack in the table without getting up. I grab two packs of unfiltered

Camels. "Here, Smokey, these should get you through a few hours." In a burst of generosity, I throw him a pink Bic lighter Mick must have left behind.

His chin goes slack. His shoulders shrug. "Okay." After lighting a cigarette, he stands up. Squeezing by me, he heads to the bar, AKA the cupboard under the sink. He groans as his arm extends behind the garbage disposal to retrieve a fresh, unopened bottle of Canadian Club. He favors the blend with the word "Canadian" in raised block letters on the side, repeated like Mary Tyler Moore's name in the opening credits of her show.

Canadian. Canadian. Canadian.

I assume he chooses that brand because Valerie would be able to find it for him.

As a Christmas gift, his company carpenter, a huge suck-up if you ask me, cut a bottle in half, removed the neck, and polished the sides so it could be used as an ashtray. So clever and efficient. One bottle. Two addictions.

"You win," he says with a smirk, pouring whiskey into his nearly empty can of Coca-Cola, thinking he's getting the last laugh. Same horse. Different rodeo. Nothing new here.

Looking back on this moment, I'm sad to remember that I had no hope. There was no expectation of anything improving until I left his house. A sixteen-year-old fatalist. "Knock yourself out, Dad." Literally. Please.

I start to leave the kitchen when I remember that addiction is a family disease, so I grab a couple of Little Debbie's before heading upstairs.

About four hours later, the light inside my ice storm igloo darkens to a lavender gray. The sun must be setting. I hear someone coming up the stairs. I briefly hope that means Mom and Butch are back but realize I've not heard a car pull up. It's Dad. He lets himself in without knocking, carrying a candle as the power still hasn't come back on.

Very *Little House on the Prairie*, which I've never seen. I've read the books, of course, with my mom. They're very good. I didn't want to risk ruining the memory by watching the TV show.

Pa stands in the doorway, briefly taking in the divide of the room. Butch's side is, for the most part, simple and clean. The bed is made, best he can. A few Special Olympic trophies on a shelf above his twin bed. Boyishly masculine.

My half is more theatrical. Show posters. A picture of me, Howie and Cowboy Eddie taken when the show was canceled, and they left town.

The last birthday card from Grandma Caruso before she passed away. To appear more like a real boy, I've put People Magazine covers of beautiful women on the wall of the angled wall above my bed. Valerie Harper, Liza Minelli, Barbra Streisand—yep, I'm fooling the world.

"What do you want, Dad?"

"It's getting dark. Come downstairs before we lose the light."

Watching him, he's a little unsteady on his feet, on the brink of being drunk. I should probably get dinner started. Get some food in him before things go too far.

You know, the normal thoughts and concerns of any sixteen-year-old.

Following my father down the stairs, inspiration strikes. Mom called. They're spending the night at Art's house. There's no one here to worry about. Why fight the inevitable? Let him drink as much as he can, as quickly as he can. I can invite Michael to spend the night.

I like this plan. Everyone gets what they want.

When we get downstairs, I run to the beige touchtone trimline phone in the hallway. I quickly punch in Michael's number and extend the invitation, which he accepts enthusiastically. My mood soars. Sex twice in one day. First time for that. Look at me, world. I'm a fat, gay Hugh Hefner. Huge Hefner!

Let the record show I have enough self-esteem that I didn't include heifer in the wordplay.

After quickly walking Bo on the ice-skating rink that is currently our backyard, I set my plan in motion. "What would you like for dinner, Dad?" I ask in a voice so warm he gets suspicious.

"What?"

I relax my tone and play it more casually. "What would you like for dinner?"

"That's … nice of you. But no need to bother. Whatever is easiest."

I quickly take a mental inventory. Best to avoid bread and crackers. They absorb booze and slow down getting drunk. "Mom has some nice lettuce here. A ton of cold cuts and cheese. I'll make us some chef salads, like the ones they have at Rennebohm's Coffee Shop. It'll be easy."

To my shock, he doesn't complain. "Sounds good."

I grab a fresh high-ball glass and the bottle of Canadian Club, now about a third drained. I quickly steal one precious ice cube from the cooler and pour him his drink. Big smile. "Here, Dad, while you wait." He takes his first sip, gulp really before I casually mention Michael coming over to spend the night.

"That's fine."

I make Grandma's vinaigrette which is still called Italian dressing, in late 70s Wisconsin. I put it down on the table beside the salads and sit down to enjoy a candlelight dinner with my dad. As this is a special occasion, he wears his finest t-shirt and boxer shorts.

"This looks great. Nice job, son." His appreciation seems sincere. Way to throw me, Dad. Still, a plan is a plan. Michael will be here soon. "Let me freshen that drink."

His fork is in his mouth before I return. As he chews, he gives me a thumbs up. "Something fresh. This is just what I needed."

"I'm glad."

"Since it's never just the two of us," oh good God, what's he going to say? The inevitable slur starts to begin as he repeats himself. "Since it's never just the two of us, I wanted to tell you I'm sorry."

"For what?" I ask. He can't seriously expect me to know. I mean, he has so many things for which he could apologize.

"I know there's not enough time and attention for you."

He's looking down at his plate. I hope that means he can't see my shocked face.

"With Butch and Val, the business, everything else takes a hit; especially you. It's not fair. I know that, and I'm sorry." He looks up, needing to know that I've heard him.

"Dad, I'm not a kid anymore. It's fine." He starts to protest. "Thank you, but really. I'm fine. Concentrate on Butch and Val. I can take care of myself."

"That's very generous. I'm glad you feel that way. Suzy is out there doing God only knows what. Then there's Emily. Why did she marry that wet blanket? She needs someone who can challenge her. He isn't up to that."

Can't argue there. It's almost as though she wanted to have an easy, predictable life. How weird of her.

"And nothing is working out for Art. Work isn't going well. Your mom gives him money. She thinks I don't know, but I do."

"What? What do you mean?"

He starts to say something, but the doorbell chimes. It takes a little effort to force open the iced-over door. When it's finally pried open,

Michael is waiting on the other side. Frost clings to the furry trim of his parka hood. Adorable.

He wipes his feet on the welcome mat, rubbing his mittened hands over his hips. "I fell on my way up to the door," he says with a small laugh. Thinking we're alone, he leans in for a kiss.

"*No me beses Mi padre está en la cocina.*"

We're in Spanish class together, which is convenient. We can usually discuss very private things publicly. He replies, "*¿Qué carajo? Dijiste que estaría dormido.*"

"*Se paciente. Se paciente.*"

"What's going on? Why are you talking in gibberish?"

Really, Dad? "We're just practicing for Spanish class," I say, pulling Michael into the kitchen. "Look who's here!"

"Hi, Mike. Sit down."

Michael does as he was asked while I bring him his salad. Dad uses the time for a quick visit to the Canadian Club. When he's done pouring, instead of putting the bottle down, he says, "Would you boys like some?"

We exchange a glance before smiling.

I get two juice glasses. Dad smiles and pours about an inch in each glass. "Not enough to do any real damage," he says.

He graciously holds up his larger, fuller glass. "Cheers!"

Michael and I both take tentative sips. It burns, a fact neither of us attempt to hide. How can Raymond drink this poison? Dad laughs. "That was a test. Glad to see you aren't too used to the hard stuff. How old are you, Mike?"

"I'm seventeen, Mr. Barnes."

"Call me Ray. Call me Ray. Seventeen? Jesus. That's how old I was when I joined the Army. Infantry. 14th Armored Battalion. Had a choice between that and the Navy. I figured getting shot was quicker than drowning."

His mood shifts. His eyes retreat. "Quite a choice to make at that age." He looks up, making eye contact with both of us. "I'm glad you won't have to do that. Very glad."

Maybe I gave him too much booze. I can see him struggling, trying to outpace his demons, but the demons never lose. "You boys ever been out of the country?"

"Yeah, Dad. Don't you remember? You took me to Paris last week."

His eyes narrow, but he smiles. I know he likes and gets my sense of humor, which I appreciate. "Smart-ass. How about you, Mike?"

"Yes, sir." He falters. "I mean, yes, Ray. My family went on a vacation to Nassau in the Bahamas." My mind flashes on the playing cards he brought me back from the Straw Market.

"I spent my eighteenth birthday in Italy. Rome." Quick swig. "Rome! Beautiful city. Met a nice girl, beautiful girl, next to that fountain. Oh, God. What do they call it? *Trevi. Fontana di Trevi*! Spent the night with her at a boarding house." He smiles nostalgically. "I think we fell in love a little bit. She looked like your mom, Warn. Gorgeous." He pauses before adding, "Great memory. Great."

There is a silence, but it's pleasant. Sweet even. "I hope you boys have experiences like that. Nothing like the first time you fall in love, no matter how it ends." His posture changes. His smile gets bigger. "Either of you ever been in love?"

I'm glad the candle is near my dad. I'm sure I'm blushing. I can't bring myself to look at Michael, but peripherally I can tell he's looking at the floor.

"Warn, you and Pauline ..."

"Paula."

"Okay, Paula. Are you in love?"

"Yeah, Dad. We were going to get married tomorrow, but the storm ruined it."

"Well," pause to light a cigarette, "anyway, after that, I ended up in Anzio."

"That was a hell of a battle. It lasted for months. The Germans flooded our side with saltwater. Mud, bugs everywhere. Knee deep in muck. Dead bodies. You could smell it everywhere." He takes a gulp of whiskey. "Remember that the next time you're pissed off that you've got to work at that Mexican restaurant."

He's slurring more. Even when he's laughing at this own joke. It's as though he was recorded at 45 but being played back at 33, slower than natural.

"There was this moment where everything got quiet. That's how I remember it. I was on sentry duty and saw this kid. A German. Blonde hair, like you, Mike. I raised my rifle, took aim, and fired without thinking. By instinct. He looked up when he heard the sound. The bullet hit him at the bridge of his nose. By the time he hit the ground, he was dead." His voice starts to crack. "Dead. His whole life ahead of him. Artillery shells started landing. Things got really crazy. Bullets flying everywhere. That's when I got wounded. No one could get to me. I got hit a second time. Thought I might bleed out, but someone made it over to put a tourniquet on my thigh."

He starts laughing. "Good thing that bullet wasn't three inches higher, or you wouldn't be here, Warn!"

Now he's sullen. "I look at you two. Everything that's ahead of you. Your whole lives. I stole that from someone." He looks up at us. Tears have fallen down his cheeks. The first of two times I ever saw him cry.

"Dad, you should go to bed. Come on, Michael. Let's help him"

Flanking Raymond on both sides, we get him upright and slowly head toward the master bedroom. He keeps mumbling, "Why did I do that?"

Michael folds back the covers and fluffs the pillows. He is, after all, a homosexual. I sit my dad down on the edge of the bed and take off his slippers, studying the familiar scars on his legs in a completely different, new way.

That poor German kid. And his family. He was probably someone's brother. Thank God Art got discharged early and never had to go to Vietnam.

As I'm helping him lie down, Dad says, "and to think I didn't even know it, but I was already a father."

"What?"

"A woman I met on leave hunted me down after I had gotten married. Turns out she had a baby. We had a baby. Together. But Suzy had already come along by the time I found out. There was nothing to be done. I have a son that I'll never know." He looks at me intently.

"Don't let that happen to you, Warn. Don't let it."

"It won't," I say, trying to ease his mind.

Now he's angry. "Don't be so goddamn cocky, Warn. No one knows what's going to happen. You think I wanted that to happen? How can you be sure you won't make the same mistakes? Knock some girl up?"

"Because I'm gay."

Raymond's head snaps back. He looks dumbfounded. To be fair, so do I. Never did I expect this would be the moment. That the words would just tumble out of me but tumbled they have. The confession hangs in the air waiting for someone to react.

Michael puts his hand on my shoulder.

Dad looks at me with clearer eyes. "I wondered. Hm." His head bobs a bit. "No offense Mike, but are you two, you know…uh…"

Michael doesn't answer, so I do. "Yeah, Dad. Michael is my boyfriend."

He starts to rise again, but the effort is too much. He falls back into the bed. Turning on his side. "Okay then. That's the way it is. I don't get it, but I love you. You," he says, staring at Michael, "you be good to my boy. You hear me? Be good to him."

Dad, about to fall asleep per my selfish plan, moves his focus to me. "Because I don't tell him this often enough but Warn is worth ten of me. Twenty if he lost some weight. HA! No. Twenty either way. He's worth twenty of me."

One statement - touching and hurtful at the same time.

I walk toward the bed, smooth out his blankets, take off his glasses and brush the hair out of his eyes.

"Goodnight, Dad." I feel sorry for you, but I love you too. I do. I love you.

Michael is waiting for me in the hallway. I kiss him. He pulls away quickly. There's enough light from the candle in the kitchen to see that he's upset. He stares at me, giving himself a moment to find the right words.

"You may have been ready to tell your dad, but you should've asked me first."

Oh, God. Of course, he feels this way. He's new to this community theater version of *Who's Afraid of Raymond Barnes?*

I put my hands on his shoulders and look him in the eye. "He won't remember any of it in the morning."

"Are you sure?"

"Even if he remembers, and I truly don't think he will, he won't talk about it. He never deals with the morning after drama."

"But my parents…"

The perfect Mr. and Mrs. Drake. I get it. The stakes are different for him. He has more to lose. I start to feel guilty but stop myself. I know I'm right.

"It's going to be fine, Michael. You've got to believe me. Even if he does remember, he won't deal with it."

"But all that stuff about another kid."

"Yeah. I'm not sure that's true."

"What?"

"He's drunk. He doesn't know what's real and what's not when he's like that. Once, he told me barns are called barns because my grandpa invented them."

"But still, another brother? That's huge. If you want to talk about it..."

I kiss him again, more excited knowing my dad is on the other side of the door. "Why would I want to waste tonight talking?"

Michael smiles. "You called me your boyfriend."

"I did."

"I liked that."

"Prove it."

We walk upstairs, and he does. He proves it until we're both exhausted.

We fall asleep, a teenage tangle of arms and legs sharing a twin bed while a sweet old dog wonders what he's just seen.

Michael and I wake up early rather than risk getting caught by someone. The sun is coming out brightly. The ice has a prismatic effect on the light, forming little rainbows around the room. It's pretty and feels rare. Like the Northern Lights. Slowly I feel the arm beneath my shoulders come to life. Michael starts stirring and gives me a drowsy kiss that is sweet, despite our morning breath. I start to get excited, thinking we're going to have a replay of last night, but something even better happens.

We don't.

We just lie there. Quiet. Connected in a way I've never felt before. I wait for the silence to get uncomfortable, but it doesn't. Of course, nothing this good lasts forever. The silence is replaced by the clatter of pots and pans in the kitchen. Mom must be home. We kiss again, which further breaks the spell. It's not a kiss of potential. It's a real life has intruded kind of kiss. Michael starts to look worried. I can tell he's wondering if last night's coming out story will have daytime consequences.

I grab his hand and squeeze it before we get out of bed and dress quickly. I bundle up any forensic evidence by stripping my bed and throwing the sheets in the hamper. If anyone asks, I'll blame Bo.

We head downstairs, where a stranger awaits. He looks like my dad, but it can't be my dad. He's dressed in clean clothes, and he's cooking breakfast.

"There you guys are. Sorry about the noise. I didn't mean to wake you up. I found my hunting stove. It's propane. I thought I'd make us a hot breakfast. We've got coffee too. No cream, so you'll have to drink it black. That's a good habit to build. Makes life a lot simpler. I always feel sorry for the people who waste time running down the right creamer. Milk. Half and half. Don't get me started on sugar."

Who is this domesticated person? It's like he was possessed by Mrs. Drake.

"Uh, dad?"

"Yes?" he says without stopping.

"Do you remember last night?" I ask out of what I like to think of as kindness rather than to prove a point to Michael. "Is there anything you want to talk about?"

"No. No. Other than to say it was nice to spend a little time together."

"Do you want to finish talking about the war? Or the girl you met on leave?"

"I met a lot of girls on leave." A nervous flash paces through his eyes. "Oh. Did I talk about that? No. Nope. Nothing to discuss. Here," he says, handing us each a plate. "Sit down and eat."

"Thanks."

Michael takes a deep breath as though he's getting ready to speak, which makes me nervous. I don't know what his stupid functional family has taught him to say in moments like this.

"Is there anything else we should talk about, Mr. Barnes?"

Because God loves a dramatic moment, my dad doesn't answer right away. He looks up as though he's deciding. His eyes shift between the two of us several times, and then his face relaxes. If he remembers, he's not going to deal with it.

"Let's just enjoy our eggs."

So, we do. They're good.

CHAPTER TWENTY-THREE

WHEN IT RAINS, IT POURS

"Can you believe we missed ten days of school because of that stupid storm?" says Skipper in a boggled tone as he aggressively unpacks today's lunch. "I'm going to miss the first three days of stage make-up camp because of the make-up days."

"So, you'll be missing make-up because you have to make up?" says Bijon, tucking his red and gray napkin into the collar of his Elvis Costello concert t-shirt. Skipper's eyes roll as he hands Bijon a small handmade clay pot full of Thai ginger chicken.

"With fresh ginger, I grew myself in a hydroponic farming kit I got for Christmas in middle school."

"Ginger, hm. I used to watch *Gilligan's Island* on Iranian television. It was funnier over there because they were speaking in Persian. I remember thinking the island was cool since I was living in a desert. I would've just stayed there and enjoyed the beach." Looking over my shoulder, Bijon eyes flash the way they do when he sees a pretty girl. Paula is walking toward our table. "Here comes your Mary Ann."

She's with my Michael.

"Hi guys!" she says with the enthusiasm of an auditioning cheerleader. "Excited about the show opening tonight? Here are invitations to the cast party. Mr. Burdick let me use the mimeograph!" She passes us each a copy. We all take a thorough sniff. Anyone born in the post mimeo era will never know that joy. Mimeographs are like training poppers. A tiny, age-appropriate head rush follows. "The party is at my house," she reminds us.

"I'll stop by after school to help decorate. We're turning their rec room into a dancehall!" Skipper says, slapping the table for emphasis.

"You're the best, Steven." She's the only one who calls Skipper by his real name. "Michael and I are going to split a cookie in the commons. Opening night treat!" says Paula before giving me a long kiss. Michael gives me a long glare. He doesn't look like he's particularly thrilled to share the cookie, let alone me.

Come on, though. It's not like I'm cheating on either one of them. I'm not that kind of person. My dad is, but I'm not. I'm in two totally different relationships. Besides, Michael knew I was dating Paula when things started between us. He knew. Besides that, I don't have time for a guilt trip today. I have an opening night audience to think about.

We're soon backstage of the auditorium in the male dressing room, which is basically an advanced training course for gay bars. Of the twelve guys sharing the space, ten that I know of will come out during college. Eleven in total because Tim, the muscular senior with the most dazzling smile I've ever seen, is already pretty much out and has a sugar daddy who's an executive at Oscar Mayer.

Eight of us make it to thirty-years-old.

There's a knock on the door. I hear my mom say, "May I speak to Warn, please?" Vinnie Mancuso, with wavy, thick, long brown hair and sleepy eyes, one of the guys who doesn't make it, turns to make sure I heard. I finish outlining my eyes before heading to the hallway.

When I pass him, Vinnie says, "Looking good, Cover Girl." He's smiling. It's a joke between friends, not a put down.

"I'm sorry to interrupt," Mom says, looking beautiful in a simple black dress and pearls. I love that she dressed up for the theater. All the other moms will be in Packers sweatshirts and sweatpants, with a fried home perm. "I wanted to give you these," she says, handing me a grocery store bundle of daisies and carnations, the first flowers anyone has ever given me. "It's what they do in movies, so I thought why not? You can press one in a book when they start to wilt."

"Thanks, Mom."

"We'll all be out there. Even your dad. It's a big night. Art and Ruth left the baby with Shirley. We had a nice dinner at the Golden Rooster," our family restaurant of choice. A bar for dad. A deep fryer for me. "I got you a BLT. No fries. They'd just be cold and soggy by now." She checks the small feminine Timex on her wrist. "Oh goodness. Look at the time! I'll leave you alone. Finish getting ready now. Break an arm!"

"It's break a leg, Mom, but I know what you mean. Thanks."

I quickly search for Skipper, who I find reorganizing the prop table backstage right.

"Do you have any tissue paper?"

His eyes narrow. "Always. Why?"

"Just give me some."

"Color?"

"I don't know. How about—it doesn't matter?"

Skipper gives me a disgusted look. "It always matters," he says before handing me several sheets of fluttery paper in our school colors. I divide the bouquet and wrap half the flowers in the paper.

"Thanks," I say over my shoulder as I walk away. When I pass Michael and his stage crew buddies, I discreetly hand him an opening night card. I keep navigating lighting cables, taking care not to trip before arriving at the female dressing room. I knock on the door. Paula answers. I pass her the flowers and her card.

"You're going to be awesome tonight."

She exhales loudly and makes a silly face. "I hope so. Both of us."

"Break an arm," I say.

"Hilarious," she says.

Paula is featured in the first big group number that people recognize. "Big Spender" goes over huge. Paula totally steals the number from Lesley Dallas, the senior who is only playing Charity because seniors always get the lead. Paula looks amazing. Her dancing is perfect. Skipper's sister's skating dress captures the light beautifully, just as he said it would. Three of the varsity football players in the third row are up on their feet, screaming Paula's name. She notices and likes it.

I get jealous … of Paula. Those guys are hot. Don't get me wrong, so is Paula.

Paula.

What am I doing to her? Paula deserves to experience how guys like that see her. Not just football players, other guys. Straight guys. She deserves to know how special she is.

Shake off the distractions. It's time for my first entrance.

She's my girlfriend and all, but I'm Warn Barnes, Edgewood acting school alumni, Cowboy Eddie co-star. Forget charity. *Sweet Charity* will be mine.

At the end of the show we get a standing ovation, which I've gotten before, of course. This one, however, feels more real—not your typical Wisconsin audiences think audiences are supposed to stand up, standing ovation. It's like their enthusiasm and appreciation forced them out of their seats. We leave with the audience still cheering, only to see Mr. Burdick frantically waving.

"Get back out there. They love you!"

We all run back out. In the chaos, Paula and I manage to stand next to each other. She grabs my hand, and we bow together.

As we walk off-stage, Skipper runs up to us. "That was a-maz-ing! You're like the LaFollette High School Lunt and Fontanne!"

Ah yes. Celebrated theater couple Lynn Fontanne and her rumored to be gay husband Alfred Lunt, who grew up in Wisconsin. Coincidences galore.

Butch and some of the Special Olympics kids push through the crowd. He hugs me, "You were so good! Everyone," he says to his friends. "This is my brother. He was best." Then, seeing Paula on whom he has a small crush, he adds, "You were best too."

The rest of the family isn't far behind. "Where is he? Where's Warn?" Val demands. Once she realizes she is next to me, she smiles. "You sounded so good. I could totally pick your voice out from everyone else's."

Art and Ruth each give me a quick hug. Ruth first. Then Art. "You were great Warn," he says. "Really good."

Emily tells me I'm going to be a star while her husband Martin counts the number of lights on the grid. He's super fun. A real catch. They'll last forever.

Mom hugs me while I look for Dad over her shoulder. He's off to the side with Michael. Dad just handed him something. I can't tell what. Now they're shaking hands. So, okay. I guess everything is fine over there.

"Mom, I'm spending the night at Michael's house after the cast party."

"You didn't tell me that."

"I told Dad. He said it was okay."

Mom turns to Dad with an exasperated look. He grins and shrugs his shoulders.

Paula's parents' rec room is transformed. The furniture is gone. All the lighting fixtures have green bulbs. It would be seedy, but cords of white Christmas lights cut through and give the room a nice warm glow. Paula's older brother Thompson, a wedding DJ, has set up his stereo rack in one corner of the room. Some of the kids are already dancing, trying to teach the jocks like Clint Smith how to do Fosse moves.

Mr. and Mrs. Pellham are dressed in derby hats and little bowties, with trays of party food. The girls in the show kept their beehive, teased out and up, hairdos. They're all wearing vintage dresses from Ragstock on State Street. The guys are just wearing normal street clothes.

Skipper is wearing a white dinner jacket with tight Calvin Klein's, but to be fair, that's what he wears to most parties. He also made a *Sweet Charity* dip he calls, "There is Nothing Better Than This," which he's serving with homemade pita crackers.

Skipper is clearly competing with Mrs. Pellham for Best Party Food. He was working the room for a while, but now he and Vinnie Mancuso seem deep in conversation in a dark corner where for some reason, Skipper didn't hang any lights.

Paula is busy teaching a couple of seniors a line dance. Perfect time to look for Michael. I finally find him on a bench in a little alcove underneath the stairs, as though he doesn't want to be found.

"Hi."

I get a nod. His lips, while still perfect, are pursed. I sit next to him but can feel him tense up. He's got a flask. That must've been what Dad handed him.

"Can I have a sip?"

He passes it to me silently.

"You gave me the card you meant to give Paula."

"Yours must be in my bookbag. I can go get it."

"Do you remember what my card says?"

"Something about your hard work paying off." I smile and move closer. "A little dirty talk about looking forward to tonight's sleepover."

"How did you sign it?"

"The way I sign all my notes to you. Capital W." Lessening the paper trail.

"You should've written our names on the front. Here's the note you wrote Paula," he says handing me an envelope identical to the one I meant to give him. He's smiling, but sadly. "Read it."

I do as asked.

"Aloud," he says, with a slight tone of impatience. "Read it aloud."

"'*Dear Paula—you're the best dancehall girl ever. The audience is going to love you almost as much as I do. Warn'* ... yeah, okay. So what?"

"Why don't you say things like that to me? Don't you think two guys can have that?"

"What do you mean? I told my dad about..."

"Stop it. That was about hurting your dad." I wish I felt justified to protest, but he has a point. Michael stands up. "Thanks for not lying to me. I'm going to get out of here."

"But you're my ride. I was spending the night at your pl…"

"That's not a good idea." He hands me the flask. "Goodnight, Warn."

Not even a kiss goodbye. I hear him walking up the stairs while I take a long swig from the flask and try to make sense of what just happened.

I hang out in what I've come to think of as my little room under the stairs. Perhaps I could just live here and avoid whatever happens with Michael. Sure, the alcove is small, but Skipper would help me decorate. It could work.

The flask is empty. As it turns out, so is the basement. Most of the guests are gone. Time to face whatever happens next. I pop a piece of Trident to freshen my breath and cover the Canadian Club before wedging my way out of the alcove.

Paula, Skipper, Vinnie, and that one kid who never knows when the party is over remain. The lights are up, and they're all cleaning, except for the obtuse kid, who for some reason has three pigtails. I think she volunteers in the box office. She's just dancing in the corner, by herself. That's weird. Especially now since there's no music.

"Oh, there you are," says Paula. "We couldn't find you."

"Just off in a corner talking about the show."

Skipper, who moves into my line of vision, arches an eyebrow as if to imply, "Yeah, right." Out loud, with his actual voice, he says, "Vinnie and I are going to my house for dessert. Anyone want to join us? I made a layer cake from scratch."

I take a breath about to say, "Yeah, I'll come," when Paula cuts me off.

"We're going to stay here." Paula gives Skipper the "take her with you" signal pointing toward the girl so weird that even I'm not friends with her.

Skipper sighs and pulls the macrame keychain he made last year out of his pocket. "Come on, Jules," Skipper knows everyone, "time to go."

Under his breath, Vinnie says, "We're dropping her off before we go to your house."

Again, clever Skipper positions himself so only I can see him and gives me a thumbs up. I know I'm a little drunk. Was that thumb for me or him and Vinnie? I'm too buzzed to be sure. "Goodnight."

"Goodnight, Skipper." Remembering what Michael said, I add, "you're my best friend. I love you."

Skipper, not used to such public displays of my affection, stops dead in his tracks, turns around, and gives me an uncomfortably long hug before leaving with his entourage. Tiny Dancer, whose name is evidently Jules, leads the way like a bodyguard. She doesn't see Vinnie's hand wander onto my best friend's ass as they walk outside toward Skipper's Pacer.

Paula lowers the lights when they leave. She pours us two glasses of water at the wet bar before sitting down next to me on the sofa, which is magically back in its usual place beside her Dad's felt top poker table.

I take a big, refreshing gulp. Then another. Paula grabs the glass when I'm done and puts it on a coaster on the end table.

"That's funny," I say.

"What?" she asks.

"Your parents have coasters on a fiberboard, veneer table. The coasters aren't really necessary."

Paula smiles, moving closer and closer until she pushes me back into the arm of the couch. Then she gives me the slowest, wettest kiss we've ever shared. I close my eyes, trying to get into it. When I open them, Paula hands me her bra; so recently removed that it's still warm.

"The only thing that would make tonight better is going all the way."

The little part of my brain that is still sober knows that this is a bad idea. The part of me that is angry at Michael for leaving with no explanation loves the idea. And I'm sixteen years old, so the rest of my body is cooperating.

Even the little part of my brain that's still sober starts to get in line. How do I know what I want unless I try both options? Besides, there's no denying I love Paula. If I'm ever going to be in love with a woman, it's her. We're Lunt and Fontanne, dammit.

I take a second to look at her at this very moment. Remember a lifetime of knowing her. That sweet face. Her big heart. Wetting her pants on the first day of Kindergarten. Who knew then this is where we'd be now?

This is going to happen. I want this.

Paula is four days older than me, so no statutory concerns. That's good. Preparing my mind, my body, my heart, sword raised, ready for battle. We're going in!

I quickly undress, as teenagers do in these moments. We've been naked together before, so it's not a big deal. Paula stops me gently.

"My parents went to bed. They shared a valium. We can take our time."

She takes a deep breath and wrinkles up her face like she's getting ready for a shot. "Paula, you can relax. If ever this doesn't feel right, just tell me. We'll stop."

"Oh. Okay. Thank you. Thank you." Then she gives me a little nod of consent.

So, it begins. Paula winces a little bit, but this is her first time. My first time I did more than wince, that's for sure.

Sometimes with Michael, I fantasize about John Travolta or Starsky & Hutch. Not tonight. I want to be present. Paula needs to know, no matter what happens in the future, I was with her tonight.

The actual sex isn't all that different. I mean, it's different, but it probably is with any two people. It's *who* you're with, not what you're with, right? I've only done this with two people. I don't know.

We finish. I mean, I finish. I don't know if Paula finished. I doubt it. I mean, I'm a sixteen-year-old boy. No one hits a home run their first time at bat.

We lay next to each other, silent. No-need-to-talk kind of silence, not nothing-to-say silence. It's nice. Both of us appreciating that we know each other in a new way.

"Have you done that before?" she asks.

"Huh?"

"Have you done that before?" she asks louder and with a little more attitude like the resolve of her suspicion has increased. "It felt like you've done that before."

Finding the loophole, I answer. "You're the first girl I've ever done that with."

The answer must satisfy her. She kisses me. "This was the perfect night to do this. I knew I was ready the minute I read your note."

I don't have abs, but my stomach suddenly tightens.

"Note?"

"The one with my flowers."

The note I meant for Michael.

CHAPTER TWENTY-FOUR

DEFECTIVE TYPEWRITERS

I stay longer than I wanted to. I leave sooner than Paula wants me to, thus leaving us in that wonderful middle ground where no one gets what they want. As we kiss goodbye, I look into her eyes, hoping I haven't taken away a moment that should've belonged to someone else. I hope this wasn't a mistake. I hope Paula doesn't have regrets about this someday.

I zip my JC Penney coat up. The zipper digs in under my chin. It's uncomfortable, but, thanks to Michael, I have a long, cold walk home. I pull on the stiff, snow-mobile gloves my mom bought me at Farm & Fleet. They're ridiculous. They're also unnecessary, as I'm not the snow-mobile type, but they're warm.

Outside I can feel the moisture in my lungs freeze. I fumble for the cap I was hoping not to have to wear since my post-show hair still looks great. I walk about a block when I see a car flash its lights on and off.

It's Michael's navy-blue Buick Skyhawk.

I'm angry with him but scared too. What if he can tell I had sex with Paula? I want to Marlo Thomas it the fuck out of here. You know, the way she gets all huffy and makes Ted Bessel chase her on *That Girl?*

The car will be warm. I begrudgingly head his way. When I get there, the door is locked, which pisses me off. I know he did that on purpose because I would've done the same thing.

He slides over to pull the lock up. I fumble with the latch, thanks to my snow-mobile gloves. He opens the door. I get inside, sit down and stare ahead. He does the same. Cheap Trick plays, "I Want You To Want Me" on WISM. It is followed by Peaches & Herb's "Reunited," which makes me smirk. Michael turns off the radio

"I wasn't waiting for you."

"Okay. Sure," I respond. "You were out here because it's fun to sit all alone. In the dark, waiting ..."

"I had too much to drink. I need you to drive us home."

"I was drinking too," I remind him.

"Not as much as me," Michael says.

"Fair enough." I start to slide over, but he stays put before leaning in and kissing me. He pulls away almost immediately. "Your lips taste like Dr. Pepper."

"Yeah. Well, Paula's Lip Smackers ... "

"Shut up. Shut up about Paula." He opens the car door on his side, steps out, slams it, walks around the car, opens the passenger door, sits down, slams that door, fastens his seatbelt, and then glares at me. It's like a hissy fit fire drill.

If he's this angry about kissing, I better not tell him anything else.

"Let's just go back to my house."

"Okay. I'll walk home from there."

"I thought you were going to spend the night."

"That's not a good idea," I say. Not a good idea until I've taken a long, hot shower. Not a good idea until I've had time to think. Not a good idea, period.

Michael starts to breathe shallowly. His eyes begin to tear. "Are you breaking up with me?"

"When did this become the gay version of *Grease?*"

His tone more direct. "Is this over?"

Saying yes would make everything so much simpler. Say yes, throw the car in reverse and head back to the land of the normal. End it now. Take control. Just look in his eyes, his perfect blue eyes, and say yes.

"No, Michael. No. It's not over. Not for me."

A few tears meet his smile. The tension he's been holding in comes spilling out in a deep exhale. A little laughter follows. He kisses me. My face gets wet from his tears.

"God, am I drunk," he offers as an explanation.

"That's what guys usually say the morning after a frat party, right?"

We laugh a little. Crisis averted for now.

"Warn," says my mom, yelling upstairs. "It's for you!"

I quickly turn down the stereo and pick up the trimline extension. "Hello?"

"Hi," says Paula. "How is my," I can hear her checking to see if her parents are within earshot, "lover?"

My cheeks get red, and I smile. "Yeah, that was great."

"My sister told me to tell you we should only do that on special occasions."

Phew.

"Okay. That's fair." I say, trying to sound a little put out that she doesn't want to always put out. "But I did want to ask you something." My turn to make sure no one can overhear me. "We didn't use," God, I hate this word, "protection last night. Is that okay?"

Paula laughs. "That's hilarious. Boys can be so naïve."

Yeah, I'm the naïve one.

"What do you mean?" I ask.

"You can't get pregnant the first time you do it," explains Dr. Pellham OB/GYN. "So, since we were both virgins, it's fine."

I try not to betray my crushing sense of overwhelming, horrific dread. "So, both people have to be virgins, and it's fine?"

"Uh, yeah. Everyone knows that."

"Did you talk about it in that class that only girls get to go to in 4th grade?" I ask.

"No. My sister told me. She and her boyfriend have been doing it since 9th grade."

I know that. He tells *everyone*.

"Okay, Warn. The baby has everything she needs," says Ruth as Art tries to gently push her through the door. "We're just going to the movies and out to dinner. Emily and Martin are coming too."

"What are you seeing?"

"*All That Jazz.*"

"So good! Especially *Airotica*. I've seen it three times!"

Skipper and I call it *All That Jizz*.

"We should be home by ten," says Ruth. "She's asleep! Shouldn't be a problem!" as Art finally gets her through the door.

I look around the cluttered room for the TV remote. It's not cluttered like a hoarder or anything. It's just a lot of baby stuff, which will morph into toddler stuff someday, I suppose. I find the remote sticking out of a pocket on the side of the diaper bag. It's a little sticky in a way I don't want to think about, so I clean it off with a baby wipe.

I settle into the mandatory Dad reclining chair in front of the TV when the perfect silence of the room is shattered by the most ear-piercing sound I've ever heard. Either a smoke alarm went off, or the baby is awake. If the baby is awake, she's being attacked by locusts. Checking my ears for blood, I rush to the nursery down the hallway. I get there and do the checklist Ruth walked me through. Dry, check. No fever, check. Doesn't need to burp, check. Doesn't want a bottle, check. Hates her Uncle, check.

That's the only explanation.

This baby hates me.

This baby hates the world.

Five weeks later, at 9:30 pm, I hear Art's car pull up in the driveway. Kristina must have heard it too, because she immediately stops crying, begins sucking her thumb, starts breathing normally, and turns her head toward the garage.

The door begins to open. Ruth is already talking. "Did she give you any trouble, Warn?" Before I can answer Ruth is rushing up the stairs. "Why is she still up?" I start to stammer. Ruth says, "Never mind!" With that, she snatches the smiling baby, puts her over her shoulder, and heads down the hallway to the nursery.

It might be my imagination, but the baby seems to be waving goodbye or giving me the finger. I can't be sure which.

Ruth, ever polite, says, "Thank you, Warn. Art, you can take him home. We're fine," as she disappears into Kristina's room. Art shrugs his shoulders, putting back on the coat he had just taken off.

We snake our way through a labyrinth of baby debris. Mainly items that Kristina has outgrown or for which she no longer has use. I feel my lips involuntarily shift to the right. "Why do you guys keep this stuff?" I ask, trying hard not to sound judgy.

"You never know. Might need it again."

We climb into Art's 1974 celery green, 4-door, AMC Hornet, we call Kato. Emily is in the car.

"Why are you here?" I ask, surprised to see her.

"Martin and I argued. Art is driving me home."

We make our way past Badger Bowl and a few other local businesses before turning onto the highway. Seems like a good time to jump in with something I've wanted to discuss, although I try to keep it sounding casual.

"Did you know that a woman can't get pregnant the first time she has sex?"

Art and Emily both laugh.

"Really. Paula told me so," I say, trying to keep it light.

"That's ridiculous," Emily says in an incredulous voice. "What do you think? Sperm is all gentlemanly, or there's a barrier that dissolves after the first time. That a vagina is like a hotel toilet sanitized for your protection?"

My keep-it-light poker face dissolves. My voice gets lower and quiet. "Really?"

Art's head keeps twisting between me and the road. He signals to take the left turn onto Monona Drive before pulling into the PDQ parking lot. "Why are you asking us that?"

"Uh, nothing. Nothing! No reason. Just making conversation."

"Warn. Tell me what's … "

"Uhm, well, you know, me and Paula, uh. Well," I eloquently explain.

Art slaps the steering wheel. "Wow. I owe Ruth five bucks."

"What?" I ask.

"Nothing. So, you and Paula?"

"Yeah. She said that if both people were virgins, it was fine. Do both people have to be virgins? Do they have to? Do they?"

"Wait," Art says. "You're saying a lot here. Are you saying you weren't a virgin?"

"Uhm, well. You know. I just want to know."

Emily's turn. "Okay. Well, first thing. If a woman is fertile, pregnancy can happen anytime there's unprotected intercourse whether either person is a virgin or not."

Oh, God. Oh, God. Oh, God.

"And secondly—you were already active?" she asks.

"No. No. I wasn't. No," I say in one of my worst performances ever.

"Warn. Who with? What's going on?" says Art.

I try to talk. No words come out.

"Warn. You can trust us with anything. You know that, right?" asks my big brother.

I nod. "Almost anything."

"Anything," he says. "There's not an adult involved, right? No one forcing you to do something you don't want to do."

"No."

"Then tell us."

"Well, the thing is. Uhm. The thing is, it's not an adult, and … it's not, it's not a girl."

"Oh," I see the lightbulb go off. Art gets it. "Ruth owes me five bucks."

"What?"

"Never mind. Not important. So, you're telling me you've been with uh, with guys."

"Guy. One guy," I clarify.

"Skipper," Emily says with certainty.

"NO! Not Skipper," I say adamantly.

"You could do a hell of a lot worse than Skipper," says Emily.

"What's wrong with Skipper?" asks Art.

"Nothing. He's my best friend, is all," I say. "That would be like you and … "

"Okay! Okay! I get it." Art continues. "That part probably isn't my business anyway. I don't have a lot of experience talking about stuff like this. Which one feels most, I don't know, natural?"

"The, uh, the guy. That's what feels, like, better, you know. Whatever."

"Okay. Thanks for telling us. Should we talk to Mom about it?" asks Emily.

"Do you talk to her about your sex life?" I ask.

"No. No, I don't."

"Well then let's not bring her into mine. Besides I already told my dad."

"What?" they say in unison.

"He was drunk, so I knew he wouldn't remember."

They laugh as Art puts the car back in gear. We begin to move again.

"Being gay is huge. But you know what's huger? Getting a girl pregnant. So be careful. You want to be an actor? You want to move to New York? A baby would ruin all of that." Art's face grows concerned. "There's no way Paula is pregnant, is there?"

I didn't *think* so.

I grab the tray with our two slices of Rocky Rococo's Uncle Sal's Spectacular and find Michael in a booth by the back. He's waiting with our pops, napkins, and silverware all organized. "Here you go," I say, handing him a box that is piping hot. "Careful. Don't burn yourself."

We click our glasses to make it fancy and a little more date-like before taking our first doughy bite of pizza. Michael hands me my bag from Capitol City Comics. I hand him his bag from Chess King. "The shirt you bought is cute," I say.

"The Batman t-shirt you bought isn't," he says with a grin.

I look around to make sure no one is eavesdropping before I start. "I want to talk about the other night," I admit.

Michael wipes his mouth and nods.

"Do you want us to be a couple?"

"No," he says. "I think we are a couple."

"I think so too. I do. I even talked to Art and Emily about us."

I could have timed that better. Michael looks shocked, nearly choking mid-bite. "What?"

"They won't say anything. Maybe his wife Ruth, but not my parents or anything."

"What about Martin?"

"Come on. Are you kidding me?" I ask.

"Okay. I believe you."

"But talking with them, I realized I've got some stuff to take care of."

"I hope you mean Paula."

"Yeah," I agree. "With Paula. I'm going to meet her for ice cream after we're done with lunch, okay?"

He nods. We finish our pizza before heading up State Street toward the Chocolate Shoppe. Michael quickly pulls me into an alcove and kisses me. "Good luck. I'll talk to you later. I'm going to go home and study for my advanced chem test tomorrow."

"Sounds exhausting."

Paula shows up a few seconds later, looking a little burdened.

"Let's get some ice cream."

We go inside and wait in line. Bev, the store manager, waits on us, starting with Paula. "What'll you have kids?"

Despite the line, Paula pauses, biting her lower lip. I know what she wants, but I also know she doesn't want to sound like a kid. "She'll have Blue Moon on a sugar cone."

Paula, not wanting to be outdone, says, "He'll have a cup of Vanilla and Rainbow Sherbet."

I hand a crumpled wad of dollars to Bev, "Keep the change."

"Thanks for the quarter, kid."

The store is crowded. All the tables are taken, so we head outside. We walk toward the Capitol.

"So, listen," I begin, "I talked to Art. He says women can get pregnant their first time, whether they're a virgin or not."

"What?" says Paula, not looking nearly as shocked as I thought she'd be.

"I think your sister is wrong."

"Okay. Well, what if I am pregnant?"

"You're not, though, right? Right?"

"I don't know, but what if I am?" she asks, oddly calm.

"We'd figure it out," I weakly offer.

"I'd want to keep it," she says resolutely.

"Maybe you'd feel different if we found out you actually were pregnant."

She shoots me a steely glare. "I know how I'd feel."

"Okay, that's cool. I want kids. We'd raise it together," I say, knowing I mean it.

"It? That's nice," Paula says, sounding wounded.

"Her then. Her," I concede, starting to picture the daughter we might have together.

Paula smiles. "What's her name?"

"Let's say Emma Phyllis, after my grandmas."

"Too old-fashioned," Paula counters. "Could we call her something like Emphyl?"

"That sounds like a drug," I say with a wince. "How about Eppie?"

"That's kind of cute. Unusual."

"Very *Dreamgirls*," I remind her, referring to a soon to open Broadway show for which Skipper has a bootleg rehearsal recording.

Paula looks at me very intently. "Would we get married?"

"That's a big question," bigger than I'm willing to admit. "You're the only girl I'd ever marry," I offer as a concession. "But I don't know if that's fair to you."

"What do you mean?" she asks, looking like she's expecting a specific answer.

"Well, I'm always going to have responsibilities for Valerie and Butch. They'll need my help. They might have to live with me," I remind her.

"I love them, Warn. I could handle that. What about college?"

"I guess I wouldn't go. I'd work for my dad," I say, hating how much I mean it. Feeling claustrophobic at the very thought.

"You'd do that?" she says in a tone bordering on boggled.

"For you and Eppie?" I say smiling. "Yeah. I would."

"I'm not pregnant."

I'm relieved and sad at the same time. "You're not?"

"No. I got my period this morning."

"Then why did you … "

"I wanted to hear what you'd say. It was perfect. Thank you. Now it's my turn to talk."

"Okay."

"The night of the party, before we, you know," her voice trails off.

I nod and offer a little smile.

"I kissed one of the jocks that crashed the party."

"Which one?" I say, getting angry, despite doing the same thing to her thousands of times. God, I'm a hypocrite. It's how I feel, but it's so unfair.

"Tom Hilsenhoff," good choice. He's a decent guy and so damn hot. Great hair. Jeans like skin. I want to kiss Tom Hilsenhoff too. So, am I jealous of Tom or Paula? Why is life so complicated?

Oh. She's still talking. Focus.

"I felt bad, so I thought us doing, you know, what we did, would make it up to you. I felt kind of guilty, so I did what I did."

"We did what we did," I say, wanting her to feel, I don't know, better?

"Yeah. I wanted my first time to be with you. And..."

"And?"

"I wanted to prove that the things people say about you weren't true," she says in a mumbling voice.

Oh.

"I'm sorry you have to hear those things," I say.

She looks at me and says, "I'm sorry you have to hear those things. But those people aren't wrong, are they? How they say it is wrong, but they're not."

"Paula..."

"Warn, I saw Michael kissing you."

My mouth drops. My heart begins to race. I start to stammer.

"Don't apologize. You are who you are. I know you don't want to hurt me. I don't want to hurt you either, but I'm not going to be one of those girls who pretends not to know the truth."

"So?"

"So, let's start being the friends we were probably meant to be anyway."

Part of me wants to ask her to keep my secret, but I know I don't have to. She's Paula, the girl I've known since the first day of kindergarten. Kind. Beautiful. Wiser and smarter than I ever would've guessed when we were kids. The only girl I'll ever love. The what-if woman who will always lurk in my imagination with Eppie, the oldest of the children I'll probably never have.

"I love you," is all I can say, knowing I mean it with a slightly broken heart, mourning what might have been if only I were normal.

CHAPTER TWENTY-FIVE
OSHKOSH B'GOSH

"MrandMrsBarnesIneedtocheckouttheprogramatUWOshkoshand
IthoughtitwouldbegoodforWarnto…" says Michael of the run-on sentence.

Mom looks confused, "Woah. Want to come up for air? I'm sorry, boys,
but that's a busy weekend. I don't know if there's time for a college tour."

I attempt to negotiate. "We'd already be in Oshkosh and could just
meet you for Butch's Special Olympics meet. It's only about 10 miles away."

"Warn, going away on your own…" says Mom into her coffee cup.

"Michael is going to graduate this year. He needs to decide where to
go to college. And then I'll be a senior, so…"

Dad, of all people, interjects. "Dorothy, these are two trustworthy kids."
He steals a glance at us and winks. "It's not like they're going with girls.
What could happen?"

"But when is a college tour 3-days long?" asks Mom.

"It's longer because I'm considering pre-med, Mrs. Barnes. I thought it
might be good for Warn to hear about science programs before he decides
on his major," says Michael in an outrageously manipulative way. Like I'd
ever major in science or take a tour of a science building or study.

"Let Warn go," Dad says in his best, white, straight, heteronormative
way. Of course, being 1980 I'm not sure the term hasn't been invented yet.
Still, that's what it is.

To seal the deal, Dad grabs Mom's hand and says, "Butch will be with
the team, sweetie pie. The two of us could go up early. Get a hotel room
and make a night of it."

Confused by my dad being a dad and a husband, she stares at him
quizzically like she's suppressing a giggle. I start to feel a grossed-out
glimmer of hope.

"If it's a college tour, we should go too."

Hope has died. Dashed. Crushed. Back to reality.

"No, Dorothy. No," says Dad. "I want you all to myself."

She giggles and gives a begrudging, "Okay."

The drive from Madison to Oshkosh is very rural. Mostly farms. We
stop at Hiccup Hill in Beaver Dam for lunch. We make a pit stop at the
Kwik Mart in Rosendale to grab a couple of Cokes and fill up Michael's

car. I keep my hand on his leg unless we're driving past a semi. Otherwise, it's an uneventful 86.76 miles.

Michael could get into any school he wanted. He's in National Honor Society. He's getting scholarships. He's already been accepted to Carleton in Northfield, Minnesota, and is sure I'd get in too, but then we talked to Art.

"Guys, that's too far. Get the hell out of Madison, for sure. Go away, but not so far that Warn can't get home quickly if something happens." We looked at a map and agreed we'd go no farther than 90 miles away. That left us with 35 schools from which to choose, in theory. Some were bible schools, so thanks, but no. One was an engineering school in Milwaukee. Some were just too expensive.

"Do you want to graduate with student loan debt?" asked my dad. "We can afford to help out, and with the money my mother left you, but that probably means a public school."

Michael thought we should just go to the UW, but I was against it. I don't care how good a school it is; I want the chance to go somewhere new, with people I don't know. Except for Michael.

Oshkosh, Wisconsin, is on the shores of the not so mighty Fox River. Despite a population of about forty thousand people, it feels like a small town. I like that. It's probably my only chance to ever live in a city this size since I'm going to be an actor and will have to live in New York.

Wait. I'm already an actor. Language creates reality. So, I should be specific. I'm going to be a *professional* actor. I'm going to be a famous, professional actor right after I get done with college.

We pull into the parking lot of Gruenhagen Conference Center, which is an old dorm they don't have enough students for anymore. Being in the transition between Boomer and Gen X has its advantages. Everything was overbuilt for the post-war babies, so it's kind of clearance by the time we need it.

"Gruenhagen, that's a hell of a name. Who did they name this building after?" I ask rhetorically.

Michael, who is far more literal than I, has an answer. "Oh, I read about that." His eyes roll back so he can visualize that which he read cover to cover in the UW-Oshkosh Prospective Student pamphlet. "Richard Gruenhagen, of Orihula, Wisconsin, was an industrial arts professor at the university."

"An industrial arts professor? Doctor of Power Drilling? Ph.D. in varnish?"

"No," he says in all seriousness. Some days I wonder if he has a sense of humor. "Back when it was just a teacher's college. He later retired from teaching and became one of the best woodworkers in the area. He actually … "

Michael continues, but I tune him out, taking a few seconds to look at the building. Gray and white brick. Mid-century design. I crane my head around. Looks as though this is the tallest building on campus. Michael said our room is on the top floor, so we might have a view of the river.

We check-in and are given keys to our room. We take the elevator to the 10th floor. Waiting in the lobby is a tall lean blonde student, Todd, if his nametag is to be trusted.

"I'm your Resident Assistant for the college tour," he says, trying to make himself feel important. "Where you here from?"

"Madison," I say.

"Oh, me too! Which high school?"

"LaFollette," says Michael

"I went to Middleton," he says.

"Oh, so you don't live in Madison?"

"No," replies cocky Todd. "Middleton," an upscale bedroom community that borders Madison proper. It's for people who can't handle the hustle and bustle of Madison, which hasn't really got all that much hustle or bustle.

Todd of Middleton consults a clipboard before leading us to our room in the "Boy's wing. No crossing over to the girl's side!" he says to Michael in a manner that sounds flirtatious.

"No problem," I say.

He responds with a disconcerting wink. "I didn't think so," he says. Walking down the hallway, he adds, "oh, look. You're right next to my room!"

On the door, made from faded construction paper, are the silhouettes of a baseball and bat with our names written on them in felt tip marker. I'm the bat. Michael is the baseball.

Kill me now.

"I wasn't sure which one should be which," says skeevy Todd.

Thinking he's being cool, he grabs his master key off his belt loop, like he's Schneider on *One Day at a Time*, to unlock our door. "Here's your suite," he says with a grand sweep of his arm. "I'll let you get settled." Turning his attention to Michael, he adds, "if there's anything you need, I'm right next door, and my door is unlocked. If I don't see you tonight, be in the lobby at 10 am tomorrow morning, for the campus tour."

I make sure to hear the click of the door before saying, "Well, that was subtle."

"What?" Michael says with modesty. "He's just doing his job."

"Blow job if you ask me."

"Sounds good to me," says Michael with a grin.

I remind him, "Todd is next door. It's unlocked."

The room has a long bank of windows on the exterior wall. Nice light. Cinder block walls painted mint green. Two twin beds with storage bolsters. Two side-by-side desks with bookcases above. Two closets with wicker folding doors. One dresser each, with a towel rack bolted to the side. Green wall phone. Florescent lighting fixtures. Vinyl floor tiles sure to contain enough asbestos for anyone wishing to safely walk on the sun.

Michael kisses me, longer than usual. While my lips are still tingling, he takes time to look around the room. "Welcome home," he says with a sly smile. "We aren't expected anywhere until the campus tour tomorrow. What do you want to do?"

"Let's start by pushing the beds together," I say with a smile.

Morning comes too quickly. Sunlight floods the room. *A Chorus Line* coming from our next-door neighbor, Todd, wakes me up. Michael sleeps more deeply than I do, so I get to steal a few moments to watch him before he gently wakes up.

"Good morning, Warn."

"Good morning, Michael." Look at him. This seems like the right time. A way to match how open he's always been. "I love you," I say in a very serious voice.

His hands go up to his ears. "I'm sorry. I had earplugs in. What did you say?"

"I love you," I repeat, trying not to get annoyed that the first time I tell a man I love him, he missed it.

Michael opens his empty hands. "I heard you. I just wanted to hear it again," he says with a smile that's more of a smirk. "I love you too," pulling me in for a kiss.

45-minutes later, lips a little chapped, we get up, take quick showers, and head to breakfast. Inside the very creatively named River Commons, which borders the river without taking advantage of the view, is a cafeteria. We grab our trays and snake our way past mountains of bacon, heaping piles of waffles and pools of warm syrup.

"You're not getting much," says Michael, who is holding a slotted spoon of loosely scrambled eggs.

"For some reason, I'm not all that hungry," I reply.

We grab coffee. I get an orange juice. We make our way through a maze of tables to a two-top near the windows. As Michael devours some sort of a midwestern delicacy called a Cheddarwurst, I look around. The tables are full of happy students. I could see myself being one of them. I could see us here.

The day blurs into a haze of tours and information, friendly guides encouraging us to choose the University of Wisconsin, Oshkosh. Not long after, we're in the dorm room going over our notes.

"Let's celebrate," says Michael enthusiastically. "Let's go into town for dinner." The living, breathing travel guide continues. "While I was in the shower this morning, Todd," the evil Resident Assistant, "suggested we try a burger place called Leon's. It's a drive-in just past campus."

"Okay," I say in a deadpan voice.

"You don't sound very excited."

"Todd. Showers. You. Naked. Not cool."

Michael's face breaks into a wide smile. "First, you tell me you love me. Now you're jealous. My boyfriend is jealous. This is the best day ever!"

We pull into Leon's crowded parking lot. Neon lights pulsate in rhythms that matches the music coming through our radio, which a sign said to set to 90.5 FM.

Soon a chubby anywhere but Wisconsin carhop walks up to Michael's car.

"Hi boys," she says in the midwestern twang we all share. "What'll it be?"

Michael answers. "We'll have two Spanish burgers with fries, a chili dog to share, two Cokes, and two large turtle sundaes for dessert."

I translate, to remind myself that I can test out of the foreign language requirement for a B.F.A. if we choose this school. "*Tendremos dos hamburguesas españolas con papas fritas, un chili dog para compartir, dos Coca-Cola y dos grandes helados de tortuga de postre.*"

"*Muy bueno!*" says *mi novio*.

The carhop returns quickly. They must get customers out as quickly as possible to accommodate the cars lining up waiting for a parking spot. "Oh shoot, guys, I forgot to have them cut the dog in half."

"No problem," I say. I unwrap the sloppy chili dog. We'll figure it out." I hold it between Michael and me. We each start on one side, eating until our lips meet in the middle. The chili smears between our faces as we steal a quick kiss.

Best chili dog ever.

We eat our Spanish burgers, which are more like a sloppy joe than anything I'm guessing they have in Spain. The carhop, who we've discovered is named Carla Jo, brings us our turtle sundaes and the check which I pay from my Taco Palace money.

After the spicy sandwiches, the rich frozen custard tastes wonderful.

I notice Michael hasn't started his yet. I look at him quizzically.

"Hasn't this been a great day?" he says with a simple smile. "Just the two of us."

"It's like tasting what it'll be like after I graduate. Just us. No family. Nothing to worry about."

"Yeah. Your family is kind of complicated."

"You think?" I say in the most facetious voice I can muster.

We're still laughing when there's a knock on the passenger's side window.

"Warn, is that you?"

I turn in the direction of the voice and roll down the window.

It's my sister Suzy.

CHAPTER TWENTY-SIX

SIBLING REVELRIES

"It is you." says the sister I hardly ever see. "Girls! It's him!" she screams over her shoulder. "My little brother!"

Two beautiful women wave in our direction. A blonde and a brunette. Together with Suzy, they are the Wisconsin version of Charlie's Angels.

I'm seventeen, so Suzy is thirty-two. I don't know what thirty-two is supposed to look like, but this ain't it. She's wearing a low-cut black tank top, a wide-shouldered black leather coat cinched at the waist, and jeans with heeled boots. Her full chestnut hair is cut in layers, made bigger with spray. The cut obscures her jawline, so it's impossible to tell if it has begun to soften. Belonged-to-an-old-boyfriend sunglasses complete the look.

"What are you doing here?" we both say at the same time.

"You first," says Suzy.

"College tour," I reply. "You?"

"Me and the girls, Patty and Chesty," it's pretty clear to tell which one is which, "are dancing at a club called Scarlett O'Hara's, on Lake Butte des Morts."

"Dancing?" I say more skeptically than I would have liked.

"You know. Showgirl kind of stuff."

"Oh, like in *Gypsy*!" She stares at me blankly, without recognition. "Can we come?"

"You're underage," she says way too quickly.

I pull out my wallet and show her my fake ID. "That's not a problem."

Suzy laughs. "Little Warn with a fake ID? I'm impressed," she lifts her sunglasses to read the card, "Norman Nolen of Gadsden, Alabama. Nice to meet you."

"So?"

"Fine. If they don't believe you're," she looks closer at the ID before handing it back to me incredulously, "twenty-three, I can still get you in. Early show. Starts at 10 o'clock."

"What? The early show is at 10?"

"Yes, for the headliners." She sticks her head inside the car. "Who are you?" she says to Michael.

"I'm Warn's - "

"Friend. Michael. This is … my friend Michael," I say, not being sure if Michael might've added boy to the front of the description. "He's eighteen, so no issue for him."

"Nice to meet you, Leon."

"My name is Michael," says Michael, whose name I already clearly established as Michael.

"Okay, Leon," says Suzy. "Get there a little before 10."

She turns away and starts to walk toward the other women, pausing to wave at a middle-aged dad in a station wagon. I can tell he's into it by the way his wife is slapping his shoulder.

"She's your sister?"

I nod.

"Our college tour is about to become *Faster, Pussycat! Kill! Kill!*"

"What's that?" I ask.

"Never mind. Not important," he says with laughing eyes.

9:45 arrives. We park in a dark corner of the parking lot, away from the pick-up trucks and one lonely tractor. The harsh fluorescent lights and bug zappers don't reach out here, allowing time for a few deep breaths before I use my fake ID for the first time.

We dressed a little older. Michael is wearing a rugby shirt and pants that used to belong to his dad. I'm wearing blue jeans and an orange shirt, the official colors for Auburn, where I've decided my character, Norman Nolen of Gadsden, Alabama, majored in architecture. I am also wearing my old plastic horn-rimmed glasses, which luckily were in my duffle bag.

"$2.00 cover," says the guy working the door. The *Saturday Night Fever* dance floor reflects off his sweaty bald head and white jumpsuit. I hand him $4.00, and we start to walk into the club.

"Just a second boys," he says, throwing his thick arm up to block our path. "I need to see some ID."

"Really?" I say in a thick southern accent. "I declare. That's a surprise." Michael hands over his driver's license while I reach for my Velcroed wallet. I pull out my damp from ass sweat fake credentials, which I hand to him.

He pulls a little pen light from his pocket and shines it on Norman Nolen's ID. "You're 23?" he asks like Perry Mason. "When's your birthday?"

"Why?" I ask. "You gonna send me a card or something?"

"Okay, smartass," says the bouncer. "This thing is as fake as your southern accent."

"How dare you, sir!" I say in as self-righteous a manner as possible. "To challenge my heritage in an establishment named after Scarlett O'Hara, the most revered of southern ladies."

"You're kidding, right?"

I double down. "No sir, I most assuredly am not!"

"Well, I am!" he says with a big grin as he passes back our cover charge. "I know you're Suzy's little brother. Come on in!"

He returns my crumpled dollars and leads us into the club, which smells like my dad. Sweaty booze, cigarettes, and thwarted dreams.

"Great job, Rhett Butler," says Michael.

"Fiddle dee dee," says Norman Nolen.

The audience, all men except for one very unhappy looking woman, appears to be made up of farmers, truckers, and a future serial killer.

"Let's grab this table," I say to Michael. It has a pretty good view."

"It's kind of far away," he says.

"I don't want to distract Suzy from giving her best show," I say, being the show biz veteran in our relationship. "You see, if you're in the spill from the stage lights…"

"Uh, yeah. Okay. Warn, I think we should talk."

"About what?" I ask, just as the server comes to the table.

"Hi. I'm Renee. What'll it be, fellas?" asks a woman I'm guessing was a dancer before aging out. That's just instinctual. I can't be sure, but she seems very at home in her halter top and Daisy Dukes despite being in her, I'm guessing, late 50s.

"I'll have a Miller Lite," says Michael.

"Hm. Let's see. What do I want?" I ponder out loud. "Oh, I know! I'll have an Amaretto Stone Sour, please."

"Since you're Suzy's brother, okay. But I shouldn't," says the waitress.

"Why, is it because I'm," I look to make sure no one is listening, "underage?"

"No. It's because who the hell orders that?" she says as she walks away.

"So, I wanted to talk," reminds Michael.

"About what?" I say while looking at the pulsating checkerboard of lights on the dance floor. It is open, interrupted only by a pole at center stage which must be structural. It obscures the view and messes up staging. Occasionally a fogger belches to haze the lights. I cough a little before repeating myself, "What did you want to talk about?"

"I think you should be prepared for the kind of show we're about to see." Michael fans away a bit of the fog, takes a breath, and tries to talk, but the music crescendos as the house lights dim. Michael shrugs his shoulders and turns toward the stage.

Chaser lights move around the club. A single spotlight lands on three women at center stage. The exaggerated frozen angles of their poses accentuate the curves of their bodies. Their hands are on the brims of the hats each of them wears.

"Lady and gentlemen," says the announcer, "welcome to Scarlett O'Hara's bringing the exotic and the erotic to Oshkosh, Wisconsin, since 1979."

"What?" says Michael. "They're proud of being open for a year?"

"Yes, we are, smart-ass," says the waitress dropping off our drinks.

Drums start to roll in. "Please welcome that British blend that's just your cup of tea, Miss Suzzanah Scott with Lady Jasmine and Little Peggy Lipton!"

Lights to full.

Each of them wears a tight three-piece power suit with a fitted raincoat over it. Chesty and Patty in gray. Suzy in pure white. The trio separates when the girls move upstage, and Suzy takes downstage center as the opening bars to "Fool in the Rain" by Led Zeppelin fade in.

"Hello, Scarlett O'Hara's! Who's ready to get a little wet?"

The crowd cheers.

Their dance begins. Farmers are holding $5 beers up to their mouths but not drinking. Truckers are removing their hats and smoothing their hair, wanting to look more gentleman-like. The serial killer is trembling. One of his hands is obscured by the table, but that just means the act is working for everyone, I suppose.

The first part of the song is all about the moves and slowly removing the raincoats they're wearing. When the song's tempo builds to the instrumental bridge, Suzy takes to the pole, wrapping it around her strong legs and doing a very graceful, gravity-defying act that seems like it belongs in Vegas. The other women leave the stage and start dancing with men in the audience, including Michael, who is really into it.

As the instrumental wraps up, the dancers head back on stage to meet Suzy. Just before the lyrics come back in, rumbling thunder fills the room as the lights flicker off and on and strobe to look like lightning.

It begins to rain.

Suzy rips away her pants, leaving her in jeweled square cut trunks and a vest. Chesty and Patty rip away their vests, leaving them in very skimpy bejeweled bras. They're backlit, but the water picks up light and defines their sinewy movements and reflects off their skin. The thunder returns as percussion and climaxes, along with the serial killer. The lights blackout quickly. The center special returns to an empty stage. The dancers are gone.

"Oh my God," says Michael, my very gay boyfriend. "That was amazing!"

The girls come out, dressed down, not wanting to steal attention from the dancers working the audience while the crew dries the stage.

"Suzy is waiting for you out back. Just head through the emergency exit door by the lady's room," says Chesty.

"Won't it set off an alarm?" I naively ask.

"Not in a club like this," says Patty. "Gives the girls a chance to get away from the wrong kind of guy without him noticing."

"We take care of each other," says Chesty, who I suddenly notice is wearing brass knuckles on her left hand.

I look at Michael for permission. "Go," he says, making a shooing motion. "I'll hang out here."

"We'll make sure he's okay," says Chesty.

I find Suzy outside, on a cozy deck, hidden from the parking lot by a fence. There are a few comfortable chairs, some Christmas lights, and a few candles. It's nice. She's wearing a robe, smoking a cigarette, and running a towel through her wet hair. I quietly walk up to her.

"Should you be out here? It's a little cold," I say, noticing my breath.

"No one is allowed backstage, and I wanted to see you," she says, walking into brighter light. The rain smeared her eye make-up, making it look as though she's been crying. "What did you think?"

"It wasn't what I expected. I thought I was going to have to go up to guys and say, 'that's my sister,' Instead, I wanted to go up to them and say, 'That's my sister!' You were great."

For a moment, it seems as though she isn't sure I meant what I said. Then she brushes her wrists under her eyes, and for the first time I can remember, hugs me. I can't help but notice she smells fresh, like chlorine.

"So, I should get ready for the next show," says Suzy as she breaks the embrace.

"Yeah, we should probably get going. We've got a big day tomorrow. Michael is meeting with the pre-med advisor, and I'm doing my monologue for a professor in the theater department."

"Still doing Grandma proud."

"Then we're heading over to Neenah," I say, thus completing the recitation of tomorrow's plans.

"No one goes to Neenah unless they have to."

About this, Suzy isn't wrong. Neenah is the home of Kimberly Clark paper factories. The whole town smells like a giant lit match. "Butch has a Special Olympics meet there," I say.

"I didn't know he did that," says Suzy with more than a little self-awareness.

"Come with us. Everyone would be so surprised! Afterward, we could—"

"No. No. I can't."

"Why?" I ask, feeling like I've just been hit by a bucket of cold water.

"I've got a matinee."

I stare at her.

"Okay, so that's not true. I'm just not into family reunions." She kisses me on the cheek. "Gotta fix this face. Got a show to do. You should go get Leon."

"His name is Michael."

"He'll always be Leon to me," her face twists as though she's considering what she wants to say next. "I'm glad you have a friend like that."

She starts to walk away like Sally Bowles at the end of *Cabaret* when she stops and turns back to me. "Don't tell anyone you saw me, okay?"

We stare at each other for a beat before I say, "You were wonderful tonight."

She smiles and leaves.

Morning arrives; I wake up, smiling and excited. I untangle myself from Michael, who doesn't have to get up for another 45 minutes. Quietly closing the door, I stumble toward the showers, take off my robe, soap up, rinse myself and shampoo my hair quickly. Public showering isn't really my thing.

I quickly get dressed and wave goodbye to a just stirring Michael. He mumbles a drowsy, "Good luck," before giving back into sleep.

It's a gorgeous spring day. The air is brisk. The sky is blue. A day full of potential. I walk to the Arts and Communications Building on the opposite end of campus. Per the instructions they mailed, I enter the doors on the left side of the plaza. Inside, I find the small green room between the black box theater and the scenic shop and wait. There are two other prospective students inside, reviewing their scripts. I know my piece forward and backward, having won state competitions with it last year. I recognize one of the kids I beat. He came in fourth. He's noticed me too.

"Warn? Warn Barnes?" says the brassy redhead who has been proctoring the auditions. "I'm Liz, one of the student directors here at UWO." She takes my hand to shake it. "The committee will see you now."

She walks me down a wide hallway and through a door into the most beautiful theater I've ever seen. Modern. Clean. Cavernous and intimate at the same time. We walk past the ghost light and onto the stage. Sitting at a battered, folding library table on three wildly different chairs are the professors.

"Hello. I'm Warn Barnes, from Madison. I'm a junior at LaFollette High School. I'll be doing 'The Man with a Flower in His Mouth' by Luigi Pirandello."

The man at the table chuckles, which I decide not to focus on. "Why did you choose this piece?" he asks.

"He's a Nobel Prize winner."

"Good for him. That doesn't tell us why," says the alpha woman, who is biting on the bow of her glasses as though she's studying me.

Okay, since they asked. "My grandfather was an immigrant. My dad is too. Pirandello is from Sicily, like my mother's family. The language is heightened, which presents a challenge. The use of personification is fun to play. I like the control the character assumes over his life."

"How so?" asks the other woman, who looks a little like a puppet.

"He chooses the date he will die. What's more in control than that?"

The alpha permits me to begin by extending her arm and giving me a limp wrist flutter of her hand, so I begin.

At the end they applaud, and the red-head proctor comes back to collect me.

"Liz," says alpha. "I'll walk him out."

Liz's eyes bulge a little bit before she says, "Okay, Dr. Link."

This woman, Dr. Link, I guess is her name, stands up. She's much shorter than I expected. Dressed all in beige. Normally I would think it boring, but she looks elegant. She puts her chewed glasses back on, grabs some notes, and joins me at center stage. "This way, please." I follow her deeper into the building.

"You've done that piece before, haven't you?" asks Dr. Link.

"Yes. I won the state Forensics tournament with it."

"I thought so. It felt a bit rote."

"By rote, do you mean consistent?"

"If that makes you feel better, very well. Consistent. The note is this—nothing about today was affecting your choices. You weren't in the moment. It was good but, it could've been great."

"I could do it again," I offer.

"No, you can't. That's the point. Everything we do in life, we only get to do once, in the moment, when it's happening." She takes note of the gold watch she wears on her wrist. She starts walking faster.

"That piece was fine for academia, but you'd never play it in real life. You're forty years too young. If you apply and audition as a senior, please pick something more appropriate for your age. It will show us range. Spend time thinking about what kind of theater professional you want to be."

Now I'm confused. "What do you mean?"

"Access yourself. You're an attractive fellow. Handsome even. But you're carrying extra pounds that could make you or limit you, depending on your goal." She lights a cigarette, "it's also unhealthy. Do you want to be a leading man or a character actor? While you're a student, you can be both. The real world isn't nearly so accommodating."

I've been listening so intently I didn't realize it, but we're in an office. I'm assuming it's hers, as the door plate says Dr. Gloria Link. She grabs some papers and starts to lead us out of the room, signaling that our time together is ending. "Mr. Barnes, you may have some things to unlearn."

The drive to Neenah is short, so we stop by Leon's for a turtle sundae to celebrate. Michael was offered scholarship money and had a good meeting with the pre-med people. I recount my meeting with Dr. Link and end with, "Unlearn? Go to college to unlearn? What does she mean by that?"

I may not know what she means, but I suspect she's right.

Why else would her words linger?

We get to the Paper Valley Inn, a nice hotel near the high school. The front desk clerk hands me a key and a note from my parents saying to get settled and then meet everyone in the lobby for dinner.

"Here's the key to our room," I say.

"Who are we sharing with?" asks Michael.

"I hadn't thought about it, but no one, I guess. Val isn't here yet. Butch is staying with the team. It's just us," I realize, breaking into a smile.

The celebration continues.

CHAPTER TWENTY-SEVEN

A VERY SPECIAL OLYMPICS

When we arrive at the restaurant, it's just my parents in the cocktail lounge. Mom gets up to hug me while Dad finishes paying for what I'm hoping is the first round.

"Where is everyone?" I ask.

"We wanted to talk to you boys first," answers my mother.

My mind starts racing. I can feel my heart beating faster. Are they in the room next to us? Did they hear something before we came down? Is this finally it?

I breathe through the anxiety, the way they taught us to in the gifted and talented program at school. I smile, hoping it looks casual instead of stressful.

"About what?" I say, using an ideal mix of head and chest voice.

"About the college tour!"

We happily recount everything we learned. Mom says, "It sounds like a contender." With that, my dad lifts what appears to be his first Canadian Club and clinks his glass with Mom's crème de menthe. Only then do I notice that Mom is leaning into my dad, and he has his other arm wrapped around her shoulder.

"Hello everyone!" says Emily, trailed 20 feet behind by her husband Martin. "We would've been here sooner, but shit for brains," note, she means Martin in case that was too subtle, "forgot about a last-minute meeting with his diamond supplier."

"Two vodka screwdrivers, please," Martin says to the cocktail server I didn't realize was standing behind me. "What will you have, Emily?"

"A bottle of white wine, please."

Mom, wanting to change the subject says, "Where are Art and Ruth, and the baby? Didn't they ride with you?"

Emily's face registers a little shock and annoyance. "Didn't he call you? They had to cancel. Something came up."

"Oh no," says Mom, thinking of the impending addition to our family. "I hope Ruth is alright. She's just out of her first trimester."

"They didn't mention anything about the baby, Mom. Don't worry," offers Emily, who knows how our mother loves having something or someone to worry about.

"Hm. We already paid for their room," says Dad. "What will we do with it?"

Worth noting, my parents have taken Barnes Home Improvement to a new level. Thanks to rising interest rates, people are remodeling their old homes rather than getting new mortgages and moving.

Mom and Dad now drive brand new cars. They just bought me a little orange Dodge Colt. We spent my sixteenth birthday at Walt Disney World and Planet Binger in Orlando.

They're very generous.

"You're right, Ray," echoes Mom. "What will we do with the extra room? Val doesn't need it. She doesn't get here until tomorrow."

"Martin can sleep there," offers solution-oriented Emily.

Nervous laughter from the table follows.

"Oh well," says Mom, shooting Emily a look, "we'll figure something out."

Dinner is nice. The hotel sponsors a Friday night fish fry. "Tonight's profits are being donated back to Wisconsin Special Olympics. Order up!" says Dad, with his glasses slipped down his nose so he can read.

The food is delicious because how can you ruin battered, fried stuff? The coleslaw is creamy. The tartar sauce is tangy. The lemon for the fish cuts through the oil. The only surprise is how much I'm enjoying this triple date.

Dad had one drink and switched to 7-up. Mom is smiling and totally at ease. Even Emily and sad ol' Martin are starting to relax. Michael keeps finding excuses to touch my leg or rub his foot against my calf. I keep waiting for something to ruin the mood, but it never happens. The concern evaporates.

I have no concerns.

At the end of the meal, after our server has cleared the table, a strolling accordion player approaches the table. He's not very good, jowly, sweating profusely as if playing the accordion is the first cardio he's done in years. I can almost make out the melody of "Happy Birthday" as the restaurant staff starts to gather behind Martin. The second time through, they all begin to sing along. Michael and I join in. So do Mom, Dad, and Emily, while Martin blushes until his face is nearly as red as the accordion player's.

As they finish, the staff parts and Butch shows up carrying a cake holding 30 candles. He laughs as he places it on the table. "It worked, Emily. He's surprised!"

Martin kisses Emily on the cheek before blowing out the candles. The restaurant cheers as he gives her a more passionate, lingering kiss.

"I know it's not your birthday until next week, but since we're all together, I thought it would be nice. So happy birthday Martin. And Butch, congratulations! We all hope you do great in tomorrow's meet!"

I take a good look at the cake, clearly from Barnes Bakery. In honor of Martin being a jeweler, there are toy rings, bracelets, and frosting necklaces. For Butch's, there is a young athlete running around the outer track of the cake. It is clearly a special order done by my cousin Karen, who's in charge of the cake decorating department.

She's very Catholic, which means there's usually a subversive little nod to her faith embedded in the cake. *Cakebedded*. Ah, yes. There it is. One of the frosting necklaces is a little crucifix. I'll make sure Dad gets that slice. It'll be the closest he's come to taking communion in years.

Butch sits down with us to enjoy dessert.

Dad shoots me a look when I grab a second, okay third, piece of cake, but I try to let that go. You've got one athletic son. Let me be, you old drunk. If my extra weight doesn't bother Michael, it doesn't bother me. Besides, tonight has been too nice to let anything ruin my mood.

Butch rises to leave. "I got to get back. There's a party tonight!" Mom beams at him before grabbing Dad's hand and giving it a little squeeze.

The rest of us stay after dinner to listen to the polka band. It's not that they're good. They're not. In fact, were God to temporarily take away my sense of hearing right now, I'd be fine with it. It's not my morbid obsession with the accordion player who, were he to fall over dead right now, wouldn't surprise me. I think I'm staying because I'm, and this is new, having *fun* with my family.

In one of the earliest examples of a cultural mash-up or appropriation, Mom and I dance to "The Hawaiian Polka" before Dad breaks in so they can dance to "Sentimental Reasons."

The next morning, we head to Rocket stadium for Butch's meet. Neenah High School's mascot is a rocket. It's ironically named for Wisconsin's lack of contribution to the aerospace industry. Given the pervasive smell from the Kimberly Clark factories, they should be the Paper Tigers or the Pulp Masters, but no one asked me.

The stadium is already crowded. The wheelchair events just ended, so there's a clog of people entering and leaving. We hang on the edge of the crowd since Butch's event isn't for a while yet.

Skipper comes running up. Offering a quick hug. "Hi!"

"What are you doing here?"

"Yearbook!" says the editor-in-chief of school spirit. "Have you seen Bijon? He's supposed to be taking pictures. Always late!" Skipper turns away to search.

While he's searching, Bijon runs up behind him and taps him on the shoulder.

"There you are! I was looking everywhere for you," says Bijon as he snaps a flash picture in Skipper's face.

"Cut that out! Come on now," says Skipper. "We've got to cover the event." Before they walk away, Skipper turns around to say, "We'll make sure to get some great pictures of Butch!"

"Want to get a pop or something?" asks Michael.

"Nah. Let's just wait here until the crowd breaks up," I respond.

Before we can continue with our scintillating conversation, we're interrupted again.

"Guys! Warn! Michael!"

We look around to see who is calling us.

"Guys! Over here!"

We look around until we see a pair of waving arms. It's Val, working the MARC merchandise booth. Today that stands for Madison Area Retarded Citizens. Someday the world will get smarter and acknowledge the power of language. The acronym will evolve and become the far better Madison Area Rehabilitation Center and continue doing its good work.

"Just one second. Let me finish up here," says my bossy big sister who is waiting on a big dairy farmer-looking guy.

"Sir, you wanted the Special Olympics baseball jersey in Bucky Badger red, triple XL." Her fingers fly across the piles of shirts, before handing him a petite pink tank top that says, "Special Olympics Sweetheart."

"Uhm," says the man, his eyes darting between the shirt and Val's enthusiastic smile.

Val starts laughing and says, "I'm joking!" before quickly handing him the correct shirt. "You have a great day, mister. I hope your favorite team wins!" Once he has traveled safely out of distance, she turns to Michael and me, and in a low voice says, "You can get away with murder when you're blind."

Val's supervisor comes to shoo us away. We stop at the refreshment stand to get everyone a drink and head in.

"Did your mom say where they'd sit?" Michael asks.

"No," I say, "but we're all going to wear these Barnes' Home Improvement hats so Butch can find us. Here's yours," I say, passing him one.

"But my hair," no sooner comes out of Michael's mouth than we see a profoundly challenged kid wheel past us in a motorized chair. "Never mind," he says, putting on the hat.

We spy our area and start climbing the bleachers. When we arrive, we pass everyone's drinks. Dad scratches his head and says, "Bottled water? Ridiculous. Who would ever buy bottled water? It'll never catch on." A slight shot in the ribs from Mom's elbow reminds him. "Oh. Thanks, boys. This'll hit the spot."

Michael watches the games intently, shouting occasional variations on, "Wow!"

I don't really care about sports, so I just nod and smile.

About 30 minutes later, the announcer, a boy named Henry who lives with autism says, "Ladies, gentlemen, and the rest of you," pause for laugh. The kid is good, "it's time for the 800-meter race!"

Mom stands up and takes off her jacket revealing a Special Olympics t-shirt with their motto on it. "Let me win, but if I cannot win, let me be brave in the attempt."

"Everyone, look alive. This is Butch's event!"

We all put aside our distractions and start to pay more attention.

"Raymond, how far is 800-meters?" asks Mom.

"How should I know?" says Dad in a bemused voice.

"Well, you're from England," she starts to say before Michael heads them off at the pass and answers.

"Mrs. Barnes, 800-meters is just under half a mile," says Michael.

Butch is running against six other boys. He's in the second lane from the left. One of the coaches yells out something inaudible. The boys crouch down, with their hands on the ground and their hips in the air, ready to start.

"Looks like you last night," I say to Michael under my breath. He blushes and elbows me in the ribs but doesn't take his attention off the field.

Normally the race would begin at the sound of a starting pistol. Thank goodness someone realized that might scare the athletes. Instead, former gold medalists are on the field calling, "Ready. Set. Go!"

Butch is the only one in red, so he's easy to track. He's in the lead with two other runners. In fact, he's running right past us in the stands. I see him notice the hats we're wearing because he smiles the littlest bit. Just a fraction, but I can tell. He saw us.

After he passes, we all stand, up cheering like it was the Superbowl or something. Mom is the first to yell. "Come on, Butch!"

Dad has got the guys around him cheering, "Butch! Butch! Butch!"

Emily and Martin start hooting and hollering. Michael screams, "You can do it Butch. Come on!" The energy spreads around us, with the wonderful families around us adding to the crowd urging him on.

I add to the chorus of voices yelling, "RUN!" at the top of my considerable lungs until I no longer have air because I've forgotten to breathe.

Butch, by his own resolve, or to please the people he hears in the stands, starts running faster, breaking away from the pack. Martin keeps switching his attention from my family to the field, the field to our family as Butch keeps pushing. "He's got to be at least 100 feet ahead of the nearest kid!"

Then, just as he's about to break the tape and cross the finish line, he stops. He stops and waits while everyone in the stands screams, "Break the tape! Keep running! Cross the finish line."

Butch looks toward the crowd like he's trying to understand what they're saying. While he's doing that, the second-place kid breaks the tape and makes it over the finish line. Butch, now understanding, is the next to cross over the line.

Coach Pickarts, the man in charge of the Special Olympics program at our school, comes running over. "Dorothy, Ray ... I'm so sorry. No one knew that Butch didn't know to break the tape!"

"Don't worry about it, Doug," says my dad.

"Don't give it a second thought," adds my mother. "We've got a son who chooses not to break things. How lucky are we?"

Just as the cheering is dying down, we hear a new voice.

"That was amazing," says Suzy, giving me a quick smile before turning to look at the rest of the family. "I'm so glad I came." As Suzy shifts her weight, I see she's found Valerie and brought her along. They're holding hands. I plop the extra Barnes Home Improvement hats on top of their heads.

Dad makes a beeline to his daughters. He looks as though he's going to say something, but then he just throws up his arms before wrapping them around Suzy and then Val.

If Art were here, we'd all be together.

The rest of the weekend is nice. Butch wears his silver medal as though it ere made of real silver. We all take turns wearing it while Suzy takes pictures. Lots of laughter. Lots of telling Butch how proud we are of him.

Suzy skips her show, "Chesty can take the lead," and spends the night. Amongst all of us, there is a joy that feels fresh and new.

Michael and I drive Val home. We sing along with the radio. She keeps us laughing. We drop her off at the apartment she shares with two other challenged women and say our goodbyes.

Before we pull out of her driveway, I give Michael a slow kiss, knowing that it's dark. The neighbors shouldn't be able to see us. Valerie certainly can't. It's safe.

"What was that for?"

"It was a great weekend. I'm sorry Art missed it, but having you there with us was wonderful. Thank you."

"Not a problem," says Michael. "I love your family. Sometimes I even envy you guys."

"Right."

"Really. I envy you."

"Okay," I say laughingly. "No one has ever said that before."

"My family seems so boring in comparison," he continues as he pulls onto the road and makes his way toward my parent's house.

"Yeah. I suppose. We've been through some stuff," I offer.

"Doesn't it seem as though things are getting better?"

"I had that thought too!"

"Well then, maybe we can think about going a little farther away. About where we want to go to school, not where we should because something might go wrong with your family."

Somewhere inside me, I already had the same thought. That maybe it is possible to think about the future more openly. "The U of M?" I sadly ask, as though it were an unimaginable fantasy.

"Yeah. Great theater department. Great pre-med. The Twin Cities. Or Carleton," Michael adds, daring to say the name of his dream school aloud.

"I'll think about it," sharing his enthusiasm.

His smile lights up the car. "Great!"

As we pull into the driveway, it feels like anything is possible.

"That's odd," I say.

"What?" asks Michael.

"There are no cars in the driveway," I say, craning my neck to see an empty street. "I better get inside."

"Okay. Goodnight," says Michael with a little squeeze of my leg.

I grab my bag from the trunk and head inside the almost empty house. Bo, the world's oldest dog, thumps his tail, happy to see me but also waiting to be fed. I give him a larger portion of Alpo to make up for the wait since food is love.

The cast-iron lamp bolted to the wall of the kitchen is on. One of the two lightbulbs is flickering, but there's enough light to see a note in Mom's handwriting left by the telephone.

"Art is in the hospital. Get here as soon as you can."

CHAPTER TWENTY-EIGHT

HAVING NUN OF IT

Luckily, Michael was still in the driveway and could take me to the hospital. Driving myself wouldn't be safe. Too much to obsess about. Did Mom leave out why he's in the hospital because it's minor or because it's so big that she didn't want me to find out while I was alone?

"Which hospital should we go to? The note doesn't say," says Michael.

"Our family goes to the Catholic hospital, so Saint Mary's," I say with a slightly judgmental tone. Everyone knows Saint Mary's is best.

"But you're not Catholic," he says.

"I'm not, but my family is."

"No, they're not."

"Not my parents. My Aunts and Uncles. The bigger family." God, I sound like a jerk. "I'm sorry. Just trust me. It's Saint Mary's."

It begins to rain in heavy sheets. Streetlights and traffic signals tint the car as we make our way downtown.

I turn off the radio, so except for the rhythm of the rain and the steady beat of windshield wipers, we drive in silence. Past Olbrich Park. Past the old skating rink and toboggan run. Past the duck pond.

I eventually feel the car stop. "We're here," says Michael. "Do you want me to come in with you?"

"No. That's okay," I say. "I'll call you later."

He breaks eye contact to look around in all directions before kissing me. "Okay. I'm going to stay up until I hear from you, so call me."

I manage to get drenched running from the car to the main entrance of the hospital. My wet shoes cause me to slide and nearly fall on the slippery floor. If I did fall, this would be the best place to do it, I suppose, but that distracting thought is stopped short by the disapproving glare of a very thin nun behind the information desk.

Really thin. Like a black sleeve with white cuffs thin. The scowl on her face is the only thing that distinguishes her as human.

"Young man," says Sister French Cuff, "please don't run inside the building. Think of the infirm, the people your rash actions could—"

She doesn't know I'm the great-nephew of Sister Mary Rita and Sister Alma Rita. I assume all nuns know each other. Maybe I should drop their names for a little street cred.

213

"I'm sorry, Sister," I say, engaging with my midwestern guilt. Of course, this is my fault, "my name is Warn Barnes. I just found out my brother is here."

"Ah. Follow the blue and pink arrows to the children's ward," she says while crossing herself.

"No Sister," I say trying not to sound exasperated. "My big brother. He's older than I am. Art. His name is Art."

"Barnes? Did you say Barnes? As in Barnes Bakery?"

"Yes, ma'am."

"I knew your grandparents. Lovely people. Very important at the Knights of Columbus. We ordered all the baked goods for the convent from them," she says with a smile that is, indeed, angelic. "I'm in the same order as your Aunts Alma Rita and Mary Rita!"

I knew all nuns know each other.

"You said his name is Arthur?"

"Yes, Sister," I respond. "Arthur, or Art."

She efficiently begins to thumb through her dot-matrix printed ream of patients before a confused look overtakes her pinched face. "I'm sorry, my child. There's no Art or Arthur Barnes registered at Saint Mary's tonight."

"His name isn't Arthur Barnes," I say.

"But you just said—"

"Yes, ma'am, I know. His name is Arthur, but his last name is Holden," I say as gently as possible with a frozen smile on my face.

"So, you're *not* brothers?" asks the woman who can accept that a communion wafer becomes the body of Jesus but has a hard time understanding my family tree.

"We had different fathers," I say hoping to clear up her confusion.

"So, he's not your brother. He's your half-brother."

"Technically, I suppose. I wasn't really raised to look at it that way."

"I see," she says benevolently. "Your parents shield you from the truth."

"Okay, look," I can feel my temper starting to spill over. "I just need to know—"

Sister Literal's eyes somehow get wider and more exaggerated than her bifocals had already accomplished. Really.

"You're the son of the one that got excommunicated, aren't you?"

"Pardon me?" I ask, boggled.

"Raymond. The one who divorced and then turned around and

married a *Protestant*," she says in a hushed voice, as though the Pope is eavesdropping.

"Yes. Raymond is my father," I offer.

"Well," she says, returning to her roster, "I'll pray for all of you."

"Just my brother will be fine, Sister. Thank you."

A smile returns to her face. "Well, the Lord pointed me in the right direction. Your half-brother has been here since Friday."

Friday?

She continues. "Cardiac Care Unit. Top floor. Follow the green arrows."

Cardiac Care? He has the best heart of anyone I know.

By rote, I tag the conversation with, "Thank you, Sister," and leave.

My confusion about him having been here since Friday momentarily prevents me from realizing she just said Green Arrow, one of my favorite DC superheroes. Instead, I follow orders and walk into the maze of a hospital. The Lord works in mysterious ways, and so does the architect who designed this bunker. Cardiac Care is on the highest floor. That's just what the patients need. A sprint on their way to seeing a heart specialist.

Stopping briefly at the nurse's station to get the exact room number, I finally find Art's door. Our family is large and spills out into the hallway. Everyone appears to be listening intently. To whom they're listening, I have no idea.

I stand on my tiptoes, between Uncle Nick and Aunt Josie.

"Hello?"

Mom stands up. "Warn? Oh, Warn! Thank goodness you got here. The doctor," a man in scrubs waves, "was just about to give us an update. Will you take Butch to the cafeteria for dinner?"

Butch, still wearing his silver medal, waves from the far corner of the room and slowly starts working his way through the crowd.

My dad never fails to disappoint. He uses the distraction of everyone having to clear a path to grab a quick swig from a flask in his coat pocket. I'm the only one who notices. Well played. You almost got away with it, Dad.

"I'd like to hear what's going on," I say firmly.

The doctor jumps in. "Sorry. No minors allowed during medical discussions."

"I'm eighteen," I say in a lower voice.

Mom pushes Butch toward the door. "No, he's not, doctor. That was a lie," she says as Butch clears the entryway. "We'll tell you everything later. Get something to eat." She hands me a ten-dollar bill.

As she shuts the door, I glimpse Art. It takes a minute to find him in the tangle of monitors and machines surrounding him. He looks frail. He's usually clean-shaven, but now his face carries the stubble of his hospital stay. There is plenty of white amongst his whiskers. His jawline is softer. His eyes are sad.

He catches me staring at him and becomes less unguarded. His eyes roll mockingly to cover how uncomfortable he is being the center of attention. He follows this with a smile as he disappears behind the shut door.

Butch and I follow the arrows marked, "Cafeteria." As we make our way, the clatter of silverware gets louder. We're headed in the right direction. We each grab a tray and head to the grill. The line inches forward as doctors get the food they urge patients to avoid. An appropriately hair-netted, latex laminated cafeteria lady, why is it never a man, asks us, "What'll you boys have?"

Butch, as always, places his order through me.

"Warn, tell her I would like a hamburger with raw onions. And French fries, please."

"He would like a hamburger with raw onions and an order of fries, please."

"French fries, Warn. I want *French* fries."

"French fries, please."

"And you?"

"I'll have a double bacon cheeseburger, please. A large order of onion rings." Suddenly aware of nutrition and the cardiac concerns that evidently run in my family, I lie. "And cheese curds to share."

I'm not sharing my cheese curds.

Our food is handed to us. We get in the line for the cashier, settle our bill, paying for two desserts in advance and start to look for a table in the hospital cafeteria. There are several tables near a teary woman people seem to be avoiding, preferring to process their own concerns rather than take on those of a stranger. We find a fairly private table. Perhaps its isolation is related to the nearby poster with graphic drawings of illnesses related to social diseases. Two for the Herpes section it is.

"Warn, what's wrong with Art?" asks Butch between bites of his burger.

"That's what we're here to find out," I respond.

"He's going to be alright, right?"

"Of course. Sure. Yes!" I say for myself as much as Butch.

Time to change the subject. "Tell me more about the Special Olympics meet and the party they had for you."

Butch lights up, "I hugged a girl from Poynette! I love her."

The rest of our meal is a nice distraction, led by my best friend food.

Emily and Ruth enter the cafeteria and make their way toward us.

Emily stands near Butch. "Let's go get the desserts," she says as he quickly rises.

"How did you know we did that?" I ask.

"Hello. I'm Emily. I've known you since you were born," she responds as they start to walk away.

She turns back toward me. "Boston Cream Pie!" we say in unison.

"Ruth, I'll get you a treat too," Emily adds as she and Butch head toward the horizon line of the tray return.

Ruth. Art's wife. Pregnant. Sad. Tired.

"Who's watching Kristina?" I ask.

"Neighbors," she responds in a weary voice.

"I can help starting tomorrow," I say.

"You've got school," she says with an arched eyebrow.

I shrug and roll my eyes. "This is more important. How long have you been here?"

"Since Friday."

"You haven't gone home since then?"

"I've been home to sleep, shower, and see Kristina, but that's about it."

Emily drops off my dessert and Ruth's coffee. "Come on, Butch," she says. "Let's go visit Art."

There's something they don't want Butch to hear.

"Okay, let's!" he says to Emily. As they walk away, I hear him say, "Em, I hugged a girl! I love her. Oh boy!"

Emily responds just before they fall out of earshot. "Isn't she lucky?"

Ruth looks at me. "Your parents discouraged me from telling you, but you should know what the doctors are saying." Ruth sips her coffee. "Have you ever noticed your family doesn't talk about anything?" I breathe to answer, but the question appears to have been rhetorical. "Art was sent home from the Army because they found evidence of Ischemic Heart Disease. He says heart disease saved his life because it kept him out of

Viet Nam."

Despite my confusion, I feel the need to say it aloud. "Ishanemic?"

"Ischemic," says Ruth patiently, sounding it out for me.

Would Google have come in handy today or what?

"Okay. Ischemic. What does that mean?"

"In Art's case, it means he has a predisposition for plaque building up in his heart. The Army doctors sent him home with instructions to monitor it. He didn't. Smoking and his weight," I see her quickly look at my empty dessert plate, "have made the situation much worse. He also has an enlarged left ventricle. He had a serious heart attack at work on Friday. A reporter who teaches CPR was there. She saved his life."

Wow. "Okay. Thank God. Okay. So, why did you wait until we got back from Neenah to tell us?"

"Art's choice. He wanted Butch to have his big weekend."

"What's next?" I ask.

"We reduce stress, get Art to quit smoking, and lose some weight."

"What can we do to help you?"

"Get everyone to go home so Art can get some rest. So, *I* can get some rest. So, we can all get some rest," she says with her farmgirl smile, which carries more than a little sadness behind it.

"Done."

We stop for ice cream on the way home. Afterward, Dad pulls into the driveway but leaves the car idling. "I'm going to run and get some cigarettes."

"You shouldn't smoke," I say as I get out of the car. "You shouldn't lie either," I add, opening the glovebox to expose three packs of unfiltered Camels. "Have fun."

Mom and Butch head to bed. I wander the house a bit, getting lost in a memory or two before heading to the small foyer at the front of the house.

I stand against the wall opposite the coat closet, which has a full-length mirror on the door. I'm 3 feet away, facing the mirror, and I can't see my entire body. I am wider than the mirror.

I am wider than the mirror.

Like my big brother, I stop breathing for a second, my habit when confronting a new thought. Once my breathing resumes, my head tilts to the side like a puppy. Determination floods my jaw, which is currently obscured by the extra weight I carry. I have a plan.

The only way I can help Art is to help myself. The best way to show him that different choices are possible is to make different choices myself.

It's time to change.

CHAPTER TWENTY-NINE

RUNNING ON EMPTY

It is midnight. It's spring, but brisk just the same. I can see my breath when I exhale. Despite the cold, I am wearing one of two pairs of shorts I own. My gym shoes, a pair of socks like the ones Barbra Streisand wore on the Superman album cover, and a Barnes Home Improvement baseball shirt complete the look. It's dark, so no one can see how I look. They don't need to see what I'm about to do.

I once watched a movie in school where a man wanted to kill himself by running. He pushed himself, hoping to cause a heart attack, but the first day he didn't manage it. He ran a second day, getting just a little farther. No heart attack. He did this every day until one day he realized he was no longer depressed and had begun looking forward to the run.

My parent's home is exactly half a mile from our church. I am going to run as far as I can and then walk the rest of the way, turn around and head home. The next day I'll run farther, even if it's just one step. I'll do that until I can run to the church. That will be half a mile. Then I'll strive for a mile. I will stay at it until exercise becomes part of me.

I make it to the end of the street.

I'm near the mulberry bush I used to walk to when I was pretending to be blind. Not even a tenth of the way. I picture Art and push myself further. I almost make it to Michael's house, which I'm guessing doubles the distance. I can run one-fifth of a mile. More than I expected. Tomorrow I'll do better.

I walk to the church and then home again, which gives me time to think. I walk down the steps to the basement office and write a letter to Art before I go to bed.

Tomorrow comes. I wake up feeling great about running. Then I try to move. I can't. Lesson learned. When they say you should stretch before and after exercise, they mean it. I hobble out of bed, passing a mirror. Even looking up hurts, but my hair looks good, so it's worth the effort.

I come downstairs to the usual bustle. Dad is nursing a hangover. Siding applicators are getting their assignments. The phone is ringing. Mom is at the stove cooking.

"No breakfast for me."

Everything stops. The cigarette Dad is sucking on dangles from his lips. The fried egg my Mom was flipping slips off the spatula. Even the applicators sit there with their mouths open.

"What?" says Mom.

"No breakfast. Thanks."

"Raymond, did you hear him? He doesn't want breakfast. Warn doesn't want breakfast." She puts her hand on my forehead. "You don't have a fever, do you, son?"

"No," I say over my shoulder as I start to walk out of the kitchen.

"Oh my God. Why are you walking like that? Do you have kidney stones?"

"No. I went running."

"You went running?" says Dad. "What is this, the goddamn *Twilight Zone*?"

As I pass the beige trimline phone, it begins to ring.

My arm slowly moves down to pick up the receiver. "Hello?"

"Hi Warn, it's Ruth." My chest tightens. She's been crying. "Art just crashed. The doctors are in with him. Everyone needs to get here right away."

In a blur, I'm driving Dad's pick-up, getting us through morning traffic. "I'll drop you off so you can get up there quicker," I say as I pull in front of the entrance guarded by the cranky nun. They jump out before the truck is fully stopped. I gun it with such force that a young resident jumps out of the way.

He was hot. I hate myself for noticing that during an emergency.

I use the handicapped parking permit we have for Val, and Dad, to get the closest possible spot in case Art really has crashed. *Crashed.* That's a code word meaning in danger of dying. Time is critical. Despite the pain from last night's run, I sprint through the hallways.

As I round a corner, I almost run into Sister Hateful, who is rounding a different corner. Per usual, we're in different corners. I'm surprised when she doesn't try to stop me. As I pass, she says, "Your parents told me what's going on. Let the Lord carry you quickly. I'm praying for your family."

"Thank you, Sister." I hope she heard me. I'm hyperventilating.

The elevator to the top floor takes forever. As we approach our floor, I make my way to the front of the car to get out first. I wedge through as soon as the doors have separated enough to get out.

I run through the cardiac care unit convinced I'm going to have a heart attack myself. I spy Art's door on the horizon, huffing, and puffing and increasing my speed as much as I can. I run through the door and see Mom, Dad, Ruth, and trauma-free Art staring at me as though I were crazy.

Ruth looks alarmed. "Are you okay?"

Mom steps up from her chair. "Warn, sit down."

The short, stylish nurse that is in the room puts his two fingers on my wrist to take my pulse using his Binger Bunny watch to keep time. With my peripheral vision, I see him mouth the words, "He'll be fine."

I try to form words, but my breathing is too labored. I collapse in the chair, take a few deep breaths and say, "You said Art had crashed."

"I did," says the patient, "but I'm okay now. I'm fine." Only now, when staring at him blankly, do I notice that he's wearing Butch's silver medal from Special Olympics.

The nurse talks in a very distinctive Wisconsin accent. The one I try to keep at bay. "For sure. We've just got to get Arthur stable for two days in a row, and he'll be home, lickety-split!"

"Since you've got company, Art," says Ruth, "I'm going to take your folks down to the cafeteria for coffee." Art nods. "Warn, can we bring you anything?"

"No. I'm fine."

As they pass the threshold of the door, I hear my dad say, "What's going on with that kid, Dorothy? Is he on a hunger strike or something?"

My brother and I stare at each other for a second before I break out in tears. What's wrong?" he asks, straining to get closer to me despite the machines to which he is wired.

"What's wrong? I thought you were dying."

"Warn, don't be dramatic," responds my brother, currently wired to a heart monitor.

"Dramatic? I'm being dramatic?" I repeat. Unfortunately, after I say it, I can hear it. I am being a little dramatic, I suppose. But still, "Art, this is literally a matter of life and death."

"Don't start, Warn."

"Really. I don't think I'd ever get over it. Losing you would be the worst thing in the world—for me, for Mom and Emily, for Butch. Even my dad. And Ruth. What about Ruth and *your kids*? You've got to get it together."

He doesn't say anything, but for the first time, I see him cry.

The cloudburst of tears is quick. It's followed by that post cry hiccup breathing we've all experienced. Anyone who says they haven't is a liar. Afterward, there are tissues and a little embarrassment. "I don't know what came over me."

"I do. This is some scary shit." I take a second to catch his eye. "Art, it's time for you to let us be strong. Concentrate on getting well."

"I am so tired."

I start to rise. "Okay. I'll let you get some sleep."

"No. Not that kind of tired. Life tired. Old man tired. I'm only in my thirties. It shouldn't be like this."

"What can we do?"

"If I knew, I'd do it. Work isn't going well. I don't have the energy for it. Whatever energy I do have, I want to spend on Kristina and Ruth. Another baby on the way, which is great, still means more energy that I just don't have."

"You've got to take care of yourself, or you won't be able to take care of anyone else. You know that, right?"

Art smiles, but his eyes are weary. The conversation is over.

"I should get some sleep," he says.

Soon his breathing becomes rhythmic. He's asleep. I can tell because we're brothers. We shared a room. I quietly rise, tuck the letter I wrote him under his arm and walk out the door.

CHAPTER THIRTY

MOVING ON

I'm lost in my thoughts while walking to the car. So distracted am I that I literally run into my brother-in-law Martin.

"Oh geez, Warn. I'm sorry. I'm on my way to see Art. I was distracted," he says.

"No problem. Me too."

Something in his eyes is even more distant than usual. He's burdened.

"Are you okay?" I ask.

"Yeah. Yeah, I'm okay," he responds. I can tell he's deciding whether to tell me more. "But I suppose you're going to hear soon enough…" I stare at him blankly rather than interrupt him, giving him the room to decide. "Okay. Here it is. Emily and I are splitting up."

"Uh, what?"

"It's no secret. We've been having problems. I think Art's heart attack got her thinking. Me too. Who knows how long any of us have? Better to get on with things."

"So, you wanted this?"

"No. I love Emily. Very much. But maybe that's why I agreed. We don't have kids yet. I think if I fought for us to try, she'd just resent me. Who wants to be with someone because they feel obliged? Sometimes you've got to do what's best for the other person. Emily isn't done figuring out what her life is going to be about. Sometimes you've got to put everyone and everything else first. I think this is one of those times."

For the first time ever, he hugs me.

"Goodbye, Warn."

Years from now, he and Emily will be at the same party with new partners. Neither of them will acknowledge the other or the fact that they'd promised to spend the rest of their lives together. Some promises evaporate, I suppose. This one did, but at least there was kindness.

Art stabilizes and is sent home. The doctor said one week of rest, and then he can go back to work. Ruth is still working in the office of the technical school, so Mom hangs out over at their place a lot. I come over

225

after classes, so she can wrap up the day at Barnes Home Improvement. I cook dinner, eat with them and leave around 7.

I have to work tonight, so I'm leaving early.

Ruth holds Kristina by balancing her on her own expanding belly as though it were a shelf. Together we wait on the front stoop of their raised ranch home for Michael, who I've not seen much of outside of school.

He pulls up and gives the horn a quick toot. I start to sprint toward him but remember my manners, so I turn around to give Ruth a quick hug and kiss Kristina.

"Bye, sweet girl," I say.

"Bye, Unca Warn!" she says back.

Ruth and I both stare at each other, eyes wide, beaming at Kristina. "Wow!" I say before adding, "you're the best girl in the world. I love you."

She blows me a kiss, which I take as permission to leave, and head toward my boyfriend.

I open the passenger door. We hug and steal a quick kiss. When the embrace is broken, he holds me at arm's length with a quizzical face. "Something has changed," he says. "Your clothes are looser. Your face looks different. What's going on?"

I'm not ready to talk about the diet thing, so I'm vague. "Hospital food?"

"That makes sense. Want to come to my house after work? My parents aren't home. They went to check out Carleton and talk about financial aid."

His smile gets bigger. His eyebrows wiggle. He's excited, and I don't know what to say. Northfield, Minnesota, is about 5 hours, 3.5 hours farther than our agreed boundary, away. "That's great." Then, to change the subject, I add, "why don't I spend the night at your place?"

"Yeah! We can work on your early acceptance application. I've been asking my college advisor. She thinks your service and a strong essay about the challenges in your family can compensate for your grades and qualify you for a great financial aid package."

The challenges in my family. That's not an essay. It's a book.

Art doesn't seem any stronger. There's no change in his diet. He hasn't quit smoking. Emily moved back in with us. Michael is graduating and going to Carleton. He picked up his cap and gown. It's been hanging on his closet door, reminding me that everything is going to change. The only thing I seem to have control over is food.

I've lost 40 lbs. in three months. I've had to buy some new clothes, although Skipper has been altering some of my old stuff. I can now run 3 miles. I suspect I could go farther, but I don't always have the energy.

Today, I'm rushing through the hallways to get to the QRA, the meal formerly known as lunch. I run past Butch on my way. "Warn! Warn! Hi."

I overhear his best friend Jimmy say, "That's Warn? He looks so different. Are you sure that's Warn?"

"Jimmy quit being silly. I know my own brother."

Skipper is at our table, which he has festooned with red and gray table linens as today is the last day of the school year. He's wearing his cheerleading uniform because there's a pep rally for the seniors right after lunch.

"Sorry I'm late."

Bijon shrugs. "Don't worry about me. If there's not a coup, I'm fine." He then kisses Paula, which isn't weird at all. They've been dating since about a month after our break-up.

"What's for lunch?" asks Mrs. Bijon.

"I made lasagna for all of us-except Warn, who is getting a special-order broth with shaved vegetables and poached chicken."

"Skinless?"

Skipper exhales loudly. "Of course."

"Thank you. What's this floating on top?"

"5 pistachios roasted in sweet Thai chili. You know, so there's flavor."

I inhale my soup, which is delicious and, for some reason, tastes of fresh lime. I stand up, handing Skipper my Lancer's Class of 81 hand-embroidered napkin. "Keep it," he says. "It's a gift to kick off our senior year. Wait. Where are you going?"

"I've got to pick up Michael's graduation present, get a haircut, you know. Stuff."

"The pep rally is mandatory," says the high school CIA.

"Gosh I hope no one calls the cops," I say.

"Don't you want to see it? I've worked so hard on it."

"Skipper, if I don't get these errands run now, I'll be late for babysitting Kristina."

"Do it afterward," offers Bijon.

"I have to work tonight."

"Warn, you do what you think is best," says Paula, rising to kiss me on the cheek. "You've got a lot going on. We understand, don't we, boys?"

The boys give an obligatory nod of their heads.

"Thank you."

Skipper hugs me. "Remember to eat tonight."

"I'll have a Lean Cuisine, okay?"

"So much sodium, but okay. Please tell me tomorrow isn't fasting day."

"I have got to run," I say. "I'll see you tomorrow at graduation."

"Okay," says the martyr formerly known as Skipper. I turn to leave, nearly running into Mr. Larsen, the head of the English Department. The last thing I hear is Skipper saying, "He didn't eat the pistachios."

I wake up groggy.

"Look, Warn. It's raining. Oh boy," says Butch, who is looking out the window. "I hope this don't ruin Michael's graduating. I want to go to that party!"

Mrs. Drake invited our entire family over for Michael's graduation. Art and Ruth declined because she's like fourteen months pregnant. God knows where Suzy is. Otherwise, all of us will be there.

I head down to the shower. Emily, off to go for a bike ride with some new guy whose name I won't bother remembering until he's lasted at least a month, says, "Leave some hot water," on her way out.

I wash and condition my hair, taking time to feel the layers of my new cut. I use the sandalwood-scented soap I got for Christmas. I shave and use astringent to clean and brace my skin. I moisturize my face using the lotion from the Clinique counter at the mall. Then I take the can of foamy hairspray called mousse and run it through my hair.

Thus begins a new addiction. In my future, there are times I will be desperately broke, but I will always have money for hair supplies.

I put on the pleated Girbaud jeans and thin cotton madras shirt I bought at Manchester's. Then I grab a box from underneath my bed. Opening it, I peel away the layers of tissue paper and grab my new red cotton cardigan and the Ray Ban sunglasses that I found in the Taco Palace lost and found.

I got rid of the mirrors in my bedroom, so I run down to the foyer, where I can now see my entire body. I angle to the left and right, like a model on TV. I'm not sure what it accomplishes, but who am I to judge? I pop the collar on my shirt the way I've seen in Skipper's copy of "The Official Preppy Handbook."

As I turn to grab a cup of calorie-free coffee in the kitchen, I nearly run into Dad. Evidently, he's been watching me the whole time, which is weird and embarrassing. I'm startled so I probably sound more defensive than I mean to.

"What? What are you doing?"

He stammers. "I'm sorry. Sorry! You caught me off-guard."

"Me too," I say as I cross in front of him.

"Warn?"

"Yes, Dad?" No response. I repeat myself. "Yes, Dad?"

"It's just, well, I didn't realize how much weight you've lost."

Here we go again. Convincing people I wanted to lose weight. Everyone is acting like I have a telethon disease or something. "Dad, I'm fine. Fine."

"Warn, you look like a movie star."

Some people might say it's disconcerting for your father to be the first person to really notice your looks. Inappropriate even. Luckily, I'm shallower than those people, so I simply smile because I know he means it.

"Thank you, Dad."

Skipper is announcing the names at the graduation. I get to sit in as his assistant and help him figure out the pronunciation of the confusing names. We are sitting at a table on the stage left side of the University of Wisconsin Field House. Each senior passes us a slip of paper with their name on it right before they take the stage that has been set up for the ceremony. It's kind of fun because we'll get to see them all just before they graduate.

Lori Alling, the seventh student to graduate hands me her name, which I pass to Skipper, because hello. It's a pretty simple name. "Thank you," adding "Congratulations, Lori!" while we wait.

She looks at me blankly. "Do I know you?"

"Yes. It's me. Warn Barnes."

"That's not funny. Warn is a nice guy."

"Huh? Thank you, but huh?"

"Because he's a little fat, good-looking guys like you think … "

Her tirade is interrupted when Skipper announces her name. She shoots me a huffy look, before shaking off the tension, smiling and walking to get her diploma.

Variations of the theme happen 3 more times before we get to Michael

Drake. When I see him, my stomach flutters a little bit. Of course, that could be hunger, but I think it's him. The graduation gown, never a good look, falls nicely off his broad shoulders. His honor braids, red and white for medical sciences, make his smile even brighter. I see him before he sees me. At first, he looks a little confused. The new haircut. The new clothes. Then his eyes recalibrate. I can tell. He still sees me.

I snake past the beginning of the Ds and make my way to him. No hugging. No kissing. We're in public. It seems unfair, but what's a guy to do? That's the world we live in, for now. Things will change, but we don't know that yet.

I place my left hand on his shoulder. As I'm saying, "Congratulations, Michael," I shake his right hand, slipping a single rose boutonniere with a curled Carleton ribbon into his hand. Seeing that Skipper is frantically mouthing the name of a Russian kid from my Spanish class, I quickly run back to the table. By the time Michael gets to us, the flower is pinned to the left side of his chest.

Skipper announces, "Michael Drake," in a clear, confident voice. Under his breath he says, "that was easier than the Russian name." Michael looks at me and smiles before walking the stage. I can hear people cheering. I also see his mother crouching in the front row waiting to ambush him with her Kodak Instamatic.

I change into my party outfit, which is more casual. Shorts to show off my legs which are getting more toned, and a boat neck blue and white pullover I found at Ragstock on State Street.

Emily is running late for the party. No surprise. The house is humid from her shower, so I apply a little more mousse.

"Mom, I'm going to leave now. I'll see you all at the party, okay?"

She walks into the kitchen, passing me a huge Barnes Bakery box. "Gosh. Okay. Please take this cake with you." The top of the box is stapled at an angle, so the decorations don't get smashed. I peek inside. There are stethoscopes, an ambulance, a diploma, a prescription pad and a red cross. Cousin Karen came through.

I haven't eaten for twenty hours. It's all I can do not to bury my head inside and inhale every inch of the sugary temptation.

Nothing tastes as good as being thin feels.

Nothing tastes as good as being thin feels.

Okay. I'm back.

Nearly tripping over Bo, I walk out the backdoor. The cake is intact. Me and my All-American heterosexual can-do poker face are ready to celebrate the graduation of my good friend Michael.

"Oh my gosh," exclaims Mrs. Drake. "Your cousin outdid herself! Thank you so much for contributing the cake, Warn. It's a lovely graduation present! Look, it's even got teeny-tiny thermometers!"

I'm not sure Michael would have asked for a medical school cake, given this is just his high school graduation. It's kind of like putting babies on a wedding cake. It's probably going to happen, but it's a while off. I mentioned that to Mrs. Drake, but she said, "Medicine is the overall theme of the party. The cake should match. We don't want Michael to lose his focus!"

I haven't eaten for twenty-one hours, but has she always ended most of her sentences with exclamation points? I think so!

Mr. Drake walks through the screened-in porch on his way to fog the backyard with insecticides I'm sure will damage all of us on a genetic level. He gives me a friendly wave on his way. He's the strong and silent type, although I don't think of him as particularly strong. Mr. Drake is a pharmacist. "He had the smarts to be a doctor, though!" ensures Mrs. Drake. "We were just too in love to wait to settle down!"

They've been married 22 ½ years. Shelly, their oldest daughter is twenty-two. I'm not the best at math, but I'm guessing there's a story there.

Mrs. Drake's mother is already in the backyard, sitting in the swirling cloud of contraband DDT smoking a Chesterfield. Her wine glass is empty, so I grab the nearest bottle of white wine and head out to her.

"Hello, Mrs. Hermsdorf," I say, without response. She's a little hard of hearing. "HELLO, MRS. HERMSDORF!" I repeat finally getting her attention.

"HELLO, WARN!" she responds.

"WOULD YOU LIKE MORE WINE?" I offer, holding up a bottle of Chablis with a grocery store price tag.

"YES, BUT DON'T LET MY BITCH DAUGHTER SEE YOU!" says the saucy Grandma.

"YOU DON'T MEAN THAT, MRS. HERMSDORF," I diplomatically say, defending Michael's mother.

"YES, I DO!" she counters, chuckling until she coughs. After she recovers, she asks, "WHICH ONE IS GRADUATING?"

"MICHAEL," I answer.

"MICHELLE?"

"NO. MICHAEL!" I say even louder while pointing to my lips.

"OH! I LIKE THAT ONE," screams Mrs. Hermsdorf. Shelly sees me trapped and starts coming over toward me. "THAT SHELLY IS ANOTHER STORY. SHE'S GOING NOWHERE FAST."

Actually, she is, Mrs. Hermsdorf. Having overheard you, she's heading in the opposite direction.

My family shows up. When Michael greets them, I notice he's wearing the boutonniere I gave him before the ceremony. Our private little thing. I'm smiling. The backyard begins to fill up. The sizzle and smell of the grill, tempting as it's not, begins to mingle with conversation and laughter. Platters of burgers, hotdogs and bratwurst are presented. Shared bowls of potato salad, coleslaw, and baked beans are passed. Everyone starts to concentrate on their Wisconsin buffet.

It is now 24.5 hours since I've eaten.

Michael catches my eye, signaling me to meet him inside. Perfect timing. A bowl of pasta salad is two people away and heading in my direction.

Michael heads into the kitchen. I follow. He continues down the adjacent hallway before pulling me into the walk-in, very fancy linen closet. Everything smells fresh, like fabric softener. There, amongst the perfectly folded towels, is my boyfriend. He takes off my glasses and places them near his mom's stash of scented soaps before kissing me urgently.

"I've wanted to do that all day," he says pulling up his flower, so I can smell it. "Thank you for my present." We're back in our private, perfect little bubble. Just the two of us.

"I have another present for you," I say with a sly grin. I pull off my shirt before peeling off his. We lean into each other and kiss, enjoying the warmth of each other. My hands fumble through the darkness to find the button fly of his 501 jeans. I'm just starting to pull them down over his hips when the closet is flooded with light. Someone has opened the door.

It's his mom.

CHAPTER THIRTY-ONE

THROWING IN THE TOWEL

I instinctively want to cover myself. I fumble for a towel. I look down to see I've grabbed a flowery, pastel pink bath blanket with lacy edges. Remembering I'm no longer totally ashamed of how I look without a shirt, I throw it down on the ground.

I grab my shirt and hand Michael his. I notice Mrs. Drake is fixated on the crumpled towel on the floor. I honestly can't tell if she is angry about what she caught us doing or if it's because we were doing it in her linen closet.

Silence hangs in the air like her potpourri.

I will not be the first one to speak. She's too dumbfounded to form words, so Michael breaks the stalemate. "I'm sorry, Mom. I don't know—"

"I can't believe this has happened again."

I must look confused. Mrs. Drake takes note and clarifies. "You didn't think you were the first one, did you?"

"I'd never really thought ab—"

"Because you're not."

"Mom, I, uh, I don't think that's necessary," stammers Michael.

"Necessary? You're going to tell *me* what's necessary? I throw you this beautiful party, and this is how you show your gratitude? And with Warn? I never worried about him. He was so -"

She stops herself.

"What?" I ask. "I was so what? Unworthy? Fat?"

"Okay, I was trying to be kind, but yes."

Just like that, something in me changes. I used to hunch over a bit so my clothes would hang better. Not now. Shoulders back. Claiming my ground. It's not just Mrs. Drake to whom I'm speaking. I'm talking to every person who's ever tried to keep me down or feel like shit about myself.

"Well, your son feels differently."

"Aren't you even going to apologize?" she asks.

"For what?" I respond. "For loving your son?"

"Love? You think what the two of you were doing is love?"

Fuck the shame I would've felt five minutes ago. Fuck it. Fuck her.

"Yes, I do."

Damaged people have a shorthand. We see variations of ourselves in other people who've been knocked around. Bruised. Hurt. So, Mrs. Drake knows what's going to happen. Perhaps that's why she starts to back away. "Let's have this discussion with your mother. I'll go find—"

"Leave her out of this," I say without negotiation.

"Well then, your father."

"My *father*? He threw a table at me when I was in Kindergarten. What do you think he'd do here at your perfect party? By all means, invite him into this."

"I'll do whatever I want. I don't think that's your decision, Warn."

"Mrs. Drake, with all due respect, I've been making my own decisions since I was five years old. You heard me. Leave my family out of this."

"Your family?" She laughs. "We're going to talk about your family?"

"If you ever hurt any of them, I'll spend the rest of your life getting even with you."

"That's very theatrical," says Mrs. Drake, whom I suspect is using theatrical as a substitute for fag.

"Maybe it is," I offer. "Call my bluff and find out. You bring my mom into this, that sweet woman with a drunk husband and two challenged kids. That woman who has just seen her oldest son through a heart attack. The woman who lost her first husband when she was thirty years old. Bring her into this, and you'll be sorry."

"Sorry? Are you threatening me? With *what*?"

"Your biggest fear is a crumpled towel or a chipped teacup. My brother and sister face bigger things every morning before they have breakfast. Do you think your safe little world makes you *stronger* than us? Believe me; it's just the opposite. Do the smart thing for all involved." I repeat myself. "Leave my family out of this."

"Why? Because you're ashamed?"

I grab Michael's hand. "I'm not the one who's ashamed, Mrs. Drake."

"You arrogant, stupid boy."

Michael inhales. Maybe he's finally going to say something.

"Mom, enough."

"I won't be threatened in my own home. I'm going to do something about this!"

"Mom," says Michael. "I'm eighteen. Warn is underage."

She starts to understand.

"Bringing his family into this could cause a world of trouble, Mom. College. Medical school. All of that could be ruined. Just leave it be. Please."

Mrs. Drake takes a deep breath and exhales the way she imagines Jesus did. "This isn't over," she says. She smooths out her skirt while her party hostess manners reassert themselves. "My goodness, we have a houseful of guests. We should get back to the party, shouldn't we?"

She turns on her sensible one-inch heels and walks away.

Michael drops my hand and follows her.

Years from now, when I tell this story, and I will, no one will believe it took place in a closet.

When I get to the yard, Skipper heads straight my way. His gait is so quick that the Chinese lanterns I helped hang fly sway in his wake.

"Your mom is looking for you. Something is wrong."

Skipper and I both run over to Mom. She hugs me. Over her shoulder and through the Drake's fence, I spy Shirley waiting with her car running. As our embrace breaks, I see Mom has tears in her eyes. She's having a hard time speaking. Her breathing is coming in gasps.

Oh no. Mrs. Drake. What did that horrible woman do?

"Mom, what's wrong?" I ask, trying to sound braver than I actually am.

"Art had another heart attack."

THE BEGINNING
OF THE END, 1985

CHAPTER THIRTY-ONE

SEE YA REAL SOON

I force down the hatch of Sunkist, my 1980 orange Dodge Colt. The third time is the charm. It finally latches. "That's it, Mom."

We look at each other for a second. Loud silence. College graduation. A summer spent dressed as a damn clown doing dinner theater *Godspell*. Hurrying home only to leave. It's been a blur.

She smiles, as always on the verge of tears when anything regarding my move to Minneapolis is discussed. "So," she says, taking a deep breath, "we'll get up early tomorrow and send you off. Big plans tonight?"

"No."

"Why don't you see some friends? I heard Michael is in town."

"And miss my last homecooked meal? No thanks."

"Okay, then. I'll make something nice and invite everyone over."

"Great. I'm going for a run. Be back soon."

I do my stretches. For old times' sake, I start with my eyes closed. Forty-seven steps later, I'm at the mulberry bush on the corner. Angling to the left to avoid the Drake's house, I run up Johns Street, and turn right onto Dennett and circle the church before cutting over to Lake Monona via Olbrich Park.

I'm wearing very short nylon shorts. Really short. They should be called *shortests*. That does not go unnoticed by the hot guy running in the opposite direction. He turns around and begins to follow. I change my route to get a drink of water from the fountain, which, what do you know, just happens to be located near the maintenance shed by the old toboggan run. My lips are now cool and wet. I do a few more stretches which shows off my quads. Again, a total coincidence.

The other runner, whose name I will never know, uses the same bubbler and splashes a little water on his face before shaking out his ponytail. "Phew. That's better," he says, turning to smile at me.

I walk toward the shack. "It could get even better." He follows. I guide him between the two windows on the far wall so we can't be seen.

"What do you like?" he asks as he pulls my nylon shorts down over my hips.

I give him my usual answer, as his shirt joins my shorts on the floor. "Safe things. I like it safe."

Using my bandana to clean up, I give no-name a quick hug to show I'm not a total whore and resume my run. He heads east. I go west because I'm the third Pet Shop Boy.

Getting off taken care of, I can get on with all the other shit I've got to do.

Dinner tonight. Tomorrow at 8am, Skipper's new stepfather Wayne will come over with the U-Haul trailer full of our furniture, a hodgepodge of college stuff, and some very flowery Ethan Allan colonial couches with wings our roommate Donny's mom donated to us.

"I'll make slipcovers," promised Skipper.

Donny, my best friend from college, is out to conquer the world of fashion. Skipper wants to own a culinary empire. I'm pursuing acting. It's very *Three Coins in a Fountain.*

I run the lake, do another quick loop around Olbrich Park to see if there are any cute distractions. There are not, so I head home to shower and get ready for dinner.

"Uncle Warn! Uncle Warn!" squeal Kristina and Josh in unison, followed by a slow-moving Art. Ruth brings up the rear with her famous, family favorite ham she brought from Boscobel.

That means Mom made scalloped potatoes. Delicious.

Valerie independently saunters in, whacking her cane against anything in her way. She holds up a Barnes Bakery bag, proclaiming, "I brought dessert!" She then turns to Art and says, "What did I bring?"

Butch gets home from bowling just before dinner is served. Emily and Dick, her latest boyfriend, picked him up on their way here. She seems happy with him, so I'm happy for her.

Dad turns to Mom. "Dorothy, Did you call Suzy?"

"Yes, Raymond. I left a message. Never heard back."

I'm not dieting as strenuously as I used to. I have a little plate from the lazy Susan at the center of our overflowing table. A pickled crab apple. A few olives. I'm about to bite into my second celery stick when the door opens.

"Hello everyone!" says Paula, followed by her now-husband Bijon and their toddler twins, Shirene and Mitra. Kristina and Josh light up at the sight of other children. They all happily settle into their exclusive kids-only table set-up in the living room for fish sticks and Hawaiian Punch, which I pour pretending to be a French waiter named Smelly La Stinkbottom. Easiest audience of the summer.

Dinner is satisfying, but huge. I have to remind myself that it's okay. I'll eat less tomorrow. Tonight is my last night for home-cooked food, after all.

Art, who looks to have regained the weight he lost, stabs his last bite. When he's done eating. He takes a second to look over at the kids and then asks me, "Wanna stretch your legs?" Like stepfather, like son. That's his code for sneaking a cigarette.

We both stand up and head toward the side door.

"Can I come too?" asks Josh.

"No, honey," says Ruth, kissing the top of his head. "Daddy isn't going to see Uncle Warn for a while. Let's give them a little grown-up time, okay?"

Josh must have consented. He's now happily waving his hand in front of Valerie, fascinated that it doesn't register.

Art takes a couple of deep breaths before walking away from the side door. Once safely out of eyeshot, he lights up a Marlboro.

Mom calls out, "You forgot someone!" She comes toward me with Mr. Bojangles on a leash. Mr. B. happily scurries up toward Art, who always carries a treat. I found Mr. B my junior year. A ratty looking rat terrier, he was hanging out in front of the theater in Oshkosh after a rehearsal for *Tartuffe*. No one claimed him despite the dozens of flyers I thought about hanging around campus. I almost named him after a character in the play, but that seemed cliche.

Instead, I named him after a drunken tap-dancer in a folk song, figuring he'd fit in better with my family.

Bojangles sees Art's cigarette at the same time Mom does. They both scowl disapprovingly. New Bo heads to my other side. Mom heads back inside, sighing.

Given that she smokes, as do my dad, Suzy, and Ruth, Mom is being a little hypocritical. Me and my clean lungs decide not to get in the middle of it. If they try to drag me into it, I will outrun them. Easily.

"How are things going?" I ask.

"Fine," says auto-pilot Art.

"Really?" I reply.

"No," says Art breaking like a house of cards under my unrelenting cross-examination. "The station isn't happy with the sales numbers. I didn't get my bonus."

After his gig at Channel 3 ended, Art and Ruth moved to Boscobel to be nearer her family. She's working at Land's End, the preppy catalogue company. Ruth is very generous with her discount, keeping me in monogrammed messenger bags and striped oxfords I wear to auditions for business-type roles.

Art is managing a local country and western radio station, WEKZ, which is in a small building near the transmitter on the outskirts of town.

During college, when Art was short-staffed, I'd drive over to fill in. My DJ name was Cowboy Eddie. I'd get in trouble for playing too much Patsy Cline and Tammy Wynette. Sometimes I'd play Wham to piss off the farmers. Let's just say I wasn't a good fit.

Each summer, when I wasn't doing shows, Art would take me to all the Wisconsin and Iowa County Fair country concerts. We've seen a bunch of acts like Porter Wagoner, Conway Twitty, and Reba McEntire. Once I made out with Loretta Lynn's grandson in a van.

At least he *said* he was her grandson.

"Without the bonus, things are kind of tight," Art says with a worried look.

"Listen, we ended up finding a cheaper apartment, so I've got a little extra money." I grab my wallet. "Here's a hundred bucks. Maybe that'll help."

"Oh wow. Thank you."

We walk in silence for a while.

"How about you?" Art asks.

"You know me; it's a good day if no one throws a table at me."

"I was very proud of you. Watching you graduate with a 4.0," says big brother.

"In my major," I remind him. "I never would've made it without you."

He smiles. "The world can thank me for another unemployed actor."

"Yeah, right? Now I've got to figure out how to make something happen."

My brother, the father, gets paternal. "You always do your best."

I take another long shower when I get home from the New Bar, Madison, Wisconsin's, best ever gay bar. It will be my favorite until it gets burned down by some homophobic asshole in the 90s.

I'm surprised to see Butch still awake when I enter what used to be our room.

"Did you have fun tonight?" I ask.

"Don't bother me, Warn. I got to get up early tomorrow."

Butch works at the huge state office building downtown. He delivers mail. They love him there, and he loves them. Try to get him to take a day off. He won't. He makes decent money too. More than I made working at Chess King in the mall during college.

"Sorry. I'll be quiet."

I hear him sniffle a bit but decide not to say anything. It gets a little louder, and I notice his shoulders are shaking a little bit. "Butch, are you okay?"

"I'm just crying," he answers.

"Why?"

"Because you're leaving."

"I'll come home. Minneapolis isn't that far away," I say, hoping to help.

"That's not what I meant."

"Then why? Why are you crying?"

"I'm crying because that won't happen for me."

The air inside the room we've shared almost our entire lives gets heavy and sad. Once again, I'm left wondering why God did this to my perfect little brother.

"I love you, Butch," is all I can think to say.

"I know."

Morning is a blur of busy-ness. I pack the rest of my clothes and toiletries. God has a plan. My parents both slip me fifty bucks each, which makes up for the hundred I gave Art. Skipper and entourage knock on the door at 8 am sharp.

"Good morning, Skipper," says Mom.

"Good morning, Dorothy." Craning his head, he adds, "you too Mr. Barnes."

Skipper carries a clipboard, thick with papers. Around his neck there is a gold chain with a small pen attached to it. I can't tell if the shirtless bib overalls he's wearing are meant to be practical or fashionable. They're oversized. The cuffs are rolled up to show his calves. He's wearing a slight heel, which ensures the muscles are flexed. It's very Dexy's Midnight Runners.

I hand him a box. "Come on, Eileen, let's finish packing."

Skipper's stepfather and our roommate Donny are outside waiting for us. Skipper consults his notes. "So, Wayne, you're taking the trailer with your truck." Mom shoots Dad a look. She's pissed he didn't offer to do the same. "Donny and I will ride in my car," a two-tone green Impala he inherited from his grandma. We call her Double Mint. "Warn, you and the dog hair," he shoots a look at Mr. Bojangles, "will ride in your car." Skipper then consults the watch brooch he has pinned to his overall straps. "It's 8:15. We don't have to be on the road until," pages flipping, "8:45." He breaks out in his first smile of the day. "Dorothy, I believe we have time for a cup of your delicious coffee!"

Today is the end of my life in Madison. Everything is about to change. I take a second to look around the kitchen. Mom's red and white checkered café curtains, the message pad on the table, Grandma Caruso's African violets keeping watch under the window, everything about it is precious.

Then I spy the little chip in the table.

The caravan pulls away, leaving Bojangles and me alone with Mom and Dad. We all watch longer than we should to avoid what has to happen next. Finally, I turn around to face them, hoping the right words will come.

"Well," I say with all the eloquence of a recent college grad.

Mom says, "Yes."

Dad says, "You've got a schedule to keep. Skipper runs a tight ship."

We walk toward my car, which is parked on the street between our house and the Nabors. Bojangles, always ready for an adventure, happily jumps in the passenger's side. I shut his door and walk toward my parents. We're standing underneath the tree the first Warren planted. The one I fell out of 16 years ago this month on Valerie's birthday.

Dad reaches for his wallet. "Did I give you any money?"

"You did. Thank you."

"Here's some more," he says, passing me a twenty, some ones, and a few quarters.

"Everything is going to be great. Just great," says Mom.

"Thank you. Thank you for everything."

"Do you mean that?" asks my dad.

I manage to catch his averted eyes. "Of course, I do. Thank you."

Dad starts to say something but stops himself. Instead, he smiles.

Mom and I stare at each other for a minute.

"We love you. So much."

"I love you too," I say, hugging them both at the same time.

They move to what I think of as Grandma's front steps and sit down to watch me get in the car. I take a deep breath before putting my key in the ignition. I look up. They've got their arms around each other, waving back with their free hands. I turn the key. The engine just makes a horrible whirring sound, refusing to start. I laugh and cry simultaneously, which makes me laugh harder. I take another deep breath and turn the key. The engine starts.

I wave before pulling away.

They get smaller and smaller in my rearview mirror until I can no longer see them or my little gray home that's actually white.

CHAPTER THIRTY-TWO

I'M GONNA MAKE IT AFTER ALL

The drive from Madison to Minneapolis is about 4.5 hours without traffic. Unfortunately, it's August in Wisconsin, which means road construction. Skipper told me via the walkie-talkies he'll return to K-Mart after we're done with them, that he has decided we had best stop for lunch in Millston, Wisconsin.

Through the static, I can make out, "Grandma Smrekar's. I repeat Grandma Smrekar's!" the name of a *legendary* roadside restaurant with the best pie in the Midwest.

Skipper has a t-shirt from the restaurant. He also has the cookbook, a magnet, and a rolling pin they sent after he wrote them a fan letter. His fanboy crush on Grandma Smrekar borders on obsession. He even went as her for Halloween at the New Bar last year, and believe me, everyone wanted his pie.

"I'll have the pot roast please," I say to a waitress so old she's writing with a quill.

"That'll take forever, and we've got to get back on the road," says Skipper, the time management expert.

"Okay," I say in a deadpan voice. "I'll have the house salad with grilled chicken," turning to shoot Skipper a look. "If that doesn't take too long." My eyes return to the pile of dust taking my order. "House dressing unless it's creamy."

"It's Italian," says Lincoln's babysitter.

"That's fine. Thank you."

"I'll have the same," echoes Donny.

"I'd like cherry pie ala mode and a slice of pecan pie."

"Which one should I wrap up?" asks the woman who went to prom with Methuselah.

"Neither. I'll have them together," answers Skipper in a voice that managed to be both confused and patronizing at the same time.

"The chicken fried steak platter please," says Skipper's stepdad.

Skipper glares at his stepdad. "That'll take forever!"

Wayne looks at Skipper with wide eyes and says, "Oh!" before returning his attention to our very patient server. "In that case, I'll have the chicken fried steak platter."

Lunch is delicious but rushed, of course. "If we finish now, we can beat rush hour," says Skipper, who is taking his name a little too literally at the moment.

"Relax, Steve. Enjoy the meal," says Wayne.

We rise, pay the bill, and head to the parking lot.

"Okay, Warn," says Skipper. "You have 5-minutes to walk Bojangles." Handing me a little to-go container, he adds, "here's the leftover chicken from the salads for his lunch. We'll see you at the apartment."

Bojangles and I do a couple of laps around the parking lot, pushing our 5-minute break to 10. We're almost back to Sunkist when a good-looking trucker leaning against his cab says, "Cute dog."

"10-4 good buddy."

He opens the door to his cab.

Looks like I'm going to be at least 30-minutes late.

I end up being an hour late, but I'm smiling all the way.

I park my car in front of our stately new digs at the Windsor Apartments at 3rd & Franklin. The building is an old hotel from the 1800s that has been transformed into really cool apartments in an almost ready to gentrify neighborhood.

Bo and I are almost to the front door as we pass Skipper heading to the U-Haul. He shoots me a disapproving look and says, "I hope it was worth it."

"Oh, but it was."

Jangles and I walk into the apartment. High ceilings. Polished wood floors. Built-in cabinets. A wall of windows looking out onto an alley. A small dining room leads to a smaller kitchen. An industrial-like bathroom with commercial fittings. A huge bedroom for Skipper and Donny. My bedroom is smaller. That's fine. All I need is my bed, a nightstand and a phone. The built-in dresser can hold my stereo, my albums, and my ever-growing collection of colognes. As Sally Bowles says in I Am a Camera, excess furniture makes seduction more difficult.

I feel lips on the back of my neck. "Mmmm. You taste salty," whispers a voice I suspect to be Andy, the boy I've been seeing when I'm in Minneapolis.

I slowly spin around to meet his lips. "Moving day," I say. "A man is going to sweat." We kiss again, but Wayne is still here. Better not to start anything we can't finish. Delayed gratification. Besides, a post-trucker shower is just good manners.

We walk into the living room. Everything is perfectly organized and well on its way to being put away. Skipper walks in with a flatbed dolly holding everything that had been in my Dodge Colt.

"This isn't a great neighborhood," says my best friend. "Start locking your car." I move toward the door to do so. "Don't bother. I already did it."

"Where's Donny?" I ask.

"He went out to get us some Chinese food," says Skipper. "I didn't order any for you because Andy, your *boyfriend*, said he's taking you to dinner."

Sister Skipper can be so self-righteous. Everyone knows it's only cheating if you're in the same state. Anything that happens outside the borders of Minnesota doesn't count. In fact, given that it's across the Mississippi River, even St. Paul is a safe zone.

Skipper gets up early the next day. I hear him rattling around the apartment, so I untangle myself from Bojangles and Andy, my Minneapolis boyfriend. My uptown Minneapolis boyfriend. I'm not sure. I'm still working out the logistics.

I join Skipper on the as-promised, slipcovered couch.

Today is Skipper's first day as a food stylist for a media company that shoots all kinds of stuff, including Target and Dayton-Hudson's print ads. "Are you excited?" I ask. He beams. The first step on the way to making his dream of a cooking show a reality.

"So excited! Here," he says, passing me a beautiful mini-pastry with a little demitasse of what I will soon learn is called espresso. "It's a hazelnut torte. I'm bringing savory to breakfast!" I take a tentative but optimistic bite. Delicious.

"What are you going to do today?" asks Skipper. "Hang out near the Mississippi River and pick up sailors?"

"Yeah, but that only takes 25 minutes," I respond. "After the sailors I'm going to pick up my resumes and new headshots. I found 2 auditions in the paper I want to go on."

Skipper notices I have the contact sheets. "Which pictures did you choose?"

I point out the one I had printed.

"Really?" he says smiling. "That's my favorite!"

Skipper crosses to the wall of windows in our apartment and throws open the blinds. "We are going to conquer you Minneapolis. The Twin Cities shall be ours!"

"You're screaming into an alley full of trashcans."

"Yes. The receptacles for all the broken dreams of people we'll step over on our way to the top."

"Top? That rules you out," I joke.

Okay, it's not a joke. It's the truth, but I didn't want to be tacky.

From the bedroom, we hear Donny. "Will you two shut up? I don't have to be up for another hour!"

My first audition is in a church basement.

"Hello," I say to the woman behind the reception desk, which in truth is an old dining room table. "I'm here to audition for the Minnesota Shakespeare Players."

"Yes," says a booming, theatrical contralto proctoring auditions until they need a Lady Macbeth. "You're at the right location. The Globe Theatre of South Minneapolis," she says, chuckling at her own theatre joke, which I would normally spell theater. There's no doubt that this woman spells it theatre. "Have you an appointment?"

"I do. Warn Barnes. I'm a little early."

"We can see you now."

"Really?"

"Yes. We've had quite a few no-shows."

I'm escorted into the social room of the church.

"Hello," offers a bald voice at the far end of the table. "My name is Scot, with 1 t, if you please. Last name Bellwether. You are," he consults the audition list. "Michelle Hutchison."

Lady Macbeth corrects him. "No, Scot. This is Warren Barnes."

Handing him my resume and headshot, I point out the usual mistake. "Warn."

"Yes, well, we'll commit that to memory if you get cast," says Scot the as(s)hole.

My monologues go reasonably well. They have me read several parts, including Voltemand and Osric.

"Thank you very much, Mr. Hutchison," says Scot Bellwether. "Is there anything else you'd like to read?"

"Barnes."

"Pardon? There is no such character in the Bard's *Hamlet*."

"I know. I was just reminding you of my last name."

"Yes. Barnes." He consults my resume. "I see you're from Wisconsin. That shall help me remember," he says facetiously.

"Where are you from?"

"Iowa," he responds with no sense of irony.

"I see. Well, yes, actually. I was hoping to read for the Gravedigger."

"It's your funeral," says the Queen of Des Moines.

I get all the laughs the scene offers, much to the shock of Mr. Bellwether.

Barnes tip for young actors, #1—try for the comic relief characters in dramas. You're the other. The change in tone. Therefore instantly memorable.

Barnes tip for young actors, #2—don't fall under the spell of Shakespeare. It's been done consistently for over five hundred years. Everything old is old again and buried under centuries of dust. It's the McDonald's of theater. Billions served.

I wouldn't have come to this audition, but they're doing *Hamlet* in repertory with *Rosencrantz and Guildenstern Are Dead* by Tom Stoppard. That's the exciting show.

I walk to my next appointment. It's a couple of miles, but it's a nice day. I appreciate the chance to explore a bit and get some exercise before I join a gym. I stop at a place called Capers for lunch. My waiter is cute. He slips me his number with the check. Best of all, he lives out of the six-block radius I've established as Andy's territory.

I make it to my appointment at 26th Street and Hennepin in plenty of time. Stopping at Super America for a Diet Pepsi to cool down, I wait across the street on a bus bench staring at Dudley Riggs' Brave New Workshop, America's first improv theater.

When it's time, I cross the street and open an old wooden and glass door. Turning left out of the alcove into the lobby is like a portal to a different world. You can feel the laughter and joy these walls have held.

"May I help you?" asks a woman with a warm, sexy voice. Her name is Denise, according to her nametag.

"I'm here to interview for the improv classes."

"Have a seat," she says. "Someone will be with you soon."

At the far end of the lobby, there is a huge window parallel to the street. The light at the end of a tunnel. The box office is to the left. On the other side, there is a small café, with beer and wine, candy, popcorn, and what looks to be an ancient hot pretzel machine. Someone forgot to turn it off last night, so it spins around, waiting for an audience.

Opposite my chair is a wall of company photos. Two companies, actually. One resident. One touring. 2 musicians. 2 tech directors. One artistic director. The photos by a woman named Connie Jerome all are set in ironic or iconic Minnesota landmarks. Hubert Humphrey's grave. The Electric Fetus record store. Someone is posing in front of First Avenue, the club where Prince was discovered; where someday I'll see the Bangles, k.d. lang, the Talking Heads, Joe Jackson, and more.

When I get into the company, and I shall, my photo will be taken in the Mary Tyler Moore intersection, throwing a knit hat in the air. Skipper will be dressed up as the old lady giving attitude.

A very fit man, about ten years older than me, dressed in a University of Minnesota sweatshirt, walks into the room. "Are you Warn Barnes?" he asks warmly.

I stand up and hand him my resume and headshot. "I am."

"Hi," he says, offering his hand. "I'm Jim."

Without knowing it, I've just met someone I'll be friends with for the rest of my life. We will perform together. He will direct me. We will cycle together all over the country. I will watch his daughter grow into a lovely young woman. He will become a new big brother.

"Why do you want to learn to improvise?"

"I saw the Workshop in Madison when I was 16. The show was amazing. It's why I moved to Minneapolis. To study here," I answer, hating how vulnerable I sound. Aspirational rather than realized.

We begin to talk about comedy. I stop thinking about what I'm supposed to say, only what I want to say. The interview breezes by. If I enjoy the classes as much as the interview, getting in will be life changing.

Walking home takes about 45 minutes. When I arrive, I'm a sweaty mess, but Bojangles is waiting at the door with a wagging tail and anxious eyes.

"Come on, good boy. Let's go for a walk!"

We head toward Morrison Park, which guards the entrance to the Minneapolis Institute of Art. Jangles looks at me to see if I'll let him go off leash. I'm not ready to trust him yet. Too unfamiliar an area. Too much traffic. Instead, we walk around the park twice, or about a mile, before heading home.

I peel off my clothing and head to the shower. When I'm done, my clothes are gone, which means they have been folded and placed in my bedroom. Skipper is home. I sprint to my room to throw on a pair of shorts and a tank top before heading to the living room.

"How was your day?"

Skipper's face lights up. "Everything I was hoping for." His smile gets even bigger. "The test kitchen is state of the art. As you know, the last time I did a mental inventory, there were 102 different spices in the world. They have 101, and they're getting a delivery of Amchur tomorrow!"

Skipper finishes the story of his first day before pausing. There's something else. I can tell. He's practically bursting.

"I have a little news for you too."

"Really. What?"

"The Shakespeare Players called. They're offering you the role of the Gravedigger in *Hamlet* and the Player King in the play by what's his name? Tom Stoppit."

"Stoppard."

"Whatever."

"And then the improve place…"

"Improv. It's called improv," I correct.

"Okay, again. Whatever."

"What did they want?"

Skipper squeals a bit. "You got into the classes!"

I have just been handed a pedestal from which to fall. For the rest of my career, the fact that I booked the first two things I auditioned for in Minneapolis will screw with my head. I'll go into each audition with a false sense of security.

Skipper's voice raises an octave as he starts to sing, "But there's more…"

He looks me in the eye, gets up, and heads to the kitchen. I follow, momentarily distracted by the pot rack I didn't know we had hanging from the ceiling. Skipper hands me fresh lemonade.

"I found you a job!"

"Really?"

"Yes. We're going to work together!"

I sip while Skipper continues.

"I just happened to put your contact sheets into my bag this morning, and then I just happened to be looking at them when the director of photography just happened to be passing by. She loves your look!"

"What does that mean?"
"You're Mr. Skyway."

What's a Mr. Skyway?

CHAPTER THIRTY-THREE

I DID IT SKYWAY

It's like the first day of school around here. Skipper laid out my clothes. I'm wearing gray jazz shoes, gray Willi Wear pants, a crisp, oversized white linen shirt, and an expensive Perry Ellis jacket, which Skipper swears we can return to Dayton's immediately after I meet the Mr. Skyway crew.

We take the bus up Nicollet Avenue before getting out near the Amfac Hotel. From there, we walk over to Hennepin. Skipper's office, our office, I guess, is on something called Block E. Walking past a bar called *Moby Dick's* with a sign promising, "A whale of a drink." We head to a door on the far side of the building. Skipper has to hip-check it to force it open. I would have done it, but it's filthy and this outfit goes back tomorrow. Two flights of stairs later, we are in front of a door marked "Twin Cities Media."

Everything is dark, dank, and dusty. Creaky stairs. Cobwebs and little piles of dirt fill in the corners. It's not much of a first impression.

Skipper opens an industrial, riveted, metal door, and the hallway fills with light. Past the door jamb is a white loft with high ceilings and sleek modern furniture. Behind a hive of people staring at a storyboard, a man wearing only a pair of very brief briefs briefly passes by. His dark skin underneath white mesh is a lovely distraction.

"Skip, what kind of photography do they do here?" I ask.

"That's Scottie. He's a model for a catalog called International Male. Huge client from what I hear." Under his breath, he adds, "Best of all, we get to take home the samples! I'm wearing something called a Bulge Thong right now!"

I'm so busy staring at Scottie that I plow into someone carrying a pile of clothing, all of which fall to the floor. We both squat down to pick them up as I mutter variations on an apology.

I'm face to face with a beautifully stylish man, which is different than being beautiful. Without his style, you might not notice him. The hair, the glasses, the jewelry, the clothing, the cologne, the arrogance, it makes him impossible *not* to notice.

"This is the new Mr. Skyway?" he says, looking me up and down. "I'm Jerome, the lead stylist."

I give him a big smile and some eye sparkle to buy a moment to take in all that is him. Facially he kind of looks like an African-American version of Ernie on *My Three Sons*. His almond-shaped eyes are huge. They are framed by horn-rimmed glasses, which I normally hate, hence my contact lenses. On him, the glasses work. It's almost as though he's so busy being fabulous that he couldn't be bothered to think about his eyeglasses, which he pushes down his nose to assess me critically.

His hands, a little small, carry long nails. I'm sure he does that to extend the line of his arm. He wears many silver rings, some of which hold polished turquoise stones. Working down his wrists, on the right side, there are many silver bracelets. On the left side, there is a very masculine, expensive-looking watch I have on my wrist right now. It's a Rolex, one of my prized possessions.

His long hair, a Chaka Khan wild mane, is held in place with a silver and turquoise hair clip. His clothing is simple but expensive. His oxford is made of heavy white cotton and open at the collar on which he wears a loosely knotted polka dot tie. The deepest color in the tie's design matches his oversized pleated pants perfectly. Cowboy boots with more turquoise trim and a two-inch heel completes the ensemble.

"Nice to meet you. I'm Mr. Skyway."

"What's your real name?"

"You may call me Mr. Skyway." He looks shocked. I start laughing before saying, "My name is Warn. Warn Barnes. May I ask a question?"

"Of course," he says with a smirk as he begins refolding clothes. "We are all here to serve Mr. Skyway."

"What is Mr. Skyway?"

"Oh, that's right. You just moved here. Fresh-faced freshness. So," he pauses to ponder, "Mr. Skyway promotes the businesses and events in the Skyways." Awkward silence. Jerome continues. "Skyways are the enclosures that connect buildings throughout downtown Minneapolis. To monetize them, there are a variety of retail shops between department stores and offices."

"Oh, they're the things that Mary Tyler Moore walks through during the opening credits!" I say after finally getting it.

"No," says Jerome, the stylist. "*Ordinary People* is set in Illinois. Not Minnesota."

"I was referring to her TV show."

"Oh, did Mary Tyler Moore have a TV show?" says Jerome.

I can't even. How is that possible?

He continues. "Anyway, we have shoots later this week. We need to start building your wardrobe from the Dayton's, Donaldson's, and the retailers in the skyways." He hands me the bundle of the now refolded clothes that fell on the floor. "Try these on," he says, moving me toward what appears to be a dressing room.

"Sure. I'll let you know what I like," I say.

"That won't affect what's chosen, but okay."

"We'll see," I say before opening the door to my dressing room. Only after the door is shut and I've begun to unbutton my shirt do I realized it's a shared dressing room.

"Oh, hello. You're Scottie, right?"

The wardrobe tests go well. I defer to Jerome and make a mental note of which clothes to keep if they're offered. "Let's break for lunch," says Jerome, pulling out a baggie of carrots and almonds. "We'll do shoes this afternoon."

"Shoes will take all afternoon?" I say incredulously.

"No," he says.

"Yeah. I thought so," I respond.

"It will take tomorrow morning, too," he says with an arched eyebrow.

Skipper, who has been helping out, says, "I'm going to check on the spice shipment and make sure the duck confit is ready for the afternoon shoot. Wait here. We'll go to Eddington's for soup. You'll love. Be right back!"

"Jerome, may I make a long-distance call? I can charge it back to my home number if it's a problem."

"Listen up, Mr. Skyway, we can call anywhere for free. Just dial an 8 instead of a 9 to get a long-distance line." He starts to walk away, muttering to himself. "He thinks we've got to pay for calls. Is he Amish or something?"

I dial Mom, but it's busy. I wish they'd get call waiting. What is it, like a buck a month? So annoying. Okay. I'll call and leave a message for Art. At least he has a machine.

I punch in the numbers and prepare to leave a brisk message so as not to take advantage of this free long-distance perk. To my shock he answers on the 4th ring.

"Hello?"

"You're home?"

"Is this Warn?" says Art, in a loud voice as though he has to push his volume all the way to Minneapolis himself.

"Yeah. It is! What are you doing home; it's the middle of the workday?"

"Are you getting settled?"

I run him through an abbreviated update. The whirlwind of the last few days. He asks about Andy. It takes me a second to realize who he is asking about. That might be a sign. Just as I'm about to ask him again what he's doing home in the middle of the day, Skipper walks up, pointing to his watch and mouthing, "Soup. Come on!"

"Art, I've got to run. Skipper's blood sugar is crashing, or he's just being Skipper. We've got to get lunch before the wicked witch sends out the guard to hunt us down."

"Huh?"

"It involves shoes."

"What?"

"I'll call this weekend to explain. Got to run. Bye!"

Click.

Why was a bowl of soup more important than talking with my brother?

"Okay, we're done with half the shoes," says Jerome as he checks his Rolex. "We'll pick it up again tomorrow. Got a man to get home to!" He starts to walk away before his manners get the best of him. He turns around to add, "goodnight. Thanks for a productive day."

Skipper walks up with a plate of duck, watching Jerome exit. "Sad story," he says before handing me a plastic fork.

"What?"

"Jerome and his man. Everyone in the test kitchen says his boyfriend has a heroin problem. Screws around for drugs and money."

"He seems too smart to put up with that," I say.

"People probably say the same thing about your mom," Skipper reminds me. He wisely plows through. "Come on. I told Donny we'd meet him at the 90s for dinner. Let's go have some fun!"

The Gay 90s. The exterior is old and decrepit, like many of its patrons. Inside it's a gay Disneyland. We walk into a tavern that usually has go-go boys slinging their strings on the bar. To the right, there is a dance club with a separate cover charge called the Annex. Very *Saturday Night Fever*, which is kind of sad since that was nearly ten years ago. Upstairs there is a piano lounge featuring Mr. Jimmy Martin and fabulous Lori

Dokken, Twin Cities icons. There's also a drag cabaret. To the left of the entrance, there is a supper club, straight out of the 1950s. For $6.95, you get a relish tray, a glass of wine, house salad, grilled chicken breast with teriyaki pineapple, a baked potato with the butter or sour cream and a choice of three desserts.

If you're under forty and don't get free drinks sent to you, hang it up and start dating women. The place is packed with gentlemen of a certain age, ready to be generous, especially at the beginning of the month when they've got Social Security money burning a hole in the pocket of their elastic waist pants.

Skipper gets us a table in the middle of the action. Donny arrives which does not go unnoticed by the AARP crowd. Tall. Blonde. Good build. Donny usually causes a stir, but he's a sweet guy. I'm not sure he even realizes it.

"What a miserable day," he says as he sits down with a harumph.

Skipper passes him a complimentary tomato juice. "Tell Aunt Skipper everything."

"I applied for a job at Dayton's. They told me I didn't have enough experience."

"What did you apply for?" I innocently ask.

"PR assistant."

"Well, they're right," Skipper says. "You don't have any experience."

"Uh," says Donny mid eyeroll. "According to my resume, I do." Deep breath. "I'm so screwed, you guys. I didn't want to say anything, but I've got to get a job right away to make rent."

"We'll figure something out," I optimistically offer.

Just then, a 90s employee stops at our table. "I'm sorry. I couldn't help overhearing."

"Oh really?" says Skipper. "How's that?"

"It's a gay bar. There's no privacy here. Get over it, lady." Turning his attention to Donny he adds, "You need a job, right?"

"Yeah…" admits Donny haltingly.

"Finish your dinner and then find me at the bar," says the intruder.

Donny inhales his teriyaki pineapple chicken breast and leaves. Skipper and I leisurely enjoy the three drinks each we've been sent. I have two bites of an industrial slice of dry carrot cake. Skipper has the ice cream with a chocolate sauce drizzle, saying, "How did they ruin ice cream?"

When we try to pay the bill, we find it has been taken care of, compliments of the house. We leave a great tip before rising to leave. "Let's go see if we can find Donny," says Skipper.

We tour all the clubs without luck. Having decided to have a nightcap, we head to the front bar. I order a Miller Light, which is tonight's special. Skipper peruses the specialty cocktail menu. "I'll have a Frozen Dick please," he says.

"What's that?" I ask.

"I don't know, but it sounds delicious!"

As our drinks are served, a cheesy fanfare plays over the sound system.

Skipper, who is kind of a lightweight and already drunk, gets excited. "Oh boy, oh boys! It's time for the go-go dancers!" He pulls out his wallet, carefully facing and ironing out the one-dollar bills with which he intends to tip.

I hear someone ask, "Is there room for another?" I pivot on my barstool to say no when I notice it's Jerome.

Skipper lights up and semi-slurs, "Oh my gosh! You're here!" He stands up unsteadily and hugs Jerome, forcing him toward me. Despite it being dark in the bar, I can see his eyes are bloodshot. He's been crying.

I throw a ten-dollar bill on the table. "Drinks are on me, fellas!"

Jerome smiles. "Thanks, Skyway!"

I turn to get the bartender's attention. When I look up, my face is nearly buried into the ample crotch of a newly arrived dancing boy. I look farther up to apologize when I see that it's Donny.

He already has quite a bit of money in his, I'm assuming borrowed G-string. It looks like rent will be on time.

CHAPTER THIRTY-FOUR

BEGIN THE ROUTINE

"Can we get together Friday night?" Andy asks on the phone.

"Booked. Boys' night out. Skipper says it's mandatory."

"Tonight?" he offers.

"I'm working at the Riggs café."

"Sunday?"

"Improv class."

"I meant Sunday night," he counters.

"No," I say, trying to sound disappointed. "I have dance class."

"Dance class?" he says with a bit of attitude.

"I got cut during the dance audition at Chanhassen last week. That's not happening again." No need to mention that I usually go home with Grant the instructor.

"And you're working all day," says Andy.

"And rehearsing at night," I add.

"Okay then. Got it."

As I hang up the phone, I suspect that Andy and I just crossed the finish line. He's a sweet guy, but not my guy. He deserves a happy ending.

God knows I've had my share.

Sunkist is acting up. I don't have the money to fix her. Skipper and I get up early to push the car to a new parking spot each morning because Minneapolis has stupid ass alternate side of the street parking rules. Sometimes Mary Jo and Lorna, the lesbians across the hall help. I don't mean this to stereotype, but they're much stronger than we are.

Broken car means bus. I meet my friend Mo at the bus stop to get to improv class.

Walking toward her, I can't help but marvel at her beauty. Long, flowing, honey-colored hair, the fit of her clothes hinting at a killer body, but not obviously. Somehow, she makes it seem effortless. To top it off, she's funny. That's a rare combination.

"Coffee," she says, handing me a steaming cardboard cup so hot that I can feel the warmth through my gloves. Mo always brings the coffee. Her roommate Judith is something called a barista at Uncommon Grounds.

"Here's your muffin," I say, handing her a Skipper baked good.

Generous roommates keep us caffeinated and fed. In some kind of sick service trade competition, they can't stand each other.

"Anyone can make coffee, Warn," says Skipper. "It's glorified mixing. The bean does all the work, not Judith."

After class everyone goes across the street, to day drink at the Green Mill, home of cheap liquor and cheaper appetizers.

Today it is me, Mo, Tom, box-office Denise, Mary, Michelle, and Melissa.

Our server comes over to take orders. I want chicken wings, but have salad, "And a Virgin bloody Mary please," because I'm taking dance class after this.

I get everyone's attention by standing.

"There's something I want to tell you all."

Silence. Deep breath. Smile. Continue

"I wanted you all to know I'm gay. I figured it should just be said, so people didn't feel like I was hiding anything, or you know, embarrassed or ashamed."

Tom, former marine, prototypical straight guy, is the first to say something. "Wait, Barnes. Wait. Are you telling me you're into guys? There are going to be a lot of disappointed ladies in Minneapolis."

"St. Paul too," adds Mo. "Wait. Is *Skipper* gay too? There go my hopes of having children."

Denise stands up. "As long as we're making confessions, I guess I should tell you I hooked up with Tom a few weeks ago."

"Oh, you poor girl. First Warn's news. Now this!" says Mary.

Michelle Hutchison, the "one T" Scot confused me for at my Shakespeare audition, stands up. She's in *Hamlet* and *Rosencrantz and Guildenstern Are Dead*, and my improv class. "My turn. This is hard." Pause for effect. "I'm a member of the Minnesota Shakespeare Players." After her announcement, she drains her drink and motions our server for two more.

Melissa goes last. "I think we have to applaud Warn's bravery at telling us something we already knew. I too, have a confession. I'm right-handed."

Tom stands up and begins applauding. "Melissa, for the win!"

What a bunch of assholes. I love them.

Tonight is *Rosencrantz* rehearsal, which is better than getting dust-born allergies from our tired production of *Hamlet*.

"Want to go out for a drink at Oliver's after rehearsal?' Michelle asks. Sweetening the deal, she adds, "They give a discount for theater people!"

"No. I've got a shoot tomorrow."

"What's Mr. Skyway doing now?"

"Having lunch at the Dayton's."

"You're eating at a department store?" she says, implying I'm sneaking BBQ into the lady's lingerie department. "And they're filming it?"

"Top floor restaurant. Sky Room. 8 am," I say in my most put-upon voice. "My roommate arranged it." Donny who scored the Dayton's job by way of being a go-go boy at the 90s. The third night he danced there, he met the Vice-President of Dayton-Hudson PR. Donny got the job by promising to never mention how they met. "Dayton's always does Sky Room photo shoots before the store opens."

"Why not after?"

"Donny says because the early bird gets the Chanel."

The phone on my nightstand rings. I roll over and grab my totally cool red, retro, dial desktop phone which looks like the Bat-line on *Batman*. "Hello?"

"Hi. It's Jerome."

"Business or pleasure?"

"They're the same thing. Shut up and listen. Meet me at the Hair Police in the Skyway 23B, off the IDS Corridor before the 8 am shoot at 6:30 tomorrow morning."

"Okay, but only if you quit talking like an evil robot. Why so early?"

"It's a surprise."

Yawning. Carrying the largest coffee I could find. Slightly annoyed to be up so early, I squat under the semi-opened gate to enter the Hair Police. Why they feel the need to have the flashing red lights on before sunrise on a bleak November morning is beyond me. Tossing my free Mr. Skyway leather jacket on the waiting room couch, I walk down a short hallway to find a hive of activity, with Queen Jerome at the center of the buzzing.

"Boys, get the lights focused on station three. I repeat station three!"

"Hello."

Jerome continues. "And put a gel on it. The lighting can't be harsh. Mr. Skyway ain't in his teens anymore."

"Hello?" I repeat, now slightly offended.

"Oh! You're here." Jerome checks his watch. Adding "And you're only 5-minutes late," with an almost subtle and impossible to detect passive-aggression.

"Why am I here?"

Jerome puts his arm around me.

"How do I say this? From the neck down, you're totally on point. Skyway, all the way. From the neck up, it's still Wisconsin. We need to get a little more Minneapolis up in there. A better cut," says the man in a man-bun back when man-buns were just buns.

"Okay. That's fine."

"I'm thinking Merchant-Ivory. Edwardian. A slight wedge on the sides, with a dramatic cascading bang."

"Ooh. I like that!"

"Now about the color..."

"I hate it. Hate it!" says Scottt. "Why would you color your hair during a show?"

"Well, technically, it's not my hair."

"Pardon?" says my bald director.

"I'm Mr. Skyway. I signed a contract relinquishing control of..."

"So, the gravedigger in *Hamlet* bows to the Skyway instead of the grave?"

Does this man listen to himself?

"I shall perpend on this. Please give me a moment."

"Perpend?"

"The Bard's word. To think. Ponder. Use one's wits. Try it."

"By all means, perpend away."

"Wait. Why should I bear this burden to my own bosom?"

Oh my God. He's from *Iowa*.

"What do you propose we do?" says he of the missing T.

"I don't know. A hat?"

"A hat indeed! A character of your status would wear a biggin."

"I don't care about the size..."

"No, you merry dolt. A biggin is a skullcap worn under the hats of the elite. Worn, Warn, in an aspirational manner by one of your station."

"My station or the gravedigger's?"

"Is there a difference?"

Friday night arrives. Me and my boys head to the Sweat Shop for aerobics. I wear ACA Joe fleece shorts slit up the side, a faded Planet Binger sweatshirt, and leg warmers from the store Sox Appeal in the Skyway. I've piled my cherry coke reddish-brown hair into a Rosie the Riveter bandana.

The minute Jerome saw me, he said, "That's quite a look," so yeah. It's working. Skipper, however, has got to stop raiding the sample room. He's wearing some sort of fetish wear latex thing from the International Male Catalogue inventory. Donny is wearing a wrestling singlet from high school. Jerome is dressed all in black with a red cap and matching sneakers. We are, as Jerome is known to say, styling.

Good calves require effort. I pay the extra dollar for ankle weights. We take our spots in the front row so we can see the instructor's ass. While waiting, I watch the foot traffic going past the huge window overlooking Loring Park as the sun sets.

The routine starts with "We Are Family" by Sister Sledge, an old tune, but it works, and it's true. Except for Emily, Suzy, and Val, I've got all my sisters with me.

The bass from the sound system is really powerful. The glass windows pulsate with the beat. I used to be intimidated by this class, but I'm slowly getting the hang. Once I walked into the plate glass wall dividing the studio and the lobby. Everyone noticed when I fell, including Marcus, the instructor, so I pretended it was deliberate and did ten crunches while I was on the floor.

Class ends with "Don't You Forget About Me" by Simple Minds, which was my song with Randy. I mean my song with Andy. *Andy*. Why can't I remember his name?

It must be hunger. All my simple mind can think of is dinner.

We wait while Jerome checks his machine. He tries not to show it, but I can see he's anxious. His boyfriend hasn't come home for three days. Major bender. It's really pulling Jerome down, the poor guy.

When I see him grab the quarter from the payphone, I know there was no answer.

Jerome returns to us and says, "Carbs."

The autumn air is brisk, reminding us that soon we will be experiencing our first Minnesota winter. Tonight is probably the last night to get away with wearing shorts. The trees lining Loring Park are losing their leaves, giving each step a pleasant crunch.

We walk past the Basilica of St. Mary, which reminds me to call Sisters Mary Rita and Alma Rita. They've retired to St. Paul. I try to meet them for breakfast a couple of times a month at their convent, which is basically a nursing home for nuns. We, of course, pray before our meal. I always ask God for better food. The eggs taste like scrambled communion wafers.

We turn right on Hennepin and head over to Café DiNapoli, the best Italian restaurant in the world. Their red sauce tastes just like Grandma Caruso's. The whole place is a freaking time machine. Everything about it is pre-WWII cool. The tiled façade, the red and green interior, the heavy diner-like plates with the red circle, broken by the restaurant's logo. Heavy matching cups with real saucers.

A coven of waitresses case the dining room wearing brown and white jumper dresses which zip up the front. Over their left breasts, they wear plastic nametags with daisy wheel embossed nameplates. They're always crooked. Why they go with temporary nametags is confusing. No one quits. The women who work here love it. A mafia in hairnets and sensible shoes.

I eavesdrop while we wait for our table.

"Here is your check," says Jill, one of the more awkward servers. She's a bit shy. In hindsight, I think she's probably on the spectrum. We love her.

"The manager gave me permission to tell you you're the worst table I've ever waited on. Don't come back. Just pay your bill and leave." Remembering she is from Minnesota, Jill turns back and adds, "enjoy the rest of your evening."

When she comes over to greet us, we applaud. She blushes and takes our drink order. Jerome gets up to check his machine again. "If she comes to ask about food, I'll have lasagna."

Carbs. Cheese. Meat. He's in a bad way.

He returns quickly. Rather than pry, I push the conversation in another direction. "Andy and I broke up."

"Andy?" asks Jerome.

"My boyfriend."

"Huh? You fooled around with three guys this week, including Scottie."

"Well, Andy was my boyfriend. My uptown boyfriend."

"Skyway, he was never your boyfriend."

"What does that mean, Jerome?" I ask, getting a little pissed off.

"Sleeping with him more than once doesn't make him a boyfriend. Did you love him?"

Despite myself, I laugh. "No, I didn't *love* him."

"Have you ever been in love?" asks Jerome, clearly assuming the answer is no.

"Yes. Yes, I have. Twice."

"Twice?" says Skipper, who has obviously taken sides.

"Michael and Paula," I say, feeling defensive.

"A woman? You loved a woman," says Jerome.

"A girl," says Skipper.

"That doesn't count," says Jerome.

"It counts," I say. "Don't tell me who I did or didn't love."

"What about the boy? What did you say his name was? Michael! What about Michael?" Jerome presses.

"It was a long time ago," I say. "I'm not even sure it was love. We were kids."

Skipper looks me in the eye. "Don't say that. It was love."

"Of course, it was love. That's why we're still together. He and our six kids are picking me up after dinner. There's Greg, Marcia, Peter…"

"Stop it. Stop it. Don't dismiss love. Don't act like it doesn't matter," Jerome says in a small voice.

"Okay. I'm sorry. I won't." I put my hand on his. "Are you okay?" I ask.

A heavy silence, as though something is about to change, follows. "Carlos and I had a doctor's appointment today. He didn't show." Jerome pauses before looking up. "And, well, there was some bad news."

"Oh."

Oh.

Bad news. In 1985, there's no mistaking bad news. HIV if you're lucky. AIDS if you're not. As the conversation continues, there is no denying it. Jerome is not lucky.

As he shares details, I think of Grandma Barnes, staring at a picture of my Uncle Greg. "The first soldier to die in a war is the one everyone remembers. That's the most heartbreaking loss—the one you never forget. The ache in your heart that never goes away."

Gay men are at war. There will be many casualties. It's not going to end anytime soon.

Each day there's something horrible in the newspaper about AIDS.

People turning loved ones away. Gay bashing. Funeral homes refusing to bury the dead. Shit which should be impossible to imagine when you're twenty-two-years old. Things that should be unimaginable at any age.

Each morning at our breakfast table, I pray for strength. I pray to be brave enough to be there if Skipper or Donny got sick.

We're just Midwestern boys starting to explore the bigger world, hoping to live long enough to become men. A scary world, in a frightening time to be gay. That which we have been dreading has found us.

I'll include Jerome in that prayer starting tomorrow.

Skipper crosses the table to hug Jerome from behind. Donny, on his left, grabs his hand. I kiss Jerome on his impossibly well-defined cheek.

Jill brings our drinks, placing a glass of chianti in front of Jerome.

"Bring the bottle," I say.

Jerome laughs. Loudly.

CHAPTER THIRTY-FIVE

I'LL BE HOME FOR CHRISTMAS

It sounded like such a good idea. Take Amtrak home for Christmas. Sure, it's a lot more expensive than the bus. Sure, it's never on time. Yes, it means Emily driving thirty miles to pick me up because, for some reason, the train arrives in Columbus, Wisconsin instead of the capitol city. Stupid details. None of those things matter.

At least it's uncomfortable.

I head to the bar car, which is nothing like the elegant scene depicted in movies. It's more like a fast-food restaurant in a dying mall that started serving liquor to people desperate for self-medication. I wait in line, wondering what the hell is taking so long. Turns out some poor guy who doesn't speak English got drafted when the real bartender called in sick.

I start translating orders. The line picks up a little speed. Finally, it's my turn.

"*Gracias mi amigo,*" says the substitute bartender.

"*¿Puedo tomar un vodka?*" I ask.

"*Si. Doble!*"

"Oh Jesus," says the kind of hot, already drunk guy behind me in the line.

"Is there a problem?" I ask, patronizingly.

"You're in America. Speak English."

"Have you ever been to Mexico?"

"Yeah," he admits. "Why?"

How can he not see where this is going?

"*¿Hablaste español allí?*"

I laugh. So does the bartender. Laughter makes guys like this angry, which makes it even more fun. I put an extra $3 on the counter.

"*Le compraré una cerveza a este idiota,*" I say to the bartender.

"*Eres demasiado bueno,*" he responds.

When the drunk realizes I bought him a Corona, he smiles. "Thanks. I get your point. Sorry for before." He moves closer. "Maybe I can make it up to you."

"You're a little drunk. I don't want to take advantage," I say, trying to be a Christmas gentleman.

"I'm not that drunk." He smiles again before moving me toward the restroom, adding, "You're Mr. Skyway, right?"

Emily is waiting on the platform. As I get off the train, the drunk who got me off gives me his phone number. "Merry Christmas!" As he walks away, he turns around to add, "*Adios!*"

Emily hugs me. "We better hurry. Mom said supper is in 90-minutes."

I throw my luggage and gifts into the trunk of a white Corvette I've never seen before. "You look wonderful." Her long hair, pulled back and off her face, cascades into the fur collar of her suede coat and show off the tasteful diamond earrings she's wearing. Her makeup is perfect. Even Jerome would agree.

"New car?"

"My new job comes with a different car every six-months."

Emily is now a sales manager for one of the Chevy dealerships in town. She is, like this car, firing on all cylinders. We drive to Madison, serenaded by Aretha Franklin's "Who's Zooming Who."

"Can we make a quick stop at East Towne?"

That's our local mall. The E in Towne makes it fancy.

We drive down East Washington Avenue and pull into the mall parking lot. Emily parks a mile away because, after all, we're in a Corvette. We head to Gimbles. They have the best menswear department. Mick works in the shoe department, so we can say hi.

"Are you dating anyone new?" I ask Emily.

"Not yet. Dick and I only broke up a few weeks ago. How's Skipper?"

I begin to answer her when something catches my eye. When some*one* catches my eye. Past the arcade, I see Michael Drake shopping with his mom. My first urge is to go over and say hello, but I don't. Instead, I will myself to shrink, hoping if I take up less space, I'll become invisible.

Once I'm confident he doesn't see me, I give myself a moment to really look at him. Still handsome, dammit. His hair is shorter, and he's wearing glasses. He's gotten a little bigger, but it's probably muscle. Dammit again. He's still perfect. Triple dammit. The trifecta.

Sometimes when I see someone I've been with, I wonder what the hell I was thinking. With Michael, I know the answer, because I'm still thinking it. The attraction is still there. The affection too. I still feel drawn to him, which is why I don't go to him. He's with his mother. His hateful mother.

Emily breaks through my distraction. "Hello? Where did you go?"

"Wha? Sorry, I saw someone I used to know."

"Did they drive to Columbus to pick you up?"

"No."

"Okay then. Remember that. You can buy me a soda to make up for it."

We stop at the food court to get two Diet Cokes, before heading to Gimbles. I need to get Art a Christmas present. Something a little impractical, I think. Something he'd never get for himself. We find ourselves at the tie counter. Rather, we're at one of the tie counters. There are many. It's a football field of ties. Too many. It's overwhelming.

"How about this one?" asks Emily, holding up typical dad stripes.

"That's nice," I lie, "I was thinking of something a little more unique. More Art."

"He likes stripes," she says, oddly committed to the tie she's chosen.

"Then you should get it for him," I say.

"I already got his present," she says. "Just get it so we can go."

I grab the tie and we start toward the cash register when I see something better.

There in the Ralph Lauren section are an assortment of wider ties, with embroidered or woven animals you'd expect from Ralph Lauren. Polo horses. Hunting dogs. Fish. Peeking out from underneath the pile is a jungle green silk tie full of little gorillas. There are gorillas pounding their chests. Gorillas reading books. Gorillas eating bananas. Gorillas playing with each other. Happy gorillas.

The price tag says $39.99, which is more than I'd normally spend. This is a decision. I start doing an inventory of outstanding bills. Bargaining that perhaps someone will give me money instead of a Christmas gift. And, of course, the biggest variable. People buying me drinks when I go out. The numbers don't work. I shouldn't do it.

A clerk walks up to us.

"I'll take this one, please," I say, handing him the gorilla tie.

"Excellent choice."

We pull into Mom's driveway, snow crunching under the Corvette because no one has shoveled. I'll try to do it tomorrow. Time is tight. Because of work and the show, I can only stay for two days. I've got to leave Christmas night for an evidently critical post-holiday shopping special insert in the Skyway News. I could barely steal the time to come home, but the minute I force the side door open, I know it's worth it.

The door stuck because Mom's kitchen is holiday humid with various foods boiling on the stove. Butch runs up to say hello and then heads outside to help bring in the packages and luggage. Valerie is sitting at the table reading one of her braille books. Christmas carols play in the background. Mom and Dad rush into the room to say hello.

I'm home.

Paula and the kids stop by on Christmas Eve.

"Surprise!" says Paula, which is weird. She called before coming over. The kids run over to my dad, knowing that he'll have candy for them. He really stepped up when Paula's dad died. Raymond Barnes is a much better grandad than dad. "My goodness," he says. "It's my two favorite kids in the whole wide world."

Under his breath, he adds, "Don't tell Kristina and Josh that I said that."

Paula hands us gifts to unwrap. Artwork from the kids. My parents love it.

I pour Paula and me each a cup of coffee from Mom's Corningware cornflower blue percolator. I split a brownie from Barnes Bakery in half, giving Paula the larger piece. We sit down to talk, like my mom and her girlfriends did years ago.

"How are you?" I ask.

"Eh," she says, rolling her eyes. "Okay."

"That was unconvincing," I say.

"Since my dad died, my mom is constantly making demands. I've already got two kids. And a husband," she inventories. "There's not a lot of time left for me. I mean, I'm only twenty-two!" I take a second to really look at her. She's in full Mom drag. Fried hair. Badger Sweatshirt. Fanny pack, sticky with candy residue.

Running my finger up and down her look, I say, "Can't disagree."

"Fuck you, Mr. Skyway."

We hear a gasp. Her daughter Shirene is standing in the doorway. "Mommy swore!" she says, galloping toward the living room to share the news.

"See?" says Paula. "I can't even say fuck."

"What do you want?"

"So many things. For now, I'd just settle for a date with my husband."

"We can make that happen!" I say, smiling as I run to grab her Christmas present.

"What's this?" she asks, eyes wider than her daughter's when she found out her mom has Tourette's. Paula tears through the wrapping in record time. Holding it up, she exclaims, "Oh Warn, it's perfect! Inspecting the tag of the slinky, sexy, silky dress, she adds, "and it's the right size! How did you know?"

"Mr. Skyway knows everything." What *Paula* doesn't know is there's a Ms. Skyway too, and we trade swag we get to keep from shoots. This dress cost me a Jack Nicklaus golfing ensemble I wouldn't have been caught dead in.

"My parents are going to babysit for you tonight," I tell her. "There's a restaurant gift certificate from them in the box. Bijon is in on the whole thing. He says he can't wait to show you off. Merry Christmas!"

In her eyes for a nanosecond, I can see the spark we used to share. Knowing a remnant of that is still there is my real present.

My parents leave about 4 o'clock. While they're gone, Butch, Val, and I string the lights on the outdoor tree and clean up the house to surprise Mom.

"How are things going, Val?" I ask while I straighten out the light cords.

"Great! I'm shift supervisor," she says. Valerie is working at the Madison Opportunity Center, doing light assembly line work since she's so good with her hands. "The girls think they can get away with murder because I'm blind. I had to write three of them up last week. I did it in *Braille*. I got the last laugh."

"You always do Valerie," says Butch.

Christmas morning is all about the parade and Mom's egg strata. No sooner does she finish serving that than she starts making dinner.

"Can I help?" I ask.

273

She looks at me quizzically.

"What?" I ask.

"No one has ever asked me that before. Not since your grandma died," she says, getting that wistful look she gets whenever Grandma Caruso's name gets mentioned.

"It can be our new holiday tradition," I say.

"Well, it's my favorite gift this year," she smiles, giving me a quick hug. "Big news, by the way. We're all going to be here for supper!"

"What?" I ask, unable to remember the last time that was the case.

"You're here until 4, at which point you need to go catch your train. Art, Ruth, the kids, and Suzy all are supposed to be here by 2:30, so that gives us 90-minutes to eat, open some presents and get a picture!"

"God bless us, everyone," I say.

Mom, to my surprise, attempts a British accent. "Yes. And Mr. Scrooge too!"

Mom then pushes a bowl of potatoes, a brush, and a vegetable peeler my way. I commence scrubbing and peeling before she says, "Have you talked to your brother lately?"

"Which one?" I ask.

"Art, of course," she says in a heavy voice.

"No. I've called, but come to think of it, he hasn't called back. Why?"

"If you get a chance find time to talk to him," is all she says.

Emily shows up with Valerie at 1:30, which allows us to rationalize opening some presents. My parents hand me a card. Expecting money to be inside, I'm surprised to see they've ordered me new dishes, all white, being shipped to Minneapolis. Emily got me the matching service pieces. Florence next door, my godmother, bought the cups and saucers.

"You don't look very pleased," says Mom. "I thought you'd love it."

"It wasn't cheap," Emily adds.

"It's not that," I say.

"Then what?" Mom asks. "We even went through five sets before we found one Skipper would agree to."

"Oh great! Skipper approved it. That's wonderful. Makes my life a hell of a lot easier."

"Warn, don't say hell on Christmas Day," says Valerie.

Suzy shows up at 2:15 with an exceptionally tall, bearded guy named J.J., who doesn't appear to own a coat. She was in on the plan and gives me white linen napkins and a tablecloth for Christmas. Nothing from J.J. Oh well.

"You're hard to buy for. Mr. Skyway gets everything for free," Suzy says.

She's right. Her gift is a trade-in. I gave Ms. Skyway a fishing reel in exchange for $75 worth of cosmetics at Dayton's in Suzy's colors.

2:30 comes and goes. 3:00 arrives to take its place. At 3:15, Mom offers a defeated, "Well, I suppose we should eat," to no one in particular. Mom's, "Sorry if it's a little dry," meal commences. "Ruth is bringing the ham. So, there's no main course yet."

At 3:50, the door opens. In walks Ruth, Kristina, and Josh.

"Where's Art?" I ask.

Kristina takes over. "We each got a puppy for Christmas! Mine is named Kris, like me. Josh's is named Kringle!"

"That's why we were late. We had to stop every 5 miles so they wouldn't do their business in the car. Art is walking them now because it was his idea," says my sister-in-law, with a frozen smile.

I'm nearly done gathering together my things when Art walks in with the dogs, with whom I have no choice but to quickly play. "Time to go. Catching a train." Handing Art a puppy and his Christmas package, I add, "Open this before I leave."

Art hands a package to me. "Here's yours."

"You first," I say.

Art tears his package open. "Oh my gosh. Gorillas! Like Samson."

"Yeah. You got it. Good."

"I love it. Thank you. Your turn."

I tear away the paper. As I do, the shape and size reveal it to be something framed. As the last of the tissue paper floats away, my family loves tissue paper, I see it's a photo of a skyway under construction.

"I took that on a class trip to Minneapolis. The only time I've ever been there." Art says shyly. "I printed it myself and signed it."

In the corner, scribbled in his handwriting, it says, "Art Holden, brother of Mr. Skyway."

It has hung in my home ever since, no matter how often I've moved. No matter how far I've gone. It has stayed with me.

"It's 4 o'clock. I've got to go!"

Emily, mid-bite, says, "Can't we leave a little later?"

I hesitate to ponder my options. "Amtrak is always late. We'd probably make it."

"No, you can't," says Mom. "You might miss your train!"

"Okay. Everything's late because of me. I'll take him," says Art.

After hurried goodbyes, we run outside with my presents and luggage only to realize it has begun to snow. We're just about to load up Art's car when we hear honking from about half a block away. The snow makes it hard to see who it is. Two houses away, near the Smiths, I can see it's Skipper and his stepdad Wayne.

Skipper jumps out before the car fully stops. "My car broke down. I'm taking the train too. We can take you to the station," he says, grabbing my bags and loading them into their car.

"Good," I say to Art. "You can eat while it's still hot."

"Yeah. That's great," he says flatly before hugging me. "Safe travels."

"Sorry, we didn't get to catch up."

"My fault. Puppies. Kids."

"Life! It's okay. We'll talk soon. I lov-"

"Warn. We've got to go," says Skipper. "The snow is going to slow us down."

"Okay. Okay!" I say, heading toward to car.

I jump in and put on my seatbelt before looking up to wave goodbye to Art.

I will always be thankful for the instinct to look up.

There in the front yard, framed by the branches of the maple tree his Dad planted 30 years earlier, is my big brother; kind, generous, self-sacrificing, Arthur Bradley Holden. Snow is clinging to the Christmas sweater he wears every year, no matter how tight it gets. Unshaven, the snowflakes also stick to his whiskers. Of course, he forgot to put on a coat. Despite the cold, he smiles.

The car pulls away from the curb and toward the future. I don't look back, but in my heart, I know Art stayed there until he could no longer see our car. That's what my family does.

CHAPTER THIRTY-SIX

CALAMITY EVE

"Warn, can you move a little farther left of center?" asks Scot.

"I'll be out of my light," I respond.

"Is the play called *Hamlet* or *Gravedigger?*"

I resist the temptation to say, "I think the working title was *Go to Hell,*" before doing as asked.

"Was that so hard?" asks Scot in a very patronizing voice.

We wrap up the final tech rehearsal after running the closing fight scene several times. Our fight Captain, Chang, should be demoted to Private. He's sweet, but that doesn't mean he knows what he's doing. I'd say something, but we're sleeping together. He's much better at that.

"Want to grab a bite to eat?" asks Chang.

"Sure. Let's do Vietnamese," I say, picking up my duffel bag.

He trips on a cable on our way out.

"Jerome," I fib. "You look great!"

"Skyway, don't lie to me," he responds. "Turns out Diana Vreeland was wrong. You can be too thin."

"Well, I'm here to help with that," says Skipper with a flourish. "I've been baking all day!" Like a magician, he pulls open the contraband picnic basket he snuck past the nurse's station. From that, he grabs the two Tupperware containers, putting the smaller one on Jerome's nightstand. "I brought brownies, blondies, lemon bars, and some sugar-free cookies for poor Tracy."

"Why?" I ask. "Why poor Tracy?"

"She's diabetic, Warn. We talked about it. Can't you remember anything?" he says self-righteously, which when describing Skipper seems a little redundant.

"How are you doing, sweetie?" I ask Jerome.

"Well," he says, "the infection is under control. The thrush too. So, I might be out of here soon."

We are at Hennepin County Medical Center, one of the first Twin Cities hospitals to see AIDS patients. Not in the nicest neighborhood.

Not the most modern. It's the most generous. The most aware of what a hospital's primary mission should be—putting patients first.

Skipper and I are dressed in hooded HAZMAT coveralls, which we've accessorized with turquoise jewelry and scarves to make Jerome laugh, which he did until he started coughing. Every victory comes at a price, I suppose.

Despite the coughing, he manages to say, "You should always wear those. It makes it nearly impossible to see the little lines starting to form around your eyes."

Whenever I worry about Jerome, I remember he's too mean to die.

I'm bundled up for February weather and just about to leave the apartment when the phone starts ringing. I run to pick it up in the kitchen. "Hello?" I say while lifting the stocking cap Skipper knit me up over my left ear.

"Warn, it's me. Your mother."

"Hi," I say in a breezy tone. "What's up?"

"I'm in Boscobel," she says.

"Fun! Say hi to everyone."

"Not fun, Warn. Not fun," she says. "Art is in the hospital again. They think he had another heart attack."

"Oh my God. Was it serious?"

"It doesn't seem to be. I mean, when is a heart attack not serious, but no. The doctors think it might be angina. They're testing."

I try not to sound anxious, knowing it would make things worse for Mom. Instead, I take a cleansing breath before responding. "Can I talk to him?" I ask.

"Not now. He's with the doctors."

"That's right. You said they were testing."

"Yes," she confirms.

"Mom, my show is opening tonight. I don't ... I don't know what to do. I feel as though I should come home," I suggest, already anticipating Scot's reaction if I leave. "Or head to Wisconsin after Sunday night's show."

"No, don't. It's not that serious. If you did come home, Art would think he's sicker than he is. Don't come."

I unzip my coat and can feel the steam leave my body. For a moment, I'm a little dizzy. I take off my coat and sit at the breakfast table while Mom gives me the address and phone number of the hospital in Boscobel, Wisconsin.

I wish he were in a bigger city, but I push that concern out of my mind.

"Okay, Mom, I've got it. I'm going to the theater now. I'll check my machine as often as I can."

"Have a good opening," she says, which sounds trivial against the news she just delivered.

I get to the theater early to walk the set, check my props, and relax. I grab my cup of coffee to walk through the art exhibit they've set up in the lobby. It's kind of creepy. Elizabethan death masks on loan from whatever sick kind of person collects such things.

Scot says it's meant to be a portal from contemporary society to the time of Hamlet. I hate to compliment him, but it's very effective. Winding around each corner to discover more masks, all lit with pinpoint spotlights that give the impression the masks are spirits hovering in mid-air.

I wish he'd worked this hard on the lighting for the show.

Flowers from Skipper and Donny are on my dressing table. I can smell them as I do my make-up. Lining my eyes, I realize there is water pooling in the corners. I grab a tissue to blot them dry and repair the damage.

I rationalize checking my messages so the make-up can dry.

"You have two messages," says Ernestine, our name for the answering machine.

"Hi Warn, it's Paula," I hear.

"And Bijon!" I hear from farther away.

"We wanted to wish you a good opening. Knock 'em dead!" says Paula.

"And then bury them!" yells Bijon.

They laugh and hang up. Delete.

Beep!

Message two. It's Art.

"Mom said you wanted to talk when she called. Sorry. I was with the doctors. Everything is fine. It's fine. Nothing to worry about. I know how you are. Don't let it ruin your night, okay? Have a great opening. Knock 'em dead!"

"And then bury them!" says Ruth in the background.

They laugh and hang up. Delete.

How many actors playing the Gravedigger in *Hamlet* have heard that joke.

Upon my first entrance as an auxiliary character, I can make out a very full house. The lights are too bright to see specifically who is there, but I'm pretty sure I can make out Skipper's reactions.

My scene gets all the laughs I could find and applause at several points, so I'm happy. The rest of the show blurs a bit. The battle scene, during which I am a swordsman who dies, goes well enough. Chang positions himself upstage and at an angle, so the audience can't see his face when he stabs me. As I fall to the floor, he blows me a kiss. It's sweet. Unprofessional, but sweet.

He and I have no future.

The curtain call is respectable. It starts slowly but builds. When I enter in my Gravedigger costume, pockets of the audience stand. The ovation continues to grow, and by the time Claudonious or Gerphelia enter, the entire audience is on their feet.

Just like that, I'm a working actor in a major US city.

I find Skipper and Donny by one of the partitions in the lobby. They applaud when I walk up to them, which causes people around them to applaud. Various compliments are thrown around, which is nice. Neither of them is a huge Shakespeare fan. They're coming back tomorrow for the other show. My friends. Loyal to their own detriment.

"We have a surprise!" says Donny.

Skipper begins a drumroll as the two of them part, and around the corner, Jerome walks in carrying a dozen red roses.

I scream and fall into his arms for a hug.

"Skyway, you were good," he says.

We break our embrace. I glance toward the floor. "Thanks."

He lifts my chin, so we're looking eye to eye.

"Don't play that humble game with me. You're good. Much better than I expected."

"Uh…"

"Shut up. I don't mean it that way," he explains. "I mean, I thought you were just pretty. You know. Mr. Skyway, not Mr. Actor. You've got something here. You make it work."

He looks at me with great intention.

"Make it work."

Rosencrantz & Guildenstern opens well. Sunday sucks because the reviews will come out. That means lots of competition and bruised egos, maybe mine, on a day when there's a matinee of R&G and a nighttime performance of dusty old *Hamlet*. We're expected to help change the set between performances, so it's an exhausting day. Especially since I have improv class before the first show.

I walk into the workshop at the last minute, having tried to get as much sleep as possible. Judy Spanberger, the café manager, is behind the counter as I rush to class. "We miss you. Finish with Shakespeare so you can get back to comedy, where you belong."

Tom Winner steps onto the stage when I enter the theater.

"Ladies and gentlemen, the mighty Warn Barnes is amongst us." Opening the *Sunday Star Tribune*, he begins to read. "*To See or Not to See Hamlet, a review by Kenneth Parks. 'While it is exceedingly hard to find anything fresh in a Shakespearian production, the Minnesota Shakespeare Player's repertory productions have plenty of bright spots ... blah, blah, blah. Director Scot Bellweather does a nice job inspiring the young cast ...*'"

He liked Scot (1 T). Kenneth Parks is a hack.

"'*Rounding out the stronger performances is Warn Barnes, a newcomer to Minneapolis stages. He buries Ophelia and his competition by offering a delightfully comic performance as the Gravedigger in the oft-told tragic tale. According to his bio, he is originally from Wisconsin, which makes sense. His Gravedigger is equal parts Elizabethan and Green Bay Packer. We look forward to more from this funny young man.*'"

Give the man a Pulitzer.

Judy, who has been listening from the back of the theater, enters with two bottles of champagne and distributes glasses to everyone. Jim, my improv teacher, hands me a pair of sunglasses and offers a toast. "To Warn. A future so bright, he's got to wear shades."

The matinee goes well. Smaller, older audience, but responsive. *Hamlet* is a little slower. Double show day. Less energy. The gravedigger scene hits, but not as hard. When it's time for the closing fight scene. Chang jumps ahead in the choreography. He turns upstage to kill me, but he goes down instead of up. I see what's happening. He does not. I pull my thrust. Having anticipated getting a block, Chang gives it full momentum, but my blade is not there. He makes contact.

The pain is startling. It radiates across and then through both my legs. My woolen leggings are red. The audience cannot tell I'm bleeding. I decide to say nothing and wait until the end of the show to get help. I position my body to minimize the bleeding best I can.

During the blackout, I hobble backstage to find the stage manager. "I was cut. Call an ambulance." I fashion makeshift tourniquets, for my legs before returning to take my bows. While I'm bending over, I put my hands on the front of my shins. Blood pools through the wool.

Chang is waiting for me backstage. "I'm so sorry," he repeats on a loop.

I hate moments like this. People expecting to be taken care of during someone else's crisis. Someone's guilt eclipsing my needs.

"I know," is the best I can muster. Chang is a decent guy who made a mistake. I'm just tired of paying for the mistakes of others. Tonight is a case in point. I just end up with more scars, and I've had enough.

The ambulance arrives. The paramedic inquires if Chang is coming to the hospital with me. "Should I?" he asks.

"No. That's fine," I say, grateful that he asked instead of saying yes. "Just call Skipper and ask him to meet me there, okay?"

He nods. "What about your mom?"

"No!" I say automatically. I repeat myself in a softer voice. "No. Thanks. She's dealing with enough right now. One hospitalized kid is enough."

The gurney is lifted. They carry me out through the lobby. The audience is still milling, waiting for friends in the cast. As we pass through, I overhear one of them say, "I wish the show had been that dramatic."

Skipper enters the Emergency Room in full Shirley MacLaine, *Terms of Endearment* mode. A Karen before Karens were Karened. "This man has been slashed. Slashed, I tell you! Get him a room. Get him a room now!"

They do. Quickly.

The autopilot admissions clerk knocks on my door. She doesn't introduce herself. "May I ask you some questions?"

"Do I have a choice?" I ask.

"No, I don't suppose you do!" she half giggles, having come out of her coma. I think I liked her better before.

She gets my insurance information, address, phone number, banking info and then moves onto personal information. Marital status. Education.

Emergency Contact.

She looks at Skipper and then back to me. "Sexual preference?"

"Pardon me?"

"Sexual preference."

"I don't think you can ask me that."

"Very well. Allow me to rephrase per our HIV protocols." She clears her throat. "Have you ever had sexual relations with … another man?"

"No. No, I haven't," I say.

"Very well," she says, rising to leave. "That's all."

There is a moment of silence.

"Well," says Skipper. "That's the best acting you'll ever do."

It's cold and snowing, but we get home. Me on crutches. Smelling of Betadine and peroxide. Stage make-up long past its expiration date. Leg warmers. Dried blood. 24 stitches. I wear it well. It's a very sexy look.

I check our machine. No messages. That's good.

I hobble into the bathroom, wash my face and douse my hair to get rid of the product.

"Do you need help going to the bathroom?" Skipper offers.

"What? NO!" I say, horrified at the mere thought.

It's not easy, but I manage without assistance.

"Let me help you get into bed," says Skipper. After I'm lying down and tucked in, he hands me a glass of water and an ibuprofen.

"Thanks, Skip. I really appreciate all you've done."

"So, this is when it finally happens," he says.

"What?" I ask.

"I've been waiting for years for you to acknowledge my efforts on your behalf." We smile before he adds, "I'm exhausted. If you don't need anything, I'm going to bed."

I'm finally alone. The tension I've been carrying seeps out of my body and into the mattress. Under the safety of my matching sheets and feather comforter, I process the day. Art. Class. The review. The shows. The accident. Lying to the clerk at the hospital. Knowing that I can lie, but Jerome can't. Highs and lows. I'm glad it's over.

The red phone on my nightstand rings at 3:34 am.

CHAPTER THIRTY-SEVEN

BATHTUB BAPTISM

"Mom?"

"Yes. Uh, well - Art just died."

I can feel myself shrinking. Getting smaller. I can feel my world getting smaller.

"I was spending the night at the hospital. I was asleep but heard an alarm. People started rushing in. A nurse, I think she was a nurse, led me out of the room. The noise didn't stop, so I came back in. I tried to smile so Art wouldn't be scared. He smiled too; I think. I think he was smiling. Then the alarm stopped. Everything was silent, and then this horrible, steady beep started. I looked at the little screen. It was a flat line."

I hear her take a deep breath.

"His heart ruptured. He never had a chance. Warn, I'm sorry I told you not to come. I'm sorry I did that. You could have seen each other another time. You could've said goodbye. I'm so sorry."

"Mom don't do that. Don't. It doesn't accomplish anything." I hear someone walk by. She's still at the hospital. "You're not alone, are you?"

"No. Ruth is here. And your dad. They're calling other people."

"What can I do?" I ask, knowing how futile it sounds. How rote.

"Get home. Please. As quickly as you can. Fly. I don't care what it costs. It's fine. Just get here, please. We need to be together."

I get out of bed, which is hard because of my legs. I steady myself on the footboard, before crossing to the window. I open the curtains to see what the world looks like on this sad day.

The freshly fallen snow is perfect and silent. Comforting, were that possible. In the distance I hear the quiet beginnings of a rumble. A scraping sound moves closer. Orange lights flash across the white blanket. A plow truck comes by and pushes the snow away. Trapping cars in drifts. Blocking paths. Creating obstacles.

I want to wake up Skipper and Donny, but they both need their rest. Besides, what could they do? What has happened has happened. There's no need to share something that can't be fixed.

I stumble to the kitchen, choosing pain over crutches, balancing myself with walls and furniture. I quietly make a pot of coffee before grabbing the phonebook to find the number for Northwest Airlines and book my one-way, 40-minute flight to Madison.

"That will be $900," says the overnight operator.

"I told you, this is for a funeral," I say, feeling myself getting angry.

"Do you have a death certificate?"

"My brother died an hour ago," I say. "I don't think the paperwork is ready."

"And that's why it's $900," says the overnight operator at no-longer exists Northwest Airlines.

Obligations feel ridiculous, but necessary. I convince Scot I'll be back in time for the next show. The critical business of Mr. Skyway is handled. The Twin Cities will learn about the Winter Skyway Scarfopalooza via Skyway Jr. and Little Miss Skyway, the kids with whom Jerome hates working, so at least there are a few laughs on the horizon.

My cane becomes a boarding pass for early seating. I get on a plane for the third time in my life. Sitting down, I can't help but think how little of the world Art saw.

I turn my head toward the window and cry all the way to Madison.

I'm still someone's little brother.

Emily is waiting for me at the gate. I fall into her embrace and cry, vaguely aware that I could be harming her fur collar, which feels so good against my face.

Emily looks different. No make-up, no eyelashes, her hair pulled back in a simple ponytail. For a minute, I think of the wiglets she used to wear. Art was just a room away when I used to watch her get ready for school. The vacuum that thought creates, that hole, is going to be part of all my memories from now on, I think. Everything is different.

Everything.

Years from now, I will have two cats from the same litter, a brother named Bo Dean and a sister named Bo Derek. It will always seem to me that they're the luckiest cats in the world, to be living together from birth. They'll just blithely go about their business accepting each other as a given. A fact of each other's lives because they don't know the difference. Dean will die. Derek will never be the same.

I suspect that's what this is like for Emily.

We load my luggage into the white Corvette, the luxury of which feels disrespectful this morning. We don't play music. We don't talk. We just sadly and quietly drive to Mom's house in the flashiest car on the road.

We make our way through a maze of hotdishes, fruit baskets, plants, and flowers to get into the house. Mom's all-girl posse is in full swing. Florence, who knew Art every day of his life, is organizing the refrigerator. Aunt Lil is cleaning. Mick is serving everyone coffee. Shirley walks up to me, looks as though she's going to speak, but hugs me instead. Geneva rubs my back.

Mom is asleep on the couch. Dad is sitting beside her sobbing.

Butch stands up when he sees me. "I'm glad you're home, Warn."

It takes Valerie a moment to realize I'm in the room. "Warn, you look sad," she says. Despite myself, I chuckle.

We're in my room at the only motel in Boscobel. The walls are paneled. There's a very firm king-sized bed. Gray indoor, outdoor carpeting, the steady hum of traffic from the highway outside becomes white noise. This is the kind of motel room in which Willie Loman planned his suicide.

Mom, Emily, and I came ahead to help with the plans. The rest of the family will join us for the funeral. Kristina doesn't want to see anyone. She's not ready to be reminded of her dad. "Maybe you can each stop by alone, so it's less overwhelming," suggests Ruth. Art married his mother, that's for sure. She's behaving a lot like I suspect Mom did when the first Warren died.

I've been plagued with a nagging thought ever since Art passed. Maybe it's the bargaining of grief. I keep thinking it would've been better if I'd died, not because I don't love my life, but because I am less necessary than Art.

I catch myself wondering if Ruth has thought the same. Not in a cruel way. Not because she wishes me dead. Just in a way that honestly assesses the situation.

"Dorothy, Emily, and I have to go to the funeral home. Can you watch Josh?" Ruth asks, pointing at my nephew sleeping on the foot of my bed.

"Why? Does he do tricks?"

"Thank you, smart ass," she says after kissing me on the cheek. "There's a change of clothes in case he spills or has an accident." She crosses over to her bag to point them out to Uncle Clueless. "Oh. I almost forgot. Art had a little box of things that the kids and I understood were just for him. His camera," which she hands to me, "family pictures. A birthday card from his dad. And this."

Ruth hands me the letter I gave Art in the hospital after his first heart attack.

The paper is worn. The back flap of the envelope is missing. It has been read many times. "Keep it," she adds as she puts on the gloves I gave her for Christmas.

They leave. I sit down to read the letter. Josh starts to stir. I freeze, hoping he's just stretching and will go back to sleep. Naive optimism is my constant companion.

"Uncle Warn?" says a groggy little boy. "Where did everybody go?"

"Errands. You're stuck with me, kid."

"That's okay. I like being with you. Can we play?" he asks, which suggests he's been told not to play during this sad time. A co-dependent, midwestern, Protestant form of shiva for children.

"Did you bring any toys?"

"Transformers!" says the boy smiling for the first time in days.

As most people know, Transformers are two toys in one. When you first get them, they're sort of autonomous, weaponized robots. When twisted and turned, they become something else, a dinosaur, a vehicle, a vibrator for your mom. Whatever. I love them. They plant the subversive thought that things can evolve and change.

We go into the bathroom. I begin to fill the bathtub with water. Josh's face contorts. "You said we could play!"

"This is an underwater research facility the Transformers protect."

His eyes get huge. "Oh yeah. Now I see it."

"You want to know something that makes your granny great?" I ask my nephew.

"That she makes good cookies?" I shake my head no.

"That she's always nice to me?" I shake my head no.

"Can she fly?" he asks.

"Yes," I say. "But that's not what I was looking for."

"What makes Granny Barnes great?" he asks.

We move back into the bedroom. "She runs a construction company with Gramps." We leave our room and head toward hers. "Since she runs a construction company, she has weird little habits. For example," I say, opening the unlocked door of her room and heading to her travel tote, "she always has duct tape. She thinks it can fix anything."

I open the bag and allow Josh to look inside. Per usual, she is carrying three rolls of duct tape. The rolls we are looking at are rainbow-colored, which only makes it better for such a little boy.

"Wow," says Josh. "What else is in there?"

"No. No. We respect other people's privacy. We just need the duct tape and some of her towels."

We head back to my room. Using our supplies, we create bridges and ramps between the bathtub and toilet, then up to the towel rack and back over to the showerhead. Another set of towels acts as a pole to lower the Transformers into the bathtub.

Fun and educational. Josh learns that almost anything can become a toy, and the rainbow duct tape gives it a nice gay pride vibe for me.

We spend about 20-minutes playing, letting the bathtub splash over the edge, soaking us and our clothes, laughing. Each time Josh thinks I won't do something, I do it.

"Uh-oh," he says. "Headquarters says you have to jump into the bathtub. Now."

"Right now?" I ask. "Wearing all my clothes?"

He manages to say, "Yes," between giggles.

"Well, if HQ says so," I walk into the bathtub and sit down while Josh jumps up and down, laughs, and screams.

"Uh-oh," I say. "I'm getting a message from Headquarters too."

Josh gets very serious. "What? What do they say?"

I grab him by the waist. "They say you've got to come in too."

I lift him in the air. He's giggling to the point of almost hyperventilating. I move him over the water without dropping him in. I lift him up into the air and bring him down quickly, pulling him up at the last second. Then I hold him up in the air until he settles down.

"I knew you wouldn't do that to me," he says with a cocky swagger.

So, I drop him into the water.

Best water park day we ever shared.

Since we're already wet, we hang out in the bathtub for a while. Josh keeps morphing his Transformers from one shape to another. I make sure he doesn't fall below the waterline like a responsible adult probably should.

289

Josh looks like a little engineer. He keeps twisting and turning his toy, looking for new shapes and forms. Seeing what he can make happen. Keeping his attention on the work, he says, "Uncle Warn?"

"Yes?"

"My dad didn't want his heart to break, did he?"

"No, Josh," I say, trying not to give in to the tears pressing behind my eyes. "The last thing in the world that your dad wanted was to leave you."

"Then why did this happen?"

"I wish I knew. Sometimes things can't be explained." He puts one of his toys into my hand. "But you know what?"

"What?"

"Maybe we should think of it like Transformers. Your dad isn't gone. He just became something else."

"What did he become?"

"A spirit."

Josh looks confused. "What's a spirit?"

"A spirit is like the wind. It's the best part of us. A force that helps keep us in touch with God. A force that keeps us in touch with the people we love forever. Even after our bodies die."

Someone said something similar to me when I was a little boy.

CHAPTER THIRTY-EIGHT

THE GODFATHER

I'm about to walk into the funeral home when someone hugs me from behind. I turn around to discover it's Ruth. Kristina is with her.

When our eyes lock, she turns away. Ruth gently puts her hand on Kristina's shoulder to keep her from walking away.

"I'd love to have a moment alone with Art. Why don't you and Tina take a little walk?" suggests Ruth.

I put out my hand, which Kristina chooses not to take. We walk toward Wisconsin Avenue, Boscobel's Main Street. She doesn't talk, so I don't either. It throws her. I can see it on her beautiful little face. She expected me, the grown-up, to force the conversation. Finally, she can't take the silence any longer.

"Where are we going?"

"It's Boscobel. How many choices are there? Want some ice cream?"

"It's February," she says, rolling her eyes.

"Don't let anyone tell you we can't have ice cream in February."

"Well, if you want some ice cream, I guess we should go get it," says Kristina.

We head over to the Unique Café, the best diner ever. You don't think the best diner ever would be in Boscobel, Wisconsin, but it is. I should know. I've lived in New York City. Or rather, I will live in New York City.

It gets a little awkward when we walk into the restaurant. One of the downsides of a town this small is everyone knowing your business. People know you're in mourning and want to imagine that you're too overcome to even think about eating.

Our server walks up to us. "Hi Kris," she says in an empathetic voice, meant to be kind. "What'll you have?"

"A strawberry milkshake, please," she says like it's a punishment.

"And you?"

"Nothing, thanks."

Kristina shoots me such a look I almost laugh. "I thought you wanted something to eat," she says very self-righteously, looking a little like Emily. They really are a lot alike. Genetics are real.

"Fine," I say flaring my eyes at her. "I'll have a scoop of vanilla ice cream."

"Thanks," says Bonnie, our server.

"With a slice of peach pie, some fries, and a cup of coffee."

Kristina laughs a little. Perhaps the thaw has begun.

A few thoughtful people stop by our table to express their condolences. My niece, who it turns out can be a bit of a brat, introduces me as "Warn. My father's brother."

After the condolence parade passes us by, Kristina steals a bite of my pie.

"Oh no, you don't."

"You always let me have some of your pie," she says, sounding a little wounded.

"Uncle Warn lets you have some of his pie. Your father's brother, on the other hand, is kind of a bastard. He only shares with kids that call him Uncle Warn."

"Why?" she asks in an annoyed tone. "Why does that even matter?"

"Because that's my name," I say with wide eyes. "That's always going to be my name, no matter what has happened or will. You and me? That doesn't change. Okay?"

"Okay! Jeez!"

"Now, is there anything you care to talk about?" I ask.

"No," she says adamantly. "Okay. Yes. There is."

I'm busy chewing pie. I gesture for her to continue.

"What happens if my mom dies too?"

Wow.

I wipe my mouth and take a sip of my coffee before answering.

"Well, first off, that's not going to happen, so don't worry about it. But you're my goddaughter. You could always live with me."

"Josh isn't your godson. Where would he live?"

"Do you think I'd ever let anyone, or anything split you two up?"

She searches my face for a moment. Her head tilts to the side.

"Okay. I believe you."

"I'd love to live with you."

"I'd love to live with you too," she says, finally relaxing.

"You could do my laundry and make the beds. You could scrub the floors and walk my dog. It would be just like *Cinderella*," I say, trying to look very smug and entitled.

"But then what would Uncle Skipper do?" she says, smiling at her own joke.

"You know, sweetie, your dad was almost an adult when I was born. He kind of raised me."

"What do you mean? Granny and Gramps—"

"They were there too. And my Grandma. It's a long story. But you want to know what I think?"

"What?" she politely responds.

"He made all his mistakes with me," I say with a smile. "You and Josh are his masterpieces. You're going to be fine. Better than me. Better than all of us. You had a wonderful dad. That's why this hurts so much. Pretending it doesn't hurt is just going to make the hurt last longer. He wouldn't want that for you."

She nods. I think she understands or is at least starting to; that's enough for today.

I push my pie toward her. "Are we good? Anything else you'd like to talk about?"

"Not now," she says, grabbing the fries and digging into what's left of my pie.

An Ichabod Crane of a mortician walks me into the room in which Art, or rather Art's body, rests. It is a somber space. The goal seems to be sadness rather than peace or contemplation. I immediately hate it. When I notice the organ music droning in the background, I hate it more.

Pink lightbulbs give the room a rosy glow. I'm guessing they do that to make the bodies look more alive, which is ridiculous.

"May I lead you to the deceased?" asks Olive Oyl's brother.

"No," I say, more firmly than intended. I need to relax. The poor Crypt Keeper is just doing his job. Besides, this is Ruth's hometown. It's best to be polite.

"No, thank you. I'd just like to be alone with my brother before the visitation starts."

"As you wish," he says before leaving.

Evidently, I just wasted a wish on being alone with my dead brother. If I truly get a wish, bring him back, you god-damn cricket. I wish my brother wasn't dead.

To avoid looking at Art, I concentrate on the flowers, of which there are many framing the casket, which in turn frames Art.

I will never be an in lieu of person. Send flowers. Life can be for the living tomorrow. Reading the little notes, I see arrangements from Ruth's family, Richard Nabors and his wife Linda, Aunt Lil and the rest of Mom's all-girl posse, Uncle Nick and Aunt Josie, the Barnes family, and Nancy.

"For one of the best guys I've ever known."

In the end, love transcends disappointment.

I'm just about to get good and sad when I spy a very dramatic bouquet next to a peace lily sent by Paula and Bijon. The foundation of the arrangement is a hat woven from palm fronds. Spilling out from the hat are birds of paradise, ginger, and Hosta. It is over the top, tacky, and breathtaking at the same time. I smile imagining Jerome making the poor florist's life hell.

I look inside the casket.

The tears I've been expecting don't come. Instead, there is a pressure from deep within me, building. Getting stronger. I exhale in a way I never have before. I can feel it in every part of my body, as though I've just lost a piece of my soul.

Ruth chose his clothes well. A crisp white shirt. A brown sportscoat that would match his beautiful eyes if they could be seen. If they could see. His tie is green silk. Tiny gorillas playing together, forever. Samson and Art, reunited for eternity.

He looks old. Thirty-seven going on seventy-seven.

He deserved to live forever.

I can hear Grandma Caruso from her new home inside my head.

"Deserving doesn't make it so."

For the first time, I'm glad someone is dead. This would have destroyed her.

Old photos and keepsakes are hanging on bulletin boards to the right of the casket. Glorified scrapbooking, representing the entirety of Art's life.

Mom pregnant with Art. Looking young and hopeful. Faded pencil identifies the era as June 1948. The first Warren holding Art as an infant. A mole on the left side of his head warns of future threats. Art holding baby Emily. A picture of the house on Johns Street before the roof was raised. Art, dressed up, standing ramrod straight next to Grandma Caruso and Grandpa Sam, looking so happy and proud of their first grandchild.

Warren and Grandpa Sam disappear from the timeline. There's

a picture of Grandma in her gardening hat standing next to Art and one of his cornstalks. Art and Richard Nabors on parallel bars. The first color photo is of Art, Emily, Suzy, Val, Mom, and Dad at their wedding, looking so full of promise. Art holding a baby tightly. Kind of daring the world to get past his line of defense. I think it's me. Could be Butch. It doesn't matter.

The family photo of everyone but me because I chose to walk away.

Time to walk away again. These pictures are too hard to look at. The moment beyond the photo being taken, Art was still alive. Speeding toward this horrible conclusion. Everything in the photo seems infinite when it's not.

It's like watching *Gandhi*. I know the ending.

I grab the letter from my left breast pocket. I gently pull the contents out of the envelope and begin to read the letter, written on Barnes Home Improvement letterhead, aloud.

Dear Art,

Remember when I was a kid, and you had to break me out of the garage the day before you left for the army? I was screaming, "I don't want you to die! I don't want you to die!"

That's what this feels like.

You have got to take care of yourself if you want to take care of others. Your devotion to everyone else is one of the most wonderful things about you. I'm not asking you to change. I don't think you can. It's who you are, and I love you for it. It's just time for you to matter as much to yourself as you do to other people.

You, more than anyone else, have made me who I am. Any strengths or talents I have, exist because of you. You'll be part of anything I ever accomplish. I owe you more than I could ever repay.

Please let me know how I can help you get through this stronger than before. Stronger than ever. Healthier than you've ever been. For Ruth. For your kids. For Mom. For me.

I want us to grow old together. I want you to outlive me because I don't know if I could handle a world without you in it. As I said years ago. I don't want you to die. So, don't. Live. Heal. Thrive.

I love you.

> *Your brother,*
> *Warn*

I gently fold the letter back into the envelope and slip the letter into Art's left breast pocket. The pocket next to his oversized and ruptured heart. I smooth the jacket back into place, kiss his cold forehead, and whisper, "Thank you," to anyone who might be listening.

CHAPTER THIRTY-NINE

THE SEQUEL

This church makes me miss the funeral home. It's old, imposing, and stuffy as hell. Perhaps that's to keep the parishioners in line. Remind them what's on the other side if they covet their neighbor's wife.

It seems like a place people come to be punished rather than comforted. Closed minds instead of open hearts. There's probably a dungeon in the basement for farmers who don't tithe.

My cherry coke-colored hair, the Skyway clothing, the disdainful bordering on flirty looks from the very uptight organist, it all feels isolating rather than welcoming.

Shake it off, Barnes. You're not going to change them and they're not going to change you. Do not judge lest ye be judged more than you're already being judged and judging.

Just listen to the minister.

"Though I didn't know Art Holden well when I visited him in the hospital, I could see the Lord's love shining in his eyes. The Christian fellowship we shared, though brief, left me with no doubt that we shall see each other in heaven."

As much as I want to believe this guy, I can't. Those cliches don't capture Art at all. I don't doubt Art's redemption. I doubt the *minister*. He looks a lot like that creepy undertaker. They're probably brothers running some kind of mourning monopoly, praying on the innocent townsfolk of Boscobel, Wisconsin.

Check yourself, Warn. That's cynical and unfair.

I'm sorry, God.

But, since I have your attention, shouldn't funerals be about the person that's passed? This seems more about putting on a show for the mourners. This service isn't about my brother. I don't see him or feel his spirit in any of it.

So let me just say this, God.

Thank you for the gift that was and will continue to be my brother. Carry him into whatever might be next, peacefully and well. I don't understand why he's not here anymore. That makes me sad and angry, but

I will not become a sad, angry person. I will live my life being the best man I know how to be, in his honor. To thank him for all he was and for all he taught me and for all he may have missed while doing that.

Amen.

Looking up, my eyes land on Mom. Ten years older overnight. She's lost her son, the most tangible tether to her first husband, who, let's be honest, had to be the love of her life. To lose any child must be hard. To lose that child must be the hardest of all.

I've got to figure out how to turn these feelings into action. It seems the only thing that makes a tragedy more tragic is if no one *learns* anything from it. I'm not going to let that happen to me or my family.

Uncle Nick is near the stained-glass windows, talking with Josh. After he leaves, I plow over to my nephew. "What were you two talking about?" I ask, trying to sound breezy.

"He says I'm the man of the house," says Josh, sounding confused.

"How silly. You're a kid, right?"

"Yeah. I'm only this many," he says, holding up his little fingers.

"That's right. And you've got a bunch of grown-ups waiting to take care of anything you need." I pick him up and fly him around, the little amount of room the crowd allows. He shrieks and giggles until we almost hit someone I don't recognize. I put him down gently and kneel to be on his level.

"What are you?" I ask.

"I'm a kid."

"That's right," kissing him on the cheek. "You're a kid."

"Is this a funeral or a wedding?"

"Shut up and get in this receiving line. Stand next to me, or I'll scream," promises Emily. As always with my big sister, my best choice is the path of least resistance. I get in line.

People file past us. I am drowning in a sea of sincere conversations. Emily cries when Kathy Olson, her best friend from high school surprises her. She and her two beautiful daughters drove all the way from Chicago. Uncle Nick and Aunt Josie, looking so old and sad. Mom's all-girl posse. Ruth's wonderful brothers and sisters, all ten of them, their children, the cousins.

Many, many people.

They always speak to Emily first. She's instinctively smart about these things. If she thinks I won't know a name, she repeats it several times, so I'm spared the embarrassment of having to ask.

The minister who conducted the ceremony steps up to speak with her. Pastor Dronesalot is a little chubby. Been there. No judgement, Rev. His skin has a pink glow, as is the case with many orange-haired people. I did not notice the I Heart Jesus button during the funeral.

"Hello," he says, "you're Emily, Arthur's sister, correct?"

"Yes, I am."

"Blessings," he says while making a cross-like gesture in her direction.

"Thank you for leading the ceremony," she replies, sounding rather half-hearted, as though she's thanking a fast-food clerk.

"Your brother was thirty-seven when he passed away. The same age as your father when he died if I understand correctly."

"Yes," says Emily looking a little skeptical.

"And you're what, thirty-five?"

Run while you still can, preacher-man. Run like the devil is chasing you.

"I'm thirty-four," she says with more than a little ego.

"Wow," he says. "You must be freaking out wondering if you're next."

"Okay then. We should keep the line moving," says Emily.

He moves in a little closer. "Are you going to be here long? Perhaps we could go get a drink. Of course, we'd have to go a couple of towns over, so no one would see- "

"No. I'm in mourning. I'm sorry, but that wouldn't be appropriate," says the sister I've never really thought of as being hung up on appropriate.

Emily turns to me and says, "What the actual fuck?"

I laugh. I get several dirty looks, but I laugh.

Valerie, with eagle ears says, "Language, Emily."

I laugh louder.

It's by no means a consistent pattern, but it seems I enjoy talking to every fifth mourner. I've just been released from mourner number 4, so I have a giddy sense of anticipation for whomever is next. New number 5 is an older guy with snowy white hair. I think I recognize him, but I can't be right.

"Mr. Olson?" I ask shyly.

"Please Warn; I think it's time you call me Howie."

"Oh my gosh. It's really you."

"I thought very highly of your brother." He looks over to Ruth and the kids. "Such a beautiful family. You and Art were always close. I'm sure this is very hard," he says.

I nod rather than try to talk.

"Eddie is out in the car, listening to the radio. He was wondering if Art's children and their friends might enjoy a little show after the luncheon."

"Please tell Cowboy Eddie I can't think of anything better."

Mr. Olson starts to move on but stops. "I almost forgot," he says, pressing something into my hand. "I found this the other day and thought you might enjoy it."

A tiny porcelain clown.

More people I don't know. More effort finding different ways to say thank you. More energy spent not screaming. Purgatory is real, and this is it. This receiving line is never going to end.

Then the crowd parts like the Red Sea. Salvation appears on the horizon. Cue the angelic choir. Paula and Bijon are here. Hallelujah! Ring a bell. Give an angel his wings.

Bijon shakes my hand and kisses Emily on the cheek.

Paula waddles up to hug us both. She called last night to tell me she's pregnant again. She hasn't told Bijon because she's sure he's going to freak out.

Death followed by new life. A nice thought.

"I loved Art," says Paula. "What a good guy."

Paula's tone changes. "So, listen Warn. Someone wanted to come with us. I hope you don't mind."

"Why would I mind?" I say, confused until I see who is behind her.

It's Michael Drake, with his mother and grandma, who I'm shocked and delighted to see is still alive.

I exhale, loudly, giving myself permission not to say anything.

Mrs. Drake dressed all in black, of course, speaks first. "I'm so sorry this happened. And" she looks at Michael, "for anything in the past. I hope you'll accept my apology."

"Mrs. Drake, this hardly seems like the time," I take a deep breath, "to hold onto the past. So, yes. Of course."

"Thank you," she says, awkwardly hugging me.

"GOOD LORD, THAT MINISTER SURE SEEMED TO PHONE IT IN. WHERE'S WARN?" asks Mrs. Hermsdorf.

"I'm right here," I say, looking around to my right and left. "I'M RIGHT HERE."

"HA! VERY FUNNY. YOU'RE NOT GOING TO FOOL ME. WARN WAS FAT. NICE KID, BUT QUITE A WEIGHT PROBLEM. WHERE IS HE?"

Despite myself, I laugh. "NO, REALLY. IT'S ME," I say.

'NO, NO. WARN! THE ONE THAT WAS FOOLING AROUND WITH MY GRA-"

Mrs. Drake steps in. "Mother, let's get you downstairs for a little food." As they walk away, she mouths, "I'm sorry."

I smile and nod, bracing myself for what and who is next.

"I was hoping we could talk," says Michael.

"Maybe a little later?"

"Great. Not now, of course. You've got lots of other people to talk to," he says.

"Yes. I do," I say.

We both turn our heads in the direction of the line which has vanished. "So, we'll talk later at the lunch," Michael says, looking relieved before nodding and walking away.

My face freezes in a Botox before Botox way. I turn to Paula. If Michael is watching, hopefully he won't know we're talking about him.

"You could've told me he was coming."

"Is it a big deal? Get it over with already. Rip off the band-aid," Paula says.

"That's good advice. You're right," I say.

"Thank you."

I turn to her Bijon and shake his hand. "Paula is pregnant. Congratulations."

Emily and I walk into the church basement. Skipper, wearing a beautiful black suit from the sample room at work, is directing traffic. "People, this is Wisconsin. We've all seen hamburger, rice, and cream of mushroom casserole before. Keep the line moving, please."

"I didn't know you were here," I say, kind of dumbfounded.

"We got here just before the ceremony," he pauses for effect. "Did that minister ever even meet your brother?"

"Right?"

"We saw Kristina, and she said, 'Uncle Skipper, it's a mess down there. You're the only one with the skills we need. Please take charge.' So, here we are."

Donny pops in wearing his graduation suit with a frilly apron over it. He's carrying a can of Hi-C. "Funny, I heard her say, 'go help downstairs.'"

Skipper ignores that, instead turning toward the buffet line. "What are you people, Hassidic? You're acting like you've never seen a ham sandwich before. Grab and go, people. Grab and go! By the way," he says, turning back to me, "there's a woman here named Geneva who told me I used too much mayonnaise in the potato salad. I hate her. I mean, I love her, but I hate her too."

I spy Kristina watching with a huge smile on her face.

Josh is following Donny around refilling Hi-C.

Ruth walks up, saying to Emily. "I heard the minister asked you out."

"He did."

"What a cute way to meet. I hope you two will be as happy as Art and I were."

The sad finality of Ruth speaking about her relationship with Art in past tense hits each of us. We're all quiet for a moment or two.

"You know, during the funeral," says Ruth, "I kept having the same thought over and over."

"What's that?" asks Emily.

"Even if I knew this was going to happen, I'd do it all again," says Ruth, who begins to smile as she looks around. "I'd do it all again." She starts crying. Emily leads her to the ladies' room, no doubt to fix her make-up.

Dad comes over. "Warn, can we talk for a minute?"

"Sure."

He pulls out a pack of cigarettes.

We head outside to the back of the church.

"Wow," says Dad, "the parking lot is full."

Grandma Caruso would be so pleased.

"What did you want to talk about, Dad?"

"Well, it's just, I could have been more of a father to Art. To all of you," he says. "I was so busy drinking and whoring around…"

I hope he's not expecting me to disagree.

"Your grandma would tell me I was screwing up. That I was missing it all with you kids. She was right."

"Which grandma?"

"Both of them." He takes a long drag from his cigarette before adding, "There's nothing I can do about it now."

Kristina runs past us with some of her cousins. Josh follows behind a couple of seconds later, bringing up the rear like every little brother since the beginning of time.

"You know, I was just a little older than you when my brother Greg got killed in Korea. Killed on his first day there. His first god-damn day. Hardest thing that ever happened to me, losing him. I'm sorry you have to go through it too," says Dad. "Get through it better than I did, okay?"

"I'll do my best."

"You always do," he says sweetly. "You know I wanted to name you after my brother, but I thought naming you Warren would make Dorothy happy, so…"

"And then that got screwed up."

"What do you mean?" asks Dad.

"They misspelled it," I say.

"You want to know the truth?"

I nod.

"I misspelled it on purpose."

"You mean I've been correcting people my entire life because you were feeling a little insecure?" I ask.

"Yeah. I suppose."

"That's hilarious."

Dad smirks. "Did you see Michael?"

"Yeah. That was a surprise," I say.

"He's a good guy," says Dad. "Go hear him out."

"What do you mean?" I ask, genuinely confused.

He throws his cigarette into the nearby ashtray. "Come on, Warn. I wasn't *that* drunk."

CHAPTER FORTY

SNOW BECOMES WATER

Back in the church social hall, only the farmers have left. That makes sense. Farms don't wait for you to finish the ambrosia salad.

Paula, Bijon, and Michael are under a felt banner promoting the power of forgiveness. I guess Paula hasn't read it. She's glaring at me.

"Michael. let's go for a walk," I suggest. No need for an audience.

He takes a sip of his fruit punch Hi-C, grimaces, hands his glass to Bijon, and nods yes. Skipper sees us from across the room and raises his glass of Country Time pink lemonade.

Suzy is walking into the room as we leave. "Son of a gun," she says. "It's Leon!"

Butch is behind her. "His name is Michael Suzy, not Leon. There's no one here named Leon."

It's a warmer than normal February afternoon. The fresh air feels good. "I'm sorry about Art."

I begin to cry. The last thing I wanted to do in front of Michael, of all people. He awkwardly approaches to hug me. I step back, raising my arm. "No. No! That's okay. Thank you. I'll be fine."

We walk about half a block while I compose myself.

"How have you been?" Michael asks.

"Well, you know, my brother died," I say.

He barks a shocked laugh.

"Bad joke. Forgive me. It's just, well, I feel so bad. Overwhelmed. Sad."

"Of course, you do," Michael begins to say.

"I thought now that I've graduated from college, I could be there for Art in the way he was always there for me. That finally I'd be able to pay him back, you know?"

Michael takes a second to think. "Art wasn't the kind of person who kept score. He knew how much you loved him. Really." He locks eyes with me, "Warn, when you love someone, they know."

"Okay. Thanks. That's kind." Hating how vulnerable I just felt, I change the subject. "Anyhow, I live in Minneapolis now."

"I know. I keep up," he admits.

"Really. How?" I say, surprised.

"Through Paula, and you know, Skipper's quarterly newsletter."

"Of course," I say, nodding. "What about you?"

"What, you don't lurk in the background waiting to hear updates?" he says, sounding a little disappointed.

"I used to, but it hurt, so I stopped. Anyway," I say with a forced smile, "Give me all the wonderful details of your perfect life. I'm ready."

"I live in my parent's basement."

Unfortunately, he continues. "I took a year off to study for the MCATs. I just found out I got into med school."

"Great. Just like your mom planned," I say, being supportive and bitchy in the same sentence.

He graciously ignores my little dig. "The school is in Minnesota," says the future Dr. Drake, with intention.

"Minneapolis?" I ask.

"Rochester," he answers.

"Good. I don't have to move to Saint Paul," I say, knowing he'll know I'm joking.

Michael keeps going. "I'm still single. Is there, uh, anyone, you know, special in your life?"

"Special? No. I mean, I have been seeing someone, but he's not special. In fact, he's the reason I'm walking with this cane," I say, holding up my walking appliance.

"Yes, the *Hamlet* fight scene. I heard."

"Paula told you?"

"No. Your mom told my grandma. Then she told us you'd been attacked by a ham. We figured it out eventually." We walk a few steps.

"How are your parents?" I ask, to break the silence.

"You know. Dad is quiet. Mom is saving the world one bottle of Windex at a time."

"I think of her whenever I see a chipped cup."

"Me too," he says with a relaxed smile. Another few steps. "She's easier now. She's so busy worrying about my health that she forgets to hate that I'm gay."

"Your health? Are you- "

"No. I'm fine. The last person I had unsafe sex with was you, actually. What about, uh, what about you? Are you okay?"

"That's a big question."

His face gets ashen. "You mean…"

"No. Don't worry. I'm healthy. I'm just not sure I'd describe myself as okay."

We stop at the Unique Café. Our server brings the slice of coconut cream pie we're sharing. We both get coffee. I'm on my third sip before Michael gets the half and half and sweetener ratio to his liking.

"I want to apologize," he blurts.

My co-dependent midwestern heart wants to say, "That's okay." But I have recently learned that life is short. There are some things that must be said and known, even when it's hard. So, instead I say, "For what? Why are you apologizing?"

"I shouldn't have distanced myself just to keep my mom happy. I was worried about college, but I should've tried harder. I wasn't ready." He looks up. "I'm sorry."

"Thank you. Me too," I say. "For all of it."

He looks a little bruised. "All of it?"

I smile. "No. Not the good stuff. I'm sorry I didn't realize that you were just a kid too. I get why you handled things the way you did. None of it matters anymore."

"I was hoping it might," he says.

Same old Michael, putting it out there. I can almost taste the Corona and lime.

"I need to get back to my family." I say, throwing five bucks on the table.

"Okay," he says, taking a last swig of coffee. "Paula and Bijon are probably waiting for me so we can drive back to Madison."

"You're going back?"

"I was going to," he says before clearing his throat. "Why?"

"Why don't you stay here with me tonight?"

He smiles.

As we pass the church, I spy Shirley and Mick smoking on the steps. They motion me over. Michael nods and says, "I'll see you inside."

Shirley hugs me.

Mick says, "Dorothy could use a little company."

Mom is sitting in the front row, across from the casket, crying. Quietly.

I sit next to her, not to stop her. To let her know that she's not alone.

She looks up. "I thought the worst day of my life was already over. I was wrong."

My mind races to think of something comforting, but there's nothing to be said.

"When you were a little boy, you were sick with a bad fever. You were delirious and kept asking for Art, over and over. No one else could comfort you. That's how I feel now. I want Art."

"Mom, you once told me that bad things are inevitable."

"Did I? How depressing," she says casting her eyes heavenward.

"No—you said it's part of life we just need to accept. That which makes us stronger. That the true test of a person is getting back up and recovering with grace."

"I'm tired of being graceful," she says.

A woman from the funeral home comes in. "If you're ready, it's time," she says kindly. I watch her guide the casket up the aisle and through the door. We rise, to follow. Mom, standing next to a floral arrangement plucks two blush pink roses, handing one to me. "Press this in a book when you get home."

My perfect family is outside, waiting. Dad, standing near the door, puts his grateful hand out for Mom. Emily, strong and beautiful, is standing with Butch. He thoughtfully scans the crowd to make sure everyone is here. Val has a vice-like grip on her cane, the way she does when she's avoiding sadness. She stands next to Suzy, who catches my eye. We share a quiet smile. I join Skipper, off to the side. Ruth, Kristina, and Josh are standing nearest the car.

Art is lifted into the hearse. Ruth places a small bunch of red roses inside, kisses her hand, and touches it to the casket before putting her arms around the kids.

The door shuts. The car starts to pull away, crushing the snow in its path. Slush splashes up and lands into a nearby puddle where it mixes with dirty water. The puddle trickles toward a culvert where it will be carried away to somewhere new and unseen.

For one second, everything feels connected and infinite. Ashes to ashes, Art to dust. Leading the way to a time when hopefully we'll all be reunited.

A comforting gust of wind swirls around the eleven that should be twelve.

We linger for a moment before leaving to face whatever comes next, stronger for having been together.

EPILOGUE, 1999

CORN

The house is always quiet this time of day. I putter around, wiping here, stacking there—avoiding mirrors. I've got to get back to the gym before my new show begins. The mail truck passes by. I head outside to retrieve today's delivery. My glasses fog up, but I can still make everything out. A residual check, hallelujah. A letter from Jerome, who refuses to email. *Newsweek*. Another Y2K article, ten months from now. Surely there are better things to worry about until then.

I take a moment to look at our yard, coming back to life. Soon it will be time to plant this year's garden. Crocus are growing next to stubborn clumps of snow. Fruit trees are budding. The smell of potential is in the air.

Life in the City is so different. Bustling. Busy. Exciting, bordering on frantic. Thank God for our time upstate.

I begin to head inside when I notice a parcel from Mom on the front steps.

I squat down to pick up the box, which is heavier than expected. Struggling to balance it with the mail, I use my knee to knock on the door of my own house. The best I manage is a dull thud which I hope someone heard.

The doorknob starts to twist but stops. "Just a little harder. You can do it, buddy."

The door opens.

"Hi Dad!"

And so, it happens again. My breath is taken away by the miracle that is our kid. Wavy chestnut hair, infectious smile, carefree, confident and opinionated as hell. This morning he insisted on choosing his own clothes; hence, the polka-dot swimsuit, rainboots, sweater vest, and Halloween top hat look we've got going right now.

"What's in the box?" says the child whose hazel eyes light up whenever there is something to open.

"It's from Granny," I explain.

Our Cavalier puppy, Boregaard, follows us into the living room. All three of us plop ourselves down on the floor. I start to open the box. Thor begins pouting.

"I want to do it!"

So, Thor opens the box, throwing the tape to the puppy, who thinks it's a new toy. God knows where I'll find it later.

Thor prepares to tear through the contents. I put my hands on his shoulders to slow him down. "Let's take our time so we can enjoy what's inside."

His eyes get huge. "That's a good idea."

As usual, Mom includes magazine and newspaper clippings, she thinks I'll find interesting. Thor hands me one asking, "What does this one say?"

"You're a smart kid. You can figure it out. Start with the picture."

Thor does as he is asked for about five seconds. That's good. His attention span is getting longer.

"Dad? DAD?"

"Yes?"

"What's this?" he says impatiently. "And don't say look at the pictures." He begins to cough.

Thor has a dust allergy, but isn't everyone allergic to dust? I ask his pediatrician, but she acts like I'm being abusive or something. She treats me as though I'm a pro dust lobbyist for the dust division of the National Committee on Dust. Is it wrong to hate a pediatrician? Because I think I do. I think I hate her.

Thor continues to cough a little as he hands me a book that hasn't been opened for years. I flip it over to see the cover. The 1955 *Bear Cub Scout Book.*

"This must've belonged to your Uncle Art when he was a boy," I say.

"Uncle Art is the one I'm named after, right?"

"Yes."

"Arthor Emile Barnes. I like my name." he says, clapping.

"Good," I say, kissing him on the forehead, "because no one else will ever have it."

"I want to see what's inside."

Thor scoots next to me, still able to fit snuggly in the space between my ribs and arm. I crack open the cover. There, in childish printing is, "Art Holden, age 7."

"If he was your brother, why do we have different last names?" he asks.

"That happens sometimes."

As we look through the book, Thor says, "Why build a fire with sticks? Can't scouts afford matches? That's sad."

I'm explaining why Thor can't build fires when he notices something tucked between the pages. As he fumbles to grab it, whatever it is falls out of the book and onto the floor.

Handing it to me, Thor asks, "What's this, Dad?"

I look at the small envelope, still sealed. "Hm. Corn seed."

"What are seeds?"

"Come on; you know what seeds are," I remind him.

"Like in an orange?" he reasons.

"Right."

Thor rolls his eyes. "But what do they do?"

"Well, it's kind of like a baby," I say. "If people take care of seeds, they grow into something bigger. Everything it's going to be starts with that tiny seed. It's got to be planted. Then it grows roots. If it gets proper care—"

"Like water?"

"Yes, and light, warmth -"

"Love?"

"That too. Then it becomes whatever it's going to be."

"Really?"

"Here's the really cool part. When seeds are done being whatever they become," I pause for dramatic effect, "they give you more seeds."

"Wow," he says, holding the little envelope like it's full of gold. "What are we going to do with these seeds?

"We could try to pop them," I offer. Thor shakes his head. "Why not?"

"Because then we got nothing left. It's all gone."

"What do you think we should do?"

"Plant them. Then we'll have corn forever."

And so we do.

Arthur Radke

1948 - 1986

Photo by Emily Sobiek

ACKNOWLEDGEMENTS

As the cover says, this book strives to bring laughter to serious things. 70% of it is experience. 30% is imagination.

While cookies and furniture flew, my dad didn't go to jail for a Christmas gone wrong. I did not know the comfort of a Michael Drake in high school. Being a dad was a fantasy fulfilled, but Thor does not exist in real life. I was, of course, Mr. Skyway, but this is not a memoir.

To those who knew the people who inspired these characters, believe the best. Assume the rest is fiction. Any real-life based stories in this book are, after all, only half mine.

It does feel strange to write acknowledgements for a book that is basically one long acknowledgement; but I acknowledge that there are many to acknowledge, so here goes.

First up, my family. My one-of-a-kind, unlike any other family. The perfect family for me.

Art Radke. The brother to whom I owe so much. In a long list of life's blessings, he will always be one of the first to come to mind.

This book began as a short story called, "What Is Art?". Thank you, Nicole Humphries. Your sweet reaction planted a seed. This larger work represents an attempt to thank Art for all he was, and in my heart still is. I thought that writing this book would make me miss him less. I was wrong. I miss him more.

If you were lucky enough to have an Art when you were a kid, and he's still here, I envy you. Put this book down and call him right now. Thank him (or her) every chance you get.

Dorothy Fiore Radke Triggs. Our mom. She brought her own beautiful version of order to the chaos that was our home. When my dad wasn't living with us money was very tight. My bedroom needed curtains we couldn't afford, so she taught me how to decoupage. We used tissue paper (which my family loves) and glue to turn the windows into stained glass. To a child, it was beautiful. Lesson learned. Celebrate what you can do. Don't dwell on what you can't. Move toward possibility.

She had a wicked sense of humor. Tommy Terpening and I took her to see the movie *Cocoon*. We asked if she would get on the spaceship promising eternal youth. She said, "No, I'd stay home with Butch and Val. I'd send your father."

She was the best.

Raymond Triggs. My dad. If, sadly, there is one person I have truly hated, it's him. I loved him too. Thanks for teaching me ambiguity Dad.

In his own way he was smart, kind and generous. Other things got in the way.

There were times he was haunted by his memories of WWII. Those moments were frightening, so I avoided discussing them with him. I'm very thankful to Rick Ryerson and Penny Ziemer Ford for their help in researching his military record. I'm proud of my father's service and very aware of what it cost him.

When Raymond died, I was given his Triggs Home Improvement Company jacket. I found a wooden nickel with the Serenity Prayer printed on it in a pocket. The edges were smooth from being rubbed between his thumb and fingers many times.

I didn't know he had kept trying to quit drinking, and therefore living with his inability to do so. I was, in the same moment, proud and sad.

That little wooden nickel made me consider that he had fought for himself and us. I finally started seeing his addictions as a separate thing. Something over which he had no control.

Let your kids see you fail. It's so much better than them thinking you didn't try.

My love for him grows.

For that and many other things, I am grateful.

Emma Henke Fiore and Phyllis Tinkum Triggs. My grandmothers. Quietly lurking in the background waiting to provide anything they felt was missing. Ready to whip out a map of the stars or pay for an acting class. Wonderful, talented and intuitive women.

As in the book, sometimes Grandma Fiore lived with us. At bedtime she'd often tell me one of the things I should consider being when I grew up. On those nights the last thing she'd say before she closed the door was, "You can be anything you want to be."

Let the kids in your life know you believe in them. Make them believe in their future.

The rest of my family is still here. I can tell and show them how I feel, and so I will.

I've heard writing can be a lonely profession. That has not been my experience.

Thank you, Patty Thompson and Lisa Iverson for being important teammates in bringing this book to the finish line. Thank you also to Redhawk superstars Robert Canipe, Richard Eller, Tim Peeler and Aurora Brianna King.

I'm grateful to the friends who took time to read the book and provide feedback. The Fruchter Family readers, especially Jill, your enthusiasm means the world. Steven "Skipper" Nordberg, Patrick O'Connell, Tommy Terpening, Michele Greenwood Bettinger, Lori Alling, Bill and Donna Fellenberg, lucky is the guy who has you on his side.

Thanks also to the very accomplished people kind enough to read the book and provide quotes. Each of you is an inspiration.

To the hilarious John Connon, thanks for one of my favorite jokes in the book.

Katie Hammond and Robert Z. Grant, your partnership makes each day more fun and rewarding. Robert, seeing how you visually represent storytelling is thrilling. Katie, working with you puts the Entertainment in Strategic. Learn more about us and what we can do for you at www.StrategicEntertainmentNYC.com.

If you enjoyed this novel, please leave a review online or mention it on social media. If you or a friend is in a book club, recommend TWMUS. If you know someone going through Barnes like experiences, suggest they pick up a copy. If you're going through a Barnes and Noble experience, ask them to order a copy for their shelves.

If you didn't enjoy the book, suffer in silence so others may know your pain. Better yet, buy several copies and hide them in your attic to spare others the suffering you endured.

This book is filled with people I loved and to whom I am grateful. Spending time with my mom and her girlfriends was wonderful. I was thankful to remember teachers like Barb Jung, Susan Saunders, and Gloria Link. My friend Bonnie Beckwith and I still bring up Marlene Cummings and her life changing visit to our classroom. Mrs. Cummings was the recipient of the Martin Luther King Jr. Heritage Award in 2003. She is the perfect example of how one person can change the world.

Giving fictional Shirley and Jerome happier endings than their real-life counterparts was bittersweet, with emphasis on the sweet. They are forever missed. I was lucky to know them.

Thank you to my Narrowsburg friends and family.

My mom and her first husband Warren wanted to buy a small newspaper and live in a town just like ours. Sometimes dreams come true, even if they skip a generation.

Matt, Zuzu and Tammy Faye, you're everything. Thank you, most of all. You are now that which makes me stronger.

ABOUT THE AUTHOR

Greg Triggs tours with and co-produces the improvisational musical comedy revue *Broadway's Next Hit Musical.* He owns and is the Chief Creative Officer for www.

StrategicEntertainmentNYC.com whose clients have included the Tribec Film Festival, Slack, and Disney. He and his husband, ceramic artist Matt Nolen, live in Harlem and Narrowsburg, NY.

Learn more at www.GregTriggs.com

Scan the code above with a SmartPhone or tablet to visit the site.

Made in the USA
Middletown, DE
24 March 2022

63045510R00179